I0590876

The
RADIANT
CHILD

The Dragon Sword Histories

BOOK THREE

DUNCAN LAY

HARPER

Voyager

Harper*Voyager*
An imprint of HarperCollins*Publishers*

First published in Australia in 2010
by HarperCollinsPublishers Australia Pty Limited
ABN 36 009 913 517
www.harpercollins.com.au

HarperCollins*Publishers*
Level 13, 201 Elizabeth Street, Sydney NSW 2000, Australia
Unit D, 63 Apollo Drive, Rosedale, Auckland 0632, New Zealand
A 53, Sector 57, Noida, UP, India
1 London Bridge Street, London SE1 9GF, United Kingdom
2 Bloor Street East, 20th floor, Toronto, Ontario M4W 1A8, Canada
195 Broadway NY, NY 10007, United States of America

National Library of Australia Cataloguing-in-Publication entry

Lay, Duncan.
The radiant child / Duncan Lay.
1st ed.
ISBN 978 0 7322 8770 2 (pbk).
Lay, Duncan. Dragon sword histories ; bk. 3.
A823.4

Cover design by Darren Holt, HarperCollins Design Studio
Cover illustration: Les Petersen
Typeset in 10/12pt Sabon by Kirby Jones

An interview with legendary US fantasy author Raymond E. Feist inspired Duncan Lay to begin writing fantasy, using the time spent on the train commuting between his Central Coast home, where he lives with his wife and two children, and his work at *The Sunday Telegraph*.

This is his third novel.

Talk to Duncan Lay at:
duncanlay.blogspot.com

PRAISE FOR DUNCAN LAY

'Fast paced and dramatic, Lay writes the kind of battle scenes that I have not seen since the late David Gemmell, and booksellers should definitely be recommending this to his fans.' **Australian Bookseller and Publisher**

'This is even stronger than its predecessor, *The Wounded Guardian*, and features complex character development, gritty, realistic battles scenes and imaginative plot twists. Verdict: Highly enjoyable.' **Daily Telegraph**

'*The Wounded Guardian* promised so much in a debut novel and The Risen Queen follows it up with another engrossing read for fans of great epic fantasy.' **Booktopia**

'Isn't it great when an accomplished new fantasy author comes along? This is an engrossing tale of a credible world. Can't wait for the third and final volume!' **Aurealis Xpress**

BOOKS BY
DUNCAN LAY

THE DRAGON SWORD HISTORIES

The Wounded Guardian (1)
The Risen Queen (2)
The Radiant Child (3)

PRAISE FOR THE WOUNDED GUARDIAN

'Heroism, romance, heartache, sex, violence, death and disappointment — *The Wounded Guardian* has it all in spades.' **Manly Daily**

For Belinda

Acknowledgements

The Dragon Sword Histories, and myself, owe a huge debt of thanks to the many wonderful people at HarperCollins, and elsewhere, who worked to improve the series.

Writing this trilogy has been an amazing experience but it has certainly not been my work alone. Many people have helped along the way.

I owe a debt of thanks to cover artist Les Petersen and cover designer Darren Holt for their attention-grabbing work; to copy editors Abigail Nathan and Kylie Mason for making sure my ideas were fully developed; to proof readers Ian Tonkin, Ron Buck and Kylie Mason for ensuring my many mistakes and talent for over-using certain words remains relatively hidden; to Jordan Weaver and Natalie Costa Bir; to Anne Reilly, to the HarperCollins sales staff and everyone else who had a hand in this — and most of all to Stephanie Smith, whose ideas, advice, encouragement and support made my dream possible.

Character List

Alban	Priest of Aroaril; works with Derthals
Albiona	The continent
Argurium	A dragon
Aroaril	The Sun God, God of Light
Aviland	Fought in Ralloran Wars; defeated by the Rallorans
Barrett	The Queen's Magician of Norstalos
Bayes	Officer of Duke Gello; fights at Gerrin
Bellic	Berellian town; scene of infamous massacre
Beq	One of Gello's war captains
Berellia	Fought in Ralloran Wars; defeated by the Rallorans
Berry	Northern town; ruled by Baron Berry
Borin	Martil's childhood friend; killed in Ralloran Wars
Byrez	Berellian earl; opponent of the Fearpriests
Cessor	Count of Norstalos; obeys Duke Gello
Cezar	Champion to King Markuz
Chanlon	Former priest of Aroaril; enemy to Rallorans
Chelten	Duke Gello's former bodyguard
Conal	Ex-bandit; friend of Martil
Croft	King of Norstalos; Merren's father
Cropper	Archer officer
Darry	Norstaline innkeeper on the Tetran border
Declan	Archbishop of Norstalos
Derthals	Primitive men who live north of Norstalos; unkindly called goblins
Dunner	Ralloran sergeant; friend of Kesbury and Nerrin
Edil	Father of Karia
Ezok	Berellian ambassador to Norstalos
Fearpriest	A priest of Zorva
Feld	One of Gello's war captains
Forde	Militia officer from Gerrin
Gamelon	Bishop of eastern Norstalos
Garie	Ralloran officer; killed at Bellic
Gello	Duke of Western Norstalos; cousin to Merren

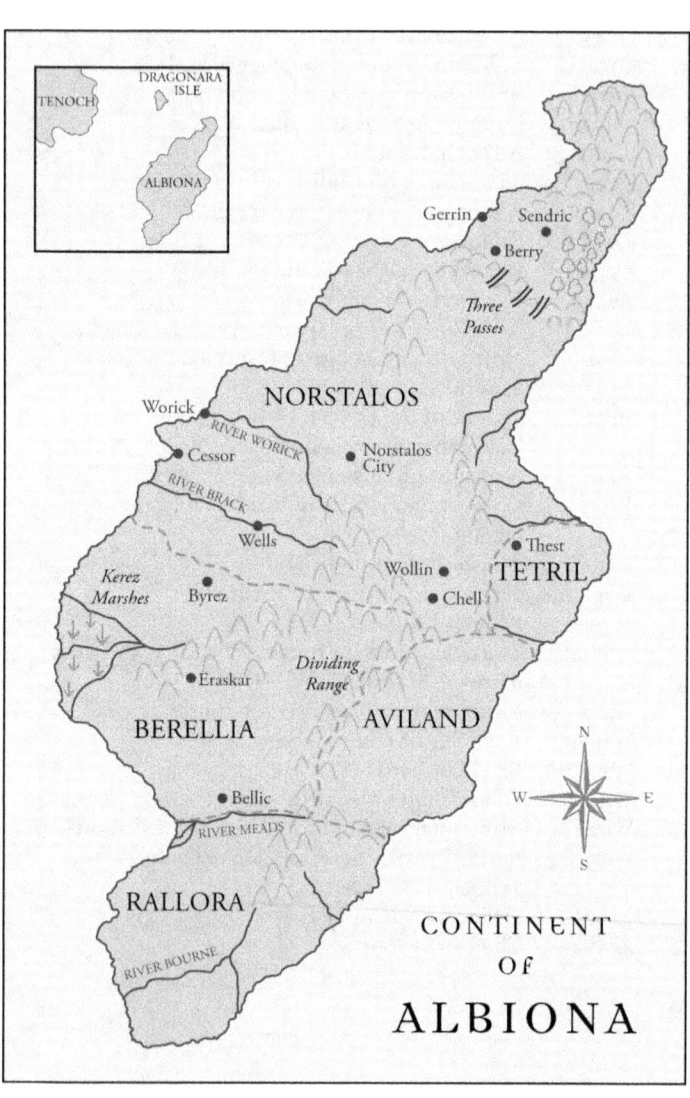

CONTINENT

Of

ALBIONA

1

Martil opened his eyes. For a long moment he just lay there, trying to remember what had happened. Then it all came back to him.

The fight with Cezar, the anger and the adrenalin — he shut that out. The agony of his wounds, where the razor-sharp spearhead had ripped him open, even the ache deep in his shoulder and arm, where he had driven himself past exhaustion — and still been able to drive a Derthal spear clean through Cezar — he pushed those aside. The fear, the despair when he had been on his knees, sure he was about to die, knowing what it would do to Karia — he tried to lock that away, although it would not go easily.

The thing he held on to was Merren. How she had looked when she'd rushed over to him and he'd fallen into her arms. She'd told him they could never be together but the way she had acted after the fight made a lie out of that. She loved him, he knew she did! She would be with him and they would be a family with the baby and Karia. Karia! Where was Karia?

'You're awake!'

Martil looked across, but saw only a blur as Karia launched herself off a stool and fastened herself around his neck, clinging on tight.

'I told you never to leave me! I would have been able to save you!' she cried.

'It's all right, I'm fine,' he said awkwardly, trying to breathe through her ferocious embrace, and hug her back at the same time. How could he have been so foolish? How could he have risked leaving her alone? Guilt was thick within him and he held her desperately, kissed her head, feeling her small arms tighten around him.

'I was so scared!'

'I'm sorry,' he told her, hoping they had not let her see him covered in blood. Suddenly everything he'd tried to shut away flooded back and the thought of fighting again terrified him, as nothing had before. Not for himself but for Karia, for Merren, for everyone in Norstalos who needed him. He had too much to live for, too many people depending on him. He had too much to lose, too many responsibilities. He held onto Karia. What if Cezar had won? He could say, truthfully, that Cezar had an unfair advantage; the fight would have been different had Cezar not had magical protection — different again had they fought with swords. But he should have lost. His arrogance, thinking himself unbeatable, had nearly cost him his life — and only Cezar's desire to gloat had given him long enough to recover. Karia deserved more than that from him.

As for Karia, she had no intention of letting him go any time soon. Waiting back at the church had been bad enough — the howls and shouts of the Derthal crowd had her close to tears. But then Wilsen had rushed up, shouting about magic and she'd known something was wrong by the way Barrett had run off.

She had feared the worst, especially when Martil did not return, as he had promised. Even though

Merren had eventually come to fetch her, the look on the Queen's face had frightened her — and the blood on Merren's clothes had only made it worse. Part of it was worrying what would happen to her, but mostly it was because she did not want to lose him. She loved him. Thinking that, she clutched him tighter, unwilling to let him go again.

The tears had come when she saw him just lying there, not waking up. Luckily Merren had been there. Back at the caves, she had thought Merren would make a good mother. She had been fun to play with, had looked after her while Martil was away and had even taught her to read. But then they had left the caves. Almost immediately, Merren had been too busy to spend time with her and she began to wonder if Merren really liked her. Still, Merren had been wonderful while they had waited for Martil to wake up. She had held Karia close, told her everything would be all right.

It had given Karia an idea. Martil was always going off and doing silly things. She needed someone else to look after her. Merren was the best one. Sitting there, being cuddled, had been as good as Martil. And Merren smelled better as well. That would mean making sure Merren married Martil. That could not be too hard, surely? It all made sense to her. They needed each other, for they were both always getting into trouble. Having her to look after would give them something better to do. She was sure that a little work from her would be all it took. And then the three of them could live together, happy, as a family. Family was a word Father Nott had spoken of many times but she had never really had one. And that was what she wanted more than anything. Something so important could not be left to silly grown-ups to get right. She would make it happen herself.

Martil kissed her again, and then glanced up to see Merren standing over the bed, smiling down at him.

'Father Alban had healed you and cleaned you up before we let Karia in,' the Queen said. 'By then you had fallen into a deep sleep — Fathers Alban and Quiller said it was better to let you rest. She hasn't left your side in four turns of the hourglass. She's barely even eaten!'

Martil's arms tightened around Karia. For her to ignore food just reinforced everything he was feeling. He gazed up at Merren, willing her to say something that proved the love he had seen in her face as she'd run to him.

'We've all been worried about you,' Merren said softly.

She wanted to hug him also, hold him close. Watching that fight had been the hardest thing in her life — worse even than the battles of Sendric or Pilleth. Certainly a part of her had been dismayed at the thought of a Derthal army invading the north of Norstalos. But the greater part was horrified at the thought she was going to watch Martil die.

Right then she had known that, despite all her father's teaching, all that had been drummed into her, she was still prepared to put her personal feelings above the needs of the country. The thought of life without Martil had been devastating.

When he had fallen into her arms, told her that he loved her and knew she loved him, she would have been prepared to put everything aside, agreed to make a life with him, even marry him in front of the whole country. At the moment of life and death, the choice had been easy.

But that was then.

While he slept, she had spoken with High Chief Sacrax, Barrett, Quiller and Alban, the Elfaran

Havell, comforted Karia — and had more than enough time to think.

She was going to return to Norstalos with an army of Derthals.

High Chief Sacrax and almost all his chieftains may have sworn loyalty to her cause — an oath that both Alban and Quiller said would not be broken — but there would be many Norstalines who would see this army not as a rescue force but as another threat. Like Count Sendric, they had been raised on tales of the evil, vicious 'goblins' that lived in the north. The cruel killers who had tried to murder a dragon and who would slaughter men, women and children. Ruthless monsters that ate babies, wore skins as cloaks and collected skulls as trophies. That almost of all of this was a lie and it was the Norstalines who had been the aggressors and betrayers was not going to go down well anywhere, let alone the rich towns of the west, who saw Norstalos as blessed by Aroaril and the dragons. It was going to take an extraordinary amount of work just to convince her people to fight alongside the Derthals. How, then, was she going to get them to accept Martil as their Prince Consort and his son as their next King? The people needed reassurance, familiarity. She was asking them to change dramatically and quickly. But she knew there would come a point where they would not accept what she was asking.

Martil could be the straw that broke the donkey's back.

She had convinced herself she'd made the right decision, that she needed to hold to her original plan, to marry Sendric and present Martil's baby as the Count's. When Martil had woken up, that decision had once again seemed ridiculous, and it took all of her control not to rush forwards and hold him close.

This was a battle between her head and her heart, between what she had learned and what she felt. It would have been so easy, if it were not for Norstalos. But she could not risk her country for something so trivial as her own happiness.

You must be strong. Think of the people, she told herself.

'Where are we?' Martil's voice broke into her thoughts.

'In the caves of High Chief Sacrax,' Merren replied, glad to be talking and not thinking. 'You were brought here after the duel.'

'What's been going on?'

She sat down carefully on the side of the crude bed — merely a platform raised a foot off the floor and heaped with animal skins. Not only did they smell as though they had never been washed, or even cured properly, but she could not help but think what fleas, lice and Aroaril-knows-what-else might be in there.

'High Chief Sacrax and almost all of his chieftains have sworn to serve me faithfully until our enemies are defeated, and then they will come to live in the Great Northern Forest, which will be theirs in perpetuity. Not all of his chiefs swore — Rath's tribe has left, along with two other, smaller tribes that were allied to him. But as only those that swore would be allowed to live in Norstalos, even those who seemed against us were eager to join. And there was your victory as well. It impressed the Derthals. Not only did you defeat Cezar, but they saw Barrett defeat the Berellian wizard, so they are sure both our strength and our magic are greater than the Berellians.'

'Glad I could give them so much entertainment.' Martil tried to smile. 'Speaking of Barrett, where is he? I need to thank him.'

'He's resting. We need more time — time to get our people to safety, time to get the Derthals far enough south that they can help us. He has been working on creating a huge storm at sea, to delay the western attack from the Tenochs.'

Martil nodded. 'And what of the Berellians?'

'They have left, don't worry about them,' Merren assured him.

'What! They should have been killed!' Martil hissed.

'They were Sacrax's guests — and he had promised safe passage to the losers. We would have wanted him to keep his word, had we been in that position,' Merren argued.

'They would have done their best to kill you,' Martil muttered. 'Now they are free to spread more mischief.'

'You forget how important it is for the Derthals to see we are honourable and our word can be trusted,' Merren said sharply. 'That far outweighs any danger a couple of Berellians hold. Besides, what can they do? Barrett has already shown their mage is nowhere near as powerful, and Ezok is just an ambassador!'

'You might be surprised at the trouble they will cause. The day may come when we regret letting them go,' Martil warned.

Ezok could remember only too well the way his predecessor had died: stripped naked, tied to a column in Markuz's throne room and then executed by Brother Onzalez. Of late, the image of the dead man, eyes bulging with terror above his gag, had loomed large in his thoughts. He could not help but imagine that was the fate waiting for him in Berellia, after Cezar had failed so spectacularly to kill Captain Martil and persuade the goblins to attack Norstalos.

Even now Ezok could not understand how it had all gone so wrong. One moment Cezar had stood above his vanquished, unarmed foe; the next, Martil had come alive and slaughtered Cezar. If Cezar had not sought to taunt his fallen opponent, if he had only stepped in and struck the death blow quickly ... of course, he had been distracted by Khaliz's failure to win his duel with the Norstaline magician, Barrett. If Khaliz had not failed, Cezar could not have been hurt, even if Martil had got up again!

Ezok could plausibly blame both Khaliz and the dead Cezar for the failure but he worried that would not be enough. Their failure had been bigger than he could have imagined, for the goblins would now send warriors to help the Queen! Onzalez, and Markuz, were going to be furious. Certainly it should not make a difference — even several thousand of these primitive creatures could not stop the three massive armies poised to invade Norstalos from the south, the east and the west. But Onzalez and Markuz were not men to reward failure.

Ezok had been tempted to flee, to persuade Khaliz to take them both elsewhere. But several things stopped him. First, he had sold his soul to Zorva. Nowhere would he be safe from Onzalez's wrath. Second, he wanted to share in the power and riches that would flow from their conquest of Norstalos. After all, he was the expert on that country — and still cherished hopes of being named its governor while the Berellian–Tenoch army marched south to crush the rest of the continent. But, most important of all, he had a secret that he hoped would forgive his failure in the north. As a matter of course he had bribed several goblin chiefs and some of the goblins who worked for Father Alban — and the information they had given him might just save his life. So now he was waiting to see Onzalez and Markuz — and hoping his secret was big enough to save his life, or if he could at least make it sound as though it were. At times like these, he almost felt like praying for help. Almost.

Martil wanted to talk privately with Merren. And more than talk. But apparently she had promised Chief Sacrax they would speak with him as soon as possible, while Karia showed no sign of wanting to let him go — and then Havell barged into the chamber.

'What were you doing?' the Elfaran shouted at him. 'Do you have any idea what would happen if you died and we were unable to find another wielder in time?'

Martil was in no mood for the Elfaran. 'No. But I'm sure you'll tell me,' he growled.

Havell's face reddened. 'Do you think I am here for your amusement? I have tried to tell you the fate of the world rests on your shoulders ...'

'And you know I don't want it!'

'You have no choice! This burden is yours and you must accept the responsibility. Your life is too valuable to waste — too many others depend on it!'

Havell's words touched the things that Martil had tried and failed to bury.

'Leave me alone!' he threatened.

Merren added her support. 'Sacrax is waiting for us. Perhaps we should speak later.'

Havell stared at them, breathing hard. 'I have served the dragons for a thousand years, more lifetimes than I care to remember. I did not devote my life to them to fail now! You are needed to restore the world's magic. It is not a hard task but it is impossible if you are dead! We shall speak again but meanwhile I would urge you to think about what you almost cost this world!'

Martil watched Havell stalk away and was afraid he would think of nothing else.

'Give me one reason why I should not have you killed for your abject failure,' Onzalez demanded.

Ezok managed to keep his face impassive only with an enormous effort. His story, blaming Cezar and Khaliz for the failure, had been received coldly by Onzalez — although Markuz had only cared about the death of Cezar. Markuz was sitting near the body now, his face ashen. He had lost all interest in Ezok — but the Fearpriest was not so merciful.

'I have an excellent reason why I should live,' Ezok replied strongly. 'I have a secret — I know all about an object of amazing power, one that makes the Dragon Sword of Norstalos seem nothing more than a child's toy.'

'Tell me!' Onzalez said softly, although Ezok could hear the interest in the Fearpriest's voice.

'Only if you swear by Zorva that I shall rule Norstalos in His name, once we have the country in our hands,' Ezok said boldly.

Onzalez's hands twitched, as if seeking to crush the life out of Ezok.

'Why don't I just put you on the rack and take your secret along with your screams and your life?' the Fearpriest suggested.

'Because you will need me to control Gello, to use him as a puppet. And because you told me I was named by Zorva, so to kill me is to thwart His plans.'

Onzalez stared at Ezok for a long moment — at least Ezok supposed the Fearpriest's hidden eyes were fixed on him — and the former ambassador knew his life hung in the balance. Then the Fearpriest chuckled.

'You are a brave one, Ezok! Truly you must be blessed by Zorva! So, I swear on His unholy name that you shall not only live, but rule Norstalos after we have taken it — if this object is as powerful as you say.'

Ezok felt the tension go out of his shoulders, and realised he was dripping with sweat. Time to speak — and time to embellish what little he knew.

'It has been made by the dragons, and can destroy the Dragon Sword. Its magic, its power, dwarfs that toy. Whoever has it controls all the magic in the world,' Ezok declared.

'Control all the magic in the world?' Onzalez snapped. 'How is that possible?' But his voice betrayed his excitement and awe at the thought.

'I do not know. But that is what I was told,' Ezok lied confidently.

Onzalez nodded slowly and Ezok felt a surge of relief. All those years of learning to mask his feelings were allowing him to lie to a Fearpriest and get away with it!

'And what is the name of this object?' Onzalez asked.

'They call it the Dragon Egg,' Ezok said.

'We have agreed to help but there is still a problem,' Sacrax told them.

Merren smiled carefully. 'There are no problems that cannot be solved,' was all she said.

They had eaten at the table of the High Chief — although there was no table as such. Instead, they had sat on stools and passed around crude bowls of nuts, berries, meat and a pungent goat's cheese that only Sacrax and Karia had eaten with any enthusiasm, while Sacrax had eagerly quizzed Martil on the Ralloran Wars. Now it was well after midnight — there were no hourglasses here, so Martil and Merren had no idea exactly what the hour was — and he was getting down to the real business.

Sacrax had spoken of his concern the Norstalines would turn on the Derthals once all was won, that they would be betrayed yet again. In reply Merren had shown him the deeds to the forest, signed by the Crown, which meant anyone harming or disturbing the Derthals could be arrested, their property forfeit.

Then he had pointed out his concern about being attacked as they marched south, and she promised Father Quiller would go with them, to ease their passage and as a guarantor of their safety, silently hoping that would be enough.

'All you have to do is help us hold those passes. I shall not ask you to do anything else. We hope no Derthal will have to fight,' she promised.

But Sacrax still had one more concern.

'This is autumn. Food is not plentiful. We must leave enough for our females and young to eat, for snow will arrive soon. If all my warriors leave with me ...'

Merren smiled with relief. 'Our wizard will bring in deer, goats, rabbits, whatever is around.'

'Good.' Sacrax grinned suddenly. 'We are happy!'

'So are we,' Merren said fervently.

Sacrax stood and stretched. 'We shall begin tomorrow.' He patted Martil on the shoulder. 'It is good to see you. You fight well. My warriors talk of how a dead man came back to life and won! No warrior has ever lost his spear and survived a fight like that!'

Martil forced a smile. He covered himself by turning his grimace into a yawn. Although that was not entirely fake. He was still bone-tired.

'You need to sleep,' Sacrax said. 'Much to get ready but we work better on a full belly, after a good sleep! Too late to walk back to the church now. My guards will show you to a bed for the night.'

'Oh, that's fine,' Merren began, imagining the skin-strewn bed that Martil had been given — and the many fleas that no doubt already called it home.

'No, we are allies now. Sign of trust to sleep in my house!' Sacrax insisted.

'Then we shall be happy to,' she lied, keeping a smile on her face until Sacrax had left.

'That took longer than the fight!' Merren sighed. 'We have allies but I'm not sure they really trust us yet.'

'Well, I can hardly blame them. But you did well — had an answer for everything,' Martil said softly. Karia had fallen asleep beside him, her head resting on his leg, some time ago. He stroked her hair gently and looked back at Merren. This was the perfect opportunity to be alone. He could feel his heart beating a little faster. 'I have been sleeping half the night already — but I am still tired. I vote we find where they have offered us space to sleep.'

Merren rubbed her eyes. 'But there is still so much to do!'

'And it will get done faster if you have some rest,' he suggested. 'Sacrax was right there.' He stood carefully, picking up Karia and ignoring the aches in his muscles. He looked up at Merren who, only a little reluctantly, joined him as they walked into the quiet caves. A pair of guards waiting outside the door pointed them down a narrow tunnel.

'Sleep there,' one gestured.

Merren tried to question them, but it was obvious they were the only human words these Derthals knew. So they gave up and took a sputtering torch from the dining area to light the way, its pungent smoke mingling with the caves' aroma of unwashed bodies, damp and animals. Then the passage ended in a blank rock wall, with just one opening leading to a small chamber, where a crude platform bed, thickly heaped with animal skins, waited.

'Did we miss the other chamber?' Martil wondered quietly.

'No, there was no other. This is the only one,' Merren said angrily. 'Is this Sacrax's idea of a jest?'

Well, it's not Barrett's idea of one, Martil thought to himself. 'It will be fine. We have Karia with us. She can sleep in the middle — that platform is big enough for three of us.'

'Don't be ridiculous — I shall walk back to the church,' Merren declared.

'Merren, that's a foolish idea. You are tired and the church is far away. We can sleep here and nothing will happen,' Martil whispered, signalling for her to be quiet, to not wake Karia.

For a moment Merren thought about walking away, but she was too tired. The stress of the day had left her feeling wrung out. Besides, if Karia was there between them, what could they get up to? Still, that did not stop her imagination from working, a little.

The platform bed was more than big enough for the three of them — she guessed several Derthals could fit in, and she could not help but wonder about Sacrax's sleeping arrangements.

Martil carefully lay Karia down in the middle of the bed, and tucked a couple of animal skins over her.

'Are you sure they're clean?' Merren kicked off her boots but kept the tunic and trousers on. She had changed out of the clothes that had been covered in Martil's blood after the fight so they were relatively clean — and there was no sense in giving in to temptation …

They found themselves talking in whispers, so as not to wake Karia.

'Clean enough.' Martil shrugged. 'You can always take a bath tomorrow.' He had felt tired but having Merren alone had woken him up in more ways than one.

Merren laughed as she stretched out on the bed. 'I doubt there will be time for that! Still, a queen always has to look her best or people talk about her. And she must put up with any discomfort without complaint. It feels like I've been on my feet all day!'

'Let me see.' Martil sat down at the end of the bed and grabbed her foot.

'And what do you think you are doing?' Merren sat up.

'Making sure my Queen is fit for duty tomorrow,' Martil said innocently, carefully massaging the ball of her foot. 'Wouldn't that feel better?'

Merren had to admit it felt wonderfully soothing, although she was concerned it might lead to other things.

'You shouldn't do that — my feet must stink,' she protested weakly.

Martil knew she had a point. They were not only dirty but sweaty and smelly. Still, he was not about to let go.

'I can't tell,' he lied with a smile, making sure he kept a firm grip on her ankle as he rubbed her foot.

It was relaxing, and Merren lay back on the animal skins, which were surprisingly comfortable.

He switched his attention to her toes and she could not stop a small gasp of pleasure escaping.

'You know, I could do this more often,' Martil offered, moving her feet subtly out of his lap and onto his thigh.

'Don't tempt me,' she muttered. 'Although I don't think it would be a good idea.'

'Why?'

She just looked at him.

'Karia's sleeping just there! I'm not trying to begin anything,' he protested, without conviction.

'Still, you can stop at the ankle,' she told him. 'And I thought you were tired from the duel?'

'Not that tired,' Martil said softly. The sight of her lying there on the bed and the feel of her skin under his hands eventually grew too much. He had to say something.

'Merren, after the fight, when you ran to me …'

'Yes?' she said guardedly, unsure of what she might have to say to him.

'I know you love me. It was written all over your face. You know I love you and we are to have a child together. You can't marry Sendric when we return,' he said in a rush.

'Oh, I can't?' She sat up, her eyes blazing. 'Do you think you can give me orders?'

'Of course not!' he protested, pointing at the sleeping Karia and lowering his voice. 'That wasn't what I meant! It's just that we should be together …'

'Well, I'm glad we are agreed that it is entirely my decision,' she snapped, hoping he would drop this but knowing he would not. *Dear Aroaril, what was she going to say to him?*

Martil stared into her eyes. 'It is your choice but it is the right thing to do. We were meant to be together!'

She smiled bitterly. 'I never thought to hear that from you, of all people. The man who hates sagas and their traditional happy endings.'

He closed his eyes for a moment. 'Let me start again. I just meant you don't need to marry Sendric. I know why you think you must but the people will accept me. And you cannot deny what there is between us. I love you and I know you feel the same way. That duel proved it to us. Why does being Queen prevent you from being happy?'

She had to look away. With him so close, with his hands on her, it was too easy to give in. But being queen was not about taking the easy option and she had never been willing to give in. So why was telling him so hard? She knew all the arguments — she had used them to convince herself earlier that night. But it was very different now, with the two of them together like this.

'It is not that easy,' she managed to say.

'Well, it should be!' he stormed, then checked himself as Karia stirred and rolled over. They both watched her, almost holding their breath, until Karia snuggled herself back into sleep.

They locked eyes again and she glared at him.

'You don't understand what the country is going through! I am asking them to accept me, when many of them never did, agree to the changes I plan — and now welcome an army of Derthals living among them, when they were all raised on tales of those evil goblins in the north. A base-born Ralloran Prince Consort and half-Ralloran Prince is too much ...'

'At least wait a little! Give the people a chance to see that I am no threat to the throne. Give your new ideas a chance to take hold!' he begged in quiet desperation.

Merren's instincts told her this was a bad idea. The Crown Prince needed to be born without suspicion. Waiting could create all sorts of problems. The part of her that was enjoying the sensation of Martil's hands on her skin, the part that had almost died during his fight with Cezar, wanted to agree with him. But she could not let her heart rule her head.

'I don't want to give you a false hope. I thought we had agreed this was impossible, and you had sworn not to bring it up again?'

'But you admitted you loved me!'

'I did no such thing,' she protested in a hoarse whisper.

'After the fight! I saw the look on your face — when you caught me before I fell. Look me in the eye and tell me you felt nothing,' he challenged, still trying to talk in a whisper.

Merren tried to stare him down, but could not.

'But that changes nothing! I cannot put myself before the people.' Merren was almost in tears.

'Then just wait a little — see if the people change. Perhaps you don't have to make a choice between me and the people,' Martil appealed.

Merren surged to her feet. 'If it comes down to a choice, you cannot win. All we are doing is delaying hurting ourselves now, only to hurt even more in the future.'

Martil jumped to his feet as well. 'How do you know the people won't accept me? I've fought for them, my men have died for them — I've just bled for them and it nearly cost me my life. Why can't they see that?'

'Because it's not that simple!' she snarled.

Martil was about to shout at her when a noise from the bed made them both turn — to see Karia stretch and then subside once more.

'Well it should be — don't your people want you to be happy?' he mouthed angrily.

'It is not about you! It is not about me, either — Norstalos is bigger than both of us.'

'Then what are we fighting for?' Martil asked.

She had to take a breath then, to keep control. 'Do you really think it is that easy, that I can just ignore what the people want and do whatever pleases myself? For down that path lies Gello,' she said indignantly, struggling to keep her voice down.

'That's not what I meant! I'm trying to say the people will change. I'm saying we can still hope,' Martil argued. He wanted to rage and shout but kept himself quiet. It seemed ridiculous to be having an argument in whispers.

'I can't allow myself the luxury of hope,' Merren said softly, hollowly. For a long moment they stared at each other, Martil trying to convey through his eyes what he had not been able to put into words. Merren wanted to tell him there was no hope but could not bring herself to do it. Not just for what it would do to him, but what it would do to her. 'After what we have been through, I will delay the wedding — for a while,' she relented.

Martil had imagined far more than this but, after her earlier words, it was enough to make him grin. He stepped in close and hugged Merren tight. She was slow to react and could not step away as her head was telling her to do. But as she felt his arms around her, sense fled and she relaxed, holding him close. He leaned down to kiss her and although she knew this was a bad idea, which could only lead to other things, her hand went to the back of his head ... only to hear a light cough.

They both turned their heads at the same time, to see Karia yawning and rubbing her eyes.

'Are you coming to bed?' she murmured, her eyes barely open.

Martil hesitated, unwilling to break the moment, but Merren slipped away from him and went around to the far side of the bed. For a moment only, she locked eyes with him.

'That is the end of the discussion,' she said gently, then lay on her side, her back to him.

With no other choice, he lay down on the bed also. It was not that big, but it still felt as though there was an enormous space between them.

2

Kettering waved Hawke and Leigh down the neat, cobbled street. Cessor was a rich trading port and the houses in this district belonged to merchants, shopkeepers and traders who all made their living on or from the sea. All were two or three storeys high, and the top storeys would have magnificent views across the water. Sadly, they would also have wonderful views of the Tenoch invasion that was set to sweep through this town. Kettering and his men were trying to persuade as many people as possible to move out. Some had gone but many remained.

'Knock on the door,' Kettering ordered.

Leigh, limping slightly from the wound he had taken at Pilleth, used the hilt of his sword to bang on the solid wooden door of the first house.

'Careful,' Hawke growled. 'You'll dent it!'

Leigh looked at him. 'Since when have you cared about damaging things?'

'That's a good door, that is. Western cedar — that door's worth more than you and I!'

'What are you going on about? I never knew you was an expert on doors!'

'I used to sleep in a doorway like that when I was a kid, on the streets,' Hawke said slowly. 'I swore to myself one day I'd sleep on the other side of it.

A door like that says you've made it. Says you're a man of substance.'

'Man of substance? Sounds like you've been on some substance,' Leigh sniffed. 'Anyway, seeing as how the Tenochs are going to burn it all down, do you really think it's going to matter if it has a small dent in it?'

'Enough,' Kettering stepped in. 'Use the bloody door knocker! Don't you know how to deal with people?'

Leigh sighed, sheathed his sword and used the brass knocker to rap three times on the door. 'Not all of us were under-managers of big inns, you know,' he grumbled, but quietly enough that Kettering could pretend he hadn't heard it. 'Besides, I thought the idea was, if we looked like criminals, we'd help scare the good people away?'

The door jerked open and Leigh hastily raised his hands as a loaded crossbow was pointed at his face.

'You may not be an inn manager, but you obviously look like a criminal.' Hawke grinned, then wiped the smile from his face and threw his hands into the air as the crossbow moved in his direction.

'We are soldiers of the Queen, here with an important message,' Kettering said, stepping close to the arbalester, a middle-aged, portly man with an enormous moustache.

'Soldiers? A likely story! You're all thieves and murderers, more likely. Look what you've done to my door!'

'Told you,' Hawke murmured.

Kettering ignored him. 'Sir, a fleet of ships, bringing thousands of warriors sworn to Zorva's service, is heading towards this town. Now, I am here for two reasons — to tell everyone to move out, and to compile a list of provisions you have with you.'

'Provisions? And what business of that is yours?' the man said suspiciously.

'Sir, we are evacuating thousands of people. Some will be without food by the time they get far enough north. We need to make sure the food is shared out equally,' Kettering said as calmly as he could. He had always hated dealing with members of the public like this when he was under-manager at the Crown and Sparrow in Wollin. Just because they had some money, they thought they could get away with anything.

'We shall also need any carriages and especially horses you have in your stables, to help others move faster,' Hawke added.

The man snorted. 'Do you think I was born yesterday? Do you know how much a good horse and carriage costs? And sharing the food equally! I've never heard theft described like that! Tell me, is your Queen going to buy this food from me? Will my horses be given the best corn? Will any damage to my carriage be repaired — and will a proper hire fee be paid?'

Kettering took a deep breath. Once he would have bowed and scraped and apologised abjectly for offending a man like this. But that had been a different Kettering. Now he could feel his anger rising. With reluctance he quelled it and tried again. 'She is your Queen also,' he said harshly. 'I would have thought that, as a loyal Norstaline, you would want to help your fellow Norstalines in their time of need? And does not Aroaril say that charity is good for the soul? Besides, everyone has to tighten their belt at a time of national crisis.'

The man's face reddened, as he glanced down at the wide leather belt fighting to keep his large stomach from bursting out of his straining trews. 'You come here and order me out of my home, tell me you are going to steal my horses, my carriage, all my food, my wine, the delicacies I have purchased at great expense to see me through the winter, without so much as a copper coin in recompense, then you have the nerve to say that it will be good for my soul! You are scum, plucked from the gutter, who know no better. King Gello is coming back to put you and yours in your place! He will have no quarrel with the likes of us, so I have no intention of leaving and I would rather burn in Zorva's pit than have you and your kind rob me of everything I spent twenty years earning!'

'That can be arranged,' Kettering spat, anger racing through him now. 'You will pack for leaving, and you will give me a full list of all the food you are hoarding or by Aroaril I will …'

'Er, Killer, you might want to look around,' Leigh said nervously.

Kettering whirled around angrily to see a crowd had gathered, attracted by all the shouting. Even now, other doors in the street were opening, and a variety of richly dressed men and women, almost all of them middle-aged, were either stepping onto the street or leaning out of ornate windows. Many held clubs, or knives; two others had crossbows.

'We don't want your kind around here!' one across the street shouted. 'Leave Fergus alone!'

'Aye, leave now or I'll send you to the pits where you belong!' Fergus, the moustached man, stepped out past his door and prodded Kettering in the back with his crossbow.

That was too much. Kettering sidestepped and, in the same action, grabbed the front of the crossbow and pointed it away. Fergus's finger instinctively tightened on the trigger bar and the heavy bolt thumped into the man's door, sticking in the fine timber.

'I told them to watch the door,' Hawke muttered.

Kettering let go of the now-useless crossbow and turned to the gathering crowd. 'Listen to me. You have to leave now — your lives are at risk!' he roared.

'So you say. But King Gello will not harm us!' a woman cried, and many others nodded or let out a shout of agreement. 'Your Queen is destroying the country! She has ended the nobility, she is giving common people the right to tell us what to do.'

'Aye! That's right!' her supporters chorused.

Kettering watched her, amazed, as she whipped the crowd into a frenzy.

'How can peasants have the right to tell us what to do? Would I let my kitchen staff and maid give me orders? It is madness. As if their voice is as important as mine! Me, a personal friend of the Countess Cessor! This action will destroy the country. And now you tell us she plans to seize all of our property and give it to scum who are jealous of everything we have worked hard for?'

Kettering stared at the woman. If she had done any work harder than ordering her servants about, he would eat Fergus's crossbow. But he could not get a word in against her tirade.

'Suppose we leave, and return to find ten families with stinking brats living in our houses, messing up our rooms and wrecking our treasures? After our horses, our wine cellars, our carriages and our stores have been stolen and handed out to anyone who walks by? This is your Queen's next step in her mad plan to ruin this country. And we will be damned before we let it happen here!'

'Herena! Herena!' her supporters applauded.

Kettering tried to push through the crowd towards her, but they locked arms in front of him.

'Get out of here, and don't come back!' Herena roared at them.

'Come on, lads,' Kettering grunted. As far as he was concerned, they deserved anything the Tenochs gave them.

King Gello waited impatiently. Co-ordinating three attacks, from three different forces, across hundreds of miles, was an enormous undertaking. The delay chafed at him. All he thought about was revenge. Since Pilleth and then the realisation he was a puppet of the Fearpriest, his thoughts had turned inwards. He was having long conversations with Mother about how he would both defeat Merren and outwit his erstwhile allies. He had thought, since his conversion, he would not need her so much — but he had found himself talking to her more and more. She would not answer him but he thought he was making progress. He was sure she was smiling at him now. He was telling her how both the Dragon Sword and Pilleth would be consigned to history, forgotten in a blaze of glory as he forged a new reputation for himself, when Prent and Feld rushed over to him.

They waited while he carefully kissed the portrait of the Duchess Ivene that he now carried everywhere, and placed it where it could listen to the report.

'Sire, there are problems. Bad weather has meant the Tenochs are delayed — they cannot leave for another three days, then there will be the sailing time of four or five days.'

Gello spat in disgust. 'I thought you Fearpriests could promise fine weather?'

Prent shuffled his feet. 'It seems the Norstaline wizard acted first. It will take days for the storm to blow out.'

'What else?'

'Ezok failed to persuade the goblins to attack the north. Martil killed Cezar; Ezok and Khaliz only just escaped with their lives. They believe a goblin army will march to help the Norstalines.'

At this, Gello threw back his head and laughed.

'Sire?' Feld said nervously.

'Perfect! Now the people will fear the goblins as well as the Berellians! Not only will they rally to me when I return, but our gallant allies can suffer to defeat the goblins! Now leave me. I must discuss these developments with Mother.'

They carefully bowed to both Gello and the portrait, before backing out of the tent.

If Conal had had two hands, he would have used one to pull his hair out. Reports were flooding in from around the country on the progress of the evacuation, and while some gave him heart, others made him despair.

'You cannot bear the responsibility for everyone,' Louise tried to tell him.

Conal sighed. 'I wish I could make myself believe you. I wish I was back being a simple bandit or, even better, a simple militia sergeant. But I cannot. These reports tell me that villages and towns are emptying, faster each day as the food shortages start to bite. But hundreds remain.'

'That is their choice,' Louise told him.

'And even those who are leaving are making little progress! Some of the roads are almost jammed with people, all moving at the pace of the slowest farm wagon. And the pace seems to slow further, as livestock and people tire. Thank Aroaril our weather has held. If we get a few days of solid rain, many of those roads will turn into mud and it will be near-impossible to get the people away. Even if it stays fine, I don't know if we can get all of them into the north in time!'

Louise put her arm around him.

'You need to rest, you've been working too hard,' she told him.

'Well, you know what it's like. If only I had an extra hand,' he told her, with a tired smile, a smile that slowly dissolved. 'There is so much to do and time is running out. We have lookouts on every cliff along the western coast — we should get a day's warning of when the Tenochs are about to invade, and that will tell us when to expect Gello and the Berellians to sweep in as well.'

Louise looked down at the long lists of parchment.

'Then Gia and I shall help you,' she stated firmly. 'After all, we are members of the Royal Council and attendants to the Queen. You go to bed and we shall keep working.'

'I can't do that,' Conal protested weakly. 'I have to write out these orders and send them out with these birds that Barrett has left us so Nerrin, Rocus and the rest know what to do tomorrow!'

'You will go to bed if I have to drag you there myself!' Louise told him.

Conal could not help but smile then. 'Well, if you put it like that ...'

Louise smiled back, despite herself. 'I don't. But get yourself some sleep and let us finish these off.'

For a long moment he looked at her.

'Wime was a lucky man,' he said softly.

'I know.' Her smile was brittle. 'Now leave me to work.'

Martil woke to find Karia's arm over his chest and her head on his shoulder. He hugged her close for a moment, until he had control of himself. He had been dreaming about the fight with Cezar, only this time a sobbing Karia was watching — and he was unable to get up and stop the Berellian. Even now he could feel his heart pounding. He rubbed his eyes with a shaking hand.

'Don't get up. This is too comfortable,' Karia declared, reaching out so she had an arm around both Merren and Martil. 'Isn't this nice, us all together like this?'

Martil looked over and saw Merren staring at him.

'We should do this more often,' Karia announced. This was exactly what she wanted! A family, all together. All she had to do was make sure the two of them saw it as well.

'Perhaps we should,' Martil agreed, gazing at Merren.

'Better make the most of it, because I don't know when it will happen again,' Merren replied.

'But it's so much fun!' Martil smiled at Karia.

'Sadly, fun isn't always the best reason to do something. Sometimes you have to do things that are not fun.' Merren's eyes bored in at him.

'That's silly!' Karia hugged them both. 'Why don't we all get some breakfast?'

It seemed to be the perfect way out of there without an argument, although getting a word in against the steady chatter of Karia was impossible for both of them. And finding breakfast was not much easier. They found the Derthal camp a hive of activity. Hundreds of Derthal warriors were lashing new spearheads to shafts, or strapping spears to their backs, while females packed food and Sacrax strode around, bellowing orders.

'They seem to be doing well without us. Perhaps we should go up to Father Alban's church,' Martil suggested.

'And get some food,' Karia added.

She slipped her hands into theirs, so they were holding one hand each as they walked. Everything was going well, she decided.

'Swing me! Please?' she pleaded.

Martil looked at Merren and saw her mouth twitch almost into a smile, then he winked at her over Karia's head. So they found themselves swinging her through the air, her laughter ringing in their ears as they walked out of the Derthal valley. As they came into sight of the church, with Argurium lying down outside it, they saw Barrett.

'Barrett! Watch me!' Karia shouted, and swung high, holding tight to Martil's and Merren's hands. Martil glanced at Barrett, and saw the wizard's jaw tighten as he watched the three of them, holding hands and laughing — and then the wizard disappeared back into the church.

'Wonderful.' Merren had also seen Barrett's reaction.

She hurried after him, while Karia hurried in hope of breakfast and Martil tried to stay with them. But he was blocked at the door by Havell.

'Martil, a quick word if you please?' the Elfaran asked stiffly. 'Queen Merren, Karia, this will only take a moment.'

Merren caught the look Havell gave her, so took Karia's hand and ushered her inside. Martil was tempted to follow anyway, then the dragon pounced on him.

'Dragon Sword Wielder, I must ask you never to risk yourself like that again,' Argurium rumbled. 'To accept a duel is bad enough but then to trick us, deliberately prevent us from protecting you ...'

'You can save it. I've heard it from your pointy-eared slave,' Martil said coldly, using anger to cover himself. 'I never asked for any of this! I never agreed to save the dragons and the magic — I didn't even want to save another country after I left Rallora —'

Then Argurium was looming over him and he glimpsed the fearsome creature that had so terrified the Derthals. 'Well, you shall hear it from me,' she said, her voice lashing like a whip. 'You won our agreement to help you but only if you fulfilled your end of the bargain by ensuring the return of the dragons and the magic. Risking your life and nearly dying is not acceptable. We must stay close to you — or I shall be forced to take you away from here, to the safety of Dragonara Isle.'

Martil spat in disgust. 'Do you think I tried to get myself killed on purpose?' he snarled.

'No, but you risked yourself unnecessarily. I want you to be more careful ...'

Martil shook his head. 'We are in a war. My life will always be at risk.'

'Well, I want you to always think of what rests on you ...'

That touched the fear inside Martil. 'Will you leave me alone?' he almost screamed at the dragon. *Why did this have to happen, on top of everything else?*

Argurium paused and looked at him carefully for a long moment before speaking again. 'I cannot leave you alone. But we are here to help you,' she promised, finally. 'I just need your word that you will not risk yourself so rashly again.'

'You have it!' he snapped, trying not to think what a wonderful excuse this would be not to fight again, when not only a little girl but everything depended on him.

'I know it is a great deal for you to take in and that we ask much of you. But we can help. What do you need?'

His first reaction was to say he wanted nothing from them but he forced himself to think before he said something foolish. 'Can you take us back to the capital?' he asked, both because he knew they needed to return fast — and wanting to give Karia a treat to make up for what he had put her through.

'Yes,' Argurium rumbled.

'Good,' Martil said, moving as if their 'talk' was over. Although Havell looked as though he had more to say, at a signal from Argurium he subsided and let Martil escape inside Alban's church.

Martil found Merren trying to get some food for Karia, and she welcomed the distraction.

'Using the dragon? What is this?' Merren asked when he told her.

Martil shrugged. 'Well, if we are going to ask Barrett to use his powers to bring in game for the Derthals, then he won't be able to take us back to the capital. But we need to get back fast. The attack could happen any day.'

Barrett appeared from the church's simple kitchen. 'What do you want?' he asked sourly.

'Barrett, the Derthals need your help. They can march swiftly, but they need food. High Chief Sacrax told me last night that they need to leave enough food here so the females, the children and the old can last the winter,' Merren said quickly. 'You can do that today, then return to the capital tomorrow, with any of us that Argurium cannot carry.'

Barrett nodded. 'I shall do that,' he agreed flatly.

'Barrett — I need to thank you for saving my life last night — and saving our cause at the same time.' Martil stepped forwards, hand outstretched.

Barrett stared at it for a long moment. 'It is becoming something of a habit, is it not?' he said coolly. 'Yet, funnily enough, it is you who is always hailed the hero.'

'That is never my wish,' Martil said quietly.

Barrett ignored his hand. 'I have duties to perform. I shall go and find High Chief Sacrax, and begin to bring in game. They will need time to smoke the meat, if it is to last the trip south.'

Martil gritted his teeth and lowered his hand as the wizard brushed past him and walked out.

Barrett could feel every eye on him but he did not care. He was not in love with Merren any more. He told himself that every day. But, still, seeing her reaction to Martil's fight, watching her run across to catch him in her arms, on top of knowing she was carrying Martil's baby — it was hard not to feel bitter.

There was silence in the church after Barrett left.

Merren thought about going after him but thought it probably best to leave him alone. She might do more harm than good, the mood he was in. And he was too important to her cause to risk offending.

'When can we fly on the dragon?' Karia asked in the silence.

Merren smiled. 'We shall need to leave as soon as we have spoken to High Chief Sacrax. Wilsen, Jaret, you can travel back with Barrett, while Father Quiller, you will need to travel with the Derthals, to make sure there are no incidents on the way south.'

'I can't believe I'm going to fly on a dragon! What a great present!' Karia laughed and then pumped her fists.

'Where did you learn that?' Merren asked, laughing.

'Watching the soldiers,' she said, innocently.

'Well, as long as that's all you pick up from them,' Martil muttered.

'Can I talk to the elf and dragon? Can I, please?'

Martil was happy to leave her with Argurium and pestering Havell with questions about the non-existent magic creatures on Dragonara Isle. Partly to pay back the Elfaran but also because he wanted to keep her away from where, thanks to Barrett, deer, goats, birds and rabbits were presenting themselves in reasonable — but not great — numbers to the Derthals. She would have loved that but hated seeing eager Derthals slit their throats, then skin and butcher them. Meanwhile, other Derthals were stripping bushes and trees of berries and nuts, again thanks to Barrett. The wizard would not talk to them but he was at least working hard.

Sacrax greeted them enthusiastically, his doubts of the previous night gone.

'We shall be able to leave this evening!' the High Chief grinned. 'All the clans are gathering, and we shall meet at the point where my guides waited for you.'

'We shall fly back to Norstalos on the dragon, so we may prepare to defeat our enemies, the Berellians,' Merren announced. 'We shall see you at the passes?'

'You shall,' Sacrax agreed. 'You have my oath, my blood. May my bowels turn to water and my loins to ice if I break that!'

Merren glanced at Martil, who kept a straight face.

'Thank you,' Merren said simply, holding out her hand. 'You have saved both our peoples.'

'I hope so.' Sacrax nodded, clasping her hand carefully.

3

Back in the capital, this had seemed like a straightforward task to ex-sergeant — now Father — Kesbury. Although he was not a real priest, not even a Brother, yet. In fact he had barely begun his training but Archbishop Nott had sent every novice out into the country. There was no point learning how to care for a flock when the wolves were already loose. His assignment had been one of the two villages on the Berellian border that was refusing to move. Attempts to remove food from villages had been far less successful than in the towns. After all, most were farmers, with vegetable gardens and livestock.

He did wonder why he had been given the hardest task of all the novices. He did not question it, because he knew he had more to prove than anyone else, being a Ralloran and also seen by some as too close to Bishop Milly.

The former priest of the village, Chanlon, had the place under his thumb but Kesbury was in no mood to play around. The attack could come any day. While Nerrin and the Rallorans had been forced to tread carefully, Kesbury had no such qualms.

He was greeted with jeers and insults, led by Chanlon, but he stopped them instantly by using his new-found powers to silence Chanlon, then hold the man. The villagers took one look at what the huge ex-soldier had done to their former leader — and swiftly decided to do whatever Kesbury asked. He sensed they feared him, some even hated him, but he could not worry about it. Their feelings about him were secondary to saving them.

Most families had a horse or two, many had small wagons or carts — and all were loaded high. Kesbury went through them, ruthlessly throwing away items that were useless, or would only slow them down, replacing them with crates of food and barrels of ale from Chanlon's store. Villagers began to protest as valuable heirlooms were thrown to the ground, then thought better of it.

He was also grabbing every man he could see, and talking to them, a little more quietly.

'Get yourself a weapon. Doesn't matter if it's an axe, a hoe, a club or a knife. Bring it.'

Against a company of Berellians, it would be pitiful, but anything was better than nothing. As for himself, he had found a lead-tipped staff in Chanlon's house. Having used something similar as a guard on the Golden Gate brothel, he was happy to adopt it.

Finally, all was ready to his satisfaction.

'Right! Our first destination will be the River Brack. We'll get there and then see which road is faster to the north. Remember, every mile we walk is a mile further away from the Berellian attack. If the children get tired, sit them on a horse or on a wagon. Let's move!'

Kesbury hid his fear as he watched them begin. They had left it late — but at least they were moving. The men and women were all farmers, used to working from dawn to dusk. He could push them hard, get them a good long way from here in a couple of days. But then it would get more difficult. People, and animals, would begin to tire. And Aroaril help them if it began to rain. He just had one more task.

'I don't want to see your face again, understand? Go where you will but stay away from these people,' Kesbury told Chanlon. 'You may take my horse. I'll be walking.'

He released the man and for a moment he thought the ex-priest was going to attack him. But Chanlon was no fool, and he came to his senses before taking on Kesbury, who was twice his size.

'This won't be the last you'll see of me,' the ex-priest hissed.

'For your health, I hope it is,' Kesbury told him, then turned his back on the man, striding after the last farm cart, which was just clearing the village outskirts.

Chanlon watched him go in impotent fury. Having been forced to watch, helpless, as his village was stolen from him, he had spent the time planning ever more fanciful ways of getting his revenge. But then his mind cleared. Revenge was close at hand. Stopping only to collect a couple of moneybags, which had been left by Kesbury, he found the horse and turned it towards the southern border.

King Markuz had become obsessed with the conquest of Norstalos. Since the death of Cezar, he had thought of nothing else. If he had had his way, the army would have already marched and smoke would be staining the sky. But Onzalez had ordered a delay. The Tenochs were late, still sailing up the coast, and the three invasions were all being held back because of them.

Without permission to attack, Markuz was bored. So when a Norstaline priest was dragged before him, he was willing to hear what the man said. If it was not useful, then it would be entertaining to hear the man scream.

'Who are you?' Markuz demanded.

'I am Chanlon, dismissed from Aroaril's service and looking to serve you, sire. I bring news from over the border!'

Markuz tried to keep the interest from his face. He had tried to slip men across the border but the accursed Rallorans were too good — hardly any of his spies made it back alive.

'What news?'

'The Queen is trying to evacuate the people to the north!'

Markuz could not care less. The fools would run into Gello coming from the east and the Tenochs invading from the west.

'Only two villages remain south of the river —'

'This is not important,' Markuz interrupted. 'Where are the Rallorans? That is what I want to know.'

Chanlon paused nervously, unsure whether he should make something up.

'Take this fool away and have him impaled for wasting my time.' Markuz gestured to the sweating Chanlon.

'No, no, I'll do anything! Just don't kill me, I'll do anything to help you!' Chanlon screamed.

Onzalez seemed to appear out of nowhere. At a gesture from him, the guards stopped dragging Chanlon away to his grisly fate. Everyone stopped, nervously waiting for the Fearpriest.

'What is going on, Brother?' Markuz rumbled.

'Summon your war captains. Launch a raid across

the border. Sack those villages,' Onzalez suggested, and Markuz sat up, a broad smile on his face.

As the king signalled for his captains, Onzalez turned to Chanlon.

'A former priest of Aroaril. Will you convert? Serve me always?' Onzalez demanded.

'Happily,' Chanlon swore.

'Bring him with us,' Onzalez ordered the guards. 'When we capture our first Norstalines, we shall see if he shall join us, or them in death.'

'You won't regret this,' Chanlon promised, sobbing with relief.

Martil did not know what to expect when it came to flying on a dragon. He had never thought such a thing would happen. Karia, on the other hand, had dreamed of little else for the past year.

'There is nothing to fear,' Havell told them. 'Riding on a dragon is not like flying on some bird or ordinary creature. A dragon flies using magic, so there is no need to worry about such things as wind and cold. The trip will be swift and comfortable, although I would caution you not to look down too much.'

'Why not? I want to look!' Karia complained.

'The sight of the ground can be unsettling,' Havell warned.

'He's no fun,' Karia muttered to Martil.

'No, but then falling off might be too much fun.' Martil smiled. 'And then no fun at all.'

'Ha ha, very funny,' she told him.

Havell, sighing slightly, showed them how to climb onto Argurium's wing, which the dragon lifted until they could step onto her broad back, then walk up to where they could sit and buckle themselves into thin leather straps that looped around the dragon's long neck.

'Is that it? It looks flimsy.' Martil tested it nervously.

'That is all you need. It is, after all, a magical trip. It is just to stop you leaning over and perhaps falling off.'

Martil made sure Karia was sitting in front of him, and he had his arms around her, as well as through the strap, just in case.

'Dad! I can barely see!' Karia protested.

'I'd rather be sure you can stay on,' Martil told her, as Merren took her seat carefully.

'Are we all ready?' Havell settled himself between Martil and Merren.

'No,' Martil admitted.

'Excellent!' Havell smiled thinly. Martil suspected the Elfaran was rather enjoying his discomfort.

A crowd of Derthals, along with Jaret, Wilsen, Quiller and Alban — but, noticeably, not Barrett — waved them off.

Martil did not know what to expect. He had imagined there would be some sort of frantic flapping of wings, followed by a struggle to gain height, before an uncomfortable trip back to the capital.

But it was nothing of the sort. The dragon seemed to leap effortlessly into the air; in moments the huge crowd had dwindled to the size of ants and they were speeding south. Martil knew what it felt like to gallop on a horse, how the wind whipped at you — and the way the ground was moving below seemed to indicate the wind should be enough to blow them clear off the back of the dragon, 'holding strap' or not. But there was barely enough wind to ruffle their hair.

'I can't believe it,' Martil gasped.

'This is fantastic! Look down there,' Karia laughed.

'This is better even than Barrett's trick with enchanting the birds! With Argurium's help, we can 'see what is happening from one side of the country to the other,' Merren exulted.

'Perhaps there is some use to this "bloody lizard", after all,' Argurium declared.

Martil glanced guiltily at Havell as a grinning Karia leaned back and nudged him in the ribs with her elbow.

There was barely time to spot the northern towns and the passes as they flew south at an impossible speed. But there was time to see, on every road, columns of refugees heading north.

'So Conal and Sendric did their job,' Merren said grimly. 'But what will this cost the country?'

'Less than if we were not getting those people behind the passes,' Martil replied.

'How is it going? Are the south and west being evacuated swiftly enough? Perhaps I should not have gone north …' Merren was worried.

'Merren, you had to go. Without the Derthals, we could offer those people only a false hope. With the Derthals, they will be safe behind those passes,' Martil told her. 'You can only do one thing at a time. Conal and Sendric have not let you down.'

But Merren was not really listening to him. 'So many are going to die,' she sighed.

'But more will live,' Martil reminded her. 'The most important thing is to keep as many soldiers as possible. It will be a hard decision to leave people behind to the Berellians and Tenochs but we have no choice.'

'Sadly, I fear you are right,' Merren groaned.

'We shall be at the capital shortly. I assume you want to be taken to the palace?' Havell interrupted.

Merren shook her head. 'I want you to go lower, fly around the city slowly. Let all see me on the dragon's back before you land.'

'Is that sort of display really necessary?'

'Dragons hold a special place in Norstalos' history. It might be a false place, given what you told us about King Riel and the Dragon Sword, but dragons are still honoured and cherished by the people. They talk of Norstalos being "blessed by the dragons". The people are afraid, worried. To see me on a dragon will give the people a boost,' Merren explained.

'And stop those rumours about the dragons not wanting a Queen on the throne.' Martil turned and smiled at her to remove any sting from the words.

Merren could not help but smile back. 'Indeed,' she admitted.

So it proved.

The first swoop around the city brought the people out in droves — rather too many people, Martil thought, when they should have been already heading north — and the second trip around the city was greeted with thunderous cheers. Merren — and Karia — waved as Argurium banked low over the city and Martil rather reluctantly drew the Dragon Sword and flourished it for the benefit of the crowds below.

'It is important. The people need to see it,' Merren insisted.

Martil felt a little foolish — in fact he felt the way he had when Rallora's King Tolbert insisted Martil and other war heroes share the stage with him at victory parades. But he remembered Merren's promise to wait before marrying Sendric, and he thought he could survive a little foolishness.

The square outside the palace was full of people by the time Merren finally let Argurium land. Many were cheering and screaming — others were crying with joy, holding up children so they could get a better view of the wondrous sight.

Out in front were Sendric and Conal.

'That's a fine welcome, but don't you think there are too many people here?' Martil said sharply, sliding off in a rather ungainly fashion, then catching Karia as she jumped nimbly down.

But they ignored him, instead addressing Merren, who slid down gracefully.

'Your majesty! Thank Aroaril you are back,' Conal said with relief.

The appearance of riders on their flank had many of the villagers crying out in fear. Some tried to run, others tried to hide but Kesbury saw immediately the riders were Rallorans. He ignored them, concentrating instead on the people who were his responsibility.

'Stop!' he roared at the villagers. 'Those men are on our side.'

'But they're Butchers of Bellic!' one elderly man cried fearfully.

'I was at Bellic,' Kesbury told him, standing close to the man. 'And you are in no danger from them. But you may be in danger from me unless you quiet down!'

'I see you've got everything in hand here, sergeant!'

Kesbury turned to see an amused Dunner. A score of grinning Rallorans had ridden in close and were now watching him.

'Sergeant no more, my friend,' Kesbury stated. 'What news?'

'You still sound like a sergeant.' Dunner smiled. 'The Berellians are stirring. The attack will come soon. We rode to give the village a final warning, found it empty and followed your tracks.'

Kesbury nodded grimly. 'Did you see that ex-priest still there?'

'Chanlon? No, I'm sure he would have taken the opportunity to scream at us if he had seen us.' Dunner shrugged.

Kesbury wondered where Chanlon had gone, for the man had not overtaken them on the road, then put it aside.

'Are you going to give us an escort north?' he asked.

Dunner's face lost its smile.

'We don't have the men. We'll be outnumbered eight to one as it is,' he said sadly.

'Then give me ten men. They won't make any difference to you but could make all the difference to us!'

Dunner hesitated, glancing up and down the column. Men, women and children stared back at him mutely. He sighed.

'I cannot order men to do this. You know why,' he said softly, then turned to his Rallorans.

'Volunteers to stay and fight with Sergeant Kesbury!' he called.

'I'm not a sergeant ...' Kesbury began but then saw every man urge their horse forwards.

Dunner looked at Kesbury. 'We've all heard too many sagas,' he muttered, then pointed to the men behind him. 'Two squad, you're now under Sergeant — I mean Father Kesbury's — orders.'

'Thank you, my friend,' Kesbury said softly. 'Aroaril be with you.'

They clasped hands.

'Say a prayer for us all,' Dunner said, then waved to his remaining men. 'We ride!'

Merren smiled as she looked out the window, seeing the crowd gathered around Argurium. This was a tale that would spread across the land!

'Your majesty, if we can continue?' Conal interrupted her thoughts.

'Of course.' Merren turned back. She had outlined what had happened in the north, now she needed to know what was happening in Norstalos.

'We have people moving on every road — we managed to get them out by taking as much food as we could and bringing it north. Much of it is here in the capital, waiting to be handed out to those from further south, who will have exhausted what they brought with them by the time they reach here. There are pockets that still remain, but we cannot do any more than we have already,' Conal explained. 'In the south, Captain Nerrin reports the Berellians are preparing to attack. In the east, Kay says Gello is still in camp and making no move towards the border. In the west, Rocus warns the Tenoch fleet has been seen off the coast, but is still three days from landfall. I don't know the reason for their delay but it is a gift from Aroaril. It will save many lives.'

'It was a storm created by Barrett,' Merren said. 'But you have done wonderfully well. If you had been unable to get the people heading north, I dread to think what would have happened! Now we can not only get them to safety, but protect them once they are there.'

Conal looked down at the table. 'It has been hard, your majesty …'

Merren stood and walked around to where the ex-bandit was slumped in his seat.

'Conal, you have done the impossible. You have my gratitude. All of you! What you have done is amazing. I am sorry you had to do that for me, but it was done in my name. It is my responsibility, not yours. Any blame is mine, any thanks is yours.'

'I cannot accept all your thanks. Louise and Gia helped me greatly. They were the ones who made the hardest decisions ...' Conal shook his head.

'We know what it is like to make a sacrifice for the good of the country,' Louise said, trying to smile.

'Well, those people should sing your praises when they are safe.'

'They are not safe yet. Most have many miles to travel,' Sendric warned. 'It would not take much to see at least half the country unable to escape, and at the mercy of the Berellians and Tenochs.'

'Which reminds me. Why are there still so many people in the capital? I thought it would be almost empty by now,' Merren asked carefully.

Conal, embarrassed, looked to Sendric.

'What is going on?' Merren demanded.

'I thought it was advisable to have a decent crowd here to witness the royal wedding,' Sendric said stiffly. 'After all, you said you wanted it to take place as soon as you returned. I held back many of the capital's residents so word of the wedding could spread far and wide.'

There was a sudden silence around the table. Martil tried not to look at Merren but, under the table, he grasped Karia's hand tight.

Merren took a deep breath. 'We need to tell them to leave. Now. Their escape is more important.'

'But ...' Sendric began.

'There will be no wedding until all are safe behind the passes. It would be the height of arrogance to waste time and money on such a thing when there are lives at risk,' Merren said briskly.

'But —'

'I have decided — and that will be the end of it!' Merren snapped. 'Besides, I shall be too busy. Apart from all the reports flooding in here, I shall take

Argurium and visit the people, as many as possible, to encourage them.'

Martil found himself smiling, a little. His heart had leaped when she declared the wedding was postponed. It was not cancelled — but every day when it did not happen was a good one.

'Next, we need to think about feeding and housing the people once they are in the north.' Merren sighed.

'We already have men up there, putting up crude shelters, just basic huts, as quickly as they can. As more people arrive, they can help,' Louise reported.

'Then what is next?'

'Waiting for an attack. We need to slow them down, but also preserve enough men to form the basis of an army that will defeat them in the spring,' Martil answered. 'Once we have withdrawn behind the passes, our soldiers can begin training every man who can lift a spear or swing a sword.'

'Well done, everyone! When Barrett returns from the north I shall have more tasks for him but, for now, I want you all to rest while I go over those reports in detail. I shall leave orders before I take Martil and Karia with me on Argurium to visit the south.'

Martil was sure that had not been part of Argurium's deal, but it would certainly help Merren win over the people.

The meeting broke up then, but Sendric lingered behind. He had sat in silence since being rebuffed by Merren.

'Your majesty, I must protest,' he said indignantly. 'Putting the wedding off — the timing, your majesty! We must be married a decent time before the baby arrives. I think not of myself but of the reputation of Norstalos!'

'Sendric, we are talking about a few weeks, at most,' Merren waved him away. 'It is not important. Not compared to saving the people.'

'It is important to the country,' Sendric growled. 'And what about Martil? What if he were to find out?' He looked at her suddenly-white face and gasped in horror. 'He knows! He has found out!'

'No!' Merren tried to protest but Sendric would not listen to her denials.

'This is exactly what I feared,' he said furiously.

'Keep your voice down, for Aroaril's sake,' she barked. 'It changes nothing.'

She swept past him, leaving the old noble fuming. Could she not see the future of the Norstaline Royal House depended on this?

Martil had been reminded by Cezar that he was out of shape. So he worked with a pair of guardsmen, sparring with one, then both of them, using heavy wooden practice swords until the sweat was pouring off all three of them, and the muscles in his back, arms and shoulders were protesting furiously.

He had left the two Royal Guardsmen to go and wash before he went to see Karia again. She would be with the dragon, who was proving a perfect child-sitter, although Havell was not too impressed. Apparently the Elfarans had been without women and children for centuries. And the first one he had to experience was Karia, Martil thought to himself with a smile.

He was towelling himself dry in his room when Sendric walked in.

'Count! What is it?' Martil wrapped the towel around his waist.

'I need to talk to you about Merren,' Sendric said sharply, standing stiffly by the door.

'Merren? Is she all right?' Martil found himself reaching for the Dragon Sword before his trews.

'She is not in danger, if that is what you mean,' Sendric said. 'But I must speak to you about this despicable situation you have put us all in.'

Martil took a few moments to realise what the noble was getting at, then he had to control his temper.

'I don't want to talk about this,' he said through gritted teeth.

Sendric stared at him. 'You don't have a choice,' he snarled.

Since Merren had ordered him to marry her, this had been eating him up inside. How could she have done this with a Ralloran, of all people? He had been a good friend of her father, King Croft, had seen Merren grow from a small girl into a queen-to-be. Everything about her education, her training, had been about the importance of propriety, the necessity of putting the country before herself. Personal feelings were not important. How could she have thrown all that away to be with this brute? He was useful, certainly, but then so were the servants. And as if one of noble blood could marry a servant!

He had come to accept the need to marry Merren, to cover up this scandal that could end the Royal House — and the throne of Norstalos. Preserving the good name of the country was vital. The disgrace, the shame, if anyone ever found out the Crown Prince was a half-Ralloran bastard ... he shuddered to think of it. And it would not just be here! The damned bards would sing of it in inns across the continent. He could just imagine the sport the Rallorans and Avish would have with this. No-one must find out the truth. But it had to be done quickly. Even commoners could count!

Then, just as he had steeled himself to do this for the good of the country, the Queen had called a halt to it. Seemed actually to be thinking about declaring this oafish Ralloran her Prince Consort! That was too much for him. The man was no more than a sheep farmer's son. The thought of someone like that on the throne of Norstalos was revolting. So the only thing was to appeal to the man's decency.

'What is it?' Martil pulled on his trousers and slipped a fresh tunic over his head.

'I order you to speak to Queen Merren, and insist that she marries me, as soon as possible,' Sendric said firmly.

'You order me?' Martil asked.

'Well, you obviously do not care about her, or the country, or you would have done this already. Therefore I must insist that you take action now.'

Martil sat down on the bed and deliberately pulled on his boots, to give his hands something to do.

'And what makes you think Merren will listen to me anyway? She won't take orders from me, or from any other man,' he made himself say.

'You have some influence over her. That much is obvious. She went away sure of her duty, and ready to marry for the good of the country. Then she returns from the goblins and suddenly she has other things on her mind!'

'Derthals,' Martil interrupted.

Sendric waved that away. 'Call them what you want. I know what they are. Somehow you have persuaded her to forget her duty. Persuade her back.'

Martil stared at him. Did the man not know what he was asking? He could not sleep, not eat, without thinking of Merren. He could no more do that than he could tell Karia to go away.

Sendric ground his teeth. Well, if the brute would not listen to reason, perhaps an appeal to his baser nature was in order.

'You know, controlling the gold trade for so many years has enriched my fief,' he said casually. 'There is quite a store of gold back in Sendric. Enough to keep you and Karia in comfort for the rest of your lives …'

'Stop there, Count.' Martil surged to his feet. 'Do you think me some servant girl, able to be bought off when the master gets her pregnant?'

Sendric snorted in indignation but managed to control his anger. Perhaps one last attempt …

'Look, once we are married, perhaps there could be some sort of — arrangement. After all, Merren and I shall have separate bedrooms. If you both still feel the need, I'm sure we could organise something to allow …'

'Get out!' Martil picked up the Dragon Sword and buckled it around his waist, his eyes on Sendric the whole time.

'This is your last chance! Believe me, you do not want me for an enemy, in a Norstalos at peace,' Sendric said coldly.

Martil stepped close to where the Count blocked the doorway. Sendric did not flinch away, but met Martil's stare coldly. He had courage, Martil acknowledged, but that was no excuse for his behaviour.

'My answer is no,' Martil told him. 'Believe me, you don't want me for an enemy, at any time.'

He went in search of Karia but had not been able to get outside the palace before a message came that Merren wanted to see him.

He tried to tell himself it was probably nothing, just a discussion about tactics or similar, still, hope rose within him and he lengthened his stride. But Merren did not look like she had any good news for him when he stepped into her office.

'I have just had Count Sendric in here, claiming that you threatened him,' she said immediately.

Caught off-guard, Martil was struck dumb for a moment before his outrage took over. 'What?' he spat. 'The man tried to buy me off, offered me money to go away. That was after he asked me to persuade you to marry him!'

Merren rubbed her eyes. 'That is not what he says.'

'Well, he is lying.'

Merren sighed. She believed Martil over Sendric but the old noble was still a great help to her. 'I cannot have my War Captain and the country's last noble fighting ...'

'Well, that is easily solved. Tell him that you are not going to marry him,' Martil said hotly.

'The one thing I cannot do — and we have been through all this before,' Merren said heatedly. 'You are fighting with Sendric, cannot be left alone in a room with Barrett and we always seem to be arguing ...'

'Now that's not true —'

'You're doing it again!' she almost cried and he fell silent. 'Look, I think we all need some space. The stress on us all has tempers short. While that's understandable, I don't have the time for it. I have decided that you shall fly south, with Argurium, and take command of the Rallorans, oversee our defences to the south —'

'So I am being blamed for everything!' Martil spat.

Merren slapped her hands on the table. 'I did not say that! And for Aroaril's sake, stop interrupting me. I am not accusing anyone. I am saying you have given me a problem, so I must solve it. You shall fly down now. I shall bring Karia to visit in a day or two — and perhaps by then things will have calmed down.'

Martil simmered in silence.

She shook her head. 'Say farewell to Karia and go. And don't let me hear that you went looking for Sendric!'

Martil saluted silently and marched out of her office, fuming. But he couldn't say too much, for fear she would go back on her word and marry Sendric. At least he could take his anger out on the Berellians.

Loft believed he was a prudent man. If he had obeyed the Rallorans and left his village by the border, he would be poor. But being dead was worse than being poor, so Loft had made sure his large store of coin was buried deep and that he had a fast horse always ready and supplies packed. If the Berellians did attack — and he firmly believed that would never happen — then he could be out of the village long before everyone else.

With all eventualities prepared for, he could get back to what he did best — selling food and drink and dismissing any suggestions that the village leave.

Last night had been a particularly good one. Despite Loft's best efforts to ridicule talk of a Berellian attack, there was fear among the people, and Loft had found fear was excellent for business. People came to his inn to talk to their friends, to find out what everyone thought — and to ask Loft his opinion on it all. Naturally all that talking worked up quite a thirst. Loft had been concerned to hear that many of the women in the village were talking about leaving. But that was only women's talk. Elsewhere in the country there might be word about women being given the right to have a say, even to vote for the village council but, as far as Loft was concerned, that was ridiculous and he would have no part of it in *his* village.

It had all added up to a profitable night, and he had both coin and bartered goods aplenty to show for it. The coin he would bury later, the goods he would either sell to the villagers, or organise a wagon to take it north to the town of Wells, on the River Brack, where he could sell it for even more money. But it had been a late night, so Loft decided to reward himself with a large breakfast of bacon and eggs. He had just started frying the bacon, the delicious aroma filling his kitchen, when the screaming began.

He ignored it for as long as he could. After all, it was just women crying out. Probably someone's idiot child had been trampled by a horse, or something just as foolish. But when it grew louder and was supplemented by the worried shouts of men, Loft left his bacon and walked outside.

Men, women and children were running around in a panic, like chickens being chased by a fox.

'What's going on?' Loft cried, grabbing the arm of one of his cronies, a stout farmer called Edgar.

'Th-the Berellians!' Edgar gabbled, tearing himself free and pointing.

Loft swivelled, and saw a line of armoured horsemen sitting on the rise that overlooked the village's southern side, leading to the Berellian border. At first glance their numbers alone were frightening but they were not moving and Loft was about to open his mouth and tell everyone they were fools, the Berellians meant them no harm — when he noticed half-a-dozen riders slightly closer than the rest. These all carried long spears, only they had strange, round shapes encasing the tip. Loft stared in bewilderment for a moment until he realised, with a shock that drove all thoughts of bacon out of his mind, that those were human heads atop the spears. He remembered, with sick dread, that some of his villagers had been planning to work in the southern fields, beyond the rise, that morning.

'Why are they waiting?' Loft wondered.

'Who cares? Let's get out of here before we're next for the spears!' Edgar cried.

Loft turned and ran for his stable, where he had kept a pair of fast horses saddled since the Rallorans had warned him. He thought, with a pang, of last night's takings in the back room as well as his house and breakfast but consoled himself with the thought he had enough gold already packed in his saddlebags to keep him in comfort until he could return here in safety and dig up the rest of his hoard. It took him no time at all to jump into the saddle, grab the reins of his spare horse and spur out of the stable. A woman and two children ran in front of him and he was forced to check his progress. He recognised her as Mabel, Edgar's daughter and parent to a pair of brats of her own.

'Out of the way,' he snarled.

'Loft! Quick! Save my children!' she shrieked.

'Are you mad? Get away!' He swerved around them and pointed the horses to the north, kicking them to the gallop.

The horses responded instantly and he concentrated on getting the last bit of speed from them. Men and women yelled at him, called out for help, and begged him to save them, save their wives, save their children, offering him everything they had if he would only stop and help. But he ignored them. Risking a glance over his shoulder, he saw the Berellians move from the walk into a canter — but they would not catch him. He felt himself relax as he galloped along the road, leaving his village behind with every stride. The only question was how to explain why he was the only survivor of the village.

He was thinking about that, so failed to see the Berellians that rose out of the tall grass and bushes on either side of the road until he was almost upon them. Screaming with fear, he tried to turn his horses, but a Berellian leaped forwards and smashed the butt of his spear into Loft's head. He was catapulted onto the road, where he hit the ground hard and did not even see the other Berellians grab his horses.

'An early one!' the Berellian captain laughed. 'And a fine prize! I'll take those horses for myself!'

'He's still alive, Captain Slokek, sir!' one of his men reported.

'Excellent! A shame to waste the entertainment. I'll wager a silver coin we don't see a villager before he dies!'

'Sir, shouldn't we leave that until the village is taken?' his lieutenant suggested carefully.

'There's no danger from a rabble of Norstalines! What are you, some sort of Aroaril-lover?'

Loft was slapped back into consciousness, then stripped and carried over to where a greased, sharpened stake had been sunk deep into the earth. The innkeeper regained his senses as they hoisted him up, and realised what they were going to do to him just before they began. But his desperate struggles were useless against the many hands holding him.

'I hope Bilek's company hurries up and drives the rest of the villagers this way soon. That noise is beginning to annoy me,' Slokek commented, as Loft's shrieks echoed across the road. 'As soon as we see the first ones, Lieutenant Harek, you can silence him then close the trap.'

They peered expectantly down the road, but could see nothing.

'Can you hear something over at the village?' Slokek asked.

'Sorry, sir, all I can hear is that,' Harek said sourly, gesturing towards where Loft still screamed.

'Lieutenant, are you criticising my orders?' Slokek growled.

'No, sir! I just don't think this is necessary. These are unarmed villagers and could have been captured without any trouble if we had just ridden in there.'

'I thought you fought in the Ralloran Wars? Or did you just make that up?' Slokek asked scornfully.

'I fought under Earl Byrez and served Berellia faithfully, sir. But I can defeat the King's enemies without massacring unarmed villagers,' Harek said defiantly. 'And let us not forget there are supposed to be Rallorans in this area. We should not split our forces with them around ...'

'I have heard enough, lieutenant! One more word out of you and I shall report you to the Fearpriests! You came to me with recommendations for bravery but a warning that you come from an area of Aroaril-lovers and do not show the right attitude!'

Harek bit his tongue to stop himself from answering but, as Loft's noises finally ceased, he had to speak.

'We should have seen something by now, sir. Bilek's company should have driven the villagers out.'

Slokek nodded reluctantly. 'You are correct. Form the companies up — we'll go and see what has happened.'

Mabel watched Loft ride away, and felt her heart go with him. He had been one of her father's friends — he had been at her wedding for Aroaril's sake! How could he not save her children? Her husband, Bernerd, had left at dawn to work in the southern fields. She knew he must be dead. She had not loved him, their match made to bring more land to both families but how would she look after a farm without him? Then she realised her future was likely to be short indeed. Her children, a pair of girls aged six and four, were wailing, and she grabbed their hands and started to run with them. Men, women and children — her friends and her family, her neighbours — were also fleeing, all trying to get away from the slow advance of the riders. The terror made it feel as though she was running through the thickest mud — she seemed to be making almost no progress. Terror seemed to have sapped the strength from her legs. Instinctively she knew she would not escape. She prayed her daughters would have a quick death, and thought that was too much to hope for, herself. She turned to see what the Berellians were doing and saw them spur into a gallop. She stared at them, hating them — then her jaw dropped open as the fields around the village came to life.

She blinked and looked again. That was impossible! Then she saw it was not grass and bushes that was standing but men! Men throwing off sacks and blankets and the earth, grass and plants that had covered them. Men in dirty blue surcoats, who now strung bows and loosed arrow after arrow into the Berellians, sending them crashing to the ground.

Mabel gaped, unable to believe what her eyes were seeing — then riders in blue appeared from behind the rise, bright swords in their hands — hundreds of them. The Berellians tried to rally, but they were wilting under the arrow storm.

'It's the Rallorans! The Rallorans are coming to save us!' Mabel found her voice, and her shout made every villager turn to watch.

Martil watched grimly as his men finished off the shattered Berellians. A handful tried to surrender but he had ordered no prisoners be taken. He was in no mood to be merciful, especially to Berellians. After leaving Merren's office with outrage mingling with his anger, he'd had to tell Karia he was going south.

She had burst into tears, begged him not to go, using the fight against Cezar as the perfect reason for him to stay with her. It had taken him the best part of a turn of the hourglass to calm her down and disentangle himself. Leaving her had been hard enough but then Havell and Argurium had taken the trouble to berate him once more about risking his life, and reminded him yet again of all that rested on his shoulders on the flight south. They had been reluctant to leave him to return to the capital and he had been forced to swear on Karia's life that he would not fight, only direct his men. Added together, it had him itching to take his anger out on somebody.

A quick talk with Nerrin had shown him he would not have long to wait, for the Berellians were moving. He had barely had time to set this trap up, to turn the Berellian ambush on itself. It had worked just as he had planned but that could not hope to balance everything else he was feeling. So he was hardly smiling as he led his men into the village where the people, ecstatic at their rescue, were cheering wildly, trying to hug or shake the hands of every Ralloran they could find. He viewed the display coldly. Nerrin had told him the last time the Rallorans had been there the villagers had hurled rotten fruit and animal dung.

'Quiet!' Martil stood in his stirrups and bellowed. 'Where is Loft?'

A young woman, clutching two children by the hands, pushed through the crowd.

'He ran away. He ran out on us, left us to die!' she cried.

Martil had to restrain a cynical smile. So the village chief, who had worked so hard to keep this village from leaving for safety, had been the only one prepared to go. He must have been the one seen galloping away earlier.

'Then he is dead, and the rest of you will die too, unless you listen to me this time!' Martil shouted.

'I need you to pack. Warm clothes and food only. You must be ready to leave quickly. There are two companies of Berellians out there, lying in wait along the road to our north. We have to kill them before we can escape in safety.'

'So you knew they were going to attack us?' the young woman asked.

'Of course. Now, I need —'

But the woman interrupted him. 'My husband was killed this morning, walking to work in the fields! Why didn't you stop him and the other men? Why did you let them go to their deaths?'

Martil glared at her. 'We don't have time for a discussion, woman!' he snapped.

'I know why, because you don't care about us! You used us as bait for the Berellians!' she accused.

Martil could not deny her words. He could have attacked the Berellians immediately they crossed the border, although a fair fight would have cost his men more lives than springing the perfect trap on the Berellians. And his men were more important than a few more villagers. But he could not say that. 'You are alive. Your children are alive. Be thankful for that. Remember, we were not the ones who attacked. We were the ones who saved you …'

'Saved us for your own purposes!'

'Enough!' Martil barked. 'There are still two companies of Berellians out there! Now, unless you want me to take my men and ride away, I would advise you to listen!'

A portly farmer came forwards to lay a comforting — and cautioning — arm around the woman. 'What do you want us to do?' he asked.

'Who are you?' Martil demanded.

'Edgar, and this is my daughter Mabel. I suppose I am head of the village council now.'

'Then, Edgar, I need six villagers to act as bait, to draw the Berellians onto us,' Martil said, seeing Mabel turn away in disgust at his words.

'We shall do whatever you ask,' Edgar said heavily.

Captain Slokek stared at the village in frustration. They had approached as close as they dared without being seen — but the last one hundred yards or so would be without any cover. As it was they had left all their horses back at the original ambush site, half a mile away.

'What do you see, Harek?' he asked.

'Villagers walking around as if nothing was happening, sir. No sign of Bilek. Perhaps he had to withdraw, sir. We know there are Rallorans in the area — if he saw something, he might've headed for the border,' Harek suggested.

'But he should have sent us a runner, at least!'

'Or maybe, sir, the Rallorans drove him off. This is just a village. Destroying it serves no purpose anyway. Perhaps we should just withdraw ...'

'I cannot go back to the King and say we ran away from a village of soft Norstalines!' Slokek said furiously. 'The King himself ordered this village destroyed, for it sits on land that should be Berellia's. Bilek must be lost, or something. Full attack!'

'Sir —' Harek began.

'Not another word or I shall denounce you as worshipping Aroaril,' Slokek warned.

Reluctantly, Harek signalled to the sergeants and led the men forwards.

As soon as the Berellians broke cover, the few villagers in sight ran for it. That was too much for many of the Berellians and they immediately broke into a run, despite the best efforts of Harek and the sergeants to keep them in a tight formation. Within moments they were strung out, the faster runners racing to be the first into the village, led by Slokek himself.

Harek watched him in disgust. He had agreed to serve again because he passionately believed he had a duty to his country. But fighting for Fearpriests and fools like Slokek was testing his patriotism to the limit. He had always been taught by Earl Byrez to fight with honour but the Earl was gone and, it seemed, all honour had left Berellia with him. Harek had hoped to provide some experience to the thousands of raw recruits who had swelled Berellia's depleted regiments. But rather than lead these men, officers such as Slokek and the King's Fearpriests used fear to keep them in line and obeying orders. It left men like Harek feeling bitter and useless. Harek followed the rest of the men, hoping he could survive this and return to Berellia. He had heard

Earl Byrez's son was trying to organise a rebellion against Markuz. He had thought it his duty to fight for the Fatherland but now he wished he had stayed in Berellia, helped fight for something he believed in.

Then the arrows began to fly through the air.

Harek saw men dropping and heard shouts of alarm, from behind and to either side. Hundreds of Rallorans appeared, on horseback and on foot, while still more poured out of the village to form a shield wall in front.

'Rallorans! Run!' Slokek screamed in terror.

But there was nowhere to go.

Harek watched his commander fall to his knees, crying for mercy, although he received none. Many of the new recruits ran in panic, or tried to surrender, but Harek knew there was no give in the Rallorans. Not after what had been done to their country. Years ago, Earl Byrez had warned Markuz that would happen, that brutality and cruelty would only be repaid in kind. Now they would reap what Markuz had sown.

Harek tried to rally men together, hoped against hope he could get away, so he could desert from the Berellian army, but the Ralloran ring tightened inexorably and he died fighting back to back with a new recruit.

Martil waved to Nerrin and Dunner. 'One company to clear the road of bodies, one to fetch their horses, and one to watch the road south. The rest on me — we need to get these villagers a long way away from here, before the rest of the Berellian army attacks!'

'And those other Berellians, sir?' Dunner asked.

Martil grimaced. As well as these three companies, scouts had reported a squadron of Berellian cavalry riding across the border, in a different direction.

Obviously they were going after the villagers Kesbury had rescued.

'Thanks to you, sergeant, we have already sent a squad of men. A squad we cannot afford to lose. This retreat is not about saving Norstalines but about conserving our men. Every one of us who makes it back over the passes can train ten men. Another villager is just a useless mouth to feed.'

Martil paused. He had already shouted at Dunner for this last night — abusing the man further would do no good. Besides, he knew Dunner and Kesbury had been friends. He softened his tone a little, although he knew it would not make Dunner feel any better. 'Besides, even if we sent men, by the time they arrived, it would be all over. He knew the risks when he went in there. Only Aroaril can save him now.'

Merren looked longingly at the wine but contented herself with a cup of herbal tea. But Gia and Louise had a glass each and now toasted her cautiously.

'This could be the most important duty I give you,' she told them. 'I need a diversion from what we face — I need people to talk to. In this room, we are just three friends: Louise, Gia and Merren. What is said in here stays in here, and you must give me your honest opinions, without fear.'

This was an unusual step, one she could never imagine her father ever taking. But she had just received the latest batch of surveys, from the refugees who had already made it safely to the north. The answers were exactly what she had dreaded, confirming what her head told her. The people, many of whom had seen Martil save themselves and their children, were strongly against him being made Prince Consort. It was not overwhelming but, if it was like that up there, what was being said in parts of the country that hated the Rallorans?

She needed to talk, needed to see if she could drop her royal persona and just be herself around someone else other than Martil or Karia. For they were the only ones who seemed to let her just be Merren, not the Queen. But if she could not be with them, then perhaps Gia and Louise might give her the outlet she needed …

There was an awkward pause when nobody said anything, just sipped their drinks. Gia and Louise exchanged glances. Both were holding their goblets of wine as though they were shields. Louise's first meeting with the Queen had resulted in Merren screaming at her in anger. She had begun to see another side of Merren as the rebellion progressed, and they had grown closer after her husband's death. Both she and Gia were older, and while they would have normally tried to offer advice to a troubled young woman, it felt exceedingly strange to offer that same advice to a queen — the hope of Norstalos. But they had seen the stress she was under, even had a taste of it themselves. They had to help her somehow.

'What did you want to talk about, your majesty, I mean, Merren?' Louise finally asked.

'Everything except invasions and war.' Merren smiled.

'How about we talk about your wedding?' Gia offered.

Merren made a face at that.

'Perhaps we should talk about who you should marry?' Louise said shrewdly. 'We have all seen the looks Martil gives you.'

Merren put down her tea. 'But would I be happy? Sometimes I wonder what is my attraction to him.

Is it just because he represents everything my father would hate, because I am rebelling against all I was taught?'

'Forbidden fruit, you mean?' Louise wondered. 'Because you should not go near him, the attraction is all the greater?'

'Exactly!' Merren nodded. 'We are so different — not just our backgrounds but our upbringing, everything. We can talk together, we can laugh together — now. He is a good man in a crisis but what would he be like in peacetime? Would we find ourselves fighting when there is no common enemy to face?'

'That, Merren, is a question only you can answer,' Louise sighed.

Another awkward silence descended. Meaningless platitudes rose to Merren's lips but, while she managed to stop herself saying them, she could not drop her guard, could not relax and be herself.

'My Queen!' Conal called through the door into the quiet. 'The Berellian invasion has begun!'

Merren jumped, both horrified and relieved at the interruption. 'Warn the dragon. I want to go down there myself. I must know what is happening!' she ordered. Then she paused and looked at the two women. 'Thank you. Perhaps we can try this again,' she said softly, before striding towards the door.

4

Barrett was looking forward to getting back to the capital. But, for the first time, not because he wanted to see Merren. Instead he was looking forward to seeing Tiera. Working with her was the only thing that seemed to stop the bitterness that threatened to overwhelm him. At every turn he had been humiliated, ridiculed, his contribution to the Queen's cause belittled, his talents overlooked. His secret love for Merren had been mocked, then trampled on as she slept with that Ralloran bastard. Now they were having a child. It was too much!

Then there was the way in which they seemed to take him for granted. He had defeated the Berellian's finest mage. Yet everyone merely wanted to talk about Martil's lucky blow against the Berellian who had been about to kill him.

Sometimes he felt he would only be truly appreciated if he left Merren's service. Then, perhaps, they would see just what he had given them. Without him, they would have been defeated a dozen times over. And here he was, stuck among the Derthals, while Merren flew on a dragon with that bloody Ralloran oaf!

There was a temptation to go elsewhere, to make them come to him, beg him for his help, admit just what he had done for them. He daydreamed about a tearful Merren apologising to him, only to have that replaced by another face. Tiera ... he knew he had promised never to touch her, to treat her only as a pupil, nothing more, but the more time he spent with her, the harder that became. She seemed to wipe the anger from his heart.

So he was eager to be back with her, talk with her. He had set out with High Chief Sacrax, Quiller and the rest of the Derthals on the march south. This high above sea level there were far fewer trees, and many of these were evergreens, so it was a full day of marching before they arrived at an oak tree he could use to get back.

'Good luck! I shall see you at the passes,' Quiller farewelled him.

'Do you have any messages for the Queen?' Barrett forced himself to ask.

'Only that we shall be there soon — I am glad I'll have the use of all your horses, because I'd never keep up with these Derthals otherwise!' the old priest chuckled.

Barrett smiled. The Derthals had set a tremendous pace, and they had to trot the horses at times, just to keep up. None of the Derthals looked tired, instead they looked as though they could just keep going. And more were joining all the time — bands of warriors clad in deerskin or goatskin, with headbands of feathers, of fur, carrying two or three of those wicked spears and bags of food. They saluted Sacrax, then joined the mass of marching warriors. The High Chief looked truly cheerful. He was carrying his massive mace of office over one shoulder and setting the pace, his chosen warriors around him.

'We shall see you soon,' Barrett agreed.

Then, with Jaret and Wilsen, he stepped into the oak tree and vanished.

Merren wanted to see the south, wanted to see what was happening. Receiving reports was all very well but she had to feel what was going on in her country. Normally she would have had to exhaust Barrett in order to do this. But now they had Argurium.

She had spoken easily enough about persuading the dragon to help, although she had been a little nervous. She had worried that the dragon or Havell would complain about the cost in magic of such flights. But they had both proved relatively easy to convince.

'Many of my kin think we should remain above all conflict, that we should be concerned only with the survival of the magic,' Argurium had said. 'We have lived for thousands of years, seen many wars, constant conflict. It is in the nature of you humans to war on each other. Kingdoms and empires rise, then fall over the centuries. Life goes on, the circle turns and new kingdoms and empires spring up. Only magic endures. But we have an agreement to help you, in exchange for the Dragon Sword wielder. So the faster you win, the better for us.'

'Yet our help only goes so far,' Havell warned. 'If you lose, we shall take Martil and leave. The magic must be reborn. Nothing else is as important. Others will have to defeat the Fearpriests if you cannot — there is no-one else to bring about the rebirth of the dragons.'

'But we shall not leave until the last moment. And, hopefully, our help will mean that will not have to come about,' Argurium added gently.

Havell nodded agreement, before adding sadly that there would be much magic returned to the circle in the next few weeks, so the cost of dragon flight would not be felt as deeply.

Merren had been happy to secure their help, although the thought they were already planning for defeat — and were already predicting that many would die — had sent a chill down her spine. But she had tried to put thoughts of death and defeat out of her mind as they circled around the southern border.

She had collected Martil from where he had been leading the Rallorans in a careful retreat away from the border, much to the delight of Karia. Merren had been pleased to hear a Berellian raid had been destroyed and a village saved, although concerned for the second village that had left with Kesbury and whose fate was unknown. Martil had reported carefully but stiffly, and she could feel the atmosphere between them. But she did not have time to deal with it.

Black-clad Berellians, looking like a dark stain, were spreading across the border and deep into southern Norstalos. Already clouds of smoke rose into the air as the closest homes to the border were burned.

'Are there still farmers left behind?'

'There're a few. Mainly ones that traded with those two villages who caused Nerrin so much trouble. We decided that there was just no way we could protect them — it would cost us too much,' Martil said absently.

He had been delighted to see both Karia and Merren, less so for Argurium and Havell, as he expected another lecture. He was also relieved he would not have to deal with more ungrateful villagers, having sent them ahead on the captured Berellian horses. They had abused and ignored his Rallorans and their warnings — now they complained when they were saved! A part of him could recognise the grief, terror and uncertainty the villagers were facing but he still felt they could be a little more grateful. As far as he was concerned, his Rallorans should just pull back over the River Brack and leave them to their fate …

'Show me one,' Merren commanded, interrupting his grim thoughts.

Martil pointed to where more smoke rose into the sky to their west. 'It is probably too late for them,' he warned. 'And I don't want Karia to see …'

'That was an order, not a suggestion,' Merren told him.

Martil clenched his jaw, then signalled to Havell. 'Take us over there.'

Argurium banked sharply, a manoeuvre that would have left Martil's stomach churning had it not been done with magic, and they flashed across the countryside, over wood and past hill, until they came across a farm in a small valley. Neat rows of crops and fenced fields of animals showed this was a fertile place to farm — but it wasn't peaceful. Not any more. The neat house was ablaze, its thatched roof sending a pall of smoke skywards. Lying outside it were several bodies, men, women and children.

'Probably two families. Don't go down too close,' Martil ordered Havell. From bitter experience, he knew none of them would have died easily. He held Karia, partly because he did not want her to look down, partly because he wanted to hold her close.

Merren sat there, staring at the broken bodies of the men, the small bodies of the children and the naked bodies of the women.

'They were warned, many times,' Martil said gruffly.

'And yet I failed them,' she said softly. 'It was by my decision that they died. A small evil to prevent a greater evil.'

'It was none of your doing — it was the Berellians, and Gello!' Martil protested.

'But it was my choice to order families from their homes rather than stay and protect my own country from invaders. Find me another,' Merren sighed.

'I don't know that —'

'Find me another!' Merren snapped.

'The road goes that way.' Martil pointed out a deeply rutted cart track heading northeast.

Argurium swooped away, and moments later, they were over another farm. Like the other one, this was well tended and prosperous. Unlike the other, it was not ablaze. Here, the Berellians were dragging women and children out of the main house.

'Take us down there now!' Merren screamed.

'To do what?' Havell asked.

'To stop them! I don't care if I have to do it myself, I will not sit here and watch people die. Besides, the Berellians will probably run once they see the dragon.'

Martil twisted around in his seat to face her. 'Merren, we can't risk it. We can't risk *you*, not for the sake of a couple of farmers …'

But Merren was not listening to him. 'What are you waiting for?' she yelled at the Elfaran. 'Get down there now or so help me I'll throw you off this dragon!'

Havell glanced at her and gulped.

Martil was about to make his protest louder, when Argurium went into a steep dive. He hung on for grim death, even though he knew by now that the dragon's magic would not let him fall.

Karia let out a whoop of delight, and Argurium answered it with a roar.

The effect on the Berellians was dramatic.

Intent on dragging out their victims, they looked up as one at Argurium's challenge to see a huge dragon bearing down on them, mouth agape, fangs glittering. As they stared in shock and horror, Argurium let loose with her challenge again, then her wings flared and she hovered almost over them.

The Berellians ran for it but, when the dragon did not chase them, some of them slowed to a stop and watched nervously as Argurium landed delicately.

Martil let go of the strap reluctantly and slid onto the ground. A cold anger gripped him. What was Merren thinking? Fighting to save the family would achieve nothing. The plan depended on speed — and meant those who had refused to heed warnings had to be sacrificed. Even if they saved this family, his Rallorans would have to risk their lives to give them time to get north in safety.

'It's the Butcher of Bellic and his Witch Queen! Ten thousand in gold if we bring back their heads,' a Berellian yelled and a group of them advanced cautiously, the thought of the gold overwheming fear of the dragon.

Martil drew the Dragon Sword, conscious of Karia watching him. He had to be careful here ... and what about the elf and dragon? Why were they not doing more to help?

Then he realised Merren was beside him, holding a dagger.

'Merren! Get back on the dragon,' he ordered.

'I will fight for my people,' she said grimly.

'I can't fight and watch you at the same time!' he shouted at her.

The Berellians raced in, but a sweep of Argurium's tail sent three flying through the air to crash into a nearby fence.

The last two pressed home their attack and Martil automatically defended himself. But his customary skill seemed to have deserted him; he was thinking too much, unable to lose himself in the fight, unable to wipe the thought that he could not risk himself and leave Karia alone. Luckily he still had the Dragon Sword, which sliced through everything. And surely it would approve of being used to protect women and children. He cut down one, then whirled to face the second man — only to see Merren drive her dagger into the back of the Berellian's neck.

'It's harder than it looks,' Merren commented, as she ripped the bloody blade out of the man's neck.

'Merren!'

She looked at him. 'I knew what you would do, and that the second man would turn to attack you, hoping to get in a lucky strike. I won't have it said that I did not fight for my people. And I will not sit back and wait to be saved by men.'

Martil shook his head. What if all the Berellians had stayed? What would have happened then? 'But you're the Queen. You're too valuable. It's foolish to risk yourself like this!'

'Remember who you are talking to!' she blazed back.

'I am talking to the Queen of this country, without whom we are lost! And I'm talking to the mother of my child. I don't want to see either of you hurt,' he growled.

'Keep your voice down,' she warned. 'I am the Queen before I am anything else. Do you know what that is like?'

Martil rolled his eyes. 'How could I possibly know that?'

'Exactly. You don't know what it's like to have everything on your shoulders. The country is being torn apart, and I am the only one who can put it back together again. And if I don't do that, then not only will thousands of people die in Norstalos, but the whole continent will be lost to Zorva and it will all be my fault! Do you know what it is like to carry that burden? Every day I must make a score of decisions that sentence people to death, in the name of the greater good. Every day I must wonder if I have made a mistake that will doom us all. And then I fly down here and see the result of my choices …'

'You have made the right choices. More people will die if you don't make those decisions,' Martil pointed out.

'I know the arguments. But what seems sensible back at the capital, while sitting around a map marked with ink, is very different down here! And, Aroaril help me, seeing it doesn't make it easier to live with.'

'That's why you need to stay above the fighting. On the dragon. Because when you get down here, it gets dangerous and confused. We need you to be apart from all that,' Martil argued.

'Well, I'm beginning to think that is a bad idea,' Merren warned him.

'Merren, listen to me —' Martil began angrily but she cut him off.

'You are not helping me! Already everyone wants something from me as Queen, so that I feel stretched in all directions, then you come along wanting even more from me. You want me to turn my back on the country and become a little wife and mother to the child that you gave me!'

'That is not what I wanted, and I didn't know you were going to get pregnant!' Martil said furiously. 'You were the one who seduced me, remember?'

'Oh, I remember,' she told him. 'And sometimes I wish I hadn't.'

'You don't mean that,' Martil protested.

Merren looked at him and had to take a deep breath. Did she mean that? Yes and no ... 'It has just led to more problems. Even defeating Gello brought more suffering on this country. There will be some saying that it would have been better for Norstalos to be ruled by Gello, to save it from these invasions.'

'Then they are idiots.'

'Are they? Tell that to the murdered families we saw at the last farm. This was all my choice and, as such, I have to live with the consequences. That is not easy. And it is even harder when I see what happens to those whose only crime was to think they could live in peace.'

Martil stepped forwards, wanting to take her in his arms, both to give her comfort and because he needed it also.

She held up her hand. 'I can't. That won't make things better. It will make them more difficult. Because the country needs me to be strong,' she told him coldly.

Martil did not know what more to say, and did not get a chance to think of anything, because Havell strode over to them.

'What are we going to do? Those Berellians will be back soon, in greater numbers.' He pointed to where the farmer's wife was sobbing over the body of her husband, surrounded by her four weeping children.

Martil ignored them, silently fuming. This argument was not over yet, not by a long way.

'We take them with us,' Merren announced.

'This was not part of our deal! Argurium is not some beast of burden!' Havell cried.

'Just to Wells, then,' Merren said instantly.

'And after them? How many more will we be forced to carry? The cost in magic will become too great,' Havell argued. 'And I don't like the idea of us swooping down to try and save everyone threatened by your enemies. The Dragon Sword wielder is not to be risked like this!'

'The Dragon Sword wielder serves me first!' Merren said coldly.

Martil stepped closer. 'I am here, you know!' he interrupted. 'And I am not some toy to be fought over!'

Merren ignored him, focused only on Havell. 'I shall not leave these people behind to die,' she declared.

'And I say we cannot load Argurium up as if she were a draughthorse pulling a wagon-load of children at a fair!'

'Kesbury is around here somewhere with some villagers. We can leave them with him,' she suggested. 'I want to find out what happened to them, anyway.'

'All right.' Havell sighed defeatedly.

Barrett burst back into the palace throne room.

He had arrived back at his house, along with Jaret and Wilsen, to find the capital in turmoil. Carriages, wagons, horses, donkeys — anything with wheels or hooves packed the streets, trying to get out of the gates and join the rush northwards. He and the two Royal Guard had to almost fight their way through the crowds at times. Men shouted for their families, women called for their children and children cried for their parents.

When they finally made it to the palace, even here was confusion. Leaving Wilsen and Jaret to rejoin the Royal Guard and discover what was required of them, he made his way to the throne room, where he expected to find Merren hard at work. Instead, it was Conal, as well as Sendric, Louise and Gia, furiously trying to compile what was going on across the country into some semblance of order.

'Where is the Queen?' Barrett demanded.

'She has left on the dragon to visit the south. The Berellians have launched their attack and she wants to see what is happening,' Louise replied.

'And I suppose she has Martil with her?' Barrett muttered. Once they would have needed his powers to move around the country like that. But now they had a dragon, he was no longer needed. Part of him knew he was being churlish, but he had expected at least a greeting, and thanks, for another job well done.

'She has. And Karia,' Sendric grunted. He was still angry about the postponed wedding, and having Merren fly all over the country with her Champion at her side was hardly improving his mood. The whole country knew what the sagas said about Queens and their Champions.

'Is everything going to plan with the Derthals?' Conal asked.

'Ask Jaret or Wilsen if you want to know. I'm off to rest,' Barrett snarled, then turned on his heel and stormed out of the room.

'What's wrong with him?' Gia sniffed.

'He'll be fine. But we need to find Tiera and get her to see him. She seems to be able to talk sense into the man,' Louise said briskly.

'Is that all she does?' Conal asked archly.

Louise slapped him lightly on the arm. 'You only have one thing on your mind!'

Conal held up the map he was working on. 'If only that were the case!' he grumbled.

* * *

The children they had rescued from the Berellians had said little on the flight, just hugged each other and cried. The woman had offered tearful thanks for saving her children but also asked why they had not arrived just a little earlier.

'It was luck we arrived at all. Be thankful for what you have,' Martil told her coldly, and she fell silent as they searched for Kesbury and his villagers.

But, watching her, Merren knew the strategy of sacrificing people, leaving those who had stayed behind to the mercies of the Berellians, was wrong. It made perfect sense but that did not make it any better. She knew they had to preserve the army if they were to ever take back Norstalos, but leaving people behind to die ... she could not do it. The strategy would have to change — and Martil would not like it. But he would just have to deal with it.

'There they are!' Karia pointed.

'Get us down there,' Merren called, looking at a ragged group of people and wagons rumbling tiredly along a road. From the look of them, they had been in a battle. Merren shuddered to think what had happened.

Argurium dropped like a stone, making Karia scream with fearful delight, then pulled up with impossible delicacy at the side of the road — the villagers crying out with surprise and fear.

'It's Queen Merren! And Captain Martil!' Kesbury roared, and the cries of fear died down.

'Keep the wagons moving! Do not stop!' Martil shouted down from the back of the dragon, as it walked beside them.

He, Merren and Karia stepped down from the dragon and hurried over to greet Kesbury.

'My Queen.' Kesbury bowed, and signalled for the rest of the villagers to join him.

'Up! Up, all of you! And especially you, Father Kesbury,' Merren instructed. 'We have a family we have rescued from the Berellians who need to travel with you. They have suffered and lost.'

'As have many of those here,' Kesbury warned. 'They are welcome to join us but we cannot guarantee their safety.'

Havell was helping the family down, and Merren waved for them to join the column of wagons.

'Tell us what has happened,' she invited Kesbury.

He explained how they had been attacked by a squadron of Berellian cavalry, how they had made a circle with the wagons and fought them off — but not without cost. More than 30 men and boys had died, including all but two of the Rallorans who had volunteered to help. Merren saw instantly there were things he was not saying, how desperate that fight must have been, what it had to have taken to hold off a squadron of cavalry.

'A waste of fine men,' Martil grated.

'Not at all. They have saved most of a village. And, more than that, look at the way they are being treated. These people hated and feared the Rallorans, now they welcome them.' Merren pointed to where the remaining Rallorans were riding with farmers.

'That is true, my Queen,' Kesbury agreed. 'The journey is changing us all.'

'Indeed! You have done well, Kesbury. I can see you are not just a soldier now. These are your people,' she told him warmly. 'But they are also my people, and I shall talk to them.'

She walked over to the wagons, taking Karia with her, speaking to men, women and children, while encouraging them to keep the wagons moving.

Martil glanced at his former sergeant.

'It will be a race to see who reaches the bridge at Wells first,' Martil warned him quietly.

'I cannot leave them, sir,' Kesbury said, without a hint of apology.

Martil glanced at where Merren was embracing a weeping mother. This was not good. He could lose every man he had trying to save these people …

'Your best chance is to leave the wagons and ride for the bridge. We will be able to hold them for a while at Wells — give you enough of a lead to stay ahead of them,' he said harshly.

'But all the food, the clothes …'

'No good if you are dead.'

Kesbury nodded.

'We captured extra horses from the Berellians — we managed to destroy three companies that tried to sack Loft's village. We'll have them waiting for you at Wells, to help you travel faster after you are across the River Brack.'

Kesbury sighed. 'How do I tell them to leave everything they can't carry behind?'

'You won't have to — the Queen will.' Martil gestured.

Merren had been delighted to find the people happy to see her. The fact she'd arrived on a dragon, bringing in a family she had rescued from the Berellians seemed to seal their pleasure at meeting the Queen. And this was a village that had been stubbornly sure it would be better off under Gello! Although, she reminded herself, they had seen only too well what Gello and his Berellian friends intended for them.

'We shall return,' she promised them. 'We have the dragons on our side now, as well as the Dragon Sword! Once we are safe, we shall train an army big enough to throw the Berellians out and restore peace in Norstalos!'

They cheered then, and she let it continue for a while before stopping them.

'But you need to move faster. The Berellians are coming — and they show no mercy, as you have already seen. Leave the wagons and ride to Wells as fast as you can. I shall send soldiers to help you — but Aroaril helps those who help themselves. You have a brave man in Father Kesbury. Trust him and he will lead you to safety!'

Martil cringed to hear those words but the people loved it, and were even happy enough to carry what food they could and leave the wagons. Because of all the men who had died, both villagers and Rallorans, they had sufficient horses, although every beast was carrying two, and sometimes three, if they were small children.

'I shall see you all in Wells — but, if you are in danger, look to the skies, for I shall try to be there,' Merren told them.

Martil, unseen, rolled his eyes at that.

'Come on. Next we must go to Wells.' Merren waved one last time to the villagers, then let them ride off.

'We have to save them,' she mused.

'The Berellians will want to catch them, also,' Martil warned. 'We can't use up all our men just to save one village. What will happen then to all the other villages and towns?'

'This is now more than just a village. They will be a symbol for unity. Saved by Rallorans and a Ralloran-born priest! That is the sort of tale the country needs to hear,' she decided. 'We shall help them, then we need to think about how we can slow the advance down, so we can get everyone away, not just the ones who have already left.'

'Merren, we don't have enough men! That is just falling into our enemy's trap,' Martil protested. 'They want us to fight, they want us to fritter away our men trying to save a farm here, a village there. It is why they are raping and burning and killing. But we have to stay strong, we have to realise we cannot save everyone!'

'But I cannot just let them die,' Merren said simply. 'These are my people. We have to do more to save those who were left behind. As the Dragon Sword wielder, you need to think like that. We don't want you getting back to the way you were before Pilleth. You have to think of the people.'

Martil felt his insides twist at her words. It made his response louder and angrier than he had intended.

'I'm thinking more of my men, whose lives will pay for this! Your bloody Norstalines hate us but are happy to have us die for their own stupidity ...'

'Enough!' She cut him off, her voice cracking like a whip. 'This is not the time or the place for a discussion. And they are not your men. They are sworn to my service, as are you. And if you feel you cannot obey my orders ...' She left the threat hanging, as she stared him down. He might have his men's lives at heart but she would not brook any disobedience to her orders, no matter what she felt for him.

Martil glared at her, holding back angry words, while Karia waved and signalled at him from behind Merren's back. She could see him getting angry and worried he was going to mess everything up again. He needed to be nice to Merren, not shout at her! She stepped in between them, grabbing Merren's hand.

'Merren, can I have a word?' she asked.

Merren allowed herself to be pulled to one side. Perhaps Karia had some plan to bring him to his senses …

'Merren, Dad's been very upset lately. But I know how to make him happy again, make everything good,' Karia said conspiratorially.

Merren smiled. 'Go on.'

'He really loves you. I think if you said you were going to marry him and make us all a family, then he'd be really happy …'

Merren did not hear any more. The blood pounded in her temples and she stormed back to Martil.

'Is all this some ploy? Are you trying to trick me into marrying you? That is bad enough but getting Karia to do your dirty work …'

Martil's anger burst into life.

'What do you mean? I feel like this because I saved this bloody country and nearly got myself killed — time after time! And if you think I would try to use Karia against you …'

'I don't care! I don't want to hear another word from you today unless it is to agree with me!' Merren roared.

She stormed back to the dragon, knowing she had left one of them looking as though they would cry, the other as if they would explode.

5

Bishop Milly looked down the road at the huge column of refugees in wonder. The trail of people and animals vanished into the distance. All seemed to have the same look of resignation on their faces. These were the ones who had left days, or even more than a week ago and had been on the road ever since. They might have begun their trek with hope and even excitement but day after day of travel had taken its toll. And they were not even at the capital yet. To those who had left from the south, the far east or west, Sendric seemed to be a ridiculous distance away.

Every priest and priestess in the church was on the road with them, trying to help those who were hurt, tired or just ready to give up.

Milly was under no illusion as to how effective they were. She had spent the day helping reunite lost families, as well as providing news as best she could. Certainly the reports that the Berellians had invaded the south, and were burning and killing everything they could find was having a definite effect on the speed of those who were trudging along. But she did not want to inspire the people through fear — that was how the followers of Zorva operated. No, she preferred to tell them how the Rallorans had destroyed a Berellian raid and saved a village, bringing the people to safety at Wells, how the Queen had ridden down on a dragon and rescued a family from certain death.

The news that the dragons were on their side cheered people immensely — many, especially the children — spent time scanning the sky, hoping to see one.

Strangely, the stories about how the Rallorans had saved a village, destroying a Berellian attack, also seemed to strike a chord with the people. After all Milly had heard about the 'Ralloran butchers' and how no child was safe around them, it was strange to hear them being praised.

'Thank Aroaril we have them on our side. There's no-one else the Berellians are afraid of,' went the common refrain.

It was ironic, but if it got them moving faster and feeling happier, Milly was willing to keep talking about it. Although doing so made her wonder what was going on down south …

She stepped away from the road for a moment and offered up a silent prayer for Kesbury. The thought he might already be dead was eating away at her. She decided to talk to Archbishop Nott. Something was telling her she was needed down south.

King Gello had had enough of waiting. The last straw came when the scouts returned with news they had discovered dozens of rotting corpses in the woods over the border, the remnants of a fight months before. Crows, ravens, foxes and the like had been at the bodies but the scouts discovered some of them had been wearing Gello's surcoat, with the badge of his personal guard.

At another time, Gello might have been sad to

finally learn of Chelten's fate. But his bodyguard had failed and, in failing, had sowed the seeds of Gello's defeat at Pilleth. He had little sympathy for that. Besides, there was a sense of relief in that Chelten was the only other person who knew the truth about Mother's death. With him gone, there could be no doubt her death was an accident. He had told her that, many times …

'Do you want us to bring in the bodies, bury them with honour, sire?' Feld asked.

But Gello shook his head, and dropped the stained, torn surcoat on the ground. Chelten belonged to another life — a failed life. He was ready to carve a new chapter now.

'Let them rot,' he declared. 'Get the men ready. We march!'

The camp was emptied in less than a turn of the hourglass, as the men were eager to begin. Behind them they left a small mound of bodies, twisted in death, with their hearts cut out. Terrified Tetrans, who had been hunted through the woods for the past few days, slowly crept back and began to search for their loved ones among the pile.

Gello rode up near the front, behind a screen of cavalry. He doubted there would be any opposition — his bitch of a cousin would have to marshal her entire forces to defeat him and he knew the Rallorans were down south, shadowing the Berellian advance.

'Sire, the first village is empty — looks like the people have fled. All that is left is this one family,' Feld reported.

'I want to meet them!' Gello commanded.

The man, his wife, three teenage children and older parents were brought into the village square, where they fell to their knees, ringed by men in armour.

'Why is nobody here?' Gello asked politely.

'Queen's men came, telling everyone to leave, sire,' the man gasped.

'Leave? Go where?'

'Sendric, sire. They want everyone to travel north, say they will be safe there.'

Chuckles broke out from the assembled troopers, who all knew how far that was.

But Gello was not laughing. 'And why do they think they'll be safe there?'

'The passes to the north. They think they can hold them until winter, sire.'

Gello stroked his chin thoughtfully. This was a development he had not expected. It required some careful thinking. The plan had been for the Berellians and Tenochs to storm across Norstalos with fire and sword, forcing Merren to commit her army to a hopeless battle in a vain attempt to stop the killing. But it seemed she, or her Ralloran dog, had come up with a way to defeat that strategy. He could imagine what Mother would say. Soft autumn sunshine was bathing them all today but, in a matter of weeks, a southerly wind would begin to blow and the rains would fall. Merren would just have to hold the passes for a few weeks and the three armies would have to pull back, probably to the capital, because there would be no way they could campaign through the winter — the wet and the cold would become their enemies and feeding such a horde would become impossible. As for the horses — they could die by the hundred without proper grazing. By spring, when fighting could begin again, Gello was under no illusions about what would come out of those passes. Thousands upon thousands of Norstalines, all furious and eager to take back their homes and country. Just the army he wanted to create — but this time it would be turned against him. He blinked away that vision. It would not happen! He would not let it happen. He would catch them on the road — his bitch of a cousin would not get away with this.

'I am concerned with this plan of my cousin's,' he warned Prent.

'I shall inform Brother Onzalez. But I shall need blood to do so. Perhaps one of those girls ...'

'Get away, priest! Feld's riders can supply you with what you need. Those girls are mine!'

'Sire?' the farmer asked nervously.

Gello waved Prent away and focused again on the man and his family.

'Why did you not leave?' he demanded.

'You are the rightful King, sire.' The farmer bowed his head. 'It ain't right, having a queen. Not natural. And she wants to change things! Says women can tell us men what to do!'

'It is appalling,' Gello agreed softly. 'So you would do anything for your rightful King?'

The farmer's face betrayed his concern.

'Sire?' he asked worriedly.

'Will you volunteer your son for my forces, and your daughters to entertain those forces?'

'Sire! I have always paid my taxes, I am a loyal subject!' the man cried.

Gello smiled thinly. 'Then you will obey me now. But I shall reward your loyalty. I shall leave you your son.'

'No! You cannot do this!' the man howled. 'Sire, I beg you!'

But Gello had already turned away as grinning, armoured men moved in.

'Down there.' Merren pointed. 'The people in that village. We must warn them.'

They had been searching for Berellians and had seen a company of them heading for a deserted village. Only the village was not quite deserted — half-a-dozen men were hurriedly loading goods onto a wagon. There was no question of fighting so many Berellians, but there might be time to let those villagers get away. Martil brooded silently at the thought. Merren might be enjoying saving families that had left it too long to flee north but all he could see was death for more of his Rallorans.

Argurium flew in low over the village, coming to a delicate stop outside the village inn. Almost before the dragon's wings had stopped beating, Merren had jumped down and was hurrying over to where the astonished men stared at them. Martil, cursing, hurried after her.

'There are a hundred Berellians on their way here. Leave that and start running!' Merren shouted.

The men just stared at her.

She paused then. Something seemed wrong. They were not bowing, they did not seem relieved to see her — although they did seem a little afraid.

'What are you doing?' she asked, looking at the wagon they were loading. Rather than food and drink, they seemed to be piling up furniture, books and paintings.

Martil arrived as the men looked from one to another, and at Merren.

'They're looters. Thought they'd profit before the Berellians got here,' Martil said softly, taking her arm and trying to ease her back, while drawing the Dragon Sword.

The men, who had been slowly moving towards Merren, froze at the sight of the Sword.

'Are you looting this village?' Merren asked coldly, shaking off Martil's hand.

The men's silence condemned them as effectively as if they had admitted it.

'What were you thinking of? Do you even live here?' Merren said angrily. 'Answer me!'

'We have nothing. Why not take something from those who do not want it any more?' one of the looters muttered.

Merren could barely believe her ears. How could anyone think of stealing at a time like this?

'You're as bad as the Berellians! I should bring you all back for trial,' Merren blazed.

'Merren, we don't have time — we should leave now.' Martil took her arm again. 'The Berellians will deal with them more harshly than we could.'

Merren wrenched her arm clear of Martil. 'Are we to let them get away with this?'

He was tempted to tell her this was all her idea but Karia had been whispering to him on the flight that he needed to be nicer to Merren and starting another argument hardly seemed the right way to go about it.

A trumpet call in the distance made any reply pointless. The looters jumped onto their wagon, whipped the horses into a trot and clattered out of the village.

'We have to go too,' Martil warned, sheathing the Sword.

Merren shook her head. 'How could people do this?'

Martil had no answer she would like, so he just helped her rush back to Havell, Karia and Argurium.

The dragon flew away as the first Berellians rode into the village. And, from up high, they saw the looters caught and killed by Berellians, the heavily laden wagon unable to get away.

'Back to the capital. I have seen all I want to,' Merren said dully.

'I need to return to the Rallorans, work out a way to save Kesbury and the others,' Martil said sourly.

'Is that wise? We shall not be there to protect you ...' Havell began.

'For Aroaril's sake! I won't be doing much fighting, the Berellians are still at least a day from Wells!' Martil snarled, happy to find a safe target for his anger and frustration.

Tiera found Barrett in his library.

'When did you get back?' she asked brightly.

'Not long ago.' Barrett had been trying to read about the weather patterns, and how to affect them, while fuming away quietly, but could not restrain a smile as he looked up at her. 'How have your studies been going?'

'Not too bad. I find some things hard — just when I think I have it, it seems to slip away from me,' she admitted.

'It's a common problem. But, with practice, you will get there,' he sympathised. She may not have anything like the ability of Karia but she had an extraordinary capacity for work.

'I was surprised to learn you were here — I thought you would be at the palace.' She sat down opposite him.

Barrett could not restrain a snort of derision.

'They don't need me there,' he growled. 'They have the dragon to move them around, a network of priests and priestesses to tell them what is going on — as well as all the birds I magicked.'

'But the Queen ...'

'Is more interested in her Champion than me!'

Tiera leaned back, and Barrett realised he had put too much venom into his voice.

'I am sorry. I am tired and you are the last person I want to shout at,' he apologised. 'It's just that ...'

'What?'

Barrett hesitated, but there were things he had kept inside too long. Besides, since Merren had told him she could never love him back, he had felt lost.

'I feel like I have wasted my life,' he confessed finally.

'What are you talking about? You are the Queen's Magician. Look where you live! Without you, the country would have been destroyed by Gello; the Queen would have been killed!' Tiera gasped.

Barrett smiled wanly. 'And yet, it probably still will be destroyed. I have all this power, and what have I really done with it? There are so many people I could have helped, but did not, because I selfishly thought of myself.'

'But you're not selfish,' Tiera protested.

'I am,' he sighed. 'I served the Queen faithfully, but also because I thought she would declare her love for me one day. All around our country there is misery. And outside of Norstalos it is even worse! You should have seen how the Derthals lived. I have this gift, I could have used it to make people happier and all I cared about was petty politics and my own glory. So I got what I deserved!'

Tiera could sense what Barrett really wanted was for her to comfort him. It was almost funny. His power was only limited by his imagination, while she was a former servant, who had been abused and almost killed. Yet he was the one who needed help.

She cleared her throat uncertainly.

'There is much you can do to help people, although I think you need to do it in the service of the Queen, at least until the country is safe. But you do not care just about yourself. I know that.'

Instantly, Barrett smiled up at her.

'Your words mean a great deal to me,' he admitted. 'You do not know what a comfort it is, being able to talk to you!'

Tiera could not help but feel a little warmth at that, at the way he smiled at her.

'Look, Queen Merren's loss can be your gain. Show me the exercises you are struggling with and I'll see if I can show you the way through,' he offered.

'But aren't you too busy?' she said doubtfully.

'If they want me, they know where to find me.' Barrett smiled. 'Helping you would be the perfect way for me to relax, after what we went through to get the Derthals on our side.'

Tiera clapped her hands. 'You must tell me about it! I heard you defeated the Berellian wizard and saved Captain Martil's life!'

Barrett smiled. 'Well, that is true. And it is a fascinating story.'

Martil watched Karia wave to him as she flew off on Argurium, feeling sick in the stomach, not just because Merren did not wave.

The problem of conducting a fighting retreat across hundreds of miles of countryside, while being pursued by thousands of Berellians and facing the threat of being cut off by the Tenochs or Gello's renegades was big enough, although reasonably easy. Stay far enough ahead of the Berellians so they did not catch up, and make it to the capital before the Tenochs or Gello.

But he had come to the conclusion that his problems were never simple.

Battle had always been the one place he could empty his mind of all problems, lose himself in the moment. But since that damned duel with Cezar, every time he drew the Dragon Sword, he was thinking about everything he was risking when he crossed swords with another man. His mind was full of Karia, of Merren and their unborn son — and of the task the dragons had laid upon him. The pressure Havell and Argurium were placing on him was understandable — but at the worst possible time.

He knew he was obsessing over his fears, for it was such a strange sensation, and that meant his anger, which he thought under control, was just below the surface. He was beginning to see what Merren was saying about everyone wanting a piece of her. He was supposed to be the war captain, as well as a dad, as well as the saviour of the bloody dragons — and he wanted to be a husband for Merren as well. And he did not know where to begin with any of them.

But what was truly tying his stomach in knots was being a dad to Karia and a husband to Merren.

As soon as they had landed, Karia had drawn him aside. She had wanted to talk to him since Merren had shouted at them, find out what had gone wrong.

'Why are you fighting with Merren? You know she won't marry you if you fight. So you've got to try harder to be nice to her. Because you seem to fight a lot.'

'I don't want to fight with her,' Martil protested.

Karia bit her lip. There was a question she wanted to ask, but she did not know if she wanted to hear the answer. 'Was it about the baby she is having?'

Martil stopped, taken aback. He could not think of an answer immediately. Not only was this a sensitive subject, but he was also horribly aware, from past experience, that she had rather more knowledge on this subject than a small girl should.

Karia saw his hesitation and felt a flicker of fear. 'It was, wasn't it? Are you going to leave me when Merren has the baby?'

'No!' Martil said instantly.

'Well, Merren never plays with me any more. We used to play dolls all the time back in the forest — she hasn't played dolls with me for ages! And you always seem to be going off and fighting, leaving me alone and scared!'

Martil sighed. She always knew the words that would strike him to the heart. 'Merren is very busy. She is the Queen. When this is over, then she might be able to play with you again,' he offered.

'But when will this be over? And by then, she will want to play with the baby! I bet you will, too! You don't even want to stay with me now!'

Martil felt a bitter pang at the thought of the baby, his son, growing up never knowing Martil was his father. But he knew he could not show any of that.

'I don't want to leave you. But there are things I have to do, to save people's lives. It is very important work ...' he tried to explain.

'More important than me?'

'No! Just ... differently important,' he tried to explain, knowing from the expression on her face that she was not convinced. 'Look, when the baby is born, you and I shall go somewhere special, do things that are fun,' he told her seriously. 'And I promise to get back to the capital for a day or two, to spend time with you soon.'

Karia cocked her head on one side and looked at him carefully. She could either throw a tantrum at this point or accept what he said. He looked sad, so she decided she had done all she could. Now to help him. 'Are you sad that Merren won't play with you, either?' she asked, a question so sharp he did not know whether to laugh or cry.

'I suppose I am,' he admitted.

'But at least we have each other,' she told him, patting him gently on the cheek. She decided to work on Merren herself. He was obviously too silly to do it properly himself. 'I love you, Dad.'

'I love you too.' He reached out and hugged her, feeling her small arms encircle him and hold him close. But strangely, rather than offer him comfort, it made his insides knot and twist. *I cannot leave her. I have to be here for her. But how can I do that and fight all the time?*

Onzalez signalled for Chanlon to be brought forwards. He had expected to find more Norstalines than this and the lack of sacrificial victims was beginning to annoy him. He intended to speak to Markuz about ensuring the raiding parties brought back prisoners. He knew the strategy was to use brutal tactics, force the Witch Queen's army to face them but dead families were no use to him. The dead could not feel fear.

'These are your countrymen. Perhaps they even joined you for a church service,' he told Chanlon, as the ex-priest stared at a young couple, who had been stripped and were being held down over a fallen log.

'Now you have a choice. Sacrifice them to Zorva, pledge your soul to Him and you shall lead the hunt for that priest of Aroaril who humiliated you and defies us. Or hold true to your old faith — and you may die with them, your soul still Aroaril's,' he told Chanlon.

Chanlon stared at the young couple, who pleaded with him to save them. He did not listen to that, although his eyes lingered on the woman. This was not a choice. He wanted revenge on Kesbury and he wanted to live. Everything else was just noise.

'Give me the knife, and tell me what I have to do,' he said.

Karia was determined to continue her attempts to get Merren to realise she had to marry Martil.

'Flying's great, isn't it, Merren? Argurium, thank you for giving us this treat!'

'It is my pleasure to carry you,' Argurium said. 'And I look forward to taking you to Dragonara Isle, and showing you around my home!'

Karia laughed. 'I know! I can't wait to meet all the talking animals!'

Havell opened his mouth but closed it again tiredly.

'And, afterwards, perhaps one of my daughters can bring you back!' Argurium continued.

Karia leaned down, unsure she had heard that right. 'Your daughters? What do you mean?'

Too late, Merren thought to change the subject.

'Well, child, when the Dragon Egg is opened by the Dragon Sword, the dragons shall be reborn. They will not really be my daughters — but I like to think of them that way.'

'But I want to see you!' Karia protested, her bottom lip trembling. 'What will happen to you?'

'I shall be part of the magic, living on through the next generation of dragons. But there is no need for sadness. I shall have fulfilled my life's purpose.'

'That's so sad!' Karia sighed, and reached back for Merren's hand. 'I wish Martil was here. Don't you, Merren?'

'Sometimes,' was all Merren said.

'You know, it would be great to be a family. The three of us together. We used to have so much fun, you and I, playing dolls back in the forest. Maybe we could play again when we get back …'

'Can't we get back to the capital any quicker?' Merren snapped.

Karia sighed. This was going to be more difficult than she first thought. Why were adults so silly?

Father Quiller was rather enjoying himself. He was riding at the front of a horde of Derthals — tribe upon tribe had joined High Chief Sacrax until there were thousands of them marching. He could look over his shoulder and see a forest of spearheads. Now they were out of the mountains and on the northern grasslands — the very northern tip of Norstalos, inhabited only by a few hardy souls, hunters and, of course, the gold and silver miners — and the sight looked even more impressive.

Quiller had two of Sacrax's personal guards carry the Queen's banner, while he rode out ahead. After all, the chances of anyone living out here having heard the latest news from the capital were slim. Most probably did not even know there was a war on.

The few Norstalines he saw did not hang around long enough to even look at the banner. They just grabbed a few items and either ran or galloped off into the distance. He thought about trying to call out to them — but they were usually too far away. In some ways it was humorous — these simple folk no doubt thought that this was the beginning of another goblin war, when in fact the Derthals were here to save them. But it was also worrying — what if one farmer loosed a crossbow bolt that turned the Derthals from allies into enemies?

All he could do was keep a close watch, and count the miles as they rolled past under the rapid tread of the Derthals.

'We must change our strategy somewhat,' Merren announced. 'Our plan has all been about speed, and preserving the army. That is still important but we must take more time and trouble to get people away. There are too many that we plan to leave behind. They must be given more of a chance to escape.'

'Your majesty, you do know the people you are talking about are the ones who doubt your rule, or even openly support Gello. It might be better all round if we left them behind ...' Sendric began.

'No!' Merren shook her head. 'They will not suffer because of that. We must redouble our efforts to get people out before they are taken by our enemies. Have the Tenochs landed yet?'

Louise produced a piece of parchment. 'Captain Rocus reports their ships will land tomorrow. It seems they have chosen Cessor as their main thrust; most of their ships are there. The rest will reach Worick the day after.'

'He must hold the city long enough to give the people a chance to get away. When the Tenochs land, the citizens will see the error of their support for Gello. The same goes for Hutter at Worick. See to it.'

'Yes, my Queen.' Conal scratched quickly on a piece of parchment.

'And the rest of the evacuation? How goes it?'

All eyes turned to Archbishop Nott, whose network of priests and priestesses was out on every road in the country.

'If we can buy ourselves a few more days, hold up these invasions, we should be able to get most of the people to safety,' he predicted. 'But our enemies are doing their best to catch up with the refugees. I fear for those who are unable to stand the pace.'

Merren rubbed tired eyes. The image of the slaughtered Norstaline families she had seen down south was still fresh.

'I shall take Argurium out, to do what I can.'

'You must be careful, my Queen. Without you, we are lost,' Conal warned.

Merren waved away the worry. 'I'm more concerned with saving the people.'

'That depends on the weather,' Nott pointed out. 'The roads are not wide enough to take this number of travellers. Those without wagons or carts are forced to walk on the grass beside the road. To make good speed, we need it to stay dry. Rain means we shall be trapped.'

'Can you predict what the weather will be?' Merren demanded instantly.

Nott sighed. 'We are able to ask Aroaril for more rain — but I have never heard of asking for no rain. Of course I can try — but I would not depend on the results. I know wizards normally leave the weather to nature and the priests but perhaps Barrett might be able to help.'

There was a pause, as they all looked around the table.

'Where is Barrett?' Merren asked the obvious question.

'I don't know, my Queen. We could not find him in the palace, and there are too few servants left to send them off to search for him through the city,' Gia apologised.

'Perhaps at his house?' Conal suggested.

Merren shook her head. She did not have the energy to deal with a disgruntled Barrett now. Let him sulk for a while — if they really needed him, he would come. She was sure of that, at least. And perhaps he would be in a better mood when he did come back.

'Leave him for now. Archbishop, as you said, this is more of your responsibility than Barrett's anyway. The wind is still blowing from the north; I have never known it to change this early in the year. I'm sure between you and Aroaril it will remain dry long enough for us to get the people to safety.'

'I shall do my best, my Queen.' Nott nodded.

Kettering swore violently and kicked the cooking pot that had held last night's dinner across the room.

'I didn't think the stew was that bad, Killer,' Leigh said nervously.

'What?' Kettering turned, then shook his head. 'Not that, this!' He held up a crumpled piece of parchment, brought to him by a magicked bird.

'Is there bird shit on the parchment again?' Hawke asked, wisely. 'I hate it when that happens.'

Kettering took a deep breath. 'No, it's our new orders. We're not to leave Cessor.'

'What? Why?' Leigh snorted.

'There're too many people still here.'

'But we'll never get far enough away now — do these people know how fast a wagon can go?' Hawke rumbled.

'They know. They want us to get the carriages from the rich streets, load them up with supplies and get north that way.'

'So that means back to that street, with the screaming hag, and the fat bastard with the crossbow?' Leigh groaned. 'They hate us!'

'But we have to protect them,' Kettering grunted.

'Pass me the cooking pot. Now I want to kick it!' Hawke declared.

Merren accepted her cup of tea with a smile. She, Louise and Gia were in her rooms, with Jaret and Wilsen on guard outside, with orders to let nobody in. Another survey had come in, with results as bad as the last. The people had spoken — and a notorious warrior with a bloodstained past and sheep farmers for parents was not the Prince Consort they wanted. Perhaps if Gia and Louise could give her the space to be herself, then her heart might agree to what her head told her she must do. Although, strangely, he was almost making it easier for her …

'So we're standing there in front of this family we rescued, having a screaming match,' she sighed. 'Everything we say to each other is another argument!'

'Have you thought of talking to him quietly?' Louise suggested. She and Gia had not expected to be called back in for another of these meetings, despite Merren's earlier words, after the last. They were not sure what she wanted from them — and less sure how to provide it.

'If I could just make the decision! It's like Martil and Sendric are symbolic of everything I face as a queen. All my lessons on how to rule, all the things I was told about royalty, tell me I should choose Sendric. But my father failed as a king; his mistakes led us to this point. I have my own ideas on how to be Queen. I know being a good ruler will take a mixture of both but it makes it hard to know which things he taught me are wrong, and which are right.'

'It's easier to make the decision when you're not a queen,' Gia admitted.

'I know — Sendric!' Louise shivered. 'Aroaril, he's ancient! I thought you needed to have as many children as possible?'

Merren put down her cup. This was what she needed to talk about. But she could not bring herself to admit the real story. As much as she wanted to, she could not break the habits, the training ingrained into her. 'Perhaps I should go and talk to Martil,' was all she said. 'Now, tell me, what is the story of you and Conal?'

Gia laughed as Louise blushed defensively, giving Merren time to cover her frustration at herself. It seemed she could only truly let her defences down around Martil. If only they were talking …

6

Rocus peered out from the harbour warehouse towards where the first of the Tenoch warships sailed into Cessor. Every Norstaline vessel had been loaded with people, or food, or both and sent north days ago. The plan had been to join them but then orders had come through to hold the city long enough to give the people a chance to escape when they saw the invasion.

Rocus had been spat on and his men pelted with everything from rotten fruit to the contents of a chamber pot by these people. He would have been happy to see them die but, even without the Queen's orders, recognised they all had innocent servants, as well as tons of supplies the others would need this winter. Besides, once out on the road, the Tenochs' massive advantage in numbers would be almost unstoppable — and there was nothing in the way of hills, passes or valleys that could be used to slow them down. It was flat country and good roads all the way to the capital.

Cessor's harbour was big enough for three score ships to berth at its long wooden jetties. Each jetty was owned by a rich merchant, or merchant company and all of these had their own warehouses facing the water. This meant these large wooden buildings overlooked everything that berthed at Cessor. He had all 500 archers hidden in the warehouses, while Kettering's men were up in the town.

Unlike Norstaline ships, the Tenoch vessels were powered by both sails and oars. Watching them row blithely into the harbour of a Norstaline city, as if they owned the place, set his teeth on edge. He would make them pay, he promised, as the first one eased alongside a jetty. He was sweating, a mixture of nerves and anger. Martil had stressed the need to preserve the men but Rocus felt released by the Queen's orders to hurt the Tenochs.

'What are the others waiting for?' Cropper, the leader of the archers, asked as just one ship slipped in towards the docks.

'They think we might be waiting for them. Pass the word — stay hidden. We shall strike when they bring the rest of their fleet in. Tell Kettering his men are to deal with the first ship's crew,' Rocus ordered.

'Father!' Karia sprinted over to Archbishop Nott and gave him a huge hug.

With a chuckle he hugged her back. With Martil still down south, he had been happy to look after Karia, although his many other duties were leaving him exhausted at the end of the day.

'Can I show you some magic?' she offered. 'And then we can do some reading!'

'Of course.'

Karia hurried over to her books. She missed Martil but she still loved Father (she could not think of him as Archbishop) Nott deeply. The only thing that would have made her any happier was if there was a mother as well. Sometimes she dreamed about her mother; a woman she had never seen. Martil was great to hug but sometimes she wished he did not smell of sweat, leather, steel — and especially blood. When Merren held her, it had felt different. Nicely different. What would it have been like had she known her mother? She hoped Merren would be a bit nicer — and she hoped Martil would come back soon.

As if reading her thoughts, Nott smiled at her.

'Martil will return. It is good to see the two of you together. And you must be strong for each other. Much depends on you both,' he said seriously, 'and I might not always be here to help you.'

'Of course you will, Father!' Karia said scornfully.

'No, my dear. When I am not here, you must always obey your father.' He patted her gently on the head.

'But what if he's not there? Will I have a mother to look after me as well?' Karia asked carefully.

Nott's smile faded. 'I cannot say,' he said, equally carefully.

The residents of Cessor had been able to watch the progress of the Tenoch fleet easily enough as their homes — although not the servant quarters — gave an excellent view of the harbour. So they knew that an army was landing in their city. All felt that, as long as they kept their doors shut, they would be perfectly safe.

Herena, for one, watched with satisfaction. At last the rightful King would be returned. The Cessors would take back their city and she could continue her ongoing campaign to marry her son off to one of Count Cessor's daughters. That had to be worth a minor baronetcy, at the very least! The sight of Gello's red flag with the double sword badge reassured her these warriors were only here to liberate her country from a dangerous radical. But then she caught sight of some scruffy-looking soldiers, the type she had kicked out of the street, sneaking through her garden. For a moment she was too outraged to do anything. How dare they trespass! Then she realised they planned to spring a trap on the warriors marching in the street outside. Well, that just wouldn't do! She knew her duty and, lifting her long dress up — so the hem would not be dirtied by brushing along the cobbles outside — she swept out her front door, intending to warn Gello's men of the foul treachery that awaited them.

'Greetings,' she called loudly.

The Tenochs reacted instantly, moving to each side of the street, while what looked like an officer rushed over.

She fixed a smile on her face — nothing too much, not like the one she reserved for royalty — and cleared her throat. 'I am here to warn you! You are about to be attacked by some foul brigands,' she declared in ringing tones.

'What? Show me!' the officer demanded.

Herena stared at his face with a mixture of horror and curiosity. He had marks etched into the skin of his forehead and cheeks, while his ears and nose were pierced with what looked like shards of gold. That sort of thing would never be allowed in Norstalos, and she began to doubt why King Gello had allowed himself to be associated with such men.

'Show me, woman!' the officer repeated. He was agitated enough as it was. The city was strange, and he did not like being the first company into its echoing streets. He grabbed her arm and shoved her back towards the house.

'How dare you! Take your filthy hands off me! And I demand you address me with some respect!'

Herena snatched her arm back. 'I shall report you to King Gello for insubordination!'

He grabbed her again and, outraged, she delivered a ringing slap to his face.

The officer blinked in surprise then struck her back. His blow sent Herena crashing to the ground. She screamed, in pain and in outrage at finding herself lying on the filthy gutter.

Up and down the street, windows were popping open and people staring out at the scene.

'Hey you! Leave her alone!' Fergus roared, waving his crossbow.

That was enough for the Tenoch officer. 'It's a trap!' he shouted.

'No, we are —!' A horrified Herena rolled onto her back and tried to explain but the officer slammed down his axe-club, striking sparks from the cobbles where its blade hacked through her neck.

'Now!' Kettering ordered his trumpeter. 'Attack now!'

In the street, the cries of outrage from the residents at Herena's brutal death was quickly replaced by terrified cries and pleas for mercy, as Tenochs began breaking down doors and windows, seeking to get inside the houses of what they thought were their attackers.

The Tenochs looked around as the trumpet call echoed down the street — then frantically defended themselves as a mass of armed men erupted out of laneways and from behind garden walls.

Kettering leaped over the wall and cut down one of the Tenoch scouts.

'Kill them all!' he bellowed, as his cavalry company thundered past.

* * *

'You need to travel south. What is going on at Wells will have a vital effect on our future. Without your help, Kesbury will be lost, killed by a Fearpriest,' Nott told Milly solemnly. 'You must save him. He has the potential to become a talisman to the people; the Ralloran who saved the village that spat on him. The Church needs him. And it also needs you to defeat a Fearpriest.'

'Why?' Milly asked.

'Trust me. It is very important. The people must know that you are stronger than the Fearpriests.'

'But what about you? I'm only a bishop — and I shouldn't even hold that position yet ...'

'You are better than you think. And you have been chosen by Aroaril for great things. Now listen to me. You would remember better than I what they teach in the seminary — how Aroaril and Zorva are brothers, but one is the God of Light, the other of Darkness. Mankind is a reflection of these two Gods, a combination of good and evil. Most of us strive to be good, to limit the darkness within us and turn to the light, but some, like the Fearpriests, embrace the darkness and are consumed by evil. They tell you Fearpriests are able to kill with a touch, can do all manner of terrible things, but they must have a weakness beyond their arrogance. And I have found it. After much prayer and contemplation, Aroaril has revealed to me how we can defeat a Fearpriest. It seems they can affect objects of stone and wood but not iron or steel. I suspect it is because they do not use those metals — in their homeland, they never learned how to work ore. Instead they use a volcanic rock for cutting tools. But we can affect metals. If they use a metal knife, for instance ... We shall tell every priest and priestess this revelation from Aroaril but it may fall to you to test this.'

'How? Why?'

'I do not know precisely. But you need to be ready. It does not take one skilled in divination to link this to your trip south. You just have to have faith, trust in me, and ask no more questions.'

Milly bowed her head, although it was almost impossible not to say anything else.

'Save me!' A screaming woman, her dress ripped at the shoulder, stumbled towards Kettering.

Kettering shoved her aside and hacked at the Tenoch behind her. The man parried, Kettering's steel sword taking a huge chunk of wood out of the man's axe-club, then Hawke's blade came over Kettering's shoulder to send the Tenoch reeling away, his throat torn open.

Kettering wiped blood from his face and tried to work out what was going on. The Tenochs had broken into a dozen houses along the street, after his cavalry had slaughtered any that stood in the street — now he was trying to hunt them down. But he was being hindered by residents deciding now was the best time to leave — and demanding he protect them.

Some had already clattered off in their carriages, servants hanging on grimly to doors and roofs. Others had decided they would not leave without as many of their treasures as they could pack, and Kettering had watched a furious fight between a handful of his men and Tenochs raging through a garden, while servants staggered past them, arms full of clothes and wooden chests.

The ambush down at the harbour seemed to have gone well — too well. After the archers had slaughtered a ship's company, the Tenoch ships were now sending volleys of rocks into the lower town, destroying any building that might serve as a hiding place for an archer. Worse, they were also hurling balls of pitch, which had started a dozen fires already — and threatened to destroy the whole town. Archers had streamed up from the harbour, dragging a score of wounded men with them — although their arrows were helping remove the last Tenochs from the street.

'Kettering! Captain Kettering!'

He turned to see a group of archers hurrying towards him, dragging a pair of limp bodies. He cursed as he recognised them.

'What happened?' he snarled.

The archer trumpeter was bleeding from a graze to his forehead.

'Catapult stones. Captain Rocus shoved me away before he and Captain Cropper were hit. They both need a priest, right now.'

Kettering swore again. Both were unconscious and, from their smashed limbs and bloodied faces, he wondered if they would ever wake.

'Sir, you're the senior officer in Cessor now.'

Kettering could not help but laugh, the sound causing the archer trumpeter to edge away slightly from this blood-splattered man with his long hair tied back.

'Right. Let's find some carriages and get the wounded on them. The Tenochs are doing a better job of slowing themselves down than we ever could. Sound the recall, we shall meet at the city gates. Find me some lieutenants from your archer companies.'

'Certainly, sir. Er, carriages, sir?'

Kettering sighed. 'Follow me.'

He turned and walked inside the nearest house, which happened to be Fergus's, flanked by both Hawke and Leigh. The fine wooden door had been smashed down by Tenoch axe-clubs, and Hawke sighed with sadness when he saw it, then quietly pocketed the solid brass knocker. Inside the house, three dead Tenochs lay where they had fallen while servants rushed around like hens disturbed by a fox, carrying plates, boxes of cutlery and leather-bound books.

Kettering reached out and grabbed one by the back of his tunic, sending silver knives and forks showering across the blood-stained wooden floor.

'Where is your master?' he growled.

'I shall fetch him!' the servant babbled, disappearing up the stairs at a run.

'Leave those,' Kettering snapped at Leigh, who had a handful of the cutlery.

'I was just picking it up,' Leigh protested weakly, then dropped them reluctantly, all but a couple of teaspoons. He winked at the archer as he pocketed them.

'What is happening? We need that carriage packed and ready to go!' Fergus stormed down the stairs, his moustache bristling, then he saw Kettering and the others and raced over, shaking their hands like a demented man.

'I was wrong about you boys! So wrong! You saved my life, my family's lives. Those monsters would have cut me down like they killed Herena, as if we were dogs. That one was about to brain me when one of your boys spitted him like a chicken. I am forever in your debt. Here, take these.'

He swept up a handful of the fallen silverware and tried to press it on Leigh and Hawke.

'Thanks, but I've already got some like it.' Leigh smiled.

Kettering grabbed Fergus by the shoulders.

'You will unpack any valuables and replace them with wounded men,' Kettering told him. 'Then you will leave immediately!'

Fergus's mouth opened and closed, he gulped, then he nodded.

'Right away. Leave those!' he shouted at the servants. 'Go with this archer and help bring his wounded around to the carriage entrance!'

Kettering left them to it, went out to see what was happening in the street and found a cluster of archer officers waiting for him.

A lieutenant saluted. 'Tenochs are all dead, or have fled! Lower town is ablaze — I think they plan to let it burn us out before they land any more men.'

'Good. Because we shall be long gone. And this fire will drive out any people who thought about staying behind. We'll load everyone we can find onto the carriages. Don't let a carriage leave if it's carrying books or clothes or silverware instead of people or food.'

'But what if they protest, sir? These people with carriages have friends in high places ...' one officer began.

'If they don't obey you, send them to me. I'll give them something to complain about,' Kettering snarled.

They nodded, then flinched as a Tenoch fireball exploded in a house at the bottom of the street, sending bricks flying and bowling over a pair of running archers.

'What are you waiting for? Get your men moving!' Kettering barked, then watched them run to obey him.

He walked out to see Rocus and Cropper now being carried away. 'Thanks very much, you bastards,' he told them.

Hutter had wanted to defend the river city of Worick, even before the orders came. Letting invaders land unopposed was like watching a crime and not acting to stop it. But he did not even get the chance to hurt the Tenochs. Their vessels had rowed into the river mouth all flying the flag of Worick, a white ship on a green background. But the Tenoch ships did not go near the jetties.

Instead of landing an army, the Tenoch ships began launching catapult stones and balls of flame into the houses.

Hutter and his men had rescued as many people as they could, loaded them into boats and set off upriver while Worick burned. But it was not a real escape. Eventually the River Worick turned south — and they would have to get out and walk from there.

It was rare indeed to see so many wizards in the one place. They never worked together and, while most knew each other — by name if not by sight — they were not friendly. After all, a wizard who had spent years building up his trade in a town was not going to welcome a competitor.

But Barrett was the Queen's Magician — and the most powerful wizard seen in a generation. A summons from him had brought every wizard who could travel through an oaken gateway to hear what he had to say.

They were clustered in the large ballroom that had been the least used part of the Royal Magician's house since Barrett had moved in. They had all eaten hungrily, drained by the journey there, now they merely nibbled on the food.

Barrett looked across the room with a soaring heart. He had felt so lost, but after many talks with Tiera, he had come up with this idea. For too long each wizard had worked against each other, labouring only for money. They were seen as aloof and arrogant, slaves to the gold that they charged. But there was so much they could do to help the people. Not just in this desperate situation but in normal life. So much misery could be averted through magic. So much good could be done. If only they listened to him!

He began to talk then, explaining how wizards had been given a gift, had been blessed to be able to work magic. How, instead of giving thanks for this gift, they had used it to make themselves rich, had refused to help those unable to afford their services.

'I know why it began — our ancestors needed rich patrons, someone prepared to feed, clothe and house them while they learned their arts, and while they experimented. But, somewhere along the way, it became all about the money. I propose we change all that. That we band together, work together, to help the people ...'

He trailed off as the angry muttering rippled through the crowd.

'Do you mean to make us lapdogs of your Queen, as Tellite wanted us to submit to the rule of Duke Gello?' someone shouted.

Barrett shook his head. Tellite, who had tried to stop him — and died in the attempt. 'No. I say we should be independent, but work together for the people. Work for free, at times. Give something back ...'

'Easy for you to say, living in this large house, with your cellars stuffed full of gold. Some of us have families to feed!' a portly mage called.

Many agreed and Barrett felt he was losing them. He glanced sideways, to where Tiera sat at the side of the room. She smiled at him, and nodded, and he turned back to them with fresh determination in his voice.

'Hear me out. I do not seek to make the rules. I say we should talk, all of us, hammer out an agreement. Coopers, smiths, leather-workers, tailors — they all have guilds. Why not mages? If we can still make a good living with more respect from the public, what is wrong with that?'

The last sally seemed to hit home. All had suffered the indignity of being abused on the street.

'Tell us more,' one invited.

'It is not just us being held back, sire,' Prent reported. 'In the west, both Tenoch landings have been slowed by resistance. When the Tenochs used catapults to crush the defenders, the towns caught fire and slowed them even more.'

Gello ground his teeth at the thought of both Worick and Cessor going up in smoke. Those were two of the richest towns in the country!

'In the south, the advance goes slowly. Markuz has discovered the Rallorans have fortified the bridge across the River Brack, at Wells. Everyone reports that the countryside is almost empty. Dust clouds indicate that they are staying ahead of our forces.'

Gello swore bitterly. This would not do at all! He needed to bring Merren's forces to battle, and the best way to do that was hurt the people. Then his soft-hearted fool of a cousin would try to stop him, and he would smash them and take back the country. But he could not force them to fight when they could keep retreating across the country whenever he got close. If they weren't careful, the bitch could actually escape into the north — and then it would be near impossible to pry them out of there before winter.

'We cannot let them escape. Tell Onzalez that we need to slow the refugees down somehow, force the soldiers to stand and fight, so we can rip them apart!'

Khaliz, the Berellian King's Magician, was more than a little frightened to receive a summons from Brother Onzalez.

He had survived the failure in the north, and Cezar's death, only because Berellia had few magicians, and none capable of replacing him. Still, being dragged before a Fearpriest was not a good sign. Khaliz was not without power, but the Fearpriest was in another realm. He was sweating when he was shown into Onzalez's tent — and shocked to find himself given a seat and poured wine.

'Tell me, Khaliz, what know you of weather magic?' the Fearpriest asked warmly.

Khaliz licked dry lips. 'Such a thing is normally the province of priests ...'

Onzalez waved his hand dismissively. 'The priests of Aroaril are blocking me. That is why I want you to try. They cannot counter natural magic, as I could not stop the storm the Norstaline wizards conjured, which slowed down the sailing of our Tenoch brothers. I want torrential rain. Rain enough to turn their roads to mud and stop their retreat, so we may defeat their soldiers.'

Khaliz took a gulp of wine. 'I can try, my lord,' he said eventually. 'But if the Norstaline wizards detect what I am doing, they will oppose me. And Barrett can defeat me. My strength is not equal to his. All they have to do is delay me, and I shall perish in the task.'

'That will be a necessary sacrifice,' Onzalez told him. 'You shall eat well, then begin.'

Khaliz felt the sweat stand out all over his skin again.

'Yes, lord. But if I am to be successful, I shall need support. Such a task is best achieved slowly, secretly. I need to let it build gently, until it is too late for them to stop me. By the time they detect it, they will not be able to stop it.'

'I don't care how it is done. Only that it is done,' Onzalez growled. 'Succeed and you shall be well rewarded.'

'Yes, lord.' Khaliz bowed his head. He knew what the alternative was.

7

Merren rubbed tired eyes and tried to concentrate on what Conal was saying. If keeping track of what was happening across the country was not hard enough, her mind kept creeping back to Martil and Karia. She wanted to go and see Martil, to talk with him and forget about Norstalos' death struggle, for a short while. But she was also afraid they would probably end up shouting at each other. He was grudgingly obeying her orders, but was sending back strongly worded reports to her. Each time one of his men was wounded or killed saving a Norstaline he was sending a note, every word a thinly veiled attack on her instructions. They made her blood boil. And having Karia constantly in her ear was not making it any easier. As well as not-so-subtle hints about being a family, Karia had begun suggesting Merren relax with her, play some games and read some books. Relax! Because she had been away from the palace, she had been up half the night as it was, going through reports and over maps, writing out fresh orders for soldiers scattered across hundreds of miles …

'Your majesty?' Conal said gently.

Merren blinked her eyes open.

'Keep going, Conal,' she said.

The ex-bandit cleared his throat. 'It's going well. Almost according to our plans. We have roads full of refugees but our soldiers are able to keep the invaders at a safe distance. Meanwhile, the Derthals should reach Sendric in the next day — and will be at the passes a day later. Father Quiller says they are in good spirits and making better progress.'

'There have been losses,' Louise admitted. 'Cessor and Worick are almost destroyed — we don't know how many people died in there. Kettering managed to get a few hundred away from Cessor, fewer made it out of Worick with Hutter. Those two are now in command in the west, we have lost both Cropper and Rocus. They were badly hurt defending the city and are on their way back here — they may not survive.'

There was silence around the table. Rocus was the last of the original leaders of the rebellion, the man who had led the charge at Sendric to save Martil, the one who had charged with the Queen at Pilleth.

'What else?' Merren said heavily. She had spent the previous day on Argurium, dropping in on refugees on roads, trying to speed them up and raise their spirits. It had worked for them, although left her feeling exhausted by the size of the crisis. Worse, she had seen more looters — and some of these had melted away into the trees rather than paying the ultimate penalty at the hands of the Berellians, Tenochs or Gello. How could people behave like that?

'Anyone south of the River Brack, barring the ones being brought out by Kesbury, is either dead or wishing they were dead. In the east, Gello is advancing slowly, Captain Kay is keeping him well back from the refugees. If we can keep this up for another week, we should be able to get the people safely away,' Conal explained.

'And where is Barrett?' she asked, suddenly aware the wizard was not at the table.

'Still locked up in his house with a bunch of wizards and his new apprentice. If you ask me, the wizard's thinking with his little staff, not the big one,' Conal grunted.

'This is not a Tetran inn, you fool,' Louise chided him.

Merren struggled to think. 'If he is happy, perhaps we should give him some space,' she suggested.

'We should tell him to get off his ... backside — and start using his magic to help us again,' Conal offered.

Merren could still see clearly the look in Barrett's eyes when she had told him she did not love him and never could love him — after using him to escape from Gello's trap at the ranger barracks. He deserved a little happiness. And perhaps he would return in a better mood and the uncomfortable feeling between them would be gone. For all his pompousness and misguided puppy love, he had been an enormous help to her over the years and she owed him a debt of thanks for saving her life on several occasions — as well as Martil's life.

'We shall leave him be for a few days. He has earned that much,' she said. 'If we really need him to transport people ahead of the invaders, we shall call on him then.'

'As you wish, your majesty.' Conal bowed his head.

'I wonder if you could visit the south again, your majesty,' Bishop Milly suggested. 'And I wonder if I might come along with you? I have a feeling I shall be needed there.'

Merren considered this for a moment. Obviously the woman had some reason and it would keep

Karia happy. Besides, perhaps she and Martil might not argue ... 'As long as the dragon is happy, I have no objections. But we shall leave now. I will be back by nightfall — and will need to know what has happened elsewhere as soon as I land.'

Louise and Conal exchanged glances. With three invasions, thousands of refugees on the roads and a rescue force of Derthals coming from the north, it meant another long day for them.

'Your majesty, if I may have a quick word,' Conal said softly, as the meeting was breaking up.

'What is it?' Merren asked.

'Your majesty, I don't know if I can keep doing this,' Conal admitted. 'Making decisions each day that cost lives or save lives. The pressure of not making a mistake. I'm ... I'm having trouble sleeping and my mind is never at rest ...'

Merren smiled grimly. 'I wish I could let you go. But I need you more than ever. You have had a taste of what I must deal with. You know what it requires. I cannot do it all by myself.'

'But surely you do not need me? I'm just an old, drunken bandit. There are many others ...'

'Where are they? Who are they? You want to make up for what you once did? There is no better place, no better time than now. Conal, I need your help.'

Conal could not meet her eyes.

'Look at me,' she said gently, and he reluctantly did so. 'Lives depend on you. I depend on you. Don't let them, or me, down.'

Conal slowly straightened up. 'I shall keep working, your majesty,' he said hoarsely. 'But can I say I now appreciate what it means to wear a crown ...'

'Thank you for your words — but I am afraid you don't know the half of it,' Merren told him, then brushed his cheek with her hand before hurrying out.

Gratt had done many unusual things since he stopped being a servant and began being the leader of Sendric's town council. But this had to be the strangest.

'Greetings!' he shouted, as the horde of Derthals faced him.

All day, terrified people had been flooding into Sendric, declaring that there was a massive goblin invasion heading for the town. Gratt had tried to explain that the Derthals were here to help, that they had agreed to protect the Norstalines — but that had done little. Only a few of the oldest residents could remember an actual goblin attack — and they had been children then — but all had been raised on those stories and nothing would convince them that goblins could be here to save them. He dreaded to think what their reaction would be when they discovered the goblins would be living in the northern forest — a fact the bards had not been broadcasting. But first they had to get the Derthals to stay.

In desperation, Gratt and the town council had ridden out of the gates to meet the Derthals. The Queen had impressed on him how important it was to show them that things had changed, that the Norstalines could be trusted. Having the townsfolk hurl everything from abuse to rocks and rotten fruit at them was hardly going to help. But now he was this close to so many gob— Derthals, the stories that his grandfather used to tell him seemed horribly real. Even though he knew they were here to help, he could feel the sweat making his tunic stick to his back.

'Gratt! A welcome face,' Father Quiller greeted him. 'Come, meet High Chief Sacrax.'

Gratt gave a nervous bow as the Derthal chief approached. Short, powerful, with plenty of scars and a broad smile that showed missing and blackened teeth, Sacrax was every bit the image of the monsters of Gratt's childhood stories.

'I am the head of the town council of Sendric. On behalf of Sendric and Queen Merren, we welcome your help and ask if there is anything you need?'

Sacrax's smile grew even more broad.

'You are afraid, town council man! But there is nothing to fear. We shall march down to the passes, and we shall stop your enemies. Then we shall live in the forest, as our ancestors did.'

Gratt cleared his throat, aware of the danger of his voice sounding too high-pitched.

'Then you shall be valued neighbours, and we shall welcome you,' he declared, as Queen Merren had told him to, and hoping it would prove true.

Sacrax smiled broadly. 'Tell your people we mean no harm. They have been running away from us for days!'

'Perhaps it's just that Father Quiller looks scary,' Gratt grinned awkwardly.

The Derthal chief stared at him, and the silence grew.

Gratt gulped, wondering how he might be able to retrieve this situation, when Sacrax threw back his head and laughed.

'You Norstalines! You say strange things!' He turned to Quiller. 'The people run because the priest looks scary!'

Still chuckling, he slapped Gratt on the shoulder.

'Will there be food waiting for us at the passes?'

'I shall see to it,' Gratt declared, weak with relief, and vowing never to joke again.

* * *

'We're almost there!' Kesbury roared.

But most of the people were too tired to do more than raise their heads. There was certainly no energy to raise a cheer. The horses had begun to falter and many of the men were walking alongside now, the horses unable to bear more than the weight of a child or two, as well as the food.

A company of Rallorans had found them as the dawn lightened the sky — and that had nearly triggered a panic, only Kesbury's calm voice and certainty that these were friends had stopped half of them running in all directions.

The villagers, who would have crossed the road to spit on the Rallorans just days ago, had embraced them like long-lost brothers when they arrived, some people openly crying.

And now Wells was in sight. Sprawled across both sides of the wide River Brack, it was one of the most important trading towns in southern Norstalos, although it stood empty, its residents gone. At its centre was a wide stone bridge, broad enough for two carts to pass side by side. All they had to do was walk out of this small wood, across a pasture and go about a mile down the road to the outskirts of the town, then through the deserted buildings on this side of the river until they reached the bridge.

'There's Berellians around. I know it,' Dunner muttered to Kesbury as they peered across the peaceful countryside.

Kesbury had mixed feelings that his old friend had led the Rallorans; he was delighted to see him, and afraid he would have to watch his friend die.

'And Captain Martil has a plan?'

'He and the Queen,' Dunner agreed.

'Well, what are we waiting for then?'

After a short delay, when everyone got back onto the horses, the group spurred their tired mounts out of the illusory shelter of the trees, across a field and onto the main road.

Almost immediately trumpets sounded. From a pair of farmhouses on their left, and a copse on the right, Berellians galloped to the attack. Scores of them. And more were appearing out of the deserted buildings ahead.

Barrett was exhausted — but exhilarated at the progress his Magicians' Guild was making.

'I think this is going to work!' he told Tiera happily.

'It's amazing to watch,' Tiera nodded. 'Every argument they have, you have an answer for them!'

It had become their custom to drink a cup of tea together and share stories of the day. Barrett found himself listening to her calm, quiet good sense. He was too quick to anger, too quick to insult those who did not agree with him. He could not suffer fools — it was a fault of his, he knew. But where he could have destroyed any hopes of co-operation, she often saw a way through that provided a clever compromise.

'It is a special skill you have,' he told her.

'Aye, well, when you're a servant, you have to think fast to get those who think themselves your betters to do what you want.' She grinned.

He looked at her and felt his heart beating faster. Where he had spent his time daydreaming of Merren, now Tiera occupied his thoughts. At his suggestion, she had let her short hair grow out, while some of the female wizards had showed her how to add colour to her eyes, lips and face, to add depth and allure. The advice had been to help her look more like a wizard, less like a servant girl — but the effect on Barrett had been dramatic. And he would not fall into the same trap of waiting too long again. He had to say something now. For many reasons.

'You know, one good thing about this guild will be the training of apprentices,' he said casually, although his stomach was trying to force its way out of his throat and the tea tasted like ashes.

'Yes! There must be so many children of the poor who never get to find their talent, as I have!' she exclaimed.

Barrett smiled, although he could feel his heart threatening to burst out of his chest. 'I meant, it will be good when you are no longer my pupil, for then we can be something else.'

'What's that?' She smiled.

Barrett gulped. 'I have feelings for you. I would like the opportunity to show you I am not just a teacher, but a man as well. Of course I would not dream of acting on those unless it was something you wanted ...'

He looked up from the table to see her ashen face staring at him.

Tiera did not know what to say. She was comfortable with Barrett, as she was with no other man. His kindness, his patience had brought her back from a dark place. But his words brought into her mind the image of Prent's leering face, as he forced her to his bed. She had thought herself beyond him but, of late, it had seemed to get worse, not better.

'I ... I cannot ...' she said shakily, then ran, because she could not stand to see what the expression on his face would be like.

'Wait! Don't leave!' Barrett cried, but she had already gone.

Before he could chase after her, a tide of laughing, chattering wizards swept into his large kitchen and bore him back to the table.

'Here he is! The champion of wizards. My boy, I think we have agreement on everything. Your idea will become a reality!' one roared, to cheers from the others.

Barrett forced a smile onto his face, and wished he did not feel dead inside.

'Keep riding!' Dunner encouraged the column of villagers — but Kesbury felt sick. How would they escape this?

Then the dragon struck.

It swooped down gracefully to their right, roaring a challenge so fearsome that many of the children cried out in fear. But it had the desired effect — the Berellian riders on that side lost control of their horses, which were rearing and plunging. Some even galloped away in the opposite direction, while others were thrown to the ground. In an instant the charge was turned into chaos.

Soaring back upwards again, the dragon turned lazily in front of them, as villagers and Rallorans alike cheered hoarsely, before it raced at the Berellians to their left, sending them running in all directions. One more time and it had scattered the company of Berellians in front of them as well. Kesbury saw, with mounting joy, the way ahead was clear. The dragon, and its riders, seemed to think the same, because it swooped down over them once more, protectively, then flew away back over Wells.

'Rallorans to the front! We don't stop until we hit the bridge!' Dunner roared.

The Berellians in front of them had not reformed their line, but Kesbury could see some of them were lurking to the side, ready to attack any stragglers. He was about to call for everyone to stay together when scores of men in blue surcoats appeared out of the buildings on this side of the river. Men with bows. Volleys of arrows struck the Berellians and the survivors ran for their lives.

The Ralloran archers gave a cheer and ran back into the town. Kesbury wondered why they did not wait. Looking over his shoulder, he could see why. It seemed like the entire Berellian army had appeared out of the countryside and was chasing them.

'Come on!' he urged them but the tired horses flagged as they began to ride through the town. Dunner's Rallorans were well in front of them, while the archers were already at the bridge. This was directly ahead, no more than a hundred yards. The Berellians, on the other hand, were half a mile behind. Kesbury was just beginning to relax when a figure in a rust-red robe stepped out of a side alley and blocked his path.

Kettering surveyed the pile of dumped goods with satisfaction. The carriages had been searched for hidden money and treasure with a criminal's eye, which of course many of his men had. All of these riches had been discarded — although he strongly suspected more than a few coins had found their way into men's pockets — and people loaded instead. Dozens of these carriages, all of them crammed with people and food, were now rolling slowly along the road north, escorted by his men. Behind him, Cessor was ablaze.

Some of the rich carriage owners had wanted to protest at the way their treasures were being treated — and particularly about having to carry servants and wounded soldiers on their leather seats.

But one look at Kettering's grim face had ensured any complaints dried up swiftly.

The Tenoch fleet had still not docked and, in fact, the ships they'd had at the jetties had loaded their surviving men back aboard and moved out into the harbour to avoid the fires they had started. It would be several turns of the hourglass before they began landing men again and it would be tomorrow before they could begin a pursuit. By then, thanks to the carriages, Kettering planned to have a big enough lead to stay ahead of them all the way to the north.

The only fly in the wine was, of course, the losses they had suffered. A score of archers, as well as a dozen of his own men were still back in the town, while another twenty or so were lying atop the carriages and might well die unless they found a priest or priestess soon. He had sent off the last magicked bird he had, asking for help. In the meantime, he had ordered the rich ladies to rip up silk dresses for bandages. None had dared question him.

He turned away from the piles of goods and climbed onto his horse, held in place by Leigh.

'Let's catch up to those carriages,' he told the slim ex-thief. 'I'll get those bastards to safety, even if they hate my guts!'

'If only we could have got the gold to safety as well,' Leigh sighed.

Kesbury stared in surprise at the single figure, who had walked out in the gap between the Rallorans and the villagers, and now stood, arms outstretched.

But he did not have the time to do more than take a look, for his horse, indeed every horse stopped, refusing to go near the figure.

'Bow down before me! Bow down if you want to live!' the figure cried, in a voice that was strangely familiar.

Kesbury did not bother trying to think who it might be. His course at the seminary might have been short but it had still been enough for him to instantly recognise a Fearpriest. He had not been afraid for many years — but he rediscovered the sensation now. Not so much for himself, but for the people.

'Off! Go around! I'll take care of him!' Kesbury roared, leaping to the ground.

From behind the figure, Rallorans turned, Dunner spurring his horse forwards to try and rescue the villagers. But the Fearpriest just raised his hand and the Ralloran horses stopped, as if they too had run into some sort of wall.

Kesbury raced forwards. His lessons had been clear on Fearpriests. Priests received their powers in exchange for prayer and good works, as long as the cause was just. Fearpriests received theirs in exchange for death and pain. He wanted to destroy this evil thing but, if that were not possible, then he had to distract it long enough to allow the others to escape. That this might cost his life did not slow him in the slightest.

Kesbury knew, vaguely, that there were ways of fighting a Fearpriest, but his lessons had not got that far. He just had to get close and trust Aroaril would protect him long enough to use his staff. As he ran forwards, he was aware the villagers were slipping away to either side, circling around the pair of them to where Rallorans waited to carry them to safety. He was also aware that the Berellian pursuit was getting closer but he put both things out of his mind. Instead he charged at the Fearpriest, wanting only to get close enough to smash his staff into that darkened cowl.

The Fearpriest let him get ten paces away, then held up a hand. Kesbury felt his legs go from beneath him and he was sent sprawling onto the ground.

'Weakling! Snivelling fool!' the Fearpriest taunted.

Kesbury dragged himself to his feet, using his staff. But it was whipped out of his hand, dragged away by an unseen force, although he used all his strength to try to hold on. The staff flew to the Fearpriest's hand, where he inspected it contemptuously.

'And you thought to defeat me with this? Did they teach you nothing?' he said disdainfully. 'But then again, you are Ralloran scum, which means your brain is not capable of absorbing wisdom.'

Something in the man's voice struck a note in Kesbury.

'Chanlon?' he asked, in wonder.

In response, the Fearpriest yanked back the cowl of his robe.

Kesbury gasped. For it was Chanlon, but not as he remembered. The ex-priest's face had new lines carved deep into it, transforming it into a visage of hatred.

'That's right! And now these people shall watch you die screaming!'

Instantly Kesbury fell to the ground, crying out in pain, despite himself.

Every wound he had taken in the Ralloran wars, every scar he wore with either pride or sorrow had suddenly opened up. Blood spurted, while the Berellian spear he had taken to the calf at the battle of Mount Shadar brought him down as effectively now as it had back then.

'You fool! You have allied yourself to the wrong God, and you picked the wrong man to insult and humiliate,' Chanlon sneered. 'I shall pay you back a thousand-fold for what you did to me!'

'You're good at talking.' Kesbury spat blood, as he prayed for the strength to get to his feet.

'I'm better at action,' Chanlon told him, striding over, a long dagger in his hand. 'I shall take your eyes first, then your manhood. But I shall leave the tongue, so you can scream.'

Kesbury tried to surge to his feet, to smash the man down, but an invisible hand held him down. And the knife was already swinging towards his left eye.

There were thousands of people now camped north of the passes, in relative safety although not in comfort. They had arrived in hope but now they waited in terror. And it was causing Quiller and Gratt all sorts of problems.

'They are here to help you!' the old priest tried to appeal to the people.

'But they're goblins! They'll kill us all and eat the children!' a woman cried.

'They're foul creatures of Zorva, abominations of nature!' another yelled.

'Stop that! They are our allies, and they are prepared to die to keep you safe!' Quiller thundered.

'I don't want any part of them!' the first woman declared defiantly. 'I won't stay here, it's not safe!'

Gratt pushed past a couple of other women to reach her. 'Would you prefer we gave you to the Berellians and your children to the Fearpriests? Open your eyes! This is the only safe place in the country. Cessor and Worick are in flames, no Norstaline remains alive south of the River Brack and you would ignore those who are here to help?'

The woman looked around for support but none

seemed willing to step forwards in the face of Gratt's anger.

'We are the ones who stole their land. We broke our promises and lied, telling everyone that these Derthals were going to kill a dragon, inviting everyone to kill them and drive them out, just so we could dig up the gold and silver they had!' Quiller bellowed, using his years of training in the pulpit to reach them. 'And yet the Derthals are still here to help you! They are standing beside you now, and you are quite safe, are you not? Has anyone had their child eaten yet?'

There was a nervous chuckle at this, but Quiller could see they were far from convinced. The open opposition might have finished, but there would be much muttering in the shelters. So be it. 'Go back to work. Get things ready for all the others, and let the Derthals do their job of protecting you.' Gratt added his voice to Quiller's and the crowd slowly dispersed.

'The people do not like it,' Gratt told Quiller quietly. 'There is much talk back in Sendric.'

'It will continue, until the Fearpriests are on the other side of those hills. Then they will learn quickly who is really on their side. Until then, we will do what we can to keep them apart,' Quiller sighed.

'And when the people learn the Derthals will be living here, among us, in the northern forest, as the price for their help?'

'One problem at a time,' Quiller said grimly.

The knife stopped before it penetrated the eye. Kesbury stared at Chanlon, wondering if the man was tormenting him, but the Fearpriest looked just as surprised. Muscles writhed in his arm as he tried to drive the knife home — but it would not move.

'Step away, Fearpriest!' a woman commanded.

Both Kesbury and Chanlon looked around to see Bishop Milly striding towards them.

Chanlon's face twisted into a grin.

'That's the last mistake you'll ever make, bitch!' he warned.

In response, Milly held up her hand, her mouth moving silently.

Kesbury wondered what prayer she was reciting — and hoped she had learned more about fighting Fearpriests than he had. He wanted to get up, to help her, but the pain and blood loss, coming after the exertions of the last few days, had left him weak as a kitten.

Chanlon turned towards her, knife held high, but found it seemed to be moving of its own volition, down towards his throat. Grunting with the effort, he tried to direct it back towards her, but it refused to obey him. Desperately he closed his eyes, muttering in a strange language, but the knife continued its inexorable progress towards his throat. Sweating now, Chanlon used his free hand to try and drag the knife hand away — but nothing seemed to stop it.

'Wait! Wait! This is all a mistake! They forced me to do this, forced me! Let me free and we can talk about it!' Chanlon cried desperately, as the sharpened tip grew ever closer to him.

'There's nothing I want to say to you, Fearpriest,' Milly snapped and closed her fist.

The knife plunged home and Chanlon, spurting blood from his mouth, toppled backwards.

'Wish you'd had time to teach me that,' Kesbury sighed.

Milly was instantly at his side, placing her hands on his head and his wounds closed once more.

'Let's go,' she told him.

Kesbury glanced over his shoulder, to where Berellian cavalry was galloping towards them.

'I won't make it. Leave me, take care of those villagers,' he gasped.

Milly's mouth tightened as she grabbed the front of his blood-stained robes.

'On your feet, sergeant! That is an order,' she barked at him. She held out her hand and his staff scraped across the cobbles and into her hand.

He gazed at her, shocked, then hauled himself to his feet and, with her help and the aid of the staff, began staggering towards the bridge.

'What are you doing here?' he grunted.

Milly snorted with laughter. 'Someone had to save you, after what you did for those people. The Fearpriest was unexpected, though. Luckily they sent that one and not a powerful one.'

'He was enough for me,' Kesbury grunted.

'Shut up and move. Once we're over the bridge, I'll tell you how to fight one,' Milly snapped, sweating a little under the weight of the large Ralloran.

They had staggered onto the bridge when the drumming of hooves on cobbles grew loud. Kesbury did not dare to look.

'Go! Save yourself,' he urged. 'I'll slow them down for you.'

'Don't be an idiot,' she told him shortly. 'I didn't go through all this just to leave you now!'

Then Ralloran archers rushed out to fill the bridge, led by Martil.

'Loose!' he roared.

Kesbury instinctively flinched but the arrows whistled past them. He did not glance over his shoulder but he heard the noise as the arrows turned the Berellian charge into chaos. He managed to get his feet moving across the bridge to safety, as cheers rang out from the watching Rallorans and villagers.

'Sorry we had to do that to you.' Martil held out his hand to help Kesbury. 'Using you as bait was risky but we needed to buy some time. Now we've stung their pride, they'll try and break through here, rather than sending their men around us. We never thought they would have a Fearpriest. Luckily Bishop Milly was with us.'

'Luck had nothing to do with it,' Milly told him. 'I was where I needed to be.'

8

Merren made sure she found Martil before she returned north — and while Karia was talking to Argurium. He had been dropping snide remarks about her orders since she had arrived. Apart from needing him, she worried what such an attitude would do to the Rallorans. Whatever some of her people thought of the warriors, she knew full well how much she needed them. If they caught Martil's mood and began to drift away ...

'We need to talk,' she stated. 'I sent you down here because you were causing me all sorts of trouble. Sendric has calmed down, while Barrett is keeping to himself, Nerrin can handle the retreat, so it should be simple to bring you back. I want you back at the palace with me, I would like the benefit of your advice. But only if I can be sure which Martil I am getting — and that you will be helping me, not questioning my orders. We cannot fight among ourselves when we are facing the Fearpriests. Do you understand?'

Martil smiled bitterly. 'Perfectly. You want to use me while you can, then you'll discard me for Sendric, like a dirty rag ...'

Merren rolled her eyes. 'Not everything is about you! I told you I have put aside all questions of marriage until the people are safe. What more do you want?'

Martil looked at her. Could she really not see what he was thinking and feeling? 'What more do I want? For us to be together!'

'So this is what your arguing is all about?' she demanded. 'If I said I would marry you then you would be happy and agree with everything I say?'

'Well, no. Your plan is wrong. It goes against everything we discussed. We are doing exactly what our enemies want, sacrificing what few soldiers we have to protect meaningless farms and villages ...'

'They are not meaningless to the people who live there! And we must do everything we can to save lives. That is why we have an army, to protect the weak and helpless. This is not the Ralloran Wars —'

'Exactly! Because my men are dying to save people who hate us and support our enemies!'

Merren looked him in the eye. 'That is the last time you shall interrupt me,' she warned.

Martil feigned surprise. 'So your majesty doesn't want to hear advice that she doesn't like from servants?'

She glared at him, and held on to her temper only with the greatest of difficulty. Then Louise's words came back to her.

'What's going on?' she asked gently.

Instantly he was wrong-footed. 'What do you mean?' he asked, defensively.

'This is not just about us, or my plan to save people. There's something else bothering you. I haven't seen you like this since you were tormented by your dreams, before Pilleth. I thought you were past that now. Is it the Dragon Sword again? I know you had the idea of not using it to kill but surely it cannot object to being used to save women and children? So tell me what is wrong. And I want an honest answer. You seem to think we should be together — prove it. Trust me, talk to me.'

Martil, who had been about to hotly deny anything was wrong, shut his mouth. The anger and fear swirling around inside him made it easier to fight than think. But he knew she was right.

'It's not just one thing but many,' he said softly. 'That fight with Cezar did something to me. Every time I am about to fight, I cannot stop thinking about Karia, about you and the baby. I so nearly let you all down against that Berellian, I cannot risk that again. And then Havell and Argurium keep reminding me that I am supposed to be saving the magic, and am too important to risk doing anything. Then I have to face the Berellians again, have to send Rallorans to their deaths when I swore I would never do so again … you told me that you felt as though everyone wants something from you as Queen. Well, that's how I feel now. Karia wants me to be a dad, Havell wants me to stay away from fighting, you want me to lead the men — I am stretched in every direction! And when I fight, I cannot empty my mind. There is too much to think about.'

Merren stared at him. From the stricken expression on his face, she could see how much admitting that had cost him. She could also understand how he felt, for it was strangely close to what she was going through. She felt like holding him but knew she could not.

'Secure the defence here and then I shall call for you, give you a day with Karia back at the capital,' she offered.

Martil sighed, then nodded. 'We should be able to keep them at bay for a few days. The way we drew them in here, using Kesbury and those refugees as bait, has their blood up and they will try and crash through here, rather than do the sensible thing and cast around for a ford to outflank us. We can give people time to get away by being here — so you need to use it, clear the countryside behind us.'

'What's going on? When can you come back?' Karia demanded, walking over.

'Soon,' Martil promised.

'Great! Father Nott's been looking after me, he says he doesn't know when he might get another chance!'

Merren and Martil exchanged a look at that. It did not sound good to either of them.

Word seemed to have spread down the roads of Norstalos almost by magic. A ravening horde of goblins was waiting for them in the north. Every man, woman and child north of the passes had been massacred — and the same fate waited any who went there.

Archbishop Nott spoke to as many people as he could, reassuring them that nobody was dead and, in fact, the Derthals were there to help them and even fight for them. But it was hard work. For centuries, the Norstalines had been raised on tales of evil goblins; strange, twisted creatures that would steal children who played in the forest and who would attack in the night, their cruel spears sparing no woman or baby. The idea that these monsters of legend, the stuff of a hundred sagas, would actually turn out to be friendly was too much for many people to grasp.

He was having some success but the pace of the refugees slowed dramatically wherever the rumour went. In some places, Nott felt it was only the sight of smoke in the sky behind them that persuaded the people that the possible danger of goblins ahead of them was better than the definite threat of Tenochs or Berellians.

And the word from Quiller was little better. Sendric, Gerrin and Berry were full of refugees who had refused to stay in the shelters and had instead rushed to get behind the towns built specially to protect against goblin attack. That would not be so bad, except the towns were not ready for such an influx of people and had sent most of their food to the massive camp being built outside the passes. It was another problem that had to be sent to the Queen. And one she would have to deal with later as well. Already upset at being driven out of their homes, forced to trek hundreds of miles to safety, the people were muttering about Merren's judgment.

More and more, people were saying they would have been better off had Gello stayed in power.

Merren came fully awake with a start. Sleep had been proving difficult to come by. There were problems in every direction — and they only seemed to multiply. For the past three days, she had been flying around the country with Argurium. The emotional burden of speaking to so many suffering people was taking its toll, not to mention the agony of seeing her people killed every day. Each time the dragon flew out, Merren knew she would see her countrymen killed or, worse, captured. And even the ones who escaped, who were still ahead of the invaders, were in a mess. Merren had lost count of the number of sobbing widows and orphans she had comforted, the number of hurt, angry, tired and confused Norstalines she had tried to talk to and encourage. But while she tried to give these people hope, encouragement and new spirit, to push them further up the road to safety, she seemed to take on a little of their despair each time.

She felt she was losing them. Even though none said as much to her face, she was afraid they were blaming her for bringing this death and misery upon them.

And there was little good news to cheer her.

The Rallorans had held the Berellians at bay in Wells for two days then, when Argurium spotted columns of Berellians heading for the fords to the east and west of the town, had pulled out at night. Wells south of the river had been reduced to a ruin, but the Rallorans had got away and, better yet, Kesbury's villagers had managed to put more than eighty miles between them and the Berellian advance. In the west the news was not so good. While Kettering had managed to stay ahead of the Tenoch pursuit, reaching the bridges over the River Worick safely, Rocus and Cropper would take no further part in this campaign. Cropper had died, and Rocus had only just survived, losing a leg and a hand. Worse still, Hutter warned he was not putting enough space between himself and the Tenochs. Once the people had to get out and walk, they would be at danger of being caught. To the north, the Derthals were still being shunned by the people. High Chief Sacrax was also asking for the Queen to come up for talks, for there was unrest back in the mountains. Barrett's trick of bringing in game for the Derthals to eat had been a great help to the tribes loyal to Sacrax but it had had an unexpected side effect. Those few tribes that had refused to come and aid the Norstalines were finding it hard to hunt food. Father Alban reported they were raiding the Derthal camp, searching for food. At the moment this was only a nuisance but Sacrax — and Alban —

feared it had the potential to get much worse. And it could result in several tribes returning north to protect their families — and weakening the Derthal army.

Meanwhile, thousands of refugees were milling around the capital, pretending to be resting and finding food for the trip north but, in reality, reluctant to go anywhere near the north.

Lurid tales of goblins wearing coats of human skin, carrying standards of human skulls and drinking the blood of children were passed up and down the roads and columns of refugees, while sensible stories of Derthals patrolling the passes and keeping to themselves were ignored as 'obvious lies'.

Also, in the east, Captain Kay had reported there was a growing number of people who refused to march any further. Some of these included those who had fled eastern villages but, after a few days of travel — and stories of goblin hordes waiting for them — decided they had a better chance of survival by throwing themselves on the mercy of Gello. This trend was increasing as there were no burning villages to accompany Gello's advance through the east. Elsewhere in the country, those palls of smoke drove people on. But without them, many in the east were staying put. Apparently there were hundreds of people in Wollin who had refused to move and Kay had been forced to leave them, or be caught by Gello's cavalry. Telling the people that they might be safe, for a while, under Gello — but would almost certainly be killed when the Tenochs and Berellians had completed their conquest of the country was not an argument that was having much success.

And now this, the news that had snapped her out of her doze.

'Are we sure?' Merren exclaimed in horror.

Nott nodded sadly. 'It is now close enough to see, out on the horizon. The Berellians have been working on the natural magic, which meant that myself, Milly and the others were unable to detect it until now.'

'And Barrett has been locked up with his nubile apprentice, wasting time with her while claiming to be working on some project to create a Magicians' Guild,' Merren said bitterly.

They all contemplated what Archbishop Nott had told them. A massive storm was heading for Norstalos. Enough to turn every road in the north of the country to mud and end their desperate bid to save the people. And this storm would not touch the southern half of the country, meaning the invaders' progress would not be slowed. It would be a disaster.

'Can we stop it?' Martil asked. He had returned overnight, to Karia's delight.

Nott shook his head slowly. 'I cannot. Perhaps Barrett might be able to …'

'Then someone get him! Now!' Merren thundered.

Barrett strode into the palace with his head held high. The messenger had not said why he was needed, just that his presence was required immediately. He had barely seen Tiera since his foolish confession. They'd both been excessively polite to each other when they had met, and she'd still been helping him organise the wizards. Except now her help was restricted to making sure the assembled mages had enough to eat and drink. Things were progressing well and he should have been delighted. Instead, he felt empty inside. Why was he seemingly cursed to fall in love with the wrong woman, and then have his heart ripped out?

He bowed to the Queen with a stiff dignity, making sure he ignored Martil completely, although he was able to smile at a waving Karia. But when Merren ordered everyone onto the roof, then pointed out the black clouds on the horizon, he felt his jaw drop open.

'Your majesty, I did not sense any of this! If I had …'

'Seems you were too busy with your new apprentice to fulfil your duties,' Merren said grimly.

Barrett almost choked.

'It is not true, I have not laid a hand on Tiera!' he protested, although the closeness of the accusation hit home, and he was horribly aware his usually sallow cheeks were flushed red.

'I'm not interested in excuses,' Merren snapped. 'Can you stop this?'

Frantically, Barrett closed his eyes, reaching out into the magic. He could barely believe he had not sensed this before. He knew he had been unable to think about much besides Tiera — it had been a huge effort to focus on the Guild work he was doing — but still …

He almost quailed when he felt how strong the storm was. He had dispersed only one attempted storm before, the work of Gello's crazed mage Tellite, and that had cost him dearly enough. He opened his eyes and did not know what to say.

'Well?' Merren demanded.

'I will need every wizard in the country to stop this,' he said shakily. 'And, even then …'

'Well, what are you waiting for? Go!' Merren cried.

'I shall send word when we are ready to try,' he promised, then ran.

'He has never let us down before,' Sendric said into the silence.

'He has never faced something like this,' Nott said solemnly. 'We must have an alternative, if he is not successful.'

'And what might that be?' Merren asked acidly. 'Get the dragon to fly thousands of people to safety? There is no alternative.' She ran her fingers through her hair. 'He has to break up that storm! We have no choice. It will all come down to this!'

'There is one other option. We could bring the army together and try and stop the invaders,' Nott said mildly.

'All that would do is get thousands of men killed for nothing — there are too many of them!' Martil protested.

'Not if the Derthals joined us,' Nott stated.

Everyone stared at him.

'We would still be outnumbered, but we would have a chance,' he offered.

'I think there is more chance of Barrett being able to break up this storm,' Martil snorted. 'Haven't you been listening to the reports? The people have hardly made the Derthals welcome. I'm surprised Sacrax and his chiefs haven't walked away before now.'

'And look at what it took to get them to come down here and help us. What would we have to sign away to get them to fight for us? Would we end up living in the mountains, scratching a living in caves?' Sendric jeered.

'If we have to!' Nott suddenly blazed, all traces of the quiet grandfather gone.

Martil felt Karia hide behind him — and he was tempted to follow her.

'Have you forgotten what we are fighting? Those are Fearpriests out there, getting ever closer! There is no price that should not be paid to defeat them. We cannot allow them to gain power here, to start raising their bloodstained pyramids to their foul God,' Nott snarled. 'We must be prepared to do anything, give up everything if we have to! Lives are not important if it means stopping their evil.'

'But what would the Derthals want?' Merren protested.

'You do not need to bribe them. Use the Dragon Sword to inspire them,' Nott pointed at Martil.

'But the Dragon Sword only works on men! It was given to us by the dragons to repay the treachery of goblins. As if it would have any effect on them!' Sendric scoffed.

'You are wrong,' Martil interrupted. 'The dragons gave it to Norstalos for another reason.'

'So, would it work on the Derthals?' Merren asked.

Martil looked around. Everyone was hanging on his words.

'I think I need to talk to the dragon,' he said slowly.

It did not take Barrett long to assemble the wizards together. Most were either reading in his library or eating in his kitchen. But nothing like this had been attempted before. And none of them were really sure how it could work. After a great deal of arguing, Barrett decided to stop asking and begin telling them what would happen.

'We must all work together. No single mage can hope to disperse it. But together we have a chance. The Berellian wizard will try and stop us but he is one and we are many,' Barrett declared.

He knew that he was making the impossible sound easy. But he was not about to fail now. He had asked Tiera to help with the preparations, making sure there was plenty of food and water, including skins of honeyed water to keep the mages' energy up.

She had fulfilled the task with her customary efficiency but he could sense there was a barrier between them. Although, when she walked over to him, he could not stop his heart beating a little faster.

'I have something important to ask,' Tiera said nervously.

'What is it?' Barrett smiled, trying not to let his imagination run ahead of him, and mostly failing.

'I would like to help.'

Barrett swallowed. 'I appreciate your bravery in offering that, and why you do so. But every man or woman here has reached at least the fifth circle. And they know the risks. What we are trying to do may cost our lives. I would not want to see you hurt. I confess you would also be a distraction. I would worry about you, rather than concentrating on what I have to do to this storm.'

Tiera reddened a little but she met his gaze squarely.

'Then I shall help as best I can,' she stated.

They stared at each other for a long moment, as Barrett sought for a way to reach her. Then a thump at the door told them the Queen had arrived.

'I'll show her in,' Tiera announced hurriedly.

Barrett sighed, then went back to his preparations. A space had been cleared in the ballroom, and the wizards were arranged in a triangle in order of power, with the weakest at the base and Barrett at the tip, facing the huge ceiling to floor windows, that looked out to the northeast, from where the storm was approaching. This in itself had taken a full turn of the hourglass in discussion to achieve, for wizards did not like to be organised like this. Barrett had had to use every bit of his authority, as well as an appeal to Norstaline honour, to get them to agree.

Even then, there was a fair bit of grumbling going on at the back of the room.

'Is everything ready?' Merren asked as soon as she stepped into the ballroom, Jaret and Wilsen by her side. It had been a nervous ride from the palace. The tip of the storm was already over the capital, the massed dark clouds filling the eastern sky and turning day almost into night. Wind gusts were whipping through the streets, while the skies rumbled with thunder. Not a drop of rain had fallen yet, although the air felt heavy and moist. It was as if the storm, as well as Norstalos, was holding its breath, waiting.

'We are ready, your majesty.' Barrett bowed his head.

'Then introduce me to these brave Norstalines, who are preparing to save us all and earn a nation's undying gratitude,' Merren announced.

Barrett had to admit she was good at this. Not only did she tell them how important this was, and how the entire country was counting on them, she shook hands with them all, men and women, asked where they were from and about their families. By the time she had finished, not only were all the frowns and grumbles gone, all seemed ready, even eager to begin, though they knew the risks.

'Your majesty, if you will sit over there.' Barrett gestured to a tangle of seats.

'I don't see Karia here,' Merren said mildly, although there was steel beneath the words.

'Well, she is a bit young, your majesty.' Barrett smiled nervously. The truth, half of these wizards would have walked out in anger had Karia been here, for Barrett would have been forced to put her in the middle of the formation, although all were old enough to be her father or mother and many old enough to be her grandparent. Besides, he would have had to ask Martil for permission — and he had no intention of speaking to the man again, if he could help it.

'And Tiera is helping you?'

'Indeed, your majesty.' Barrett bowed. 'She has been an enormous help to us all.'

Merren regarded them both carefully.

'I hope she continues to be. But let us begin. That storm grows ever closer.' Merren sat down pointedly, looking out at the ominous sky.

Barrett nodded, then signalled to Tiera, who ran from window to window, latching them open, letting the wind blow inside, setting the wizards' robes fluttering about them.

Barrett, meanwhile, took his place at the head of the triangle of wizards.

'Now!' he called.

He was vaguely aware that many of them were now chanting and waving staffs and hands around but he let them get away with this showmanship. After all, they were performing in front of the Queen.

Merren watched them begin with ill-disguised impatience. She did not know whether to be frustrated with Barrett or angry with herself. This should never have happened. Barrett should have been able to ensure the weather stayed dry, at least until the people were safe. Then he could bring in the storms to slow their enemies. It had been an integral part of the plan: use the weather against Gello and his backers. Only the Berellians had turned the tables and they stood at the brink of disaster. She had left Barrett alone, thinking he deserved a little room. She should have dragged Barrett away from this girl, as well as this guild foolishness, no matter his feelings —

and demanded he fulfil his duty as Queen's Magician. The country had to come first; personal feelings were irrelevant. Well, she had learned her lesson. She would not make that mistake again.

Yes, Archbishop Nott had suggested an alternative if this failed but, after living through Pilleth, she dreaded to think what such a battle would be like. Already hundreds of civilians and soldiers, from the farming families she had seen down south to Cropper and Rocus, had been either killed or crippled.

Part of her wanted to shut the door, lie down and not think about columns of refugees, Fearpriests and invading armies, take a break from the pressure that never seemed to let up. Every day brought more challenges, more decisions that had to be made, more lives that had to be weighed in the balance, more fear that the people blamed her for everything. Sometimes she found herself staring at an hourglass. They were all over the palace, scores of them. There were servants whose only duty was to turn the hourglasses. At these times she would watch the way the sands drained through the glass. Being Queen was like trying to stop that sand. Each grain was a life that was slipping away from her because of the decisions she did or did not make. Sometimes she felt she could get lost in the movement of the sands through the hourglass. Sometimes she felt like picking up the glass and shattering it, breaking the spell that was over her. For her life was like the hourglass. No sooner had she seemingly completed her task than everything was tipped over and she had to begin again. The demands never ended.

But she always stopped herself from going down that path. This was what she had been trained to do. And she knew there was no-one else who could do it. Either she guided her people to safety or they would die. There was no other option. So the part of her that wanted to think about Karia, about Martil, about their child — she shut that away. She had to.

Now, if Barrett would just protect them from this storm, she could go back to worrying about everything else. She looked at him, willing him to succeed.

Barrett could feel the massive storm now, could see it, hear it and smell it. It was almost ready to open its clouds and soak Norstalos in a wall of water. There was no need for words, they all knew what they had to do, so he signalled to the others then launched himself at the storm, seeking to wreck its dark menace.

For a long time, it seemed as if nothing was happening.

Merren watched the group of mages but, apart from increased breathing, and sweating, there was no clue they were doing anything. A glance out the window told her the storm was still approaching. She looked over to where Tiera watched, biting her lip worriedly.

'Can you see what is happening?' she asked sharply.

Tiera nodded. 'Yes, your majesty. The storm is resisting them.'

Merren stared at the assembly but could tell nothing.

Barrett felt as though he was trying to lift an impossible weight. No matter what he tried, it was too much for his strength. But he kept trying, kept battering the clouds, trying to break them apart. He could feel the sweat dripping off his face, while the breath sawed harshly in his throat. Then it seemed to shift.

'Keep going! It's working!' he tried to croak.

Merren sat up a little, peering out the windows. The dark mass on the horizon still loomed but the advance of the clouds across the sky seemed to have stopped.

Tiera waved at the Queen's guards.

'Help me! Bring them honeyed water!' she urged, pointing towards where a score of waterskins had been placed.

Jaret and Wilsen glanced over towards Merren, who nodded.

The pair of them joined Tiera in rushing around from mage to mage, offering them a few mouthfuls of the honeyed water, to help keep their strength up.

Barrett felt the excitement course through his veins as the closest clouds began to split apart, the massive thunderheads breaking up as they came over the capital.

'Keep going!' he gasped.

He could feel another presence there as well, the one who had created the storm. It was fighting back, trying to keep the storm together — but he could sense its panic.

He gathered himself for one final, massive effort. It would not fail. He would push on until the storm was no more and the magic calm again. Then he felt the support of the others begin to waver.

Merren could not see what was going on but she could tell, from the smile on Barrett's face, as well as the excitement of Tiera, that something was happening.

Then the wizards at the back of the triangle began to topple over.

Most fell flat upon their faces, a few just dropped to their knees, panting and gasping for breath — a chain reaction that rippled through until Barrett was the only one left standing — and one of only a handful still conscious.

'I — will — not — give — up —' he gasped, his eyes still tightly shut.

Above him, blue sky seemed to fight against the clouds — and the blue sky was winning, pushing the black mass backwards.

But Barrett was panting for breath now and dripping with sweat, swaying slightly on his feet. Merren was reminded of the time back at the ranger barracks, when she had driven him beyond his limits in order to escape. She could not use that trick again but perhaps Tiera might ...

'Go! Help him! Support him!' Merren grabbed Tiera's arm and pushed her towards the reeling wizard. 'Keep him going. Do whatever you have to.'

'What do you mean?' Tiera cried.

Merren rolled her eyes. 'Do I have to spell it out? Tell him you love him, that he's the greatest man in the world — anything to get him to stop that storm!'

'But ... I can't say those things!'

'Thousands of lives depend on it! Do it!' Merren ordered, and such was her strength that the servant in Tiera took over and she obeyed.

She stumbled towards Barrett, who was holding himself upright thanks to his staff. The agony he was going through was only too clear on his face. Her mind was awhirl. She had never planned to get involved with another man again, let alone the Queen's Magician. But she had found herself falling for Barrett. His kindness, his gentle nature and his obvious attraction to her was slowly wiping out the hideous memories she had of Prent. She could see a future with him, a future so dazzling with possibilities it seemed almost unreal. She was not ready for it yet. It was as frightening as it was exciting. But one thing was certain. That future was dying with Barrett. She could see what it was costing him — and that, alone, there was no way he could break that storm. Any other mage would have given up long before. Only Barrett's determination was keeping him on his feet. If he did not stop soon, the magic would consume him.

The Queen had told her to persuade Barrett to keep going, to not give up. The Tiera that had been raised as a serving girl wanted to do the Queen's bidding. She was the country's ruler and Tiera was gutter scum. Everything Tiera had been taught screamed she should do what the Queen asked. After what Barrett had declared to her, her head knew a few words would see him drive himself past his limits. That was the kind of man he was. He would win, or he would die.

But her heart stopped her. How could she have a new life when it came at the expense of a man who she had betrayed to death?

In an instant she had made her decision. She wanted Barrett alive. Anything else would mean Prent had won. And she could not have that.

'Don't kill yourself. You can't do it alone. Come back to me,' she whispered into Barrett's ear.

'I — can't — give — up,' Barrett panted.

'You've done all you can. Any more and you'll kill yourself!' she pleaded.

'Have — to.'

'Why?'

'It's — who — I — am —'

She glanced back at the Queen, who urged her on to greater effort. *If only she knew what I am going to do*, Tiera thought, then leaned back towards Barrett.

'You have to stop. For me. For I love you and don't want to be without you,' she told him, kissing him gently on the cheek.

Barrett's eyes snapped open and he stared at her.

'I mean it,' she told him. 'I love you and want to be with you.'

For a moment more he considered fighting on, using up his life — then the impact of her words took effect. He fell into her arms and, staggering, she eased him to the floor. He was gasping for air and she cradled his head, trickling a little honeyed water from the waterskin she had slung over her shoulder into his mouth.

'I — failed —' He swallowed heavily and stared up at her, his eyes haunted and his cheeks hollowed.

'Not to me, you didn't,' she told him and was rewarded with the ghost of a smile.

'Well? What happened? Were you successful?' Merren demanded. The closest clouds had been pushed back but the horizon was still as dark as night.

Barrett fought for breath, as well as for the words to tell his Queen he had failed her — but Tiera answered for him.

'The rain is delayed but not stopped. It could not be done, your majesty.'

'What?' Merren stormed across and stared down at Barrett. 'Why did you stop?'

'I am sorry …' Barrett began, but Tiera hushed him.

'Because the storm was too powerful. And because I told him to. Because he's better alive than dead.' She stared up at Merren defiantly, Barrett's head pillowed on her lap.

Merren was almost speechless. Did she not understand what this meant? The storm would strike home, the roads would be turned to mud and the Berellians and Tenochs would catch up with the refugees. They would be forced to fight a desperate battle, which they were likely to lose and, if they did, the Fearpriests would plunge the country, the continent, into blood and fear and sacrifice!

'Do you realise you may have doomed us all to death, and the world to an eternity of darkness under the rule of the Fearpriests?' she snarled.

'No. I just know that I saved a good man's life and I do not regret it,' Tiera told her, chin held high.

Merren was about to demand that Barrett and the wizards try again, immediately, but the sight of so many unconscious wizards lying on the floor told her that was not going to work.

She turned back to Tiera. She knew the girl probably thought her some monster, prepared to sacrifice anything for victory and she was torn between the desire to explain to her how hard it was to bear the responsibility of a country on your shoulders and the desire to call for Wilsen and Jaret, to drag the girl away so she could face the penalty for disobeying her Queen.

Then she saw the way Tiera was brushing the sweat-matted hair away from Barrett's face, and how he was gazing up at her — and she sighed. Barrett had driven himself to the edge, the other wizards had given everything they had. The limp bodies sprawled across the floor told that tale.

There was nothing more she could do here. Signalling to Jaret and Wilsen, she strode out of the ballroom.

She needed to speak to Nott — and Martil.

Karia absolutely loved Argurium. At first she had thought the dragon was like some sort of giant, magical pet, similar to the animals she used to befriend on the farm and those she summoned through the magic to help her.

But Argurium was more than that. She would enfold the girl in her wing, let Karia lie upon her broad back and answer endless questions. In some ways, it was almost like having a mother figure, albeit one with a set of wings, fangs and a body the size of three houses.

The dragon seemed happy to talk to her, which was also fine with Martil, as it gave him at least some sort of break from her questions — although Karia liked to tell him all about the conversations she had had with a dragon, even if he'd overheard them earlier that day.

This time, he wanted to speak to Argurium, so managed to persuade Havell to read Karia a saga. With a sense of malicious satisfaction, he had chosen one about dancing trees and singing bunny rabbits having adventures on Dragonara Isle. It was one of her favourites, although it set his teeth on edge.

'Tell me about the Dragon Sword,' he said to the dragon, when Karia started supplying the voices of the adventurous fluffy bunnies to supplement Havell's reading.

Argurium smiled. 'There is much to tell. Is there something you need to know?'

Martil rubbed the hilt of the sword, feeling the dragon shape. Where to start?

'I was told its power would inspire good men to rally around, to follow the wielder. Is that true? Is everything that the Norstalines boast about true? Would it really have killed me? Was it responsible for my nightmares about Bellic? Why did it let me draw it, if it only wants good men? Why wouldn't it work for me for so long? Would it work on Derthals?'

'Perhaps you should sit down and get comfortable,' Argurium invited.

Martil almost flung himself down onto the ground.

'Let me go back to the beginning and then you can ask questions along the way,' Argurium offered. 'It sounds strange but it took centuries for we dragons to comprehend that we must die and be reborn, as with all things. For time is relative to a dragon. To us, a century of your time is like a day. Our lives are not defined by the seasons but by a much greater cycle. But while birth is a natural thing for living creatures, for dragons it is something strange, for we do not breed. Our numbers do not increase or decrease. So how then could we secure our rebirth, and the continued life of the magic? And it must be done according to the laws of nature.'

'Not exactly a perfect design. I'd say Aroaril was having an off day when he created you.' Martil grinned.

Argurium stared at him. 'That is a whole new question. After all, we were given the ability to create this process. So are we apart from the power of the Gods? Beyond their command, even? After all, natural magic and the magic that priests of Aroaril or Zorva can command is different. Who came first? Were we created by the Gods or did life spring into being from the magic and then the Gods were created because humans required a spiritual manifestation of the good and evil that lurks within them ...'

'Wait! Enough!' Martil cried. 'Perhaps we should leave that discussion for another day. Can we get back to the Dragon Sword?'

Argurium inclined her head. 'Of course. But it is fascinating, is it not, to think about such things? We have pondered this debate for a millennia and are still no closer to the truth.'

'Well, I don't have millennia, so if we could just return to the Dragon Sword …'

'So. We created the Dragon Egg. All of us, making it into the female essence of dragons. But an egg by itself is nothing — it requires fertilisation to secure rebirth. Also, the Dragon Egg, by its very nature, could not be like a bird's egg, able to be cracked or damaged easily. We had to create a way to complete the cycle, act as the male to the female half of the egg. The Dragon Sword. It is the only object that can penetrate the Dragon Egg and, by that thrust inside, complete the process of fertilisation, leading to the rebirth.'

Martil found himself squirming a little at this description.

'Then the Sword …'

'Is the male essence of dragons and the missing seed to the female egg.' Argurium nodded. 'Thus we created the means for the dragons to be reborn, in accordance with the laws of nature.'

Martil regarded the Sword at his side rather doubtfully given it was, it seemed, a male dragon's private parts. How many times had he handled it?

'You should not think of it in that way,' Argurium told him. 'But surely, you are aware of the process?'

'Yes, I'm aware of it!' Martil snapped, images of Merren swimming in his mind.

'Well then. Now you have accepted why it was created you can see the problem of who was to finish the process. The men that served the dragons, the Elfarans, were the obvious choice — except they had already lived far beyond the normal span of men. When the dragons died, they would follow. No, the Sword had to be given to normal men. It could not be kept on Dragonara Isle, for it was not safe to have them both close together. If the rebirth happened too soon, who knew what effect that would have on the world? So we had to send it away, find a safe home until it was needed. But it was a piece of magic stronger than anything ever seen before. It had to be, for it had to operate by magic after the last dragon had died, and the magic had ended. What if a man used its power for evil? And it had to be a man, for it was the male essence of dragons. Its magic would never, could never respond to a female. So we used magical safeguards. The Sword would not allow itself to be drawn by someone who wanted to use it for their own glory, their own power. And those who were allowed to draw the Sword were warned to always use it for good and noble purposes. Any selfish acts, acts of anger and hatred, acts of evil — then the Sword's power would begin to drain the life from that wielder. It would offer warnings, in the form of dreams; it would give the wielder the chance to redeem himself but, if he failed to heed those, it would kill him. Because it is such a powerful source of male magic, it attracts other men. Its wielder can inspire other men, make them rally to him, especially if they are similar to the wielder. The hope was that the Sword's wielder, being a good man, would bring together other good men, to help keep the Sword safe. We could not have it used to fashion an empire of bones.'

'So why did it let me draw it? I have blood on my hands!' Martil interrupted.

'But you never wanted to use it to make a name for yourself. You did not draw it while imagining yourself as a king, an emperor, a ruler of armies and mobs. And, at your heart, you are a good man. A man scarred by life but a man capable of great kindness. The Sword saw all that. Then you began to use it in anger. You killed men who did not need to be killed — and did not deserve to be killed by the power of this Sword.'

'How did you know that?' Martil demanded.

Argurium indicated the Sword with a graceful stretch of her neck. 'I am a dragon. I helped create the Sword. I can tell its history, how it was used, every wielder through its long life.'

Martil looked at the Sword. The eyes on the hilt seemed to twinkle at him and he felt an irrational urge to apologise to it.

'But your true nature began to assert itself. Your desire to protect the Rallorans, to protect the Norstalines who served you at Sendric helped bring it to life and brought the Rallorans onto your side. You were almost ready to be its true wielder. Then came the battle of Sendric and you lost control again, killing unarmed men in anger and hatred. The Sword became afraid for you, and began to help you, forcing you to confront your past through your dreams.'

'I'm so grateful,' Martil told it sourly. The memory of those days, when he had been unable to sleep for haunting nightmares, was still strong.

'Thanks to Karia and Merren, you were able to break free of your past, escape your memories and, when you tried to sacrifice yourself to save others — the most noble of purposes — you became its wielder and began to win over men like yourself. Good men. Men who wanted redemption, who knew they should be doing the right thing, even if it meant their life. And so you won Pilleth.'

Martil looked at the Sword. 'So without Karia and Merren, the Sword would have taken my life?'

'Yes, it would. And the country would already

be lost,' Argurium agreed. 'But things happen for a reason. There is no such thing as an accident.'

Martil was about to deny that, when he thought back to the extraordinary chain of events that had brought him here. 'All right. That might explain what happened to me. But what about King Riel and all this business with the goblins, or Derthals? How come you gave it to him, only to have him turn around and begin a war with the Derthals?'

Argurium's head lowered.

'When we chose Riel, we thought we had chosen wisely. He wanted to unite his country, to protect it against its enemies. A noble purpose. And Norstalos was the biggest country of the two continents closest to Dragonara Isle. If it could be united, it would be safe, at peace. The perfect place for the Sword. Its kings would never be in danger, never really need to use the Sword — thus its true nature would not need to be revealed. It was given in secret, and meant to be kept a secret. We did not want it to become the symbol of a country or the subject of sagas. It was to be hidden but, when we needed to fulfil the Dragon Sword's true purpose, the kings of Norstalos would be ready. Riel began well. He tried to use the Sword to unite the country, in secret. But many of his nobles were not good men — and it did not work. Then gold and silver were discovered in the north of the country. So he turned to greed to unite the country. All knew of the rich farmland to the north, the vast forest. But few were prepared to risk their lives by farming or logging, for this land was inhabited by strange-looking people. They looked so different, spoke such a completely different language, that people swore they could not be men — they must be monsters. Goblins. Creatures of saga and legend. To tempt people north, he made up a story about

Norstalos being blessed by the dragons. About how the goblins, as he called them, had tried to kill a dragon. How he had rescued a dragon and the dragons had rewarded him by giving him a magic Sword. How it was the duty of every Norstaline to punish these evil creatures and all who did so would receive their own farm. Once the goblins had been driven away, he could then open mines in relative safety and use the gold from there to purchase the loyalty of his rebellious nobles. Those who swore fealty to him, who disbanded their armies and served him, were rewarded with grants of land and gold. Those who did not found themselves under siege from a king who could suddenly afford a huge army. So he won over the country — at a cost.

'The Sword tried to reform him, giving him warning after warning. It worked, after a fashion. While he did not stop the persecution of the Derthals, he convinced his sons and his relatives that only good men could use the Sword. He put the fear of the Sword into them, so they took it up as a burden and a duty to the country, instead of wanting to use it to create their own glorious legend.

'It was too late for him, it claimed his life. But while the secret was out, at least the true purpose of the Sword was hidden. And it ensured every Norstaline king after Riel did not use the Sword to turn themselves into a bloody tyrant. The few selfish ones who did dream of conquest were refused — and their refusal only secured its legend. Then Duke Gello tried to draw it, lusting to rule the world. And every other noble in the country tried to take it up, thinking of the dynasty they would forge, the legend they would create. So it stayed in its sheath, until you unwittingly drew it in Tetril, not thinking of what you could do with it.'

Martil sat there on the grass, trying to take all that in. One thing struck him.

'Back in the capital, Karia was able to use the magic from it, to help us open a magic gateway. But she's female. How did it work for her?'

Argurium nodded. 'But she was only able to use it through you. If you had not been holding it, it would not have worked.'

Martil scratched his chin. There only one more question he had.

'So would it work on Derthals?'

Argurium looked grave. 'That depends on what you want them for. You were correct in thinking the Sword would refuse to summon Norstalines across the land to form a massive mob that was doomed to defeat and slaughter. It is the same with the Derthals. If you want to sacrifice them to save Norstalines, then it will not. But if you truly believe the two races can unite to defeat the evil that is spreading across your land, then it will help you.'

Martil gave a bark of ironic laughter. 'So I just have to work out how to defeat thousands of Berellians and Tenochs?'

'Correct,' Argurium agreed.

'What's going on? Are you telling stories without me?' Karia raced over, followed by a slightly harried-looking Havell.

'Would I do that?' Martil asked with a wink, then laughed as she hurled herself upon him.

'I can beat you, you know!' she told him, as she contorted her face into a fierce expression and tried to wrestle him.

Martil let her think she was winning, before lifting her into the air.

'Are we going to be flying again today?' she asked from above his head.

'No, we have to work out how to win a battle, instead.' Martil lowered her to the ground carefully, whereupon she fastened herself around his waist.

'That sounds boring. Can we do something else?'

'The sooner we think up something, the sooner I can play with you,' he offered.

'That's a deal! Show me and I'll tell you how to win! After all, I did at Sendric!'

Martil laughed. 'Let's find some paper and ink.'

Merren rode back to the palace, deep in thought. Barrett had failed. Not only had he failed but, by extension, she had failed. She was the Queen, the one they all depended on. She should have marched down to Barrett's house, dragged him away from that girl and demanded he make sure the weather was on their side. Another choice she must live with. For a moment only she blamed herself but then she stopped. *You cannot go down that path. 'If only' is the way to madness for a ruler. You must make choices, then have the strength to live with the consequences,* she told herself.

More disturbing was how she had behaved back there, demanding Tiera encourage Barrett to push himself past his limits, even unto death, if that was what it took. The parallels between her actions and Gello were impossible to ignore. She had always thought they had nothing in common but that was a lie. They were both prepared to do almost anything to win.

But there is a difference, she told herself. *I can control myself, and my ambitions are for my people, not for myself.*

There was another difference as well. Now her initial horror and anger at not being able to stop the storm had passed, she could see Tiera had done the right thing. Still … the storm would strike tonight. The plan to get everyone to safety had failed. It was enough to make anyone give up, but Merren would not go down that path, either. There had to be another way! Despite Nott's confidence, his defiant plan of fighting Gello, the Berellians and Tenochs seemed foolish at best. Merren had been taught by Martil, who had learned his lessons in the bloody cauldron of the Ralloran Wars. Battles were fought when two sides formed shield walls and the side whose wall cracked first — usually the one whose line was shortest and thinnest — was the one that lost. But to form a shield wall took training and iron discipline. How did you learn that when you did not use shields and barely understood the language of those you fought beside?

And that supposed she could even get the Derthals to fight. What else could she offer them? And, even if she offered them the whole of the north, would the Derthals guarantee victory?

Then again, even victory would bring problems. She knew full well the muttering against her. Ironically enough, the areas that had been strongest for Gello, the south and west, had suffered the worst and were now more on her side than the east and the north, where the people were scared of what they thought was a horde of goblins waiting for them. She could save the country, only to have it turn on her.

She shook her head. *Worry about the peace once you have secured it*, she told herself. *Concentrate on the problem at hand.* But there was no comfort in that, for the problem defied belief. If only Barrett had been able to break apart that storm!

She left Jaret and Wilsen to look after the horses at the Royal Stable and decided to take a bath before trying to work out what to do next. It was her one chance to be alone, without anyone demanding she make difficult choices for them.

She was already anticipating the blissful silence when she walked around a corner and into Count Sendric.

'Your majesty! How did Barrett fare? Is the storm destroyed?' Sendric asked eagerly.

Merren composed her face hurriedly. 'The storm is reduced — but it will still strike the northern half of the country tonight.'

Sendric's face sagged. 'But what will we do?'

'There is only one thing to do. We shall have to find as many weapons as possible, arm everyone, then try and persuade the Derthals to join us.'

'Persuade the Derthals? What else are you going to give them?' Sendric snorted.

'You forget yourself, Count! This is my country!' Merren blazed.

Sendric grumbled an apology. 'But it is my land that is being given away.'

'Better to give it to Derthals than Fearpriests!' Merren told him tartly.

The Count looked ready to continue the argument but instead swallowed heavily.

'Your majesty, I bow to your wisdom in this matter. But I beg you for one favour.'

Merren regarded him suspiciously. 'And that is?'

'We need to secure the succession. What if I am killed in this battle? Then your child will be left fatherless and the country will be plunged further into crisis. It would mean the end of the royal line and Norstalos will become a laughing stock. I beg of you, arrange the marriage in the next couple of days!'

Merren stared at him. The country was about to

be destroyed by Fearpriests and he was obsessing about his dignity and the country's reputation.

'That is solved simply,' she told him icily. 'You will not fight. You will remain by my side. You will be in no danger, unless I am. And in that case, we will all be dead and it will not matter anyway.'

Leaving the outraged Sendric in her wake, she swept upstairs, hoping he would not follow her — and thinking he would regret it if he did.

It was almost the last straw, and she could feel the pressure of it all threaten to overwhelm her. She was going to have to gamble everything on one battle. She thought she had already done that before, at Pilleth. Luck, Aroaril, the Dragon Sword, whatever, had favoured her that day. Surely it could not happen again. Thinking they could win two miraculous victories against the odds was surely too much to hope for. At that moment she almost felt like calling for Martil. They had not really spoken since his return from the south, and she had tried to put him out of her mind but now she wanted to see him. She needed some human comfort, even if it were just someone to hold her. Although she doubted either of them could restrict themselves to just holding each other.

Besides, she could not help thinking, *we are all going to die anyway, so why worry about what the people think? Why not enjoy ourselves, take what little joy is left in the world? Steal some pleasure and it will be a comfort at the end.* It was dangerously tempting and she forced herself to think about lists of refugees and the shortage of shelters waiting in the north to stop herself from going to find him.

Still, the thought would not leave her and her feet dragged. She knew she should continue to her apartments and run that bath; soak herself and clear her mind before returning to work. Everything her father had drummed into her, every day of her training as a royal said that was the thing to do. But she did not want to. She wanted to run through the palace until she found Martil, throw her arms around him and tell him they would be together, for however much time they had left on this world. Tell him she was sorry for the time they had wasted — but there was a chance to make up for it all.

She had reached her apartments now and her hand reached out to the door's handle — and stopped.

Merren stared at her hand and the polished brass door knob for what seemed like an age. Her life seemed poised on a knife's edge. She could be a queen or she could be Merren. She could be proper and die with dignity, or she could have Martil and die happier. Almost unconsciously, she felt her hand draw back. It was exhilarating. She was actually going to do it!

She had begun to turn, had lifted one leg to put her foot down. When her boot touched the smooth floor, she knew she was going to hitch up her long robe and run down that corridor. Gia had been asking her to hold up her dresses, anyway. With fewer servants around, the floors were not being kept clean and the hems of her clothes were all getting dirty. Merren smiled to herself, imagining what Gia would say if she knew Merren was planning to hurl her dress to the floor.

Then footsteps on the marble floor made her spin around — to see Martil waving a piece of parchment at her, covered in what looked like a child's drawings. But she ignored that as she gasped in a breath. Had he heard about Barrett? Had he thought, as she had, that nothing mattered any more, they could be together for the time that remained?

Would he sweep her in his arms; should she run to him — would they even be able to make it into her apartment? Would some servant find them here, on the cold marble floor?

'Merren, I have it! The plan to beat them!' he declared, triumph in his eyes.

All other thought fled from her.

'Show me,' she commanded.

9

The carriages had allowed the refugees to out-pace the Tenochs, to the extent where they could rest the horses, take it easy on the run to the capital. And the type of food they carried meant each night they ate well. Kettering had been surprised to see the rich Norstalines were even happy to let his men eat with them. Probably want our protection, he had thought sourly at first. Perhaps that was true, to an extent, but men like Fergus seemed genuinely grateful. He sat with Kettering, Hawke and Leigh now. They had eaten aged ham and vintage cheese, washed down with fine ale.

'That's the best meal I've had in weeks,' Hawke announced, belching loudly.

Fergus chuckled. 'If my house is still standing, or when we rebuild it, I'll treat you boys to a dinner you'll never forget!'

Hawke grinned, then felt in his belt pouch, producing the brass door-knocker he had taken from Fergus's shattered door.

'When you do, you should put this on your door,' he said solemnly.

Fergus laughed at that. 'Why'd you keep that piece of brass, when there was so much gold going around?'

Hawke shrugged. 'I guess it was what my dad used to say to me: you can tell a man's character by the house he owns. I always wanted a special door, a cedar door like the one you had. That would have said I was a real man. A successful man. Not scum.'

'My granddad always said you could tell a man by the clothes he wore,' Leigh offered.

'And the carriage he drove.' Fergus nodded. 'My father always told me that. A man is defined by the clothes he wears, the carriage he drives and the house he lives in.'

'I can't believe you're swallowing that stinking pile of dung!' Kettering growled.

Hawke spat out the lump of cheese he was eating.

'But —' he began.

'No, you fool, that belief about what makes a man!' Kettering snarled.

They stared at him.

'What do you mean, Killer?' Leigh asked finally.

Kettering sighed. 'I've learned there's only two things that matter. What's in here,' he tapped his head, 'and what's in here,' he thumped his chest. 'Head and heart. That's what counts, not cedar doors or fancy carriages or shiny clothes. Not even gold. When you take all that away, the true man is what's left. Believing that clothes and carriages and gold and doors matter is what got this country into this mess. Maybe now we'll realise that.'

Silence greeted his words.

'You may be right,' Fergus said slowly. 'A few days ago I would have laughed at the thought. But what we've been through since then ... all the gold in this country won't stop those murdering savages from cutting us down like dogs. It's time to see what we are really made of.'

The silence this time was warmer.

'I'd still like a nice door though,' Hawke mumbled.

Their laughter made people at other fires turn and look.

High Chief Sacrax was pleasantly surprised to see a dragon circle around his camp and land in the pass. He had been asking for Queen Merren to come up and talk about the unrest in the mountains, as well as the hostility of her people.

'The Queen sees you as very important,' Father Quiller had told him — but Sacrax had not really been convinced. Perhaps this visit would prove Quiller right.

'Your majesty, I am pleased to see you here —' he began.

'High Chief, we bring important news,' Merren interrupted. 'Is there somewhere we can talk? This might take some time.'

The way Milly had saved Kesbury at Wells — in fact the way she had saved them all — had been told and re-told up and down the columns of refugees. Using their Berellian horses, Kesbury and his villagers had begun to catch up, even overtake those who had set out earlier. The tale of how Kesbury had come back to save the village and Milly had come back to save Kesbury had people flocking to the huge Ralloran and the slim Norstaline, wanting to be blessed by one or both of them.

Each night, around the campfires, they were asked to hold children, to reassure adults, to promise that all would reach safety — and to deny, time and again, there was a horde of goblins waiting to devour their children in the north.

Always behind them, they could see smoke as the

Berellians pressed forwards — although they never got too close, because the Rallorans would not let them.

But that night all could see what was waiting for them ahead.

'Is it coming our way?' Kesbury asked, as they watched the lightning flash in the distance, turning night into day every few heartbeats.

'No. It is coming no closer,' Milly confirmed. 'It seems to be contained to the north. It is unlike any storm I have ever seen before …'

'The work of our enemies. And it does not need to come any closer,' Kesbury sighed, digging his boot heel into the hard earth of the road, deeply rutted by the hundreds of wagons that had used it in the past few days, to say nothing of what the herds of animals had done to it. 'Even horses won't be able to wade through mud, past thousands of people trapped.'

Milly nodded silently. There was no need to say any more. They knew of Nott's desperate idea, of Martil's plan to win over the Derthals using the Dragon Sword; knew too well what the people thought of the Derthals and how hard it would be to defeat a real Fearpriest. The wind, which had turned around in the day and now blew cold and harsh from the south, made them both shiver suddenly. In the darkness, his hand found hers, and she squeezed his fingers in return.

The gates of the capital had been thrown open and as many people as possible encouraged to get under cover. But lightning cracked roof tiles, wind brought down trees, while rain lashed streets and flooded the lower levels of even rich houses. In the poor quarter, floods raged through tight streets and a score of people were swept and battered down the cobblestones. People took refuge on the top floors as the water drummed down. The churches were all full, as sopping wet, desperate people prayed for mercy, for help, for an end to the howling wind and driving rain.

Out on the roads, it was even worse. Everything that had four legs tried to run, to get away from the incessant barrage. Lightning crashed to the ground everywhere, while thunder cracked loud every few moments, driving fear into hearts and driving the wits from many. People sheltered under wagons, in any abandoned village hut they could find or just huddled together for warmth as the rain pelted down.

Thoughts of escape, of making it north, even tales of the goblins that everyone said were waiting for them vanished under the driving force of that storm. The temperature plunged, and people shivered, trying to keep warm when no fires would burn and all clothing was soaked through.

Survival became the only thought and death almost a welcome relief.

In the far north, the rain was heavy but without the sheer force — and without the thunder or lightning that terrorised the capital and a swathe of countryside north of it.

'So your people can't reach safety,' Sacrax said.

'No. We have no choice but to fight. We will fight them ourselves, if we must, but we cannot win. Our only chance is with your warriors,' Merren stated. 'And if we die, then you know what will happen to you and your people.'

'I thought you had strong wizards to protect you. You said this would be easy. Protect the passes and then live in peace. That not happening,' Sacrax pointed out.

'I know. We did not expect this. But just because the hunt does not go well, is that a reason to give up, walk away and come home to watch your children die of hunger?' Merren countered.

Sacrax smiled, a little. 'Big numbers on their side. Small numbers on ours. How we win? Maybe I just take my warriors home. Safer for us. Your people not want us, anyway. And my enemies raid my camp for winter food. I should return before one of my children or wives is hurt …'

Merren locked eyes with him.

'You could take your warriors home, either to protect your families or because some of my people are foolish, and have offended you. And you will live safely in your mountains, perhaps for a few years. But our enemies will come for you. Remember, you refused their offer and agreed to fight with us. They will not forget. And one day their armies will march into the far north and there will be nowhere for you to run. They will hunt you down and they will not stop until the last Derthal is dead, sacrificed to their foul God.'

She watched with no pleasure as her words hit home. Sacrax's face twisted in anger as he realised the position he was in. Before he could say or do something they would all regret, she pressed on.

'We never lied to you. Believe me, we wish this had never happened. But your people and mine will have to fight our enemies. We can either fight apart, and die apart, or we can join our forces, fight together — and have a chance to win.'

Sacrax stared at her for a long moment before, finally, acknowledging her words with a nod.

'I have never fought the Friny. But I heard from my father and his father, who had been told by his father; I know you have bows that send sharp arrows across long distance. You have horses, that cannot be stopped by spears alone. And you carry shields, wear metal clothing to protect you. Every time Derthals fought Friny warriors, we lost.'

Merren remembered what 'Friny' meant.

'But this time we are not your enemies, this time we will fight beside you, as friends.'

Sacrax looked at her, then a slight smile creased his face. 'You are not Friny any more,' he agreed.

'You will be fighting with Captain Martil. He has defeated Berellians, Avish and Norstalines. He never lost a battle where he was the commander.'

Sacrax turned to Martil, who laid the Dragon Sword on the table and tried not to think about another battle.

'I have seen you fight. You win even when you should lose. I like that,' Sacrax admitted. 'But how we win this time?'

Merren glanced at Martil. They had talked this over before leaving the capital. Lurking behind their conversation had been their arguments. But neither wanted to bring it up, while she had also tried to forget she had only just been thinking about finding him and throwing herself at him. Instead they pretended everything was normal as they discussed how to win an almost-impossible victory.

It all depended on two things.

'We cannot fight in the normal way. The Derthals do not have shields, don't have the discipline and we don't have the time to teach them to fight like that. Their spears are too short for them to stand in the second line, so we can't even use them like that. And we don't want to get into that sort of battle anyway, because the Fearpriests outnumber us. They'll just wrap around and kill us,' he had explained. 'If we fight in the normal way, we die. So we must do what they will never expect. We attack them.' Martil pointed at the drawings on the paper.

'At first we advance towards them, the Derthals leading the way. They will think us fools, and prepare to slaughter the Derthals on their shield wall. But, instead, the Derthals will split into two, run around each side of their formation, like the horns of a stag. Then our archers and infantry will strike at their shield wall, lock them in battle and hold them while the horns hook around the side and back and slice in, ripping them apart. The Derthals will not be fighting against shields, they will be striking the flanks and rear of our enemies, where their weakest fighters will stand.'

Merren had grasped the idea — but it was still a huge risk. So many lives depended on the strategy, as well as on the Derthals, who spoke only a few words of human, if any, and who had never fought like this before. Who knew how they would react in the middle of a battle?

Still, there was no other option. If they tried to hold the walls of the capital, they might succeed — for a day or two. But it was the same problem they had faced at Sendric. Too much wall and too many attackers. The Berellians could strike at one spot, the Tenochs at the other. One could be stopped, the other would break in. And that was the real worry. Another Bellic-style massacre. At least if they fought in the open and lost, there was a chance Gello would allow most, if not all, of the people to live. It was a small comfort to her.

Martil opened his parchment and explained his strategy carefully to Sacrax.

'They will never expect this,' he finished.

Sacrax patted the parchment. 'Battles easy to win on here,' he said. 'Not same when spears are flying.'

'It all depends on your warriors. Can they do what I ask?'

'We can do this,' Sacrax declared. 'But will my chiefs want to? I risked my throne bringing them here. Many of my warriors might think they should protect their families, instead. Your people give us no reason to fight.'

'My people will accept yours, after this,' Merren promised, hoping she was right.

'Take us to your chiefs and I will persuade them,' Martil stated, laying his hand on the Dragon Sword's hilt and hoping that was right.

Dawn brought some relief. But only some.

The combined efforts of every priest and wizard saw the worst of the storm pass as the sky lightened. But the sun was invisible behind thick grey cloud and the rain, while positively gentle compared with the downpour of last night, was unrelenting.

'We have to get as many people back to the city as possible,' Nott announced.

'Back to the city? But they need to get north!' Louise protested.

They were in the throne room, but had been forced to drag tables and chairs across to the far wall. The sheer violence of the storm had sent a tree branch through one of the windows, and the floor was covered in puddles of water, as well as shards of glass. They had started a fire but its fitful warmth was not enough to counteract the bitter wind that whistled through the missing glass panes. Yet the palace had escaped lightly compared to the rest of the city. The water had subsided somewhat now the rain had eased but the streets were at least ankle-deep in water. Thatch had been blown off, homes flooded, trees brought down onto houses and shops alike and the sewers were backing up.

'They will not be able to make it. Most of the wagons out there are impossibly bogged. Food has been ruined, animals have run away. The streams and rivers are flooding, making it harder to move around and, worse, they are unsafe to drink, so people do not even have fresh water. Then there is the cold. The people are soaked. Soon they will fall sick and we shall see scores of young and old perish,' Nott warned.

'But if they come here, the Berellians and Tenochs will slaughter them! Surely they are better off with a little wet and cold!' Conal gasped.

'And the city has been devastated by the storm,' Louise pointed out.

'They will die, either here or on the roads north, if we cannot defeat the Fearpriests,' Nott said simply. 'As for the city, the more hands we have, the quicker the damage will be repaired. Meanwhile, we must trust in the Queen and Martil — and the Derthals.'

'This is ridiculous!' Sendric thundered. 'Risking our lives on a pack of goblins! I cannot sit here and listen to this any longer!'

He stormed out, slamming the door behind him.

Conal sighed.

'Let's get working. We'll send out every man and horse we have, to bring the people back.'

Martil took a deep breath then walked over to where the chiefs and Sacrax waited, looking at him suspiciously. He was confident: he just had to be honest and leave the rest to the Dragon Sword.

'I am not a Norstaline! I am a Ralloran. My country lies far to the south. The Norstalines refused to help my country when it was attacked and they hate me and my men. They call us killers, and spit on us when we walk past,' he told them. 'Yet I fight for them and for their Queen. As do my men.'

This caused a stir among the Derthals, while he could also feel Merren's eyes boring into him.

'Why do you fight then, if they hate you?' one chief, with a headband of what looked like black goat hair, demanded.

'Because not all hate me. There are many good people among them. I fight for them, and for this Queen, who wants everyone to be treated as an equal. I fight for the idea that we can all live in peace. And I fight against my real enemies, who kill women and children, who want to make everyone bow down before their God, who demands blood, not prayer. I know what the Norstalines have done to you. But the men you saw me fight, the Berellians, they are even worse. I proved that they lie. They would kill you all.'

Martil strode along the front of the chiefs, Dragon Sword in hand.

'I do not want to fight. Believe me when I say I fear this battle. But we have no choice. Either we fight or we die.'

He paused. 'But we do not just fight because we must. We fight because the Norstalines need to see that they are not as wonderful as they think. They need to learn they attacked you and drove you out because of a lie. They must learn they are no better than everyone else. By helping them, by saving them, they will see this. They may never love you. But you will be able to live in peace with them. No more will your young ones cry of hunger, no more will your old ones weep for the cold.'

As he spoke, Martil was aware of the warmth of the Dragon Sword's hilt under his hand.

'Go back to the north and you might live for

longer. But nothing will change. You will still be hated, still hunted and eventually you will be destroyed. This is your chance to change everything. Your only chance. So who is with me? Who will fight not just for the Norstaline but for their families and their tribe's future?'

Whether it was his words, or the Sword, or both, he never knew. But the chanting started at the back, then spread to the front, then all of the chiefs were stamping their feet, spears in the air, hooting out their war cries.

'We shall fight,' Sacrax told them solemnly.

The stores that had been shipped out of towns and villages across the south, east and west, and brought to the capital on Conal's orders days and sometimes weeks before, were needed now. The capital was damaged but it was still shelter, warmth and food to those who had none. Other stores, set up further along the road, had been spoiled by the rain, or simply washed away.

The rain had slackened off, now it was just an unending drizzle that added to the misery.

From the south, east and west, refugees struggled through the last few miles of road, often forced to leave wagons and carts that became bogged in the thick mud within sight of the city. Tired horses, mud caking their legs up to their bellies, struggled back and forth, trying to ferry children and supplies to the dubious safety of the city. Small wagons filled with sawdust tried to improve the road, but had a limited effect. The mud was thick and glutinous and wheels stuck fast, defying the efforts of tired men and animals to shift them.

The only option for most people was to take what they could carry and strike out across the soggy fields, which at best were only a little better than the roads.

From the north, those who had been heading for safety turned around, the way ahead impossibly blocked.

Columns of exhausted people struggled into the capital, where the residents opened their doors and welcomed them with food and drink.

Conal ordered the huge town homes of the nobility — almost all of them killed by Gello and his Fearpriests — to be opened, by sword if necessary. Mud-smeared farmers lay down on marble floors, while bleating goats and complaining chickens clattered around ballrooms and roosted on velvet curtains.

People lay wherever they could — and just one glance showed they could go no further. Already tired by days or weeks of travel, soaked to the bone by a storm the likes of which had never been seen in Norstalos, they had used their last reserves to make it here. Escape to the north was now impossible.

Luckily the rain had not been nearly as bad in the far north. The Derthals had to march as hard and fast as they could to reach the capital in time.

Merren and Martil waved them off as they headed south, under the leadership of Sacrax and accompanied by Quiller.

At first a trickle, then a flood of refugees and northerners came over to see them go.

'What's going on?' someone asked, as the Derthals strode away, occasionally giving a roar of triumph at Martil, who held the Dragon Sword aloft.

'Where are they going?' another said.

'Who cares? Good riddance, I say! Further away they get from me and mine, the better …'

'Who said that?' Merren whirled around, and the crowd, growing with every moment, went silent, where it had been rumbling with agreement.

'They are marching south, to fight our enemies. If we are going to survive this, it will be because of the Derthals!'

Silence greeted her words.

'Think about that. Despite all you have said to them, they are prepared to fight for us! They have rallied to the Dragon Sword, when Norstalines did not. If you and your children live, it will because they died for you! So perhaps next time you will not be so quick to judge!'

Merren had imagined a better response to her words than a sullen silence. Again came the nagging worry that the people thought her the cause of all their troubles.

'Will the Derthals be able to fight properly? Will they follow orders?' she whispered to Martil, as they waved to the last of the Derthals disappearing down the pass.

'Well, they are used to operating together in the hunt. Often two or more tribes will work together to bring down deer or goats,' Martil said confidently.

'Yes, but were there 20,000 goats armed with swords?' Merren asked pointedly.

'No,' Martil admitted. 'What do you want me to say? This tactic has never been used before. But if you have a better idea …'

'No,' she sighed.

'Your majesty, what now?' Gratt asked politely.

She turned, to see he had made his way through the people to her side. She noticed, over his shoulder, that the people were muttering and glancing over towards her, and towards the Derthals marching off into the distance.

She sighed. She could imagine what they were saying: this would never have happened under Gello.

'Captain Martil and I shall have to return as soon as possible. Refugees will still come in, although slowly now. Take care of them. But you should get together as many men as you can, in case things go badly for us. You are a brave man and a loyal one. I wish I could give you more comfort but either we win, or we die.'

Gratt fell to one knee. 'Your majesty, thank you for everything,' he said hoarsely. 'The people may not see it now but even if we die, to have tasted the life we have had over the past few months ... the sagas tell us it is better to die on our feet than live on our knees. I never believed that before now.'

Merren reached out and raised Gratt gently to his feet, before kissing his forehead.

'Good luck and my blessing. It is for men such as you that we fight.' She smiled.

Barrett was exhausted. In fact all the assembled wizards were exhausted. A night of trying to reduce the storm, after failing to block it, had been nightmarish. They had managed to protect Barrett's house but had been unable to do much else. Rest, food and drink had them back on their feet — but all still felt the harsh pain of failure. The Queen, the country had depended on them — and they had let everyone down.

But while that hurt, Barrett found it difficult to keep the smile off his face. Tiera was the reason of course. He had been so sure that he had made a fool of himself — again — only for her to bring him back from the brink and declare she returned his feelings.

They had not spent the night together — partly

because the ghost of Prent still lingered there — and partly because he was truly exhausted. But they had talked — as equals, not as teacher and student.

She had left to find more food for the assembled mages, while he thought he might relax, and read. However, most of the other mages were in his library already, lying on couches or sunk into chairs, talking quietly or reading or dozing. Barrett thought he might be able to slip out quietly — but they spotted him. One plump mage — whose voluminous robes now hung loosely on his slimmer frame — hurried over. Barrett recognised him as Fernal, who normally added the title 'The Great' to his name but in this company had wisely decided to drop that. He was one of the more talkative wizards, quick to raise questions about the working of the Guild and, although not one of the most talented, the leading wizard from the large eastern town of Wollin.

'Barrett! What are we going to do now?' he demanded.

'What do you mean?' Barrett sat down in an empty chair and watched Fernal flop into the facing one.

'Well, the first act of our new Guild was hardly a success now, was it? And the country is in trouble because of it. Some of the others think we might be better off down in Rallora, or Aviland. The Berellians do not have much of a reputation for treating people well and Gello has something of a long memory for those who have displeased him.'

Barrett stared at him. He really did not have the energy for this — but was spared the need to argue by Tiera's return, as she burst into the library and almost knocked over a pair of wizards. 'Barrett!'

He surged to his feet, tiredness forgotten. 'What is it?'

She rushed to his side. 'The city's filling with people. Everyone who left in the last few days is trying to get back and all the refugees are making their way here. The people say the goblins are coming down to help us make a stand outside the city.'

Everyone tried to talk at the same time and Barrett had to shout to get them to calm down.

'That's settled it then,' Fernal said into the silence. 'We have to get out of here. The army will be crushed and then the Berellians'll kill everyone they find!'

Cries of agreement took even longer to quiet down.

'We have to think about this. The Queen will not have taken this step lightly,' Barrett said heavily.

'We shouldn't think, we should act!' Tiera shouted.

Everyone turned to stare at her.

'There're people out there suffering. You should see the ones coming into the city! Covered in mud, soaking wet, children crying … they only have the clothes on their backs, and those are filthy. We need to get out there and help them.'

'But we're all tired,' someone protested.

'Aye, and they'll hate us. We couldn't stop the storm and now look what's happened!' Fernal protested.

'And what is the point of helping those who are doomed anyway?' someone offered.

'Aye,' Fernal nodded. 'This Guild did what it could but it failed, now is the time to look after ourselves.'

Nods of agreement and mutters greeted his statement.

'My friends!' Barrett appealed.

'It's too late. Don't you see?' Fernal said sadly.

Barrett did not know what to say to convince them, then Tiera stepped forwards.

'What were you all talking about when we decided to form a Magicians' Guild? We complain that nobody likes us, that they think we are selfish, money-hungry and arrogant — and then we prove them right by not helping in their time of need! We need to get out there and do what we can.'

'Like what?' Fernal demanded.

'Can we do anything about the roads?'

'Turn mud into hard earth again? It can be done but the best of us could only manage a mile or so before we became exhausted,' Fernal said doubtfully.

'It's better than nothing. People will die if we don't help them!'

Her words lashed at them, and few could meet her gaze.

'Get people back here safely, help save them from the pursuing Berellians and Tenochs, and the Queen will thank you and the people will love you!' She looked around the room. 'I do not have much control over my power but I shall do what I can,' she swore.

Barrett had been watching her, transfixed, but now he turned his attention to the rest of the room. 'She's right,' he declared. 'Who's with us?'

Nods and smiles greeted his words. Fernal, who was up the front, was also looking around the room and he seemed to come to the same conclusion.

'We all are.' He grinned.

Merren held Martil's arm as they prepared to get back on Argurium.

'Thank you for what you did,' she said softly. 'We have a chance now.'

A few days ago she would have been happy never to speak to him again. But the way her mind had jumped to Martil when it seemed there was no hope made her think anew about how she felt about him. 'Listen, if anything were to … happen … I would care for Karia. She would be raised as mine,' she promised.

'Merren, why are we denying ourselves? We should be together. We both know it is right,' he told her softly. 'Your words prove that!'

'My words prove nothing,' she fired back, knowing full well she was lying. 'I have sworn not to think about this until everyone is safe!'

'Not thinking about you is impossible for me!' he protested. 'Can't you just —'

'No. Enough!' she snapped. She could not deal with this now, not on top of everything else. 'Havell, are you ready to go?'

Martil watched her walk away with mounting frustration.

10

Merren shivered as she walked into the palace throne room but forced a smile for the benefit of everyone who was waiting there. The glass had been swept up beside the wall and wood placed over the cracked panes but it was still chilly; although not as cold as the atmosphere between Martil and herself on the flight south.

'So, the rain seems to be much lighter now?'

'Indeed, your majesty,' Nott agreed. He had been looking after Karia, who had run across to hug Martil. 'It should stop in the next few days. But there is little prospect of sun.'

'Well, the Derthals have agreed to fight with us, and are marching south now, as fast as they can. It is relatively flat and open all the way from the passes, so they should make good time.'

'Hopefully they have as much time as possible. We have been labouring all day to bring people into the city, from both north and south, but it has been hard work. The mages, led by Barrett, have been helping immensely. They have improved the roads for several miles, while they have been bringing in people trapped to the north through the oak trees in the park.'

'We stand ready to do whatever we can,' Barrett announced, still looking drawn, his eyes deeply shadowed. 'Luckily I spent that time creating the Magicians' Guild, otherwise we would not be able to offer so much.'

Merren nodded, although she was tempted to point out none of this would be necessary if Barrett had not been distracted by creating his Guild.

'I shall go out on Argurium again from tomorrow. We have done well but we must get as many back here as possible, ready for when the Derthals arrive.'

'Your majesty, if I may. Why are we even bothering with these gob … Derthals?' Sendric said disdainfully. 'They have no discipline. We cannot depend on them. Surely our best hope is to man the walls with everyone and everything we have …'

'We have been over this, time and again!' Merren snapped. 'These walls will not hold! It would be a death sentence for every man, woman and child inside the walls. If we lose on the field, there is still the hope Gello will at least spare most of them.'

That silenced everyone, instantly.

'Meanwhile, we shall ask everyone to help take in these poor people, try to feed and clothe them. And we shall all set an example. Open up every spare room we have. And any spare clothing from the palace should be distributed. Archbishop Nott, are you able to handle that?'

'Of course, your majesty.'

'Good. Perhaps this will be a valuable lesson for the people,' she suggested.

'As long as we're around to pass it on,' Conal offered.

The weak jest was still enough to raise a smile and she nodded at Conal in appreciation.

'What are we waiting for?' she asked, and chairs scraped all around the table as people hurried off.

Over the next few days, the wizards worked on the roads leading south, west and east, while Conal's militia harnessed tired horses to drag wagons off the roads, then laid logs and sawdust, so that the refugees could at least slog their way through the cloying mud and reach the capital. Meanwhile, a seemingly endless procession of muddy, bedraggled people, many of them sickening, were brought into the capital through the oak trees in the park. There they were greeted with a strange variety of clothes, as well as food and hot drinks. Animals were herded over to a series of crudely fenced fields, while people were directed towards churches or the big houses of the rich, where they could fill up the endless bedrooms. The only one that was left empty was Gello's massive home, for fear of reprisals.

The rain slowly died away but the sky stayed overcast and sullen, and pools of water just sat in the middle of the road and on the verge. Any wagon that tried to leave the road just carved huge furrows in the soft grass before eventually becoming bogged. Herds of animals, as well as hundreds of people, wagons and carts rumbled into the city from the south and the east. The northern road was just too much to attempt — there were not enough wizards, men and horses, or time. Wagons and carts littered that road as far as the eye could see — and far beyond. The people and some of the animals could be rescued but everything else would have to wait.

Looming over all of them like a shadow was the smoke on the horizon, particularly in the south. Soldiers, mostly either rangers or Rallorans, seemed to be riding back to the city with ever-increasing regularity. Hundreds of people were now making their way up onto the battlement and towers of the capital, so they could see what was going on — and spoke fearfully about what would happen.

There was plenty for them to see.

Every morning the dragon would fly off, something that every child looked forward to. She would return once, perhaps twice, sometimes even flying low over the walls so the people could see the Queen on her back, waving to them.

From the south, frightened refugees bringing stories of Berellians killing and raping and burning, as well as stories of being saved by Rallorans, poured through the gates. With them came a priest and a female Bishop, walking hand-in-hand, their robes marked and stained by their travel over waterlogged roads and grass. A pair, people told each other, who had defeated a Fearpriest. Proof that Aroaril was both stronger than the Dark One, and on their side! One event that excited plenty of comment was the arrival of dozens of carriages — albeit splattered with mud and drawn by exhausted horses — laden with women and children. Behind them, walking over the grass so as not to weigh down the carriages, came several hundred soldiers in the blue — and dirt — of the Queen.

Kettering, as well as the others, was startled to hear applause and cheering from the walls as they dragged themselves into the capital, filthy and sweating. Astonished former criminals found themselves embraced by children, kissed by women and had their hands shaken by grinning men. Even Kettering found it hard to maintain a scowl when Leigh almost disappeared in the embrace of a laughing, plump woman, his head almost getting stuck between her large breasts.

But there were many people still trying desperately to get to the capital, and not enough soldiers to protect them.

Hutter and the people he had rescued from Worick, as well as those he had picked up on the way, had to be snatched away from the teeth of the Tenoch pursuit by magic, Barrett and Fernal opening gateways for them to escape.

Martil, at Merren's request, had gathered a motley group of Norstalines and Rallorans and was sweeping around the capital, finding tired people, pockets of exhausted refugees and lost children to bring back to safety. He strongly suspected Merren had chosen him for this role so she would not have to speak to him.

'Help us!'

Father Quiller was heartily sick of the saddle. And mud, come to think of it. He would also have been happy to see the back of the rain. And as for the salted meat and hard bread that seemed to be the only food available ... but his musings were put aside when a handful of children ran out from behind a bogged wagon. He had become used to people hiding in their wagons, or cowering in half-empty villages as the Derthal horde marched by. Having people run out to talk to him was something different.

'What is it?' He spurred his tired horse over the heavy ground to where the children, the youngest barely able to walk, the oldest just in his teens, waved at him.

'Father! We need help!' the teenager called, a fair-haired boy wearing a filthy tunic and mud-encrusted trousers.

'Where are your parents?' Quiller asked.

'Dead. We live with our grandparents, but they're dying. We were going to hide from the goblins but then we saw you.'

'Take me to them,' Quiller commanded.

They led him over to the wagon, sunk up to its axles in mud, but a quick glance told Quiller he had come too late. The elderly man was already dead and his wife was moments away. The cold and wet had obviously taken its toll — even the thin blankets covering the couple were soaked.

He stroked the woman's head and was rewarded with a final gasp as she slipped away.

Carefully he covered them, before turning to the children.

'Have you any food?' Quiller asked.

'Not today,' the boy admitted.

Quiller gripped the young man by his shoulders. 'I am afraid your grandparents are dead. I shall leave you food and I would advise you to get yourself to a village and find some shelter before you all get sick.'

'What about the others?' the boy asked.

'Others?' Quiller looked down at the other four children, who stared solemnly back at him.

'There's nigh on two score of us,' the boy declared. 'They'd have come out but they were scared the goblins would eat 'em.'

'Bring them here,' Quiller ordered.

Soon a motley group of filthy, ragged children emerged from the scatter of wagons. Even more slowly, their story emerged. It seemed a village had decided to hedge its bets — many of the parents would wait and see if the returned King Gello would leave them alone — but they had sent their children away with a handful of guardians. Some of those had gone for help, some had said they were going for help but had probably just left — and the last two now lay dead under a mouldy blanket.

'What going on?' Sacrax wandered over as his Derthals marched past.

'Are you going to eat me, goblin?' a little girl with wide green eyes asked fearfully.

Sacrax roared with laughter. 'Wouldn't eat you! Not enough meat!' He winked.

None of the children laughed. They just stared at him, some in wonder, some in shock, some in fear.

'High Chief, we have a problem. These children have been abandoned. We need to leave them food, so they can last here until someone comes for them.'

'Who will come for them?' Sacrax demanded.

Quiller shrugged. 'I don't know. But someone will. We have seen people struggling past on the road. We passed a dozen of them today. And we cannot waste more time here. We are needed at the capital.'

Sacrax stared down at the children. Two were babies, being carried by girls no older than ten.

'No,' the Derthal said softly.

'No?' Quiller bristled. 'We cannot leave them here to starve!'

'I know. We take them with us. Your people have been walking past them for days and leaving them here. I cannot. They come with us. I will not leave young ones behind to die,' the High Chief said firmly.

'But the schedule ...'

'I cannot fight with them on my mind,' Sacrax declared, then shouted something in Derthal.

Burly Derthals hurried over as their High Chief went down on one knee, so he was at the children's level.

'You call us goblins. But we are not monsters. We cannot leave young ones behind. I am the High

Chief. These warriors are sworn to serve me to death and beyond. They will carry you and keep you safe until their hearts give out and the breath leaves their bodies. Agreed?'

Quiller thought the teenage boy, their self-appointed leader, might look at him for confirmation first — but the boy just nodded.

'I trust you,' he said. 'We have seen many people walk past and ignore us. You are the first to talk to us, even though you look funny.'

Sacrax chuckled. 'For that, I think you can walk with me!'

Quiller could not help but smile at the sight of the muscular Derthal warriors carrying small children in their arms or on their shoulders. But he also worried. This needed to be a fast march. Saving the children was admirable — yet they would slow the Derthals down.

Merren soared high over Norstalos on the back of the dragon Argurium and closed her eyes for just a moment. How could Martil be so clever and yet so stupid at the same time? Were they fated just to be at each other's throats? He was the one person she needed; someone to talk to, to ease her fears but she could not have him around without an argument adding to her worries. And those were endless. Everywhere she looked, she saw armies advancing through her land, her people fleeing before them, heading for what they hoped would be the safety of the capital. And that was not safe at all. From up here she could view events with the proper detachment, see the small dots desperately fleeing as marks on a map, rather than people with hopes and dreams.

At times like these, she remembered an old saying one of her tutors had been excessively fond of repeating. *Be careful what you wish for, it just might come true.*

At the time she had no idea what the man had been going on about. She had wanted a new doll for her birthday. What was wrong with wishing for it and getting it, rather than some set of law books? But now it held greater significance. She had wanted with all her heart to get another chance at being Queen. Well, she had her chance but sometimes she regretted it. The pressure, the demands, the duties, the responsibility — if she thought about it too much, it became crushing.

It was like riding a wild horse. She could not get off; she had to hang on and hope it became exhausted before she did — and pray that it did not throw her and kill her.

The only consolation was the way the country was finally beginning to wake up and help each other. The palace was now full of farmers and their families, while people all over the city had thrown open their doors to take in the refugees. Every wagon or cart that rumbled through the city gates, every family that stumbled out of an oak tree in the park, was being taken care of now.

It did give her hope.

'Dad will bring everyone back safely, he always does,' Karia said confidently, intruding on her thoughts.

The little girl was sitting in front of her, so Merren reached out and patted her on the back.

Karia decided this was her chance, and twisted around in the harness.

'Why are you and Dad fighting?' she asked. 'You seemed to like each other but now you don't.'

Merren glared at her. 'Did Martil ask you to say that?'

Karia laughed. 'No! He wouldn't answer me when I asked him, so I thought I'd ask you.' She glanced back at Merren. 'Don't you like us any more? Don't you want us to live together?'

Her heart was beating faster. Her efforts up until now to create the family she wanted had failed and Martil had told her not to ask Merren questions. She had spent so little time with him lately, she did not want to fight with him when they were together. Time with Father Nott wasn't quite the same. Every time Martil had gone, she had cried. The only thing that kept her going was his promise to come back to her, not to leave her alone. He had never broken his word, and that was a comfort when she got lonely and upset.

Merren clenched her fist around the harness. If only it were that simple! But as her head had warned, and the surveys had proved, there were bigger issues than just being happy.

'These are grown-up matters, that a child like you cannot understand,' she said.

But Karia had no intention of leaving it there. Why couldn't things go back to the way they had been in the forest outside Sendric? She had never had a dad, now she had one — and she wanted a mother as well. 'Why don't you marry Martil and adopt me? What's wrong with us?'

'Nothing!' Merren cried, her promise to Martil to look after Karia a lead weight inside her. 'But I'm not just a person, I'm a queen ...'

'But if you love us, it will all work out, just like it does in the sagas,' Karia said brightly. Making the adult feel guilty always seemed to work on Martil, so why not Merren? 'Don't we all deserve to be happy?'

Merren had had enough. 'I am not going to talk

to you about this. If you want to come on the dragon again, you will say nothing more!'

Karia, who had been about to keep arguing, stopped at this most terrible of threats.

'Maybe it would be better if Dad doesn't marry a big meanie,' she mumbled, to herself.

But Merren heard it, although she pretended she did not.

11

'Thank you for your time. I know you must all be busy.' Sendric smiled.

The men around the table nodded politely. They might have been the heads of every major guild and trade and major village and town councils from one end of the country to the other but he was still a noble — the last noble left in Norstalos.

'I am preparing a report for the Queen on the disruption to our economy this invasion is causing,' Sendric announced. 'Obviously the almost complete evacuation of the country, as well as the destruction of many villages and towns is going to significantly affect business.'

'You could say that!' someone snorted, then fell silent as everyone looked at him.

'I need to find out what it is going to cost, the effect it will have on lives and how long it will take to get our various industries back up and working again. And I need a brutally honest picture, gentlemen. If you want crown assistance on taxes and grants, you are going to have to state the full effect of this invasion on your towns, cities and guilds. Do I make myself clear?'

He could see he had their full attention.

'As soon as possible,' he told them.

'Where are the Derthals?'

Nobody could answer Merren's question.

'For that matter, where is Sendric?'

Again, nobody knew.

'Well, I don't have time to worry about him. I need to know about the Derthals. There are armies just a day or two away from our walls and they are nowhere in sight!' Merren said. 'Where is Archbishop Nott?'

'Here I am, your majesty.' Nott smiled, as he walked into the throne room with Karia in tow. 'My apologies for my lateness. I was contacting Father Quiller.'

Merren threw up her hands. 'Good! Where are they?'

Nott sat down. 'They are on their way but I fear it will be something of a race between them and the armies of Gello and Fearpriests. It seems they found a pack of abandoned children and the Derthals decided to bring them along.'

'In Aroaril's name, why? They knew the huge distance they had to cover!' Merren exclaimed.

Nott shrugged. 'Quiller wanted to leave them food but High Chief Sacrax insisted that he could not leave young behind to die. But, obviously, their pace has slowed and they will take longer to reach here.'

Merren resisted the temptation to bury her head in her hands only with great difficulty. She could appreciate the gesture but could nobody else in this country realise the importance of what was going on? For the sake of a few children a whole country could die! Then she stopped herself — this was almost the argument she had with Martil ...

she wished he was here. To everyone here she was the Queen, the woman they all looked to for reassurance, for guidance. Only with Martil could she put that persona aside and just be herself. And how she longed to forget all about being Queen, just for a turn or two of the hourglass ...

'When you think about it, it will impress the people — how the Derthals rescued these children when our own people abandoned them,' Nott continued.

'Not if the Derthals arrive too late and the Berellians have destroyed us all,' Merren could not stop herself from saying.

'If they can find someone to look after the children, they will hand them over,' Nott offered.

'Well, that is a great comfort to me,' Merren said, then held up her hand. 'I know, Archbishop. Once we have everyone safely behind these walls I shall feel a little better. Surely even Fearpriests would not try to kill half a country!'

Nott looked grim. 'I would not put anything past a Fearpriest,' was all he said.

'Speaking of the refugees — how are we coping with food and shelter?'

'Every home in the capital has opened its doors. Some are crowded but all are undercover. As for food, we have plenty. And the wizards have offered to use their powers to grow more in the parklands if necessary,' Louise reported.

She was disturbed by Count Sendric hurrying in.

'My apologies, your majesty — there are so many people in the palace now, I found it hard to make my way here without speaking to them.' He offered her a short bow.

'Well, take a seat, Sendric. What of our soldiers? Who are we still waiting on?'

'The rearguards of rangers and Rallorans are expected in today, as is Martil's company,' Conal announced. 'But all will have to fight on foot — every horse we have is utterly spent. They will need weeks, if not months, before they are ready to be used. We have barracked most of the men in Gello's old home. It was big enough and was the only place still deserted.'

'I thought we would not put anyone in there, in case of reprisals?' Sendric said sharply.

Conal shrugged. 'If Gello rides into the city, it will be because those men are already dead — so I suppose it will matter little to them.'

That silenced everyone.

'Aroaril speed the Derthals,' Nott said softly.

Martil just wanted this ride to be over. There was hardly any food, sleeping on cold, wet ground was highly over-rated, and he and the other men were exhausted, both by the pace they had been forced to set and because of the refugees they had found. As much as he wanted to get back to the capital, as much as he wanted to bring these men safely in, he could not leave behind crying women and children. They had collected dozens of them — men, women and children who had become lost or overcome with exhaustion. It meant the men had to take it in turns to slog alongside the horses, fight their way through the mud.

Not only was that hard but it gave Martil ample time to reflect on how badly he had handled Merren. In fact he could not imagine what else he could have done to persuade her to marry Sendric instead. About the only other thing he could have done to offend her would have been to turn up to a council meeting with Lahra, he reflected bitterly. He resolved to apologise to her when they returned to the capital. And that could not happen soon enough. He was trying to encourage the men, but a retreat was always harder than an advance. Heads were low and he worried that they would not be ready to take on the Tenochs and Berellians in a day or two. Even the sight of the capital failed to cheer them.

'Not far now, lads!' he encouraged them. 'There'll be baths, bed, food and women for all! Just don't get them mixed up!'

Not much of a jest, he knew, but when it failed to raise even a smile, he became concerned. Would the rest of the men be like this, also?

He was brooding not just about himself and Merren but also how to improve morale, when cheering made him look up. People had filled the battlements and towers of the city walls and now leaned down, waving and cheering and clapping.

'Here they are! It's the last of them! Our last soldiers!' The shouts echoed around the city as thousands of people on the walls took it up.

Martil looked around wildly for a moment, before realising it was for his band. Obviously Merren had organised this to boost everyone's spirits, for surely the people had seen plenty of soldiers coming in over the past few days — and they had certainly not done anything particularly special. Still, there was no harm in going with it ...

'Listen to that, lads! That's why we're fighting!' He clapped men on the back, shook hands as he let them ride past him and into the city — and was delighted to see backs straighten, sergeants form men into tight lines and smiles back on faces.

'Give them a wave! Let them know you appreciate it!' he called.

They waved and the cheering redoubled. More crowds were lining the streets inside and Martil could feel a smile on his own face. It was over the top, the equal of any victory parade he had attended after the Ralloran Wars — for nothing more than a routine patrol. But perhaps the soldiers, and the people, needed it.

He let the last man ride in, then followed a moment later, waving to the crowd above. Inside, he could see Merren, as well as Sendric, Barrett, the Queen's bard Romon, Nott, Conal and Karia waiting in the middle of the capital's entry square, surrounded by even more people.

'A welcome back to the last of our brave soldiers!' Merren called, her voice being magically magnified, so it boomed across the city. 'What we have done is a feat that will live forever in sagas! To get so many people to safety across so much country! Many said it was impossible, but it has been done!'

The cheering that followed would have drowned out even her magically enhanced voice, so she let it go on before waving for silence.

Martil knew the job was hardly done — there were three armies about to arrive at the gates. But it was probably best not to mention that.

'Thanks to the courage you have all shown, we will face and defeat this monstrous attack on our country!' Merren declared, to more cheers. 'Together we have made a New Norstalos!'

She let the cheers go on for a long while before waving for silence.

'Our gallant soldiers and our noble allies will destroy the threat that we face and we shall live in peace once more!'

But this time the cheering was distracted — particularly from the wall.

'I can see the banners of King Gello!' someone shouted.

Martil could feel the excitement drain out of the crowd.

'My people, do not fear! We are safe here! They will never be able to break the Norstaline spirit!' Merren called, and there was scattered cheering at this.

Martil began to ride over towards her, when he saw her signal for the gates to be closed.

'We have the Dragon Sword! We have the dragons! And we have Aroaril Himself on our side! Trust in them and we shall emerge victorious!' she bellowed, and this time the cheering was for real, although nothing like what it had been.

'Now return to your homes, look after your children! Leave the walls to those who need to defend them!'

The people obviously saw the sense in this, and there was a general rush to get down from the walls and out of the square.

Martil did not like the sound of the gates closing. And he was even less happy when he got closer to Merren — something did not look right. He could tell she was hiding something.

'What's going on? Why are we closing the gates?' he asked.

She offered him a brave smile but he could see the worry, the responsibility that she was carrying and trying not to show.

'It seems Gello has us at his mercy. The Derthals haven't arrived.'

Gello surveyed the city with satisfaction.

It had been an infuriating march, with frequent delays by Kay and his traitorous rangers. But now he was in the perfect position. His army had arrived first at the capital, with the threat of the Berellians and Tenochs looming close behind. Thanks to the constant reports he had been receiving from Prent, he knew the other two advances had been marked by atrocities on the people. The Norstalines would be thoroughly terrified of both the Berellians and Tenochs. His advance, on the other hand, had been positively benign in comparison. And he had collected nearly a hundred ordinary Norstalines who had not only professed their loyalty to him but were happy to show it to their countrymen.

This was his opportunity to revenge himself on his bitch of a cousin and teach the Berellians and Tenochs a lesson, all in one. Thanks to Merren's attempts to get the people north, perhaps a third of the entire country was crammed into the capital. He could use them to turn the tables on Markuz and Onzalez, who had promised him help but had tricked him and were going to take his country. If he played this carefully, he would finish as ruler not just of Norstalos but of Berellia as well. Inside that city were thousands of men scared for the lives of their families. With a few threats and a little cunning, he could use them to destroy the Berellians and Tenochs, one at a time. Markuz and Onzalez thought he was just a puppet, a fool who was in their pocket. The last thing they would expect was for him to attack them suddenly.

This would go down in history as his greatest moment, the time when he turned defeat into stunning triumph. He could feel it. Mother had even looked impressed when he told her.

'But where are the Derthals? I thought Sacrax said ...' Martil began.

'They stopped to save a group of children,' Merren said tiredly. 'They are bringing them but it has slowed their advance. We can't even guess where they are because Father Quiller's last horse went lame, and he ordered them to go on without him. He is following as best he can, but thinks he is days away. As for the Derthals, he can only hazard a guess. They may arrive late tomorrow, they may arrive the day after.'

Martil did not know what to say. By late tomorrow the capital would be surrounded and the Derthals would never be able to reach them. He shook his head, barely able to believe it. 'I am sorry. This is my fault. The Derthals were my idea …'

'An idea I agreed to. No, it is my failure. I am the Queen. And I have doomed us all,' she groaned. 'The people hate me for it — I know they do!'

Martil was about to lean over and take her into his arms when a shout made him stop.

'Your majesty! Gello is riding forwards under a flag of truce!' a guard on the main gate shouted.

Merren looked into Martil's eyes for a long moment, and sighed.

'Then we need to go and meet him,' she said.

'We need to go and kill him. That will put an end to this,' Sendric declared.

Merren shook her head. 'It would do no good. Gello is not the real power now, the Fearpriests are. Even with him dead, they will still attack.'

'So we just ride out and talk to him?' Conal growled.

'Yes,' Merren agreed. 'He is still Norstaline. If nothing else, I have to persuade him to guarantee the safety of these people.'

Gello waited, little more than a bowshot from the walls, with a hand-picked squad of men behind him, as well as Feld, Prent and several flag bearers. Excitement was bubbling inside him.

Then the gates opened and Merren rode out, flanked by Martil and a squad of what looked like men from every regiment she had, from Rallorans to rangers.

'We could end this now, kill them all,' Prent said eagerly.

'No! I want my cousin to destroy everything she has created by ordering the people to fight for me. I want her to watch as the country truly becomes mine, as my power is ultimate. She shall watch as every peasant she has promoted to power is put to death and then, finally, she will join them.'

Prent chuckled softly. 'As you command, sire,' he said.

Merren did not know how she would feel upon seeing her cousin again. This was the man who had abused and killed her friends, allied himself with Berellians and Tenochs and sworn himself to Zorva. The pain and suffering he had inflicted on her country was immeasurable. Yet she had to somehow persuade him to guarantee the safety of the people. She had no idea how.

'My dear cousin! What a pleasure to see you,' Gello called, then paused before adding: 'Like this!'

Merren controlled herself with the greatest of difficulty.

'Gello. What do you want?' she said flatly.

'Cousin! Why so rude? You should be nicer, when you realise that I have come to offer you everything you want,' Gello said expansively.

Merren stared at him coldly. 'If you plan to torment us, then we shall go now,' she told him.

Gello sighed theatrically. 'And miss my offer? Miss hearing how I plan to save this country from the Berellians and Tenochs?'

'Those would be the same Berellians and Tenochs that you allied yourself with, the ones you have led into Norstalos and encouraged to rape, burn and kill?' Merren asked sarcastically. Despite all the lives depending on her, she would not be made sport of by her cousin.

Gello's smile vanished. 'All right. No more games,' he agreed. 'The Berellians and Tenochs are not my allies. They have their own agenda. But they think me under their thumb. Here is my offer. My men to join with your Norstaline divisions. We are outnumbered but if we strike before the Berellians and Tenochs come together, we can crush them separately. Arm as many men in the city as you can, and Norstalos will be victorious! The people will be safe, they can return to their homes and will be able to live in peace once more. Look there — scores of loyal Norstalines who did not believe your stories about me, and who are safe and unharmed — and happy to be under my rule once more.'

'And why would you help us?' Merren asked. There had to be a price.

'Simple. The Berellians plan to betray me. They were the ones who summoned the Tenochs from across the sea. I want to get my betrayal in first. By helping me, you save yourselves. For the Berellians will not be as merciful as I.'

'And what do you want from this?' Merren asked cautiously. She could see the possibilities in what he said. Between the men she had, the men she could arm in the city and Gello's soldiers, they would have enough to crush one of the armies facing them. The second would then be forced to retreat, and could be destroyed on the way.

'I shall be King. You and your officers will surrender to me. And that is not just your army officers but militia officers as well. All the town and village councils you have created will be disbanded, all power will rest with me. And this must be done before we join forces. Sad to say, but I am afraid I do not trust you to hold to an agreement after the Tenochs are destroyed.'

'And what happens to the officers and their families?' Merren demanded.

'They will be imprisoned for a while. Perhaps a couple of years of working in the mines. I know you liked to impose that on my men ...'

'And what about me and my Rallorans? You said you only wanted to ally yourself with the Norstaline divisions?' Martil asked harshly.

Gello shrugged. 'You see my problem. I cannot have hundreds of veteran warriors who hate me and only serve my cousin loose in my country. While we are surprising the Tenochs, you shall lead your men out to face the Berellians. Destroying you is all King Markuz thinks about. He will not help his allies when he can see a thousand Butchers of Bellic ahead of him. And, by the time he kills you all, there will be far fewer Berellians for us to worry about. I would be disappointed if you did not take three times your number with you. But you can die knowing that you are helping to preserve Norstalos.'

'Preserving it for you and your tame Fearpriest,' Martil retorted.

'I only seek to introduce freedom of religion. For too long the people of this country have been forced to worship Aroaril. I only want to give them a choice. Worshipping Zorva will not be compulsory.' Gello smiled.

'Leaving aside the truth of that, apart from the death of Martil and his men, what happens to me?' Merren asked.

Gello grinned. 'My dear cousin. We both know the penalty for treason. There will be a short trial, then you will be executed.'

'I've heard enough of this. If you think we are going to agree to —' Martil began hotly, but Merren touched him on the arm, and he subsided.

'How about a counter-offer,' Merren suggested. 'Whatever else you might be, you are a son of Norstalos. Our forefathers devoted their lives to this country. So I ask you now, put aside what has gone before. Forgive and forget, and I will also. Join your men with mine and together we shall defeat the Berellians and Tenochs. You shall be restored to your duchy, with full powers and titles and together we shall rebuild this country. You can never take the throne but if the Dragon Sword prefers your son to mine, your descendants can be crowned. A full pardon and full restitution to every man who is with you. This is your chance to show you are a good man. Join us and history will forever remember you as the man who saved Norstalos!'

Gello looked at her carefully. He could feel the lure of her words — the man who had the power in his grasp and gave it up to save his country. He could almost hear the sagas being sung across the land. He saw that vision — and threw it away. He had not sworn his soul to Zorva for nothing. Why give up certain victory for uncertain peace? And do what? Sit in his ducal home and listen to peasants? Never command an army? Live always with the thought the Dragon Sword had refused him the right to the throne? Let down his mother, after all she had done to see him as ruler? Thoughts of his mother prompted the image of her final moments, as she fought for her life against him, and he shook that away from him, like a dog trying to rid itself of water.

'No!' he cried. 'It is me who holds the power here. You cannot tell me what to do! Accept my offer or die at the hands of my allies!'

Merren took a deep breath. For a moment there, she'd thought he might have agreed. But she had another offer ready. She did not want to say it but she had to. *Grasp the nettle*, she thought.

'I cannot accept seeing my men die. Here are my conditions. The Rallorans lay down their arms and armour and walk away. My officers also: they can take their families and leave the country, never to return to Norstalos.'

'And let you go with them? I think not. I would see you back here at the head of an army of Ralloran mercenaries within a year and Norstalos would be back where it is now.' Gello shook his head.

Merren stared at him. Inside she was cold, calm. It was all so clear to her. The people had depended on her. She had failed them. Many of them blamed her, rightly, for their losses. But there was one way she could save them, one way to make amends for all. 'I would not go with them. There would be no possibility of me finding an army and returning if I agree to stand trial, and be executed,' she stated.

'No! It cannot be!' Martil cried. 'I won't let you —' but Merren turned on him.

'Captain Martil! One more interruption from you and you shall be dismissed from my service. You swore to obey my orders: obey them now.'

If Martil had sworn on anything but Karia's life, he would have broken his oath right then and there. As it was, it took every ounce of his self-control to say nothing. The only thing he clung to was the thought she was tricking Gello. She had always had a plan until now, surely she had something up her sleeve.

Merren knew Gello was not going to let her escape a second time. She should have been afraid; should have been thinking about the child she carried. Instead she was thinking about the thousands of people who waited back in the city. Terrified people, who wanted to see their children grow up in safety. If she was going to die anyway, she might as well do so in a good cause.

'So what say you, cousin? You need us as much as we need you. We fight together to defeat the Berellians and Tenochs, then the Rallorans and my officers walk away from Norstalos and you get the country upon my death. Do you accept those conditions?'

Gello scowled as he thought furiously. Was she trying to trick him? 'But will your men obey my officers and me? They turned on me during the battle of Pilleth,' he pointed out, to give himself time to think.

'They will fight against the Berellians and Tenochs,' Merren said coolly.

'I want more. I want them to swear allegiance to me,' he pressed. 'I must have that guarantee before we seal this agreement.'

Merren sighed. 'I will need time to speak to them. I cannot order men to swear allegiance. I shall have to ask them.'

'You have two turns of the hourglass. If you want to save the country, you had better be back with your answer by then,' he warned.

'Agreed.' Merren nodded.

The two groups turned their horses and began to ride away.

'Sire, are you going to let the Rallorans just walk away?' Prent hissed.

'Of course not! Once they have laid down their weapons they shall be at our mercy!'

'Brilliant, sire!'

Gello smiled. 'I shall be left ruler of two countries, not one! And to think my idiot cousin wanted me to give that up, in exchange for a few lines in a saga!'

'Merren, if you think I am going to sit back and let —' Martil began hotly, but she waved him to silence.

'I have a plan. We shall talk about it once we are back at the palace,' Merren murmured.

Martil felt the tension leave his shoulders. She had a plan. Everything was going to be all right.

Merren watched him carefully, and breathed a sigh of relief he had believed her. She had no plan, beyond the one she had already put to Gello. Of course it was bitter almost beyond belief to think what Gello would do to the country. He would stop voting for town councils, stop the bards singing the truth, stop any hope of peace. He would build up the army once more, go back to his plan of taking over the continent. Then there was the Fearpriest with him. The source of their power was blood sacrifice — and the more they killed, the more they wanted to kill.

She did not want to see any of that. She knew this was a poor outcome for her people and her country. But it was better than their deaths. Her sacrifice would give them their lives and end their anger against her in one stroke. And also, when she was gone, all the mutterers and merchants of doom would realise how good life under her rule had been and those who had wanted Gello back would regret their words.

Brother Onzalez could feel something was wrong. Everything was going to plan — the Aroaril-lovers were at his mercy. All that remained was the final assault, and he would be the ruler of two countries. He would let Markuz and Gello sit on the thrones, as his puppets, but he would be the true power.

But still, something niggled at him, a sense of events happening beyond his control.

'Bring me a horse and get the commander of the cavalry. I want to see what is happening at the Norstaline capital,' he ordered Markuz.

'But Brother, we shall be there by nightfall as it is,' Markuz pointed out.

'I need to be there now,' Onzalez declared.

Merren rode straight to the palace, where she knew everyone was waiting to hear what Gello had said. As she rode through the streets, some waved and cheered at her — but many just stared, obviously wondering what would happen to them. She felt the weight of their silent accusations.

As soon as she was back at the palace, she turned to Jaret and Wilsen. 'I want Romon and every bard in the capital here, now!' she ordered and, when they hurried to obey, she strode up to the throne room, trying to get there before Martil asked any questions. But he was too quick.

'Merren, what is your plan?' he asked, catching her arm, so she had to face him.

'I don't have one,' she admitted. 'I shall put Gello's offer to the people. They are angry with me anyway, many are saying Gello should have stayed. But if I can buy their lives with mine, then I have done my duty.'

'No!' he cried.

'Yes,' she told him, holding his face in her hands.

'I can't let you do this! I can't live with myself knowing that you died for me, that you and our child were killed by Gello!'

'Karia,' she said. 'You have to live for Karia. You cannot leave her.'

'But you, the baby ...' Martil grabbed her in his arms. 'I can't let you do it!'

'Pilleth,' she told him gently. 'You were ready to sacrifice yourself to save me and everyone else. How can you do the heroic, noble thing and forbid me to do the same?'

'That's different ...' he argued.

She pulled his face down to hers and kissed him, hard. 'No, it's not.'

Inside it felt like she was tearing in two. She was dooming herself and her child. But it was the only way to make it up to the people after bringing them to this point. The ruler bore the ultimate responsibility for what happened to their country. That was what she had been taught and what she believed.

'How can I go on without you?' he protested.

'By living a good life. By looking after Karia. There were never any guarantees we would be together anyway.'

'No. We were meant to be,' he told her, holding her close. He could not let her go, would not let her go. There was no way he would let her die for him.

She kissed him back, then forced herself to break away.

He stepped forwards and reached for her again, but she slapped him across the face, lightly.

'Don't make this even harder than it is. I don't know if I have the courage to go through with it anyway,' she said softly, trying to hold back the tears she could feel fighting to spill out.

'Don't do this! Please, I love you,' Martil appealed desperately.

'And I love you,' she admitted. 'But love is not enough to stop me. I have to be a queen first.' She wiped her eyes on her sleeve. 'We have to go and tell the others, and put Gello's offer to the people. If you truly love me, then you will follow me now.'

Martil groaned, feeling torn apart by what she was asking.

'If you love me, do this for me,' she said softly, kissing him once more. Inside, she was at war. Everything her father had told her, everything she had learned about the throne, said this was the right course of action. But she wanted to live! She wanted to see her child, wanted to be with Martil …

'Now! We have to go now!' she almost shouted, as much at herself as at him.

Everyone sat, stunned, when she had finished outlining Gello's offer.

'We cannot trust him. He has betrayed his country, now he is ready to betray his allies! He has no honour,' Barrett said immediately.

'Barrett is right,' Martil agreed, amazed he could say that.

'I will never live under Gello. Never! After what he did to my daughter, I shall not rest until he is dead!' Sendric vowed.

'I will never live under Gello,' Kettering agreed harshly. 'I would rather die.'

Others around the table nodded in agreement.

'Does he intend to banish Bishop Milly, myself and the rest of the priesthood that is loyal to Aroaril? You cannot have worship of Aroaril and Zorva side by side in the one country. One or the other must triumph,' Nott warned.

'Nevertheless, we must ask the men if they will swear loyalty to Gello. They shall make the decision, once they know everyone's lives depend on it,' Merren said heavily.

'And he will let us walk away?' Kay said doubtfully. 'After what happened at Pilleth?'

'He needs our soldiers to defeat the Berellians and Tenochs. He does not have enough men to fight a battle and betray us by attacking you,' Merren said with a confidence she did not entirely feel.

'There has to be more to it than this. I cannot believe he will let us all just walk away,' Sendric said.

'You are correct,' Merren agreed. 'The final condition is I must die so you can live.'

'No!' Barrett gasped.

'We shall all live in shame, if we let the Queen die to save our own necks.' Conal thumped the table with his one fist. 'Better to die ourselves!'

It took all her years of training for Merren not to lose control as they shouted agreement.

'Stop! Enough!' she forced herself to cry, and they finally fell silent.

'I know what you are saying but you all swore to obey me. I will hold you to those oaths. It was my choices that brought us to this point. It is up to me to save as many of those people out there as I can.'

'What about the Derthals? We could send birds north, see where they are,' Martil interjected. 'There might be time for them to arrive before the Berellians and Tenochs get here!'

'I have been trying to send them — but the Berellian wizards have been blocking us. They have hundreds of birds of prey circling around us — I cannot get anything through,' Barrett admitted.

'What about the dragon? A few eagles aren't going to bother a bloody great dragon!' Conal snorted.

'We cannot send the dragon. Havell and Argurium refuse to leave Martil's side with our enemies so close,' Merren sighed.

'And I am not leaving Merren,' Martil growled.

'Archbishop Nott — what can you tell us?' Sendric turned to their last hope.

Nott shrugged. 'The last communication I had from Father Quiller was they were forty miles north of here. They would have to run through the day and night to get here, not stopping to sleep or eat. No man could do that. Surely Derthals could not either. They will not arrive before late tomorrow, at the earliest.'

'Has Aroaril told you what to do, can you offer us any guidance?' Martil begged.

Nott shook his head sadly. 'I must face the Fearpriest. One of us must die. Beyond that I cannot say.'

'We can send riders,' Merren offered. 'But meanwhile, Romon, I want you and the bards to put Gello's offer to the soldiers. We only have two turns of the hourglass. If we are to do this, it must be done before any Berellians or Tenochs reach the capital. And I cannot talk about it any more. Everyone seems to accept it when a man is prepared to sacrifice himself to save others. The sagas are full of such stories. This is no different. I know what the people are saying, what the results of the surveys have said, that they think Gello should never have left. I have to do this for them. For now, I need to be alone.'

She stood and walked out, keeping her face impassive until she was safely out of the throne room. *I don't want to do this, but I have to. Why can't they see that? Why are they making it even more painful for me?*

'We cannot let this happen,' Martil said, as everyone sat in silence.

'It's a shame Lahra isn't still around — perhaps we could have swapped her for Merren and fooled Gello that way,' Conal tried to joke.

Martil looked at him. At another time he might have appreciated the gesture but he was in no mood for jokes. He would not let Merren die.

'I shall send birds. As many as I can find,' Barrett vowed. 'We shall redouble our efforts, send so many that they cannot stop them all.'

'Well, I know this: I shall save Merren, no matter what. She thinks the people do not want her — well, we must show her they would rather die with heads held high than live in shame! The rest of us need to get out there, speak to everyone we can. She thinks everyone blames her for what has happened. We must show her what she means to the people!' Martil stood. 'If this Sword has any magic in it at all, not one person in this city will want to be a part of Gello's treachery!'

Merren lay on her bed, trying not to think, trying to relax. She had shut the curtains, hoping this would shut out what awaited her. If she thought about death, about the child she was also condemning, she was afraid she would not go through with it. Asking Gello for her child's life was also pointless. Her son would be the rightful heir to the throne and a deadly rival to Gello. Even promising that he would be raised in secret, told nothing of his birthright, would not be enough to save his life. No, they both had to die. There was no other way. The burden of all the other lives on her shoulders was too much. At least then she would be free, at peace.

The problem was, as much as she told herself that, she was still afraid, and sick to the stomach.

A knock on the door made her sit up, heart pounding.

'My Queen, may I come in?' she heard Martil call.

More than anything, she wanted to feel his arms around her. She was afraid that if she let him inside her bedroom, she would not be able to control herself.

'Merren, I have a message from the people.' Martil tapped on the door.

Reluctantly, she got to her feet and opened the door. Martil stood at the front, with Karia, Barrett, Sendric, Conal, Louise, Gia and Archbishop Nott.

'What is it?' she asked, her heart pounding.

'I have to show you,' he stated, walking into her room and across to the wide windows.

'What is it? Tell me!' she demanded.

Martil ignored her, instead signalling to Barrett and Conal. The three of them pulled back the curtains.

'Out here, my Queen.' He held out his hand, while opening the door onto her balcony.

Almost in a daze, she took his hand and followed him out onto the balcony.

And gasped.

Thousands upon thousands of people were packed into the square below. More still packed the streets leading to the square. Children were carried on parents' shoulders, people sat in the trees, stood shoulder to shoulder, filled the windows of every building that looked onto the square. More than the population of the capital, it seemed like every Norstaline was there, standing, waiting, in silence.

'Barrett?' Martil said softly, and the wizard nodded.

'Do you want Gello as your ruler?' Martil shouted, his voice magically echoing out across the silent square.

'No!' The answering roar shook the windows.

'Who do you want?'

'The Queen!' Their bellow would have startled every bird in the capital, if Barrett, Karia and the other wizards had not sent them north to look for the Derthals.

'Mer-ren! Mer-ren!' The chant began at the back of the square, spread rapidly and then boomed across the city.

'My Queen, you have your answer,' Martil said into her ear.

Merren just stared down at them, tears trickling down her cheeks. She vividly remembered how she had felt, during those dark days when she had been a prisoner of Gello's in this palace. Many was the time when she had stepped onto a balcony and looked across the square, hoping to see some sign of protest, some indication that the people missed her rule.

More recently, she had read the reports that said people were muttering about how good life had been under Gello — and had felt sick.

This made up for all those times — and more.

Relief swamped her as well. She would not have to die to save them. But then pragmatism raised its head. This was only a temporary respite for her, for all of them.

'What will happen to them? Do they truly know what they have just spurned?' she asked.

'They know. And whatever happens, we shall all face it together.'

She wiped her face. 'Then let us tell my cousin that.'

'What is that noise?' Gello asked as he sat in the shade of his tent, enjoying a glass of wine. It had not been properly cooled but it was a fine vintage. Besides, he had to have something to toast his triumph. Merren's followers would agree to his plan and he would become the ruler of the two most powerful countries in one stroke — and get to enjoy his revenge at the same time. It was a heady thought. But as he tried to explain this to Mother, he kept getting disturbed by some sort of noise coming from outside. He ordered Feld to find out what it was.

The captain was gone for a short while before he returned, looking concerned. 'I think they are chanting the name of your cousin, sire,' he said nervously.

'What?' Wine forgotten, Gello rushed out to listen for himself.

'Mer-ren! Mer-ren!' The noise could be heard clearly even at Gello's camp, half a mile from the city. The chant did not stop, just kept echoing across the grasslands. He was amazed he had not recognised it earlier. Then it changed: 'Down with Gello!' 'Kill the traitor!'

'What does it mean, sire?' Feld asked.

'It means,' Gello said bitterly, 'that my bitch of a cousin would rather see this country ruled by Berellians than by me. Well, she's going to pay! They're all going to pay for this!'

'And what of the Berellians and Tenochs sire? How shall we defeat them now?' Feld asked, aghast.

Gello looked back at the camp. 'Merren obviously has the people ready to fight for her. They will be destroyed, but they'll take plenty of us with them, if we let them. So we need to stay back during the fighting. The Tenochs and Berellians must do the dying — the more the better. We'll tell them cavalry is no good for attacking walls.'

'So it will be an assault, sire? We won't try to starve them out?'

'I doubt that. The city has those underground

springs. And they have enough wizards to keep the people alive by growing food. Besides, how will we feed more than twenty-five thousand men? It has to be quick.'

'Sire! There's a group coming from the city!' Feld pointed.

Sure enough, the gates were open and a much bigger group was riding out this time, albeit under a flag of truce.

'Get my horse. I'm going to remind that bitch of what she will face,' Gello ordered.

But before his horse and a squad of men could be brought up, another cry came from the camp.

'What is it now?' Gello asked impatiently.

'Berellian cavalry, sire, with Brother Onzalez!' Feld pointed.

Gello felt a flicker of fear. Did the Fearpriest know what he had been planning to do? His scouts had said the Berellians army would not arrive here until the next day!

'Do you think he knows?' he hissed to Prent, who had left the tent and joined him.

'I cannot say, sire,' Prent said carefully. 'But I would suggest acting as if nothing has happened.'

Gello nodded. 'We must meet him first. Otherwise my bitch of a cousin will start blurting out details of my plan in an attempt to drive a wedge between me and my allies.'

But Onzalez ignored the riders Gello sent over, instead bringing a squadron of Berellians across to where Merren sat under a flag of truce, surrounded by two full companies, while hundreds of archers on the walls behind her had arrows on their strings.

Gello cursed, gnawing nervously at his lip. *What would Mother have done in this situation*, he thought. *Just lie. Pretend it never happened.*

The three groups drew close together, then rode forwards slowly, until they were only a few yards away.

'Who is the Fearpriest, Gello? Did you not think one was enough?' Merren called.

Gello smiled wolfishly at her. 'This is Brother Onzalez. The man who wants the privilege of sacrificing you to Zorva. He will be the last sight you will ever see.'

Merren ignored most of Gello's words, instead studying the Fearpriest. He sat astride his horse quietly enough but there was a brooding menace about him. Not being able to see his face was both infuriating and a little frightening.

'Have you come to surrender, and agree to convert to Zorva, as I ordered?' Gello shouted loudly, half an eye on Onzalez.

Merren looked at them both. 'Do you mean your offer to give up my life in exchange for helping you betray the Berellians and destroy your allies?'

But Gello had expected this and his laugh did not sound forced.

'A nice try. But I am afraid Brother Onzalez can tell when someone is lying — and your clumsy attempt to break our alliance is doomed to failure.'

'No, it is you who is doomed. Not one person in this city wants you as their King. They will resist you to their last breath!' Merren told him.

'You fool! You don't know what you are facing,' Gello threatened. 'We shall utterly destroy this city and all who shelter inside it, so that every other person in this country will immediately surrender to us. You will all die, down to the last child. The last breath is all they shall get!'

'I have nothing more to say to you, monster. Farewell.' Merren turned her horse away. The silence of the Fearpriest was unnerving; the unspoken menace that he presented made the hair stand up on the back of her neck. She had brought Martil, Barrett and Sendric, but she wished she had Father Nott with her, although he was back in the city, looking after Karia.

Gello watched her go and licked his dry lips. He took a deep breath and urged his horse over to where Onzalez sat silently.

'You should have learned the lessons of Markuz,' Onzalez said suddenly.

'Sorry, Brother?' Gello stopped short.

'Markuz thought the Ralloran War was over after the battle of Meads. The Rallorans were broken, at his mercy. Rallora was his for the taking. Only it was not just his — he had promised the Avish half of the country, in exchange for their help in destroying the Rallorans. But Markuz wanted more. So he turned on the Avish, thinking a surprise attack would deliver him two countries, not one. But the Avish did not give in and Markuz found himself fighting on two fronts, unable to both defeat the Avish and crush the last Ralloran resistance. The Rallorans had the time and space they needed to regroup under men such as Captain Martil and, well, you know the rest. A valuable lesson for uncertain allies.'

'Indeed,' Gello agreed, feeling sweat start out along his scalp. The bastard knew what he had been planning!

'A lesson you need to absorb. Otherwise it could prove a fatal mistake. Your words to Queen Merren were strong. They were good. But words need to be backed up by action. The Norstalines are defiant — they need to learn fear. Together we shall teach them to dread what is coming, so it leaches away their ability to fight. Do that and I will see you as my trusted ally, worthy of ruling here.'

'I am to be trusted! I will do whatever you ask!' Gello promised, feeling the sweat trickling down his back.

'Excellent. My men will prepare the demonstration. Bring those Norstalines that you captured on the way here.'

'But they're not captives, they are ...' Gello began, only to trail off. He had liked having the townsfolk with him, liked having them say he was their rightful King. But they were unimportant compared to his own skin and his ambition. If they had to be sacrificed, so be it.

12

Merren kept her back straight and her head high until they were back inside the gate. But when she found the streets lined with cheering people, she could not let herself relax, even then.

'They are all going to die. And I couldn't save them,' she murmured. 'I had hoped Gello might see reason and at least spare the children.'

'We cannot give up. Conal and Hutter have got men going through the town now, finding every man who can hold a weapon — and every weapon that a man might hold. We still have Barrett and his wizards. And they still have to get over the walls or through the gates,' Martil told her.

'I'm afraid you taught me too well, Captain,' she sighed. 'We can defend against one attack — they'll send four. And they have Fearpriests, who can bring down walls and gates with a touch.'

Martil was silent for a moment. 'Yes,' he admitted. 'But we will make them shudder whenever they remember us.'

'I had hoped for rather more than that,' she said wryly. She was about to tell him to find Karia and spend what little time they had left together. Then she looked at him. Why should she worry about propriety, about Sendric's pride, about rumours of an illegitimate prince, when they were all going to die tomorrow? Why shouldn't she, Martil and Karia spend their last night together? A shout from the walls made her turn.

'The Fearpriest! My Queen, you have to see this!'

She looked up to see Captain Kay waving down at her.

'Come on,' Merren said grimly.

Everyone else in the street had also heard Kay's shout, so by the time Merren and the others reached the top of the wall, hundreds of people were lined along the battlement, although they moved aside to give Merren room, and an uninterrupted sight of what was going on below.

She wished they had stayed where they were.

The Norstalines who had left their homes in the east to follow Gello, dozens of them, were being hauled over to where the Fearpriest Onzalez stood, Prent by his side, just out of bowshot. They tried to fight, they tried to struggle but, with four Berellian soldiers to each Norstaline, they stood no chance. Their screams and pleas echoed across the silent city.

On one side a chunk had been sawn off a fallen tree to make a short, wide stump. As the city watched in horror, a man was stripped and dragged face-upwards across this stump, men holding his arms and legs, bending him over backwards so he was helpless, the tree stump pushing into the small of his back.

Then, as Prent chanted behind him, Onzalez stepped forwards, knife in hand. He plunged the strange black blade home then sliced across, carving a wide arc just below the upthrust ribcage and giving him access to the chest cavity. One more circular cut inside then Onzalez reached in and, with a well-practised movement, tore free the bloody heart. This was raised high by a triumphant, dripping Onzalez, who stalked up and down in front of the walls, ignoring both the screams and pleas of the remaining captives as well as the cries and bellows of anger from the walls.

Like a showman putting on a performance, Onzalez dropped the heart into a large fire, then turned to where a second man was being prepared. Knowing every eye was on him, Onzalez strode carefully across to where his Berellian guards had hung a man upside down from a crude wooden frame. Carefully, making sure those on the walls could see every gut-wrenching moment, he began to work on the man, whose blood-curdling screams had people on the city walls turning away, praying to Aroaril or simply vomiting.

Martil watched in horror as the Fearpriest swiftly skinned the man alive, leaving a shuddering, reddened wreck to howl in agony. But it did not stop there. With his rust-red robe stained a deeper colour, Onzalez turned his back to the city walls. Then, with help only from Prent, he disrobed. With a flourish he turned back, actually wearing the man's skin like some bloodied cloak, a dripping mask across his face. Carefully he paraded before them. He said nothing, but he did not need to. His silence was more frightening. The entire city watched him, horrified, as he pointed up at them, at all of them, then at the twitching remains of a man behind him. None could miss the message of what would be coming for them.

'Barrett, you have to stop him,' Merren managed to say past the gorge thick in her throat.

The wizard nodded grimly. 'I am a little weak after using so many birds,' he warned. 'But I can still handle this,' he said confidently, then pointed. The tree trunk altar burst into flame instantly, making the nearest Berellians leap away in shock. But, next moment, it was out.

'What happened?' Merren asked.

Barrett's mouth sagged open before he recovered, shutting it with an almost audible snap.

'Let's see how good you are,' he muttered, then closed his eyes.

The grass around the Fearpriests and Berellians sprang into growth then, just as quickly, died away again.

Barrett began to sweat, his breath sawing in his throat, but the only other evidence he was doing anything was a clenched fist. Nothing was happening beyond the walls, although the slaughter had stopped as the Fearpriest's attention was diverted.

'It's too much!' Barrett gasped. 'Each death provides power for that Fearpriest to use. I — I cannot match him!'

He unclenched his hand and leaned on the battlements, sucking in deep breaths. He looked up at Merren, and she was shocked to see doubt in his eyes.

'I am sorry, my Queen,' he groaned. 'I have failed you again. The birds, they took so much out of me …'

'No! It is not your fault. Rest, we shall need you tomorrow.' She patted him on the shoulder and looked for Bishop Milly.

'What can you do to stop this?' she asked.

Milly, whose face had gone white, shook her head.

'Their weakness is metal but they are not carrying any, they are using stone knives,' she said haltingly. 'And I would have to be out there to try something and, even then, there are two of them ... if they were too strong for Barrett ...'

'I'll order the men to assemble! If nothing else, we shall take that foul Fearpriest with us!' Martil turned away.

'No!' Merren caught his arm.

'What?'

'Look!'

She pointed out Gello's cavalry lined up to the left, ready to charge, while the Berellian cavalry, except for the company helping Onzalez to slaughter helpless Norstalines, was to the right.

'It's what they want. If we go out there the cavalry will destroy us,' she said thickly.

Martil stared in frustration, despair and horror. Down below Berellians were putting up a second frame, and a terrified woman was being dragged screaming towards it.

'So we just have to watch this?' he asked.

Merren turned to Barrett. 'Can you ensure I can be heard?' she asked him.

'Of course, my Queen,' he said weakly, although with a smile.

'We cannot help them. But we don't have to watch,' Merren shouted, her voice carrying clearly up and down the wall. 'If we go out there, the cavalry will tear us apart. It's what they want. They want us to be afraid. They want us to despair, to dread that will be our fate. Do not let them win! If we only have this last day, spend it with the ones you love. If you do not have loved ones, then go to the Palace Square — and find someone, even if it is only to talk to. Remember what the Fearpriests are doing outside tomorrow. But today we need to fight fear with love. It is the only way to beat them! Don't let them have this day!'

They stared at her then one, then a trickle, then a flood of people left the wall, heading for homes and loved ones, leaving behind the cries and the screams from the other side of the wall.

'That goes for all of us,' Merren told those around her. 'We should not spend this last day alone. Go! All of you! Don't look, don't listen to what is going on out there.'

In the bustle, she caught Martil's arm.

'See if Father Nott can look after Karia for a few turns of the hourglass,' she said softly. 'Then find me.'

Neither saw Sendric watching them, his face twisted in anger.

Kesbury shuddered when Milly finished describing what Onzalez and Prent were doing outside the walls.

'They were doing it to taunt us, to try and make us attack them — for their cavalry was ready. And that Fearpriest's power — Barrett was unable to match it. By the time all those poor people are dead, he will be more powerful still. No doubt he plans to use that to tear down walls or a gate tomorrow.' Milly sighed. 'To stand there and know we could do nothing ... it was the hardest thing I have done.'

Kesbury nodded. 'The Queen was right to order everyone away. Love is the only way to fight fear. And Aroaril knows, there is enough fear in this city. We should go down to the Palace Square, try and find some lost souls, and offer them someone to talk to, a reassurance that Aroaril will be waiting for them on the other side.'

'We can do that later,' Milly said, then leaned over and kissed him.

'But ...' Kesbury began.

'Don't ask questions,' she told him.

'I have never felt such power before. It was worse than the time when I tried to stop that storm.' Barrett sighed. 'At least then I could feel I was making some progress, could feel it weakening. Against this Fearpriest — it was like a child trying to push down the palace!'

'But you had been weakened by sending many birds,' Tiera pointed out.

'I know, but I should have still been able to do something. I'm the Queen's Magician! If I couldn't stop that Fearpriest, who will?'

'Do you have to keep talking at a time like this?' Tiera asked.

Barrett paused. 'No,' he agreed.

Conal cleared his throat. 'I know it is too soon. I know that you must still be grieving. And if we weren't probably all going to die tomorrow I would never dream of asking. But over the past weeks we have become friends and …'

'It is too soon. But today is all we have. So why not live it, while we can?' Louise agreed.

'Martil, I wonder if I might spend a few turns of the hourglass with Karia. After all, I don't know when I will get another chance,' Nott said gently.

Martil, who had not even had the chance to ask, simply nodded.

'I'll be back to put her to bed,' he said.

'No hurry. I don't think we need to bother about normal routines today.' Nott smiled sadly.

Sendric walked through the streets, ignoring those who offered him drinks, or food. The supplies, that had been so carefully hoarded to feed the people on their march north, were being eaten and drunk with abandon.

Every door in the city seemed to be open, every person seemed to be eating, drinking, laughing.

However, Sendric could feel the air of desperation. Everyone seemed to be trying too hard to have fun, the laughter was too often forced, as they tried to grab what they could from their last day and night.

He had no wish to join them.

His wife had been dead for many a year, his daughter a victim of Gello. He had one wish left, that he could be revenged on Gello. After that, he did not care what happened to him.

The frantic attempts to clutch at life that he could see all around him left him empty. Dignity was everything. He would no more sup in the gutters with drunken peasants than he would embrace Gello.

But he could not go to the palace. The thought that Merren was with a base-born Ralloran had him seething. How could he? How could she? The thought of besmirching the honour of the Norstaline Royal House was enough to make him want to vomit. Even with what faced them tomorrow, how could Merren debase the proud throne of Norstalos with a commoner? Sendric was well aware that past kings and princes had been happy to debase themselves with women from the lower classes but he could not see that as the same. Bitter thoughts such as these kept him moving through the streets, his grim face causing all but the most drunken to stay clear of him.

'Count Sendric!'

He turned at the call, to see a pair of familiar faces — the head of the Guild of Coopers, and his deputy.

'Count Sendric, we have compiled that report you asked us for — it makes ugly reading,' the Head Cooper announced. 'We have tallies from every guild and many a town council.'

Sendric had to think for a moment before remembering he had wanted a detailed picture of the economic disruption the invasion had caused. He sighed: such a thing was almost obscene at a time like this.

'If I may be so bold, we have a small gathering at our guild hall. Perhaps you could join us?'

Sendric was about to refuse, out of habit, but he had nothing better to do. At least it might stop him thinking about Merren and her Ralloran.

Besides, he knew from Merren's surveys that the business community hated the idea of a Ralloran Prince Consort almost as much as he did.

'Lead on,' he indicated. If nothing else, he could read their report.

'So you're a captain in the Queen's army?'

Kettering laughed harshly. 'Only because the others are dead.'

'Don't listen to him! This is Killer Kettering, the man who turned the Battle of Pilleth and rescued hundreds from Cessor, led us all out safely after Rocus and Cropper were wounded,' Leigh announced. The three of them had been walking along the street when they had stumbled into a huge party that stretched from one side of the road to the other, adults and children eating and drinking.

Kettering shook his head at Leigh's words — he cared nothing for what people thought. Not any more. He had once tried to be liked — and failed miserably. Now he did what he wanted and let others judge him as they wished.

'And where are you all from?' Hawke asked.

'We're from villages down on the Berellian border. Why don't you come and join us? Everyone is a friend tonight.'

'Why not?' Leigh agreed. 'What's your name?'

'I'm Mabel, and these are my girls. Get some food for these brave soldiers.'

The girls disappeared into the crowd, while Leigh and Hawke allowed food and drink to be pressed into their hands. They moved into the crowd, leaving Kettering standing uncomfortably with Mabel.

'And where's your husband?' he asked, for want of something more intelligent.

Mabel's smile vanished. 'Dead. At the hands of the Berellians.'

'I am sorry,' Kettering said awkwardly. He had always had problems talking to women, always feeling self-conscious about his hair. Even now he could not stop himself from reaching up and checking it was tied tightly back from his face. He did not know what to say. Anger had helped him deal with men. But it was no use here.

'No need. Many have lost loved ones. But tonight is not about that. It is about enjoying what we have left.'

'I cannot enjoy this night,' Kettering said sadly. 'All I can think of is the bastards who ruined my life and now think they can get away with it. I want revenge, not just for me but for everyone.'

'I can understand revenge. But what about afterwards? The Berellians who killed my husband are dead — do I keep on hating their rulers, the ones who gave the orders? Or the Rallorans, who let him die for their own purposes, although that saved me and my girls?'

Kettering sighed. 'Anger, revenge — they are the only reasons I am alive. I will let them give me strength tomorrow. Aroaril grant they might save the likes of you and your children. I am sorry, Mabel, I am no fit company for a night like this. I shall go.'

'Wait!' Mabel grabbed his arm. 'No man should be alone on this last night of life.'

Kettering smiled sadly. 'But I am alone. I have always been alone. And this night is nothing special. The man I was died months ago. I shall merely join him tomorrow. Take care, Mabel.'

She watched him go, wondering how a man could live with such anger and pain. She almost started after him, but her children grabbed her hands, and she allowed herself to be dragged back into the celebrations.

'We should have done this earlier,' Merren admitted.

'I got here as fast as I could,' Martil mock-protested, then yelped as she twisted the hairs on his chest. 'That hurt!'

'You big baby! I've seen you cut open by spears, swords and axes and not even whimper!' She laughed. 'And you complain about a tiny chest hair!'

'Yes, but that hair was on a really big scar!' He grinned.

She rested her chin on his chest. 'Not hurting you, am I?' she asked with a smile.

'No, that's fine,' he admitted. 'Although I also wish we had done this earlier.'

'I know. But it wasn't possible. You know that as well as I. You knew from the beginning that I could not put myself before the people. While there were so many people in danger, I could not indulge myself.'

Martil did not think anything could puncture his mood. Inside this room, they were safe. It was like a cocoon, insulating them from the world outside. But that comment struck home. 'Indulge yourself? Merren, is that all I am?'

'That's not what I meant! It's just that we've argued about this before — we don't have the time to argue now and I don't want to waste what time we have left fighting.'

Martil ran his hand gently down her back.

'You'll get no argument from me on that,' he agreed. 'Although I thought you would want to spend the time planning a defence of the city? Hoping against hope that we can find a way to defeat our enemies?'

She sighed. 'After all we have been through in the past turns of the hourglass, on top of what has happened these past few weeks, my mind has had enough. Planning would be useless, for I cannot think straight.'

'Then you made the right choice to be here with me.' He grinned.

'Although it can lead to more problems,' she said wryly, running a hand over her still-flat belly.

'I can't tell. But I wouldn't care even if I could tell.'

She smiled. 'Thank you for what you did today with the people. Although it has doomed us ...'

'Gello would have betrayed us. I know it. And anyway, that Fearpriest turned up. We were not going to do a deal with Gello in front of him.'

'True, but I was going to say we can't really surrender to spare the people's lives now.'

'But would it save their lives? You saw what that Fearpriest did.'

Merren rolled over. 'I'd like to be able to give

244

our son a safe, peaceful country to rule,' she sighed, looking down at herself.

'I'd like to give him a chance at life. A future. Like to see him grow up, play with Karia.'

'Tell me a bedtime story. About the life we should have,' she invited.

Martil thought for a moment. 'Well, you should make me the Prince Consort. The people may not be over-fond of Rallorans but after we save them, they see me, as the Dragon Sword wielder, as the best choice for their beloved Queen. Our son becomes the Crown Prince and, when he comes of age, takes up the Dragon Sword and the throne, with you to offer a little advice. He appoints Karia as his Royal Magician and we can leave the country in their hands while we go and live on an estate somewhere, where you answer the odd scroll and my only duties are keeping you pleasured.'

She laughed. 'And I thought you 'hated sagas! By then I'll be old and grey and you'll need an apothecary's herbs to perform your duties!'

'You'll dismiss me in favour of some other young warrior.' He winked.

'Why only one? I'll need at least two!'

'So I'm worth two? That's some compliment, at least.'

She laughed, feeling as if the cares and worries of the throne were a thousand miles away. It was what she had tried to achieve with Louise and Gia but it was only around Martil she could put aside the Queen and just be Merren. Seemingly only he could see her as a woman first, a queen second. She kissed him. 'I don't want to talk about the future any more. All we have is now. So let us live in the now.'

'As you command, my Queen.'

The frenzied partying across the city slowly died down, as people fell into drunken stupors, or stumbled into bedrooms, or just fell asleep in the streets. Birds flying back from the north circled high above the city before flying down and waiting on the roof of Barrett's house. Scores of them. Then hundreds, until the roof itself seemed to be covered in a living carpet of birds. And still more arrived, filling the surrounding trees. But although there was a light on in one of the bedrooms, the shutters were locked tight and nobody came out. The birds waited.

Onzalez could feel the power coursing through his veins, finer than wine, stronger than any narcotic. The sacrifices had brought their usual reward. There was nothing to compare with it. He had power from his God, enough to do almost anything. The only thing to top it was what he'd felt as he'd stood before the walls, feeling the city's terror pulsing out. Fear and horror were effective weapons; they would leach the courage from the defenders. All would imagine themselves on those frames, under the cruel knives, and would hope for death instead. He planned to grant their wish.

Today he had defeated their magician, tomorrow he would bring down the city gates. After they had failed to best him today, he had no doubt they could not stop him tomorrow. This was his plan, the grand scheme he had worked on for the past ten years. And it was all coming to fruition. He had been a minor priest in Tenoch until he had seen that one continent was not enough for Zorva. That vision, which he knew had to have come from Zorva

Himself, had first propelled him into the highest ranks of the priesthood and then given him the opportunity to come here. He alone of his brethren had seen the possibilities of conquest beyond their own continent.

Back in Tenoch he sat on the Seventeen, the council of Fearpriests who ruled in Zorva's name. There had never been individual leaders there, not when every man was as ruthless and power-hungry as the next — until Onzalez had come along. The others were old men, most of them, happy to preserve the power they had, unwilling to take risks. First he had bent them to his will, then he had persuaded them to support his quest to bring new glory, new countries to Zorva. The Seventeen did what he wanted, had even sent him the Tenoch army when he asked for it.

Certainly there were those who hated him, who resented the purity of his vision and his fanatical dedication to converting the world by fire and blade. They supported him now but hoped he would stumble, give them the chance to wrest back the power. Once he returned home in triumph he could deal with them once and for all. And triumph was but a day away.

The thought was simply intoxicating. Onzalez could not wait for tomorrow. All his dreams would come true.

13

Merren yawned.

'How are you feeling this morning?' Martil reached out to her.

'Pretty good,' she admitted. 'My mind is working again, although we didn't get much sleep!'

'It's because you weren't worrying about everything,' he explained. 'See? We should have done this earlier.'

'Get away with you!' She laughed, pushing him back.

He kept going, and rolled out of bed.

'Where are you going?' she asked.

'I need to raid the kitchens for every sweet treat I can find before going to see Karia.' He stretched.

'I'll come too,' Merren offered. 'She has been begging for me to play with her — I might not get another chance. After all she has been saying to me during the dragon flights, I thought we should give her what she wants — act like a real family for a few turns of the hourglass, at least. It will be something for her, before the end. I never thought things would end this way. It always seems easier in the sagas.'

'This is real life. Not the sagas. Besides, they tend to have happy endings,' he offered.

'Yes, thanks for telling me this is real life and not a saga. Aroaril knows I wouldn't have realised it otherwise,' she mocked him gently.

'Anyway, it is not the final ending,' he pointed out.

'What do you mean?'

'The dragon, Argurium. She cannot let me die, I have to use the Dragon Sword on the Dragon Egg. And I shall not leave without you and Karia. At the very least, we three shall escape.'

Merren sat up in bed. 'I cannot leave the people to die!'

'I don't want to leave them either, but I don't think Argurium is going to be able to carry everyone to safety ...'

'Barrett!' Merren struck herself on the head.

Martil looked at her blankly.

'Barrett and his Magicians' Guild brought many of the people here by opening gateways through the trees. So they could send them away just as easily!' Merren cried.

'Well, not that easily. There's too many people,' Martil warned.

'But we could get many away! We just have to buy as much time as possible — time for the people to escape, time for the mages to recover from their exertions and try again,' Merren exclaimed. 'It is so obvious — why in Aroaril's name did I not think of that before?'

'Probably because you had me on your mind,' Martil said wryly.

Merren looked up at him. She had never imagined she could regret last night — but now she did. She had spent the night enjoying herself, when she could have been helping her people. How many might have escaped in the turns of the hourglass she had selfishly wasted? But she could not say that.

'We cannot waste time now, we have to get Barrett,' she decided, searching for clothes.

Martil began climbing into his.

'We'll make a token stand on the walls and then fall back to the park where the oak trees are. We need to protect them for as long as possible. And we have to send the families of the soldiers first. We will ask them to fight to the death. The least we can do is promise them their families will be safe.'

Merren paused. She could see his point. But she could also see this ending in disaster. Deciding who would go and live, and who would stay and die — it was going to be a nightmare. And the end, when the Berellians and Tenochs were pressing in, the last few soldiers trying to buy time for one more person to escape ... her mind rebelled at the thought. But she would not shy away from the responsibility. Time was slipping away and they should have begun yesterday.

'Agreed,' she said. 'I shall order the families of all soldiers to go to the city park to receive a gift from me. No sense in causing a panic and having thousands of extra people rushing to the park. We shall need a regiment of men to maintain order and ensure there is no crush or stampede as it is.'

'I'll go and find Barrett, get him to prepare,' Martil decided.

'And no attempts to make Argurium take me away from the city early! If I am leaving people here to die, they have to know I am risking my life with theirs.'

'Would I do that, my Queen?' Martil said.

'Yes. Now hurry!'

Martil smiled as he pulled on his tunic. She knew him. But the smile faded as he contemplated what lay ahead. While he was confident the dragon's magic would prove equal to the task of saving Merren and Karia, the thought of the men he had commanded all dying — from the Rallorans to the Norstalines he had worked with and trained — was too much. And as for Merren — he could see this coming back to haunt them both. She would blame herself for not saving the people.

He found Karia asleep in the bed, Nott in the chair beside her.

'Ready to breakfast and a ride on Tomon?' he asked softly, waking Karia gently.

'Dad!'

She was sleepy at first but soon warmed up as she worked her way through the various biscuits and cakes Martil had found in the kitchen.

'Save a couple for Archbishop Nott,' Martil suggested.

'I think we shall all need our strength today,' Nott agreed, standing with some difficulty. 'Chairs are never comfortable to sleep in, and even less so when you're as old as I.'

Martil rushed over to give him a helping hand. 'Thank you for looking after her last night,' he whispered.

'It was my pleasure. I wanted a last night with her,' Nott murmured.

Martil did not want to ask what Nott meant by that.

'I'm ready for that ride now,' Karia suggested, through a full mouth.

'Then let's go,' he said, forcing a smile.

The city was still sleeping after its big night as they rode towards Barrett's house. Some of the people were only now stumbling towards their beds, or were lying in doorways or in gutters. Martil had to guide Tomon around a few of them.

'What are all these people doing? Why are they sleeping in the street?' Karia wanted to know.

'They had a big party here last night,' Martil said.

'A party? Were you there? Why wasn't I invited?' Karia asked indignantly.

It was only when they rode into Barrett's property that she forgot all about the party she had missed.

'What are all these birds doing here?' she gasped.

Barrett was equally surprised when he came outside, although he took great care not to show it.

'They must have just arrived. I checked through the night,' he lied. In truth, he had been far too occupied to think about the birds. But he was not about to reveal something like that to Martil.

'Well, what have they seen?' Martil asked impatiently.

After a few moments, Barrett turned back with a sigh. 'The Derthals are still fifteen to twenty miles away. Their view is imprecise, because it was dark, but it is certainly no closer than that. They won't arrive until this evening, at the earliest.'

'And you are sure this information is only a turn or two of the hourglass old?' Martil asked sharply.

Barrett drew himself up. 'Listen, I have just about had enough of you questioning me,' he began.

Martil held up a weary hand. He needed the mage's help. 'All right. I just had to be sure.'

'Well, you can be!' Barrett answered defiantly. He was never going to admit he had been asleep on the job to this Ralloran oaf. 'What did you want, anyway?'

So Martil explained, quietly, while Karia played with the birds.

'You realise there will be a panic. It will be bloody work, at the end. People will be rushing to get to safety as the Berellians and Tenochs close in,' Barrett warned.

'It will be up to you to judge when to go,' Martil told him. 'My men and I will give you as much time as we can.'

Barrett nodded. 'I'll get the wizards ready and meet you in the park.'

'I'll bring you Kettering's regiment. The people will be happier having their own Norstaline soldiers telling them what to do. Having Rallorans hold them back from safety could just cause problems. Besides, Kettering can be relied on to be ruthless.' Martil picked up Karia. 'I'll see you later.'

Barrett watched him go, a nagging sense of unease eating at him. He had no idea when the birds had seen the Derthal advance. Perhaps he should send out more? He shook his head. He needed all his energy to get people away. Besides, even if they had arrived early in the night, the Derthals had to sleep as well, did they not? They would not arrive before nightfall. After all, the roads were solid mud, the surrounding ground little better. Men had been unable to manage better than a mile or two in a turn of the hourglass while returning to the city from the north.

As Barrett and Kay had feared, and Merren predicted, the park was soon chaos. The request for just the families of soldiers had seen long columns of people heading towards the park. Many others had not heard this was just for the families of soldiers, and came along to see what was going on. Some thought this was a continuation of the party, and staggered in hoping for more free drinks. Then some families of rangers, who had been told by Kay the real reason for going to the park, began telling friends that they would be taken to freedom.

This tale spread like wildfire through the city. When Sendric heard it, he immediately marched down to the park, flanked by scores of merchants and guild members, determined to see those he regarded as the most valuable members of Norstaline society make it to safety.

The sight of the Berellian and Tenoch armies marching towards the city, regiment after regiment appearing from the south and west, only speeded the process. Even those who had hoped their soldiers might be able to hold the walls of Norstalos City took one look at the massive armies and knew it was hopeless. Escape was the only way to survive.

Kettering met the crowds with a double line of men, who linked shields but kept their swords sheathed. They had been ordered not to threaten the people but would not have done so, anyway. Yet, while they tried to let only those they recognised through, they were being pushed back all the time — and some people were using back alleys and the like to slip past them and race towards where the wizards waited.

Martil ordered the men to stand firm, but was afraid people were going to get crushed against the armoured lines. He could see the men were also wavering. Many people in the crowd pressing against them were crying, holding up money to pay for safety, or holding up sobbing children, which was worse.

'Hold them! We need to keep this in order!' he snapped at Kettering.

'I'm doing what I can, sir!' Kettering fired back.

Martil glowered at him but left him to it. He was plainly doing everything he could.

Kettering stalked up and down the line of men.

'If you know them to be soldiers' families, let

them through! But slowly! We can't have a panic! Any man who does not hold his ground, by Aroaril I'll make him wish he had been stretched out over a Fearpriest's altar!' he bellowed at them.

It seemed to be working. The lines were not so bowed now, although the crying and begging had redoubled.

'Kettering! Kettering! Help us!'

He spun, to see Mabel holding up her crying children. He turned away instantly. He knew she was not married to a soldier. Then he stopped. He had lain awake last night, listening to the celebrations, thinking about her words and about his reply. He hesitated, then tapped the nearest men on the shoulder.

'Let those three through!'

The two men closest to them adjusted their shields for a moment, letting a shaken Mabel and her children through.

'Thank you! Thank you!' She hugged him and, after a delay, he awkwardly held her back.

'I'll never forget this,' she promised. 'How can I ever repay you?'

He did not know why he had let her through. There were scores of others who were pleading just as hard. But it was something the old Kettering would have done. He hoped it did not mean he was going to be too weak for the bloody work that the day would bring.

'Repay me? Live well. Teach your children not to live in fear,' he told her. 'Now go! Go with Aroaril.'

She stood on tiptoe and kissed him quickly on the lips. Stunned, he watched as she ran towards the trees, and the lines to safety. It was a long moment before he could turn back to his duty.

But there were so many others trying to get through; it was almost impossible to know who were really families of soldiers and who were lying to save themselves and their children.

And more were flooding down the streets every moment.

'We can't do this, sir!' Kettering warned Martil.

Martil agreed with Kettering's judgement, and raced Tomon over to where Merren, Barrett, Karia and Havell waited. The dragon Argurium sat nearby, watching sadly. Orderly lines of weeping women and children were waiting their turn to go through an oak tree, while a ring of soldiers was trying to keep back two score others who had got into the park through back ways.

'This is going to turn into a disaster! We need to use some magic or something!' Martil cried.

'How can we? If we use magic, it is power that we cannot use to rescue people!' Barrett protested.

'We have to do something — otherwise there won't be anyone getting away,' Merren told him.

Watching the crying, wailing mob was tearing at her heart. To say who was going to go, who was going to stay and die ... she had thought deciding who should be evacuated and who was not worth sending in soldiers to rescue was almost impossible but this was beyond belief. The thought she could have done this last night, had half of these people away safely, when instead she had wasted time with Martil, was ripping her apart. Yes, she had been tired, her mind unable to think clearly — but if she had not been focused on her own selfish pleasure then maybe she would have thought of this earlier.

'We shall have to form them into a queue and then send as many as we can. It is the only way,' Merren decided. 'Karia, you know how to make someone's voice really loud?'

Karia grinned, bouncing up and down. 'Of course!'

'Martil, I need your horse.'

Merren rode Tomon back to where the crowd of people was slowly, slowly pushing the soldiers back, and where she could see a furious Sendric arguing with a defiant Kettering.

Karia clung on to her, while Martil ran beside her. Her mind was racing. What could she say to cut through the panic? The noise was indescribable — soldiers shouting, men and women screaming, children crying.

'Silence! People, listen to me!'

Her magically enhanced voice cut through the noise but, while many people looked at her, others, especially those pressed up against the shields, just ignored her.

'My people, I beg you, please listen!'

She tried again, without much success. The sight of Sendric ignoring her, as he tried to haul aside a shield to push through the lines, was the last straw.

'Sendric? What are you doing?' she cried. 'We are trying to save the women and children!'

'I am trying to save your country for you!' he bellowed back. 'These men will feed and clothe the women and children!'

Merren was in no mood to have an argument at the top of her voice so, in frustration, turned Tomon away. She would have to stop appealing to reason.

'Who wants to die?' Merren thundered, her voice echoing off the buildings and ripping through the park.

That got their attention, the noise died away, although there were still many children wailing and crying. But, compared with the bedlam of a few moments ago, it was nothing.

'We shall get away as many as we can. First, let all the children come forwards. All children and mothers with babies!'

The mood of the crowd changed with that, people at the front stepping back to allow children to come forwards, although the noise rose again as men embraced wives, mothers hugged children, most knowing this would be their last embrace.

Merren had to lock her jaw to keep her emotions in check, seeing a thousand final goodbyes.

At an order from Martil, the lines of soldiers opened and stepped back, forming a funnel shape to allow the children to move through. Some did not want to go and clung to their parents, who were openly sobbing as they pushed their children towards safety. The ones at the front were shouting hopeful promises to see their children again but Merren, on Tomon, could see those further back, who knew they had no chance of making it through. Women and men clung to each other as their children, not understanding what was going on, sobbed and wailed. Parents, tears running down their faces, pushed their children away, knowing they would never see them again.

The crowds seemed to part and Merren's eye was caught by one particular scene. She watched in horror as a pair of boys, one about ten, the other a few years younger, sobbed as they embraced their parents, then the older pulled his crying younger brother towards the soldiers, while the father had to hold back the screaming mother, who finally collapsed completely, unable to watch her children walk away.

Merren took a deep breath, knowing she had to say something, but not knowing what could comfort them, or the hundreds like them. The knowledge this was her fault, this suffering was because she had put her happiness ahead of the country, had been selfish and spent time with Martil, was like a knife to the heart.

Then the trumpets sounded.

At first some people cried out, thinking the attack had begun, but the trumpets went on and on, a strange call Martil could not recognise.

'What?' Merren turned to Martil, who could only shrug.

Then, from the vantage point of Tomon, Merren saw Captain Kay galloping towards them, waving furiously and shouting something that was lost in the noise of the crowd.

'What?' Merren shouted, but was frustrated when an obviously excited Kay could not be heard in reply.

'Karia!'

Karia closed her eyes and pointed at Kay, who was trying to shout something.

'... Derthals! The Derthals are here! Thousands of them here to save us!' Kay's voice echoed across the park.

The effect on the crowd was almost like magic.

Two days, even a day ago, half the people would have run a mile to avoid a Derthal, the other half would have run a mile to spit at a Derthal. Now people were on their knees, thanking Aroaril, men were embracing each other, people were crying with relief, hugging each other, hugging soldiers.

Many were even rushing back towards the walls, eager to see their saviours.

Merren was stunned. Barrett had assured her it was impossible for the Derthals to be here before the evening. She leaned down to Martil, after making sure Karia had taken the power from her voice.

'They've come so far, so fast. Will they be ready to fight?' she whispered.

Martil paused. 'We shall have to speak to Sacrax,' he admitted. 'They might need a day to recover. But their arrival alone will give our enemies pause.'

She nodded. 'But we shall act as though they are ready to fight now. We must give the people hope. And if we do not fight until tomorrow, it will give us more time to get people away.'

'Agreed,' Martil turned to Karia. 'I need you to …'

'I know, I know,' she sighed, then patted him on the shoulder. 'You're just lucky you have me around to help you.'

Martil had to hold in his feelings as he turned to the disappearing crowd. He knew he would have to fight now, knew it would be worse than Sendric, worse than Pilleth. He clung to the thought that Argurium would save him if she had to, that Karia would not be left alone.

'All soldiers to the walls!'

14

Gello had been enjoying a leisurely breakfast with Mother's portrait, and anticipating an afternoon of entertainment. He was sure the Rallorans would fight like the cornered rats they were, and the close confines of the city would ensure the massive numerical advantage of the Berellians and Tenochs would mean nothing. Both would suffer terribly, he hoped, before victory.

But his appetite vanished when Feld burst into his tent.

'A relief force, sire! Ten thousand strong, approaching from the north!'

Gello had felt a moment's terror then. Once more he was in the throne room, once more he was at Pilleth, failing at the moment of his triumph.

Dropping his plate to the ground, he had rushed out with Feld, Livett and Heath. Where had this force come from? How could Merren have found and armed so many, so quickly?

Scouts had been hurriedly sent out, while riders from the Berellian army and runners from the Tenoch forces raced across to find out what was happening.

It had been a nervous wait, and Gello's fingernails were ragged by the time the scouts returned.

Mother had always told him not to bite his nails and he could feel her baleful stare but could not stop it.

'They're goblins sire! Goblins from the north!' the scouts reported.

Gello and his captains roared with relieved laughter.

'Goblins! We can scatter them like children! Our cavalry will go through them like a hot knife through butter!' Gello chuckled.

'Sire, Martil will surely know that. He has more than a thousand archers. What if he tries to tempt us into a wild charge, so he can destroy us?' Feld pointed out quietly.

Gello chewed on another nail. 'You are right,' he admitted. 'We must tell our allies our horses are not ready and we must fight on foot. Let Markuz use up his men on goblins and Rallorans.'

'Sire, surely they do not mean to face us in battle — isn't it more likely they will use the goblins on the walls?' Heath suggested.

Gello rubbed his chin. 'Allow goblins into the city? Surely not even my cousin would defile the capital by allowing such creatures inside the gate?'

'They are desperate, sire.'

Gello shuddered. 'The thought of goblins inside the capital. Inside my palace! We'll never get their stink out of the city. I cannot stand such an abomination! Besides, they must be exhausted after marching down here. We cannot give them time to rest. We must attack immediately, so they have no choice but to face us. Get my horse, I must speak to Markuz and Onzalez.'

The people were already delighted to see the Derthals but the final seal of approval came when they brought forward more than two score children, from babies to teenagers, the ones they had rescued. And the tale of how these youngsters had watched Norstalines walk past them for days before being saved by Derthals quickly spread across the city.

Martil had ordered food to be brought outside for the Derthals and the people rushed to obey. By the time he joined Merren and Barrett outside the city, High Chief Sacrax and many of his clan chiefs were eating and drinking.

People were packed onto the walls, pointing and waving at the Derthals, who stared back in astonishment, both at the warmth of the greeting and the size of the city. Sendric was the largest human settlement they had seen, and the capital dwarfed that provincial town.

'Sorry we are late.' Sacrax smiled. 'We had to stop to look after little ones — and then the priest's horses became too tired.'

'But you are here now, and Norstalos will not forget that you stood beside us in our time of need,' Merren declared loudly.

'How did you get here so fast? Will your warriors be able to fight?' Martil asked urgently.

Sacrax chuckled. 'Every warrior of mine can run fifty miles and still fight. We are just warm now.'

Martil found that hard to believe, but every Derthal did seem to be healthy enough. If a man had marched across forty miles of rough country in little more than a day, they would be exhausted, needing at least a day, and probably more, to recover. But the Derthals seemed able to laugh and joke; the faces did not look drawn or haggard and they did not drag their feet as they walked.

'Amazing! No man could have done that,' he marvelled.

'But we are not men. We are Derthals,' Sacrax said proudly.

'You are angels, sent from Aroaril,' Merren said fervently. Not having to decide which people lived and died had her almost giddy with relief. Her mistake in giving in to temptation and spending the night with Martil had not proved a fatal one for her people.

'So your people do not hate us any more?' Sacrax glanced up at the smiling faces lining the walls.

'It looks that way,' Merren agreed, trying not to think of Sendric, and others, who had remained back at the park.

'What is this army that has arrived?' Onzalez demanded.

'Goblins. The same army of goblins that you suggested attack the north of Norstalos. But, thanks to the failure of Ezok and Cezar, they are here to help our enemies,' Gello said harshly.

Onzalez seemed unmoved. 'That they are here shows the desperation of the Aroaril-lovers, allying themselves to creatures who are not even human. Goblins! Even to speak their name invites contempt.'

'Goblins, what are these creatures like?' Itlan asked. 'We have nothing like them in Tenoch.'

'Small, foul-smelling, backwards, deformed half-men,' Gello dismissed them. 'My ancestors drove them out of the north of our country easily. They are vicious and brutal but they lack warlike skills. One-on-one they are dangerous, but they will break upon shields like waves on a beach.'

'What will the Witch Queen do with them?' Markuz rumbled.

'Bring them into the city and fill the walls with them. It will make breaking into the city a great deal more difficult. But if we attack now, before they can get inside the safety of the city walls, we can crush them,' Gello said urgently.

'Attack now? Our men have only just arrived. We need the rest of the day to rest and eat,' Itlan said doubtfully.

'Perhaps a cavalry charge?' Markuz suggested. 'Your cavalry could shatter these goblins while they are pinned against the city walls.'

Gello made sure his horror did not show on his face.

'A good strategy, except that their archers will slaughter our horses before we can crush the goblins,' he said calmly. 'Besides, our horses have been tired by the march here. They are not ready for a charge.'

Onzalez turned his hooded face towards Gello, who fought to keep his face impassive.

'Then your men must fight on foot. We shall assemble immediately. The Berellians shall lead the way, followed by Gello's dismounted cavalry, and the Tenochs shall bring up the rear, for they have the least protection from the bows of the Aroaril-lovers.'

Gello raged inside the safety of his mind, for Onzalez was ensuring the men most loyal to him were best preserved in the coming battle. But there was no backing out now.

'At once, Brother.' He smiled.

'We shall be formed up within a turn of the hourglass. We shall destroy these goblins and then press on into the city. Once they see their desperate gamble has failed, the city will crack like an egg. Zorva is watching, my friends!' Onzalez announced. 'I shall go forwards with the Tenoch lines. There will be no mistakes this time!'

Martil was astonished by how much the Derthals could eat and drink. Dozens of people were bringing out casks of water and crates of food and it never seemed enough.

'When are they going to finish? We need to get them inside the walls,' he told Sacrax. 'Tomorrow we shall march out and attack but today your warriors can rest — and we can use the time to get our women and children to safety.'

The Derthal High Chief belched, then grinned. 'Many of my warriors have never tasted food like this. Soft bread. Sweet cakes. Strange meats. And we have all gone without food enough times to want to keep eating when there is plenty.'

'And perhaps the march south cost you more than you admit?' Martil suggested.

'That was a gentle stroll,' Sacrax protested with a smile. 'We are ready to fight now!'

'Well, you might be but I think the Queen wants to fight tomorrow, when she knows her people have been sent to safety.'

Sacrax grinned. 'I shall get them inside now then.'

Martil turned away, only to hear a call from the walls above.

'Captain! They're forming up for an attack!' Kay cried.

Martil raced inside and up the steps to the top of the wall, where a grim-faced Kay stood.

'They're coming straight for us. And they're coming now.' He pointed.

Breathing hard from the race up the stairs, Martil shaded his eyes, peered towards the Berellian camp — and felt his pounding heart beat even faster. More men than he had ever wanted to see were forming themselves into a shield wall, five hundred men wide. There were sixteen ranks of Berellians, another six of Gello's red-clad soldiers and thirty of the strange Tenochs. It was a massive sight, bigger than anything he had seen in the Ralloran Wars. The temptation to stay here was almost overpowering. But he knew what he had to do.

'Get the Queen, and every officer we have. We need to meet them outside,' he found himself saying.

'Go out and meet them, sir?' Kay asked, appalled.

Martil could appreciate the feeling. After all, here they were on a tall wall, behind solid stone embrasures, where the bows of Kay's men could cause havoc among their enemies. But there was no way ten thousand Derthals could get through the gates into the safety of the city before the attack arrived. And the lack of siege equipment told him that this army was not going to rely on a conventional assault. It was going to use its Fearpriests — who had already proved themselves stronger than Barrett — to smash through these walls.

'We meet them. Get everyone! Now!' Martil ordered.

It was a hasty council of war that assembled in the shadow of the capital's main gate.

Mingled together were captains and priests, Derthals and wizards, councillors and a dragon. And behind them, soldiers hurried out of the gate, forming up into lines behind the mass of Derthals, the archers and rangers weighed down with arrow sheaves, while carts were piled high with pikes to follow them. The weapons were too heavy for normal men to use but were perfect in the arms of the powerful bowmen. If the bowmen ran out of shafts, as they had at Pilleth, they were almost useless when fighting with the sword. But not, perhaps, when armed with the pikes.

Merren had not wanted to go down this path. She liked the idea of holding the walls until the people were all away to some sort of safety before trying a desperate battle. But she had seen there was no point to a calm, rational approach. Now was the time for desperate courage. Even so, she had left the Magicians' Guild, all but Barrett, back at the park, sending children, then women away to safety — just in case.

'You all know the plan.' Martil was sketching hurriedly in the dirt with a borrowed knife. 'The horns of the stag. We shall advance as though we are in a conventional formation, with the Derthals in the lead and the rest of us in a traditional shield wall, archers at the rear. When we are within one hundred yards of them, the Derthals will split in two and race around the flanks, to strike at the Tenoch sides and rear. Meanwhile our men, led by the Rallorans, will engage the Berellians, hold them in place while the horns gouge and tear our enemies to shreds.'

'It all depends on the two horns striking fast and deep, using their speed to outflank the enemy. High Chief Sacrax, are your warriors ready to do this?' Merren asked directly.

Sacrax nodded. 'They have eaten well. They are ready.'

Merren looked at him closely. 'I trust you,' she said. 'And I know the horn you lead will rip our enemies apart. But what of the other horn? Who will lead that? We need a brave fighter who understands our language, and what must be done, who can command several clans as one.'

For the first time, Sacrax looked troubled. 'My chiefs are brave but there are many who will not obey another chief.'

'This is vital,' Merren pressed him.

Sacrax looked over at his chiefs pensively, then grinned. 'Your Champion. Martil. All will follow him. He can lead the second horn.'

Martil gaped at him. He could feel his stomach roiling, as if it was full of snakes, at the thought. 'I would be honoured,' he began, 'but I am needed to help direct the battle. Besides, I will be unable to keep up with your warriors in my armour —'

'There is nothing I cannot handle,' Merren interrupted. 'Sendric shall command our sick and wounded at the gate. I led our forces to victory at Pilleth, and I shall do so again here.'

She stared around the rough circle of men, and none doubted her. She turned to Martil. 'As to the armour. Get out of your mail shirt and we shall have Barrett protect your skin, as he did at Sendric.'

Martil stared at her for a moment in mute appeal, but there was no give in her expression. He looked around the circle. So many lives depended on this. And it was his strategy. He feared for Karia, for himself, but he could not let these people down. He could not live with himself. Across this continent, his name was his reputation. The man never beaten, the invincible, unafraid War Captain. If he did not fight now, he would make a mockery of the pain and suffering he had already gone through. It was strange, but he found he was more afraid of being seen a coward than of the fear itself. Slowly he stood and began unbuckling straps.

Merren turned to the others. 'I want the Rallorans at the front, then the Norstaline divisions, with the archers behind. Kay, Ryder, I want you to conserve shafts — don't waste them, because we don't have many. Once out, your men must drop bows and use the pikes, the way we planned.'

'Yes, my Queen.' Kay nodded.

'To your regiments. We have little time!'

Argurium and Havell had been less than impressed to hear that Martil would be taking part in such a desperate fight and that he would lead half the Derthals in the charge that would make or break this battle.

'Can't you just watch?' Havell asked, plaintively.

Martil had not dared to say how much he wanted to do just that.

'We shall watch over you. If it looks like you are about to die, we shall rush down and save you,' Argurium said.

Martil liked the idea of that, although he could see a problem. 'That's reassuring but when will you know to come down? If you pull me out of there at a critical point, the Derthals could think we have lost — and run. You'll have saved me but cost us the battle,' he pointed out.

'After the trick you pulled up north, getting that soldier to stop me calling Argurium, I'll be coming down at the first sign of danger,' Havell said tartly.

Martil cast about desperately for a compromise. 'What about Karia?' he suggested. 'She'll know if I'm in trouble and won't let me die.'

Argurium agreed, while Merren also liked the idea of eyes above the battlefield.

'While she is up there, she can tell Barrett what she is seeing, and he can tell me,' Merren ordered. 'Our enemies have the numbers, but that means they will react slowly. Information on a battlefield is worth many lives.'

All seemed satisfied with that, while Karia liked the idea of riding the dragon. She gave Martil a hug that neither wanted to break.

'You'll win us the battle,' she told him confidently.

Martil kissed the top of her head. He did not trust himself to say anything. But knowing she was ready to come down and rescue him was a comfort.

He only let go when Nott came over to embrace her as well.

'Would you not be safer on the wall, Archbishop?' Martil asked pointedly.

Nott shook his head. 'There are Fearpriests out there. Swords will not help you against them. Only I can.' He kneeled down to embrace Karia again.

'Karia, I want you to always remember how proud I am of you,' he told her. 'And I know you will be happy. You are special. Always know that, wherever I am, I love you.'

He signalled to Havell, and Karia, slightly confused and afraid, let the Elfaran take her hand and lead her over to Argurium.

'What was that about?' Martil demanded.

'There is no time for explanations.' Nott waved him away.

He was right about that. By now, they could all hear the steady tramp of the marching shield wall, the horns and drums they were using to keep time and keep themselves in line. It felt like the ground was actually vibrating slightly, shaking at the thump of thousands of feet striking it in unison.

Martil raced towards where Merren, on Tomon, was speaking to the men — as well as the thousands of people on the walls behind them.

'You know what we have to do! These are the men who have driven us out of our homes, who want to see your families sacrificed to Zorva, want to see us dead! But we have the Derthals. We have

Aroaril. And we have the Dragon Sword. And after this, we shall have victory! Follow me!'

The roar that answered her drowned out the sound of the Berellian horns and the Tenoch drums. From the walls above, every person in the city shouted their support, cheered and clapped as the men formed up. Those who were not cheering were screaming for revenge, yelling for the Berellians and Tenochs to be put to the sword.

The noise from the walls above was deafening but, when Merren's standard bearer rode out of the city, flag held high, it doubled.

The man looked familiar and, when Martil ran over, he almost stopped in surprise. It was Rocus. He had lost weight, lost a leg and a hand, but he was strapped into the saddle, his good arm holding the flag high.

'What are you doing here? Get back into your bed!' Martil yelled at him.

Rocus offered a ghost of a smile. 'That's the first order from you I shall disobey, Captain,' he said. 'I was there from the start of this. I shall be there at the finish.'

'He shall stay with me,' Merren agreed. Flanking her were Nott and Barrett, both looking grim, as if they already knew what she was going to ask them to face that day. With them were the rest of the officers, Nerrin, Kay, Kettering and Hutter. He shook hands with them all. Sendric was there also.

'Make sure you save Gello — I want to kill him myself,' Sendric said wolfishly. 'I shall be cheering you on.' And with that, he rode back to the gate.

'Captain, to the front. We can delay our advance no longer,' Merren said crisply.

He stepped close to her. There was no need to

question what they were doing. It was the only option. They could fight, or they could die.

'I shall see you after the battle, my Queen,' he said softly.

'Come back to me, Captain,' she replied.

'Martil!' Barrett called.

Irritated, Martil turned, to face the wizard's angry stare.

'When you are quite finished, perhaps you might like to think about the battle?' Barrett snapped.

Martil just glared at him, then felt the unusual tingling that told him his skin was now magically protected.

'So I'm protected now?' Martil asked him.

'All the essential bits. You can still take a nasty wound to the groin though,' Barrett said with relish. 'Wouldn't that be a pity?'

Martil wanted to check but, before he could, Merren ordered the advance.

Barrett turned away, while Martil ran to the front, where the Derthals were chanting and stamping the ground in unison, a deep counterpoint for all the noise that was coming from the walls. Even though his stomach felt raw and his legs seemed to be sapped of all strength, his pride kept him moving. He was the War Captain, he was the Queen's Champion. He could not let everyone down.

'About time. Thought battle was to begin without you,' Sacrax greeted him. 'You look good now. Skin nice. Grow your hair and you almost a Derthal.'

'I'm not good-looking enough,' Martil told him, and Sacrax thought that hilarious.

'I give you the big clans, so they stay together, while I lead the smaller clans. Today you are also chief of my clan.'

Martil could not help but smile as Sacrax carefully slipped a wolf fur headband over his forehead.

They were walking towards the massive shield wall that was advancing right at them. You could not look at it for long, with its tight ranks, level shields and drums and horns sounding the beat, without wanting to think about something else.

'Glad we not going through that. Much rather go around it,' Sacrax remarked.

'We shall strike the ones in bright colours, the ones without the metal armour,' Martil agreed. 'We know they do not form lines — they will fight us man on Derthal.'

'Good. Metal blunts your spearhead.' Sacrax winked then looked over his shoulder. 'What your people on the walls saying?'

'Fight well, make us proud, kill our enemies,' Martil explained.

'I like that. They were even cheering us, were they not?'

'They were,' Martil said, watching the Berellian advance. He guessed they would have several hundred crossbowmen in the third or fourth rank, ready to break up an attack. Having had first-hand experience of the barbed bolts the Berellians used, he had no intention of being there when they landed. He looked up, trying to see Karia. The thought she was looking out for him was a great comfort.

'Makes nice change to be cheered,' Sacrax declared. 'Up north they were spitting at us and …'

'Not long now. They will loose bolts at us soon. When they do, we must run and attack, form the horns,' Martil said urgently.

'See you in the heart of our enemies. Save some for me.' Sacrax buffeted him on the shoulder.

Martil was about to reply when Berellian

trumpets sounded a familiar order — the command to the crossbows.

'Now!' Martil bellowed and began to run, leading his Derthals in a loop to the right, the mass of Derthals breaking apart. He ran hard, imagining all the crossbows being wound back and cocked. More and more Derthals were running clear with every moment, then he heard the sound of hundreds of crossbow bolts being loosed, the deep twang as the pressure on the bow tips was released sounded over the horns, drums and cheers.

Nerrin kept his eyes on the back of the Derthal horde in front of him. The recently promoted Lieutenant Dunner marched with him.

'Never thought we'd be fighting with gob ... with Derthals, sir. Sounds like something from a saga,' Dunner said dryly.

'Nothing funny about fighting Berellians again,' Nerrin pointed out.

'Aye. Hope this is for the last time,' Dunner agreed.

They could not see the Berellian line from where they were, behind nearly ten thousand Derthals, but they knew what to expect. And they knew that their two ranks could not defeat sixteen ranks, even with the help of archers and the Norstalines behind. The best they could do was hold them off, give Captain Martil time to lead the Derthals into the heart of the enemy. It was a simple plan. But, if it went wrong, if the Derthals could not put the Tenochs to flight, the allied force would be helpless.

'Be nice to be on the side with more men for once, sir,' Dunner remarked.

Nerrin could not answer him. What was he doing here? He was just a sergeant! Why were they all depending on him? Martil was with the Derthals but he wished with all his heart that the Captain was in charge. If things went wrong, if they could not hold the Berellians, it would all be his fault …

'I know you can do this, Captain Nerrin!'

He whirled, to see Queen Merren riding alongside him.

'Your majesty! Where … why …?'

Merren smiled. 'You know why I am putting the Rallorans at the front? In part because Markuz will see you and lose all control and discipline, think only of killing you. But mainly because you are the best. I know you will not let us down. Without you, we would not have made it this far. And my people know that now. You are no longer the Butchers of Bellic. You are the Saviours of Norstalos!'

Nerrin grinned as the men around him cheered her words.

'Doesn't quite have the same ring to it, your majesty,' Dunner offered. 'How about the Rescuers from Rallora?'

Merren smiled. 'If your sword is half as quick as your tongue, then we shall have an easy victory today!' she told him.

They roared with laughter at that.

'And you can all know you march under one of the finest officers you could ever have. Many of you have told me that Nerrin is the best captain you have served since Captain Martil!'

They cheered that, and Nerrin could not stop his cheeks from flushing.

'Although as some of you served under Captain Oscarl, that may not be all that much of a compliment.'

They bellowed with laughter, both at the comment and at the knowledge of Rallora she showed.

'The Berellians already dread facing you — the world shall see why at the end of today!'

Nerrin looked around as his men shouted their approval and when he looked back, saw Merren wink at him.

He smiled and nodded back, then she waved at the Rallorans once more, before turning Tomon away.

Nerrin straightened his back. He knew what she had done but it had still worked. He was ready now.

Hutter had sworn he never wanted to find himself in the battleline again after Pilleth. But many of the men he worked with, and trained, were marching and he could hardly abandon them. Still, he could feel the pressure of his bladder, while his legs seemed to have no strength and he had to grip his sword tight to stop his hand shaking. Before Pilleth, men had been vomiting their meagre rations back up, breaking ranks to empty their bowels and pissing themselves out of fear. Hutter could see other men were afraid: the faces were too drawn, the laughter too forced, the eyes downcast. He reckoned it was only the presence of so many people on the walls that was keeping the men in their ranks this time. He was right behind the Rallorans, which was both comforting and frightening. It was good to have them on your side, of course, but they were real soldiers. He was just a country militia sergeant whose stomach was bigger than his ability.

'Captain Hutter!'

He turned to see Queen Merren.

'I just wanted to tell you how much I trust you, and am depending on you. You and your men will be the backbone of this army, helping the Rallorans hold firm. Your children will be proud of you today,

Captain! You are a symbol of what this army is about. An ordinary man who can do extraordinary things! I just need you to hold firm with the Rallorans, and I know you can do that.'

Hutter straightened to his full height.

'You can depend on me, your majesty!' he told her.

'I know. I can depend on you all!'

She waved at them and they cheered her, before she curbed Tomon, and they strode past her.

Merren watched them march past, keeping a wide smile on her face. Sending Martil out with the Derthals had been the sensible thing but the rest of the men needed extra reassurance because of it.

She looked confident but she felt sick to the stomach at what she knew was going to happen. Thousands of young men, and Derthals, many of them known to her, were going to be killed or hideously wounded in the next turn or two of the hourglass. And they were going to die for her. The only way she could repay them was by sharing their risk, and by leading them to victory.

'Captain Kettering!' She spotted another of the officers she needed.

Kettering had been angry. Angry at almost everything but particularly angry at Gello and the Berellians. What he had gone through back at the park, holding back the screaming, sobbing crowds, had just put a fine edge on his anger.

'This is your time for revenge! This is revenge for all of us,' Merren called. 'The man who framed you was the Berellian Champion. Everything he did was at the orders of King Markuz. And Gello told me Markuz laughed when he heard how his Champion had left you to take the blame for his crimes!'

Kettering gripped his sword tight at that. If only he could face Markuz today ...

'But today we shall wipe the smile from his face. When I give the signal, Captain, you shall be the man to lead us to revenge, lead us to victory! I know you and your men can do it!'

She smiled as they cheered again, and she let them get ahead of her once more.

Kettering marched on, Leigh and Hawke to either side. There were many Berellians ahead but he was not worried about that. He needed as many as possible to slake an anger that seemed to fill the whole world. He would pay back the Berellian King for ruining his life.

Merren tried to joke with the others, with Nott and Barrett and Kesbury, but she strained to see what was happening at the front of the column, where Martil and Sacrax led the Derthals.

'What can Karia see?' she demanded from Barrett.

'No more than us. As soon as anything happens, she will send me a bird with a message,' Barrett assured her.

She imagined she could see Martil, and she prayed he would survive. She prayed they would all survive, even though she knew that was impossible. Then the Derthals began running and she forgot to worry over Martil, and just worried about winning this battle.

Gello marched in the middle of his men, his armour polished to an eye-dazzling brightness, his helm and shield shining silver, his sword — the fake dragon sword crafted for his coronation as King of Norstalos — in his hand. He had no doubt they would win. A mass of goblins and a few thousand Rallorans and Norstalines would be no match for the massive column marching straight for the capital.

He had been surprised to see Merren march her men out to join the goblins. He had expected her to get as many goblins inside the walls as possible, and then use her archers from the walls. She must have an inflated view of the goblins' fighting abilities, he reflected. Or perhaps she just could not count!

He, Markuz, Itlan, Yertlaan and Onzalez had held a brief conference of war. With three separate forces, two Kings and a Fearpriest, there was no person in overall charge. Gello was happy to sit back and let Markuz take the lead, though Markuz did not command, he suggested. Onzalez, on the other hand, seemed bored by the whole process.

'Just advance and destroy them. Once they are running, and have fled back inside the city, I shall show them that stone walls can easily be brought down.' Onzalez waved his hand casually.

So, with no more instructions than that, they had advanced.

'Do you think we shall even need to order the men to link shields and draw swords?' Gello asked Heath.

'I doubt it, sire. The Berellians will go through the goblins easily enough — perhaps Martil hopes the Berellians will be encouraged to chase a beaten enemy and run into his shield wall. But even if he slaughters half the Berellians, there's still enough of them to destroy him.' Heath smiled. He fervently hoped this was the case. The men he commanded were all veterans of Pilleth — and his sergeants reported they were terrified of facing the Rallorans again.

'Martil's archers will eat away at our Berellian friends, unless they keep their shields up,' Feld warned. 'And most of our men are cavalry troopers — they don't have shields. And Martil will have something planned. He always has when we have faced him before. We need to be ready to react to his tricks.'

Gello felt the first stirring of disquiet, which he quelled ruthlessly. This was to be his revenge, his moment of triumph. Nothing could stop it now!

'There are too many of us. There is nothing more that renegade Ralloran can do to us,' he declared grandly.

With both sides marching briskly forwards, the gap between the two forces was narrowing rapidly.

'Here we go, sire!' Livett called, as the Berellian arbalesters launched their bolts at the goblins.

Gello watched eagerly, expecting to see goblins fall and die but, instead, they broke into a run.

'What are they doing?' Gello demanded, his heart pounding.

None of his captains could answer.

Markuz spat in anger as his crossbow volley was wasted. A dozen goblins, the slower ones, went down, but most of the bolts landed harmlessly in the ground, as the mass of goblins had split apart and were running out to his flanks.

'Sire! Do we change formation to take care of them?' one of his captains asked.

Markuz watched the goblins, seeing them run wide of his shield wall. It could be done, but it would mean adjusting his lines and holding up the advance. Still, it was the sensible thing to do ... he glanced back to his front to see the rest of his foes still advancing, led by ... Rallorans! Butchers of Bellic!

Markuz snarled, the memory of the humiliations he had suffered during and after the Ralloran Wars wiping out everything else.

'Advance at the double. We destroy the Ralloran Butchers! We can win the battle and avenge Bellic! Pass the word for Gello and Nobles Itlan and Yertlaan to deal with the goblins.'

15

Martil ran hard, leading the Derthals wide around the edge of the Berellian shield wall and out in a big loop, to where the brightly coloured Tenochs marched at the rear of the enemy column. The Derthals could not break a shield wall but he reckoned they would rip apart the Tenochs. Like all conventional army formations, the best troops were at the front, while the ones at the back were there to add bulk and to pursue a beaten enemy. If he could attack there, where the weakest Tenoch fighters waited, then numbers would mean little.

He pumped his legs, driving himself across the soggy ground, afraid that the Berellians or Gello would somehow see through his strategy and march their men out to block the Derthal advance. They had enough men to do that — and if they did, it might just win them the battle. If that was to happen, he at least knew Karia would come and get him. He glanced up, hoping to see her.

From her position high above, the battle looked like a game of toy soldiers to Karia. Argurium swirled lazily above the battlefield, banking gently to stay over the Queen. Karia was ready to contact Barrett if she saw something unusual, so she watched what was going on — although she was particularly looking for Martil. The mass of enemies looked enormous, a huge block of men marching in time. Facing them was a much smaller force — and she watched as the Derthals split into two, running across and around the edge of the advancing shield wall.

'The horns of the stag!' she cried excitedly.

She could see what Martil was talking about from up here. The Rallorans and Norstalines made a solid block, while the two curling wings of Derthals looked like horns, reaching out to hook into the back of their enemies.

She had never seen a battle before, they had always tried to keep her away. She was excited and afraid, all at once. But she was sure Martil was going to win. He always did. Havell expected her to say she had to go and rescue Martil but she knew there was no need for that. He was the greatest warrior dad in the world. Nothing could hurt him.

Markuz ignored the goblins now streaming around both his flanks. All his attention was on the Butchers of Bellic, his mind focused only on revenge. Besides, Gello had said the goblins were primitives, easily defeated. What harm could they do to this massive army of conquest?

'Form points!' Markuz ordered.

All along his line, massive axemen pushed to the front, forming the point of small wedges. Each carried a huge, double-bladed axe. Markuz smiled grimly. He had seen this happen so many times before. They would chop a hole in the line and the rest of his men would pour through the gap. It was a technique he had perfected over many years and it had won him many battles. Certainly the Rallorans had learned to deal with it, but only when they had enough men to match him. And this time the advantage of numbers were all on his side.

'Send out the arbalesters!' One volley and then his wedges would strike home.

Nerrin saw the Berellian lines change, crossbowmen stepping forwards and axemen forming the points of attack wedges and took a deep breath. The Berellians were now about fifty paces away. That seemed close but, from bitter experience, Nerrin knew the last fifty paces were the longest and hardest, for men instinctively shied away from the bloody horror of a grinding shield wall battle.

He ordered a flag raised.

'That's the signal! Kay! Ryder!' Merren shouted. 'Now!'

The order rippled up and down the ranks and the archers stopped marching and opened arrow bags, placing their spare sheaves on the ground behind them. The rangers, who were on the flanks of the column, marched out wider, giving them a clear sight of the enemy lines before they followed suit.

'Loose!' Merren signalled.

'Loose!' Ryder and Kay echoed her order and the archers and rangers began drawing and loosing arrows, sending them over the heads of the Rallorans. Each man carried three sheaves of arrows. It was not going to be enough — to defeat such an army, they would have needed twice as many bowmen, and ten times as many arrows. Merren had not wanted to waste their best weapon, so she had held them back until every arrow would count.

The Berellian line instinctively covered up when they heard the thrum of the bowstrings — but there were arrows coming from two directions. The archers were lofting their arrows high, so that they fell down from above, while the rangers were to either side and sent their arrows snapping in on a straight line. The Berellians tried to protect their crossbowmen and axemen but those who kept their shields low to save themselves from the rangers were struck by arrows from above, while those who held their shields high were picked off by rangers. In moments scores were down, including almost every axeman and arbalester. Those crossbowmen who still lived wasted their quarrels on Ralloran shields — and those who tried to reload made themselves an easy target.

'Take them forwards, Nerrin!' Merren signalled.

Now it was the Rallorans' turn to form wedges, led by skilled swordsmen and axemen.

The advance of the Berellians had been halted effectively by the arrow storm and before they could reorganise themselves the Rallorans attacked, lines tight, wedges ready to reach out and pierce the Berellian line. As they advanced, the rangers changed their aim, sending their arrows further back, to strike at the rear of the Berellians. Then, with a crash that echoed across a battlefield already loud with trumpets, horns, drums, the thrum of bowstrings and the screams of the wounded, the Rallorans struck home. Nerrin led one wedge in. He knew as the commander he should stay back, help guide his men, but he had had enough of that. He wanted to fight, only worry about what was going on in front of him. Besides, this was what he had trained to do.

The Berellians were in disarray, trying to watch out for arrows, their lines already uneven where dead and wounded men lay.

Directly in front of Nerrin lay an axeman, two arrows in his chest. The Berellians who had planned to help him carve a hole in the Ralloran line were cowering from the arrows. With a roar, Nerrin led his men in over the last few yards. The Berellians tried to lock shields but it was too late. Nerrin drove into one man, using his speed and strength to push the man back and across, then he slammed his sword into the neck of the man to his right — and instantly there was a gap. Behind Nerrin, Rallorans widened the opening, using shield and sword to prise apart the Berellian line. The black-garbed Berellians tried to regroup but they were facing men who had dedicated their lives to breaking apart Berellian shield walls. And the arrows kept falling on the rear ranks, stopping their attempts to help the others.

Nerrin locked shields with men in the Berellian second rank. The first rank he ignored, the men there were either dead or being killed by Rallorans. He could smell the breath of the man in front of him, smell the rank fear as he hooked his shield's boss beneath his foe's and hauled it up, giving him the chance to drive his sword through the Berellian's mail shirt and into his groin. Blood spurted and he felt the breath of the man's hoarse scream. But he had already swivelled to his left, hacking furiously at the Berellian there. He cut down the man and waved his bloodied sword, flinging sticky drops in all directions.

'Back five!' he roared, hearing it taken up by Dunner and the sergeants.

The Ralloran lines took five paces back, leaving a gap between them and the Berellians — but a gap filled with dead and injured men.

Nerrin smiled as he eased himself into the second rank. The Berellians pushed forwards but their careful lines broke up as they tried to avoid treading on their dead and injured countrymen and they became easy prey for the Rallorans. More bodies were left and the Berellians hesitated, unwilling for the moment to commit themselves to another attack. That was fine by Nerrin. The longer they waited, the more time for Captain Martil.

Gello was frustrated. The advance had stopped and the careful spacing between each rank had been thrown out. His men were hard up against the rear ranks of the Berellians, while the Tenochs had pushed close in behind him. Worse, arrows were falling all the time — and not enough of his men had shields.

'We should push out and outflank them, sire,' Heath declared. 'There's not enough of them to stop us.'

'And expose ourselves to Martil's bowmen? Sire, we could lose hundreds of men to buy Markuz a victory,' Feld protested.

That sealed it for Gello.

'We stay here,' he agreed.

'And what about the goblins?' Livett asked. 'They're running past us, as if they mean to attack the Tenochs from the rear!'

'That is no concern of ours,' Gello assured him. 'There are more than enough Tenochs to deal with a few goblins!'

Onzalez was thinking about where he would build the first pyramid to Zorva. It was an important decision, for it would be the centre of worship in this country. The obvious place was inside the capital but should he build it where the Norstaline palace stood, or on the site of one of Aroaril's churches?

Putting it where the palace stood would tell Gello that he ruled only by Onzalez's sufferance, while tearing down the biggest church would symbolise the victory over Aroaril. It was no easy choice.

'High One! The goblins are approaching us!' Noble Yertlaan interrupted his thoughts.

'So destroy them!' Onzalez said dismissively. 'You heard King Gello — they are easily defeated!'

Yertlaan hesitated. There were many of these goblins, and they were threatening to encircle the Tenoch column, attacking his rear, where his weakest troops waited. His best men, who wore eagle or leopard suits, were enmeshed with Gello's Norstalines and it would be difficult to redeploy them to meet the goblins. He would have liked to order Gello to block at least one of the goblin wings to give him time to organise his men. But he was used to obeying Onzalez instantly, on pain of death. He would not dare to tell a Fearpriest, let alone one who was a member of the Ruling Council, what to do. So his hesitation was for only a heartbeat.

'Your will, High One.' He bowed.

'Now!' Martil roared, leading his Derthals towards the rear corner of the Tenoch column.

As ordered, the chiefs under his command split up, each leading their warriors towards a different part of the Tenochs, just like the individual spurs of a stag's horn.

At the back of the Tenoch ranks were mainly spearmen, wearing brightly coloured padded tunics and carrying long spears and short knives. But there were some slingers here, too, and several Derthals fell as fist-sized stones struck them. There were also spear-throwers, and Derthals fell to them also, as Tenochs launched their weapons high into the air.

Then the Tenoch ranks broke apart as they did not wait to be attacked, but raced out to meet the Derthals.

That suited Martil perfectly.

'At them!' Martil lengthened his strides, drawing ahead of the Derthals.

As the two sides drew closer, a bellow that Martil recognised as the challenge of an angry dragon rent the air. He did not look around or up, although almost every Tenoch paused to do so. Instead he raced into their ranks, the Dragon Sword carving a bloody path through the Tenochs. An instant later, the two sides collided with a crash, the Derthals striking deep into the mass of Tenochs. Their short spears, with their wickedly sharp heads, went through the padded jerkins of the Tenochs as if they were parchment. As each spearhead was ripped clear of its victim by thickly muscled arms, blood spurted high and the Derthals drove onto their next victim.

'N'gidha!'

Their chant went up with every dead Tenoch.

The Tenochs tried to fight back, but their long spears were too unwieldy. By the time they thrust these forwards, the Derthals had slipped past the point. Up close, the short spears of the Derthals were by far the better weapon. They could be pressed against a Tenoch and still have room to thrust home their spears, while the Tenoch could only hit at them with his spear haft.

As for the slingers and spear-throwers, they dropped their leather thongs and wooden atlatls and drew knives with blades of the same black rock as their unusual spears — but were no match for the Derthals.

And Martil drove them onwards, the Dragon Sword weaving a terrible path of destruction through the Tenoch ranks. His worries were still there, he could not empty his mind, but the Sword helped him cut through spears, armour and flesh.

If the Derthals had attacked only in one place, or from one direction, the Tenochs might have been able to regroup, to use their numbers. But not only was Martil's horn striking in five different places, Sacrax's warriors had struck on the other side as well. The powerful Derthal was leading his warriors steadily forwards, both his spear and his spear arm encrusted with blood. If spears broke, the warrior just reached behind his back, to where he kept his spares on a sling — or picked one up from a fallen brother.

And the Tenochs also shrank away from the merciless Derthals. These men had been told the Derthals were creatures from the foulest pit of Aroaril. The wild hair, strange faces and bloodthirsty war cries only convinced them they were facing demons of Aroaril. Tenochs backed away rather than face these blood-spattered monsters.

And as for the one with the Sword that cut through anything — nobody wanted to face him.

'N'gidha!'

The Derthal victory cry was echoing on all sides, answered only by the screams of men.

The Berellians were pushing forwards again but getting nowhere. Every time they advanced, their careful ranks were thrown into disarray by the heaving, weeping, bleeding piles of men they had to step over, and the Rallorans were able to throw them back.

Markuz's captains were telling him he should extend his lines to outflank the Rallorans or, even better, order Gello to do the same — as the Norstaline bowmen to either side would take a fearful toll of such an attack. But Markuz ignored them. Berellian pride was at stake. There were just two lines of Rallorans facing him! All must see that the Berellian soldier was far superior to a Ralloran. He would wear them down and break through. It was a matter of honour. And as for asking for help from a Norstaline …

'Get your men back there and wipe out these foul creatures! And I want Markuz and Gello to bring their men back to help us! Markuz can use a couple of regiments to hold off the Rallorans while we destroy these demons of Aroaril!' Onzalez screamed at Itlan and Yertlaan. 'Get Markuz on our left, Gello on our right.' He had expected his Tenochs to sweep the goblins away but the opposite was happening — his Tenochs were being slaughtered. And every one that fell was a little bit less power for him to wield over Markuz and Gello.

The two captains exchanged glances. The fastest way to win the battle was to order Gello to swing out and outflank the Rallorans. The goblins could be scattered once the rest of the Aroaril-lovers were defeated. But they could not question a Fearpriest.

'At once, High One.' They bowed.

'Brother Onzalez has just sent me orders — we must march out to our right and destroy the goblins we find there,' Prent reported.

'Tell him we shall do so at once,' Gello said immediately then, when Prent turned away, signalled to Feld and Heath.

'As slowly as we can,' he instructed. 'Let them weaken our allies first.'

* * *

Markuz ground his teeth in frustration. But he could not ignore an order from Onzalez. The Rallorans would just have to wait.

'First three lines stand firm! The Rallorans will not attack. The rest, with me!' He waved his sword, leading his ranks out to his left flank and back towards where the Derthals were tearing into the hapless Tenochs.

'What's happening there?' Karia saw the change first. The block of red, which she knew was Gello's men, seemed to be doing nothing but the black ranks of Berellians were marching out and back, towards the Derthals.

'I have to tell Merren!'

Merren could not believe how well the battle was going. Hundreds of Berellians were down, and the rest seemed reluctant to attack across their own dead and wounded, which had formed an effective barrier. The Rallorans were tiring but had fought magnificently, stopping a shield wall ten times larger than their own, giving Martil the time he needed to strike home. She had tried to get them to slip back, to swap places with her fresh Norstalines, under Hutter and Kettering, but Nerrin had refused, saying it was a point of honour for them to hold back the Berellians. And watching the way the two sides tore into each other, she was not sure the Norstalines could handle it, either. Besides, she had had to order the bowmen to conserve their shafts — many were down to their last sheaf of twenty and there were still far more targets than arrows. But that was the only problem. From the reports coming down from Karia, the Derthals were smashing the Tenochs, even if she took out the obvious exaggerations. The girl was proud of Martil but Merren knew it was impossible for him to have killed hundreds of men by himself.

'My Queen! The Berellians are marching to stop the Derthals!' Barrett cried.

Merren tried to peer over the heads of her troops but it was too hard to see. She had to take the word of her eyes in the sky, on the dragon.

'Kettering! Hutter!' she cried. 'Swing your men out to the right. We have to stop the Berellians. Kay, Ryder, every bowman with them — loose everything you have at those Berellians and then follow with the pikes! Archbishop ...'

'I have another duty,' Nott said softly, turning his horse.

She was about to call after him when interrupted by Barrett.

'My Queen — perhaps we should leave them. Would it not be better to keep our men together. Besides, the Derthals will extract a high cost from the Berellians ...' Barrett began, but she waved him to silence.

Martil had told her how great generals could sense a shift in the battle, could feel when everything was about to change. She could feel it now. Her enemies were in confusion, their massive numbers had made them unwieldy. They were slow to respond, when they even did respond. Karia had reported that the red ranks of Gello's men had barely moved for the whole battle. But the Berellians were still a potent fighting force. If they succeeded in driving away the Derthals, then her small army would be destroyed. But if she could stop the Berellians, then it would be her enemies who would be sundered. It was time to seize the moment.

'Barrett! Rocus! With me!'

She spurred Tomon around to where her Norstalines were advancing as fast as they could over the soggy fields, past where exhausted Rallorans and Berellians stared at each other across a small gap filled with the dead and dying.

Not for the first time, Martil was thankful he had the Dragon Sword. In the close confines of this fight, it was invaluable. Already the Tenochs had learned to fear him, and tried to stay away. Which was no mean feat, considering they were terrified of the Derthals. He was covered in blood, most of it Tenoch, and was taking advantage of the ebbing tide of battle to get his breath back, sucking in deep gasps of air. Well, that was what he was telling himself. Certainly the run around the Tenochs, followed by the furious fighting was enough to test the stamina of the fittest man. But a Tenoch spear had nearly gutted him — if not for his protected skin he would be dead and there would have been nothing Argurium could do. The thought of it had made him pause.

Now he was watching the Derthals. They may look similar to men but Martil guessed their hearts and lungs must be bigger for their size or something, because they seemed unstoppable.

Everywhere he looked they were driving the Tenochs back. Perhaps he did not even need to rejoin the battle.

Kay and Ryder's men stopped the Berellians. No troops could march through an arrow storm and the Berellians had to put aside thoughts of going to the aid of the Tenochs, instead covering up behind shields as best they could.

But stopping the Berellian advance and defeating it were two different things, as Merren well knew.

Her Norstaline companies were advancing steadily but she could feel their nervousness. Most of these men's only experience of battle had been Pilleth, where Gello's armoured troops had cut them apart. The others had fought at Sendric or at least charged with her at Pilleth and this was to be their first real shield wall. They had watched the Rallorans fight but this was, as the saying went, a horse of a different colour. Even with the bowmen, there were barely four thousand of them — and there were at least six thousand Berellians. She could smell the fear — and more.

'This is for your family! This is for your friends! This is for your country!' she told them, her voice amplified by Barrett.

Scores of Berellians were down, the others trying to keep their shields up. But the arrows were running out.

'Follow me!'

'Sire, it looks like Merren's bringing her main force around to attack Markuz! We can hit them in the flank as soon as they engage with Markuz and destroy them!' Feld said excitedly.

Gello shook his head with a smile.

'Feld — we are obeying the orders of Brother Onzalez, to go to the aid of the Tenochs. Besides, Markuz does not need our help. He's facing a straggle of militia, criminals and raw recruits, as well as some bowmen, who don't even have shields! It would be an insult for us to offer him help.'

'But, sire …'

'We shall wait and see. If it appears he is in trouble, we shall help him then.'

If I play this right, everyone's army but mine will be shattered to buy us victory, he thought smugly.

Nerrin massaged his right shoulder. It seemed to be on fire, while his left arm, his shield arm, felt almost numb from all the blows it had absorbed. Looking up and down the line, he could see many of his men were in the same state, or worse. Others were wounded but staying in the line, while more, their wounds crudely bandaged, were returning to the line. In front of him was barely five yards of ground, but every inch of it was filled with dead and wounded men. Mostly Berellians but some Rallorans as well. On the other side were what was left of two regiments of Berellians, shields locked. As the dead and dying had proved, crossing those few yards was impossible to do while maintaining the lines — which meant they were easy meat for the other shield wall. But they could not just stay here and watch others fight.

'What do we do, sir? The Queen's taking on the rest of the Berellians, and the Captain's fighting the Tenochs. There're still Gello's dogs out there, too. If the Queen takes out Markuz, they'll hit her open flank,' Dunner said. He had a rough bandage around his left thigh, while a cut on his cheek added more blood to his already stained mail shirt.

'We can't break that line.' Nerrin shrugged. 'We've done all we can, it's up to the Norstalines to win the battle now.'

Sacrax had lost his last spear, trapped in the ribs of a screaming human. But he had brought his huge mace on the long march south — and he intended to use that now. Many of the Tenochs were dead or had backed away, unwilling to fight. But new men, wearing either strange feathers or the spotted pelt of a mysterious creature, were joining the battle — and proving tougher opponents. For a start they were using different weapons, strange war-clubs that were far more effective than spears and knives, as Sacrax's warriors were finding out. He smashed down one Tenoch, then another, then was forced to duck and weave as more pressed close. His mace was a mighty weapon but more unwieldy than a spear. His breath was coming hard and fast now and he realised he was fighting just to survive here. And he was losing.

Markuz cursed with frustration. At every turn he had been blocked. Now his advance on the goblins had been stopped by the Norstalines and, in particular, their bowmen. His men had to turn around and defend themselves from the plague of arrows. The last of his crossbowmen had been lost as well to those damned shafts. The only positive was the Norstaline bowmen seemed to have run out of arrows.

He ordered his men to march again — this time at the Norstalines. Without the Norstaline longbows, it should be easy. He had more men. And when they were dead, he would attack the cursed Rallorans from the flank as well.

The wagons that had followed the bowmen into battle had carried pikes, the unwieldy weapons that had been stripped from Gello's soldiers in the fight to restore Merren to the throne. On one side was a heavy hammer-head, on the other was an axe blade, and it was topped with a spike. They were brutal weapons but needed an extraordinary amount of strength to wield. The sort of strength built up by a lifetime of using a bow. Merren and Martil had decided, after the way the bowmen had been slaughtered fighting a shield wall with just swords at Pilleth, they should be given another weapon. Now the bowmen rushed past each wagon, grabbing a pike and leaving their bows behind, before hurrying to catch up to where Merren led the Norstalines directly at the Berellians.

Martil could see the elite Tenoch warriors pushing forwards now. The Derthals were sweeping away the ordinary fighters but these ones were proving far more difficult. In fact they were driving Derthals back. Martil found a dry patch of sleeve and wiped his face clear of Tenoch blood. Now he could see what the Tenochs were pushing at — Sacrax and his bodyguard. If they killed Sacrax ... Martil began to run, ruthlessly quelling his desire to stay safe. Around him, many Derthals, without a Tenoch to fight, were turning their attention to helping wounded brothers.

'Follow me!' Martil called to them.

They may not have understood his words but they followed anyway.

Men shuffled forwards, a yard at a time, while the Berellians waited grimly. The advance was so slow that the bowmen, even carrying the heavy pikes, had caught up.

Hutter had watched how the Rallorans had formed wedges and then ripped into the Berellian lines. But he did not think he could do such a thing — and did not want to make men do what he feared. The line stopped, a few paces from the Berellians, and to Merren it seemed as if nothing could induce it to move, to close the last distance. She glanced nervously across to where Gello's red ranks stood. *If we wait much longer, they will attack us*, she thought.

'Kettering!' Merren called.

'My Queen?'

'That flag over there is the Berellian King's. He stands beneath it. He was the man who ordered his Champion to make it look like you were a murderer. He was the one to blame for everything that has happened to you!'

Kettering looked to where she was pointing.

'He was the man who had you thrown into prison, who wanted to see you hang for crimes you never committed!'

Kettering swore he could see a figure in gilded armour standing beneath the flag. It was all it took to send the anger racing through him.

'Kill them!' he screamed.

Flanked by Leigh and Hawke, he burst out of the line and at the Berellians.

Almost as if a spell had been lifted, the rest of the Norstaline line followed, closing the gap until they crashed into the Berellians.

Men shouted, cursed and screamed as the two lines ground into each other. Men tried to stab underneath or between shields, while others covered up.

'Now, Kay!' Merren cried.

Every bowman had a huge upper body, forged by years of using a longbow, where just drawing the string back to the ear was a feat equivalent to lifting a woman above his head. Now they used this strength, and the pikes, on the Berellians.

Some used the spike to stab between shields, others used the hammer-head or the axe to smash men down. Each pike was ten feet long and the top was wrapped in steel, so the head could not be cut off. The bowmen could stand in the third rank, safe from the Berellians, and bring the pikes down or thrust them through.

Either way, it was a tactic the Berellians had not foreseen — and could not defend against. Men who tried to watch out for the pikes opened themselves to the swords in front.

Markuz bellowed in rage as he saw what was happening. Drawing his sword, and heedless of the cries of his captains, he pushed himself into the fray. He was sure that no man could stand against him. After all, he had Zorva on his side.

It was easy enough to push through the ranks — men did not want to get near the front, where the relentless pikes were smashing open helmets and heads, piercing eyes and faces and crushing shoulders.

Markuz elbowed aside a pair of his guardsmen — to see a lean Norstaline cutting his way towards him. The man had burning eyes, an intense look on his face — and long hair tied back from his head.

'Come and taste death! I am Markuz, King of Berellia!' Markuz challenged, then thrust his golden-hilted sword forwards, sure this would be the first of many victims.

But Kettering deflected the blow on his shield, and cut down viciously at Markuz's arm, striking through the mail sleeve and deep into the flesh and bone beneath.

The Berellian King screamed in pain and fury as his nerveless fingers dropped his gilt sword and royal blood spurted out. Markuz's bodyguards tried to push forwards to save their monarch but found their way obstructed by the very men Markuz had pushed past.

Before they could rescue Markuz, Kettering stepped in close and rammed his sword into the King's throat.

'That's for what you did to me, you bastard!' he spat.

Markuz's screams choked off instantly.

'The King! The King is down!'

The cry went up and down the Berellian line and, in an instant, their ranks dissolved. There were still more than enough to destroy the Norstalines — but these recruits did not stop to count. Fear had kept them in line but, with that removed, they turned and ran. Behind them, the Berellians facing the Ralloran line saw their comrades run — and an instant later followed them, the Rallorans hard on their heels.

Sacrax grunted as he used his mace to block a wicked blow from a Tenoch war-club. His fingers felt numb and he doubted he could hold much longer. Most of his bodyguard was down and his warriors were only concerned with what was going on in front of them — this mass fighting was new to them.

Then a war cry announced Martil's arrival. The Dragon Sword carved its way through the Tenochs — each stroke killed or maimed a man — and behind Martil came more Derthals.

'Good timing,' Sacrax greeted, dropping his mace and taking a spare spear from a warrior.

Martil grinned back at him, blood masking his face.

'Kill them and the rest will run.' He pointed out what could only be the Tenoch leaders.

Not only were they adorned with gold, rather than bone, but they were cutting down Derthal after Derthal with their strange war-clubs.

Side by side, Martil and Sacrax fought their way to where the leaders waited.

'Come to meet your death, foul creature of Aroaril?' Yertlaan challenged, swinging his weapon in a wide arc.

Martil said nothing; he just used the Dragon Sword to cut through the weapon then, when Yertlaan stared in shock, the reverse stroke took the Tenoch leader's head.

Martil glanced over towards Sacrax, but the powerful Derthal had ignored the challenge of individual combat with Itlan and instead a dozen Derthals had swarmed the other Tenoch leader.

'Who's next?' Martil bellowed. He had to put everything aside until the job was done, the battle won.

None came forward. The sight of their leaders being killed was the last straw for the Tenochs. Again, they still outnumbered the Derthals but they scattered in all directions, running desperately to get away from these monsters of Aroaril, these hideous goblins.

Gello watched in shock at the way Merren's Norstalines were using pikes to cut through the Berellians. He had never thought to use the weapons that way; he could see instantly that this could change the way battles were fought, for no shield wall could defend against them. It was time to do something. He was about to give the orders to strike Merren's Norstalines in the flank when the cry went up that Markuz was dead. His heart barely had time to leap with delight before the Berellians broke and ran.

He could not believe his eyes — then Feld grabbed his arm.

'Sire! The Tenochs have broken!' he screamed.

Gello turned to tell Feld he was an idiot, it was

the Berellians that had broken — only to see the Tenochs running in all directions.

Gello gaped in horror. How had it come to this?

The walls erupted in ecstatic cheering as the people saw their enemies begin to scatter. Men, women and children embraced each other, fell to their knees and thanked Aroaril or cried openly.

'Don't let them get away!'

Count Sendric's shout cut through the jubilation.

'Out there are the men who despoiled our country. They are running for safety! Will we let them just walk away after what they did to us, our friends and families?' Sendric boomed. 'Those of you with weapons, follow me!'

The grim realisation of his words stopped the cheering. A flood of men, carrying knives, clubs, axes and anything they could find, joined Sendric in a rush out of the gate and after the fleeing Tenochs and Berellians.

Sendric led them, victory singing in his blood. He just wanted to get there so he could see Gello die.

Gello backed away from the slowly closing ring. Everywhere he looked there were men or goblins looking grim and bloody.

The battlefield was not silent. Men moaned, screamed, begged and cried as they lay in the thick mud, blood and brains and entrails. But, to Gello, it had all the silence of the grave.

'Sire, we need a fighting retreat to the horses and we can get away from here,' Feld said urgently.

Gello ignored him. How could it be ending like this? How could triumph slip out of his grasp yet again? This was impossible! Thoughts beat against his head, like moths against a lantern. How could he possibly lose?

'No! It shall not end like this!'

Gello thought those were his words — until he realised it was Onzalez who was shouting.

16

The Fearpriest had not run when the Tenochs broke. Gello watched him walk disdainfully towards where he and his captains stood, accompanied by a handful of frightened-looking Tenochs, the wizard Khaliz, and a scared Ezok.

'Stay with us, High One, and we shall get you away safely,' Gello said urgently. He thought, having disobeyed the man's orders during the battle — which could, possibly, be seen as a reason for why they had been defeated — he should at least try to save him.

Laughter roared out of the Fearpriest's cowl.

'There is no need,' he assured Gello. 'Victory is at hand!'

Gello could feel the eyes of his captains on him and almost hear their thoughts. But Onzalez ignored them, instead turning towards the Queen's standard.

'You think you have won? You think you are triumphant? You fools!'

Gello and his captains edged away from Onzalez's laughter.

'I did not need these soldiers to defeat you! Fall down on your knees and tremble, as I show you the power of Zorva!' Onzalez cried.

'Behind us!' Heath called.

Onzalez spun, to see a mass of Derthals, led by Sacrax and Martil, advancing purposefully.

'Away from me, creatures of Aroaril!' Onzalez warned.

He kneeled down and thrust his hands into the earth. Instantly it rippled away from him, forming waves in the ground, waves that hurled Martil and many Derthals off their feet. Then he turned towards the advancing Norstalines. The closest men to him were Kay's bowmen, carrying bloodied and battered pikes.

Another gesture from Onzalez and the pikes warped instantly, the men dropping the twisted wooden shafts in surprise.

Gello and his captains looked at each other with renewed hope.

'Form up your men, Gello,' Onzalez said calmly. 'We shall go and kill the Queen, and none shall be able to stop us.'

Gello glanced over to where the Norstaline shield wall inched closer. He licked his lips. Two-thirds of his men were cavalry who were without shields. And once he was fighting Merren's Norstalines, the Rallorans would hit his open flank. He had no doubt what would happen then.

'There is no danger!' Onzalez screamed. 'You have me with you, and none can stand against me!'

'Stop!'

Everyone turned to see an old man in the robes of a priest walk carefully across the piles of dead and wounded.

Onzalez turned to face him.

'I am Archbishop Enterius Nott, and this is my country. You are not welcome here, Fearpriest,' Nott said mildly, but not only did his words carry easily to everyone on that field, none doubted the steel behind them.

'This is no longer your country! Rise! Rise and do my bidding!' Onzalez pointed to where the Tenoch dead and wounded lay in heaps, and where Martil, Sacrax and the Derthals were only now regaining their feet.

Martil stepped back in shock and horror as the dead began to pull themselves to their feet. Instantly he was transported back to the Archbishop's office in the capital, when Prent had made the dead come to life — and remembered how hard it was to stop them.

He backed away as dead men staggered to unsteady feet and searched for fallen weapons.

'Rest in peace!' Nott thundered.

Instantly the walking dead froze in place.

'Kill! Kill for me!' Onzalez screeched.

But although they tried to walk forwards, the dead could not move. For a long moment they struggled against the unseen forces that both compelled them to act, and called them back to their sleep, then they simply collapsed.

Onzalez shuddered with fury and strode towards Nott, ignoring all those around him.

'Archbishop, I ...' Milly began as she breathlessly raced to his side, Kesbury a step behind.

'Get away! The pair of you! It is him and me! Everyone else get back!' Nott roared.

Startled, they stayed put as Nott stalked forwards to meet the Fearpriest, who was advancing quickly, heedless of the nearby Norstalines.

But the distraction allowed a group of bowmen to run at the Fearpriest. At a gesture from Onzalez, most of them were thrown backwards — while the Fearpriest merely touched the two closest to him.

Blood burst from their eyes, ears, noses and mouths and they fell backwards.

'Keep away! Leave him to me!' Nott shouted urgently.

The remaining bowmen backed away, while everyone else kept their distance also.

'You fool! You are old and weak — you cannot stop me! And once you are dead, your country will be mine!' Onzalez boasted.

Again he thrust his hand into the ground, sending it rippling towards Nott, who kneeled down swiftly and laid his hands flat on the ground. With a groan, the ground shook, then burst up between them, throwing dead and wounded men into the air.

Onzalez stood and brought his hands together.

Milly and Kesbury backed further away as the air around Nott turned cold, ice forming on the ground beneath him. But the old priest stretched out his arms and a blast of warm air melted the ice.

Onzalez stared at the man, who stood there, relaxed, arms by his side.

In fact everyone was staring at him, which Onzalez swiftly realised. Not just the men and Derthals, but everyone on the walls and all those who had flooded out of the city gates. Even many of the Tenochs and Berellians who had broken and run had stopped to watch this duel.

'Time to stop playing,' Onzalez announced and strode forwards, arm outstretched, reaching out to strike Nott down, in the same manner that had killed the bowmen.

But Nott was too quick. He ducked under Onzalez's arm and brought his own hand around in a flat slap. Everyone thought it looked an innocuous blow, the sort of thing a woman might deal to an importunate man; something to shock and surprise, rather than hurt.

Only this had a completely different effect.

Onzalez screamed as it struck his face with a hiss, as if hot iron had been plunged into icy water, and kept screaming as the blow sent him flying through the air, impossibly high and long, until it choked off abruptly as he thumped to the ground almost at the feet of Gello.

Everyone stared in shock and surprise; nobody moved until Prent kneeled beside his mentor.

'He's alive, but unconscious. I cannot wake him,' Prent said urgently.

Gello licked dry lips and looked around the battlefield. The Tenochs and Berellians who had paused in their flight now turned tail and ran, pursued by a vengeful flood from the city. Meanwhile, he could see Rallorans, Norstalines and goblins closing in on him.

'Fighting retreat! Back to the horses!' He tried to sound calm, but even to his ears it was shrill. 'Prent, Ezok, take Onzalez.'

His infantry regiment dutifully formed up a line to stop the advancing Norstalines and Rallorans, while the cavalry regiments hurried across the field, to where their horses waited at their camp.

Gello paused only to throw off his armour, before breaking into a run, to make sure he was at the front of the retreat. Prent, Ezok and Onzalez's bewildered bodyguard were carrying the limp Fearpriest across the field.

'Hurry!' he urged them, as he passed. Saving the Fearpriest was secondary to saving his own life but if he was going to keep alive the faint hope of one day extracting some revenge, he needed Onzalez.

They needed little urging.

Behind them, Heath and his regiment were attempting to march backwards and stay in line. But the Norstalines under Hutter and Kay slammed into their front — and moments later, Nerrin's Rallorans struck their open flank. Heath's men fought on for a few moments — then simply dissolved, running for their lives.

Meanwhile, Martil, Sacrax and the Derthals were angling to cut off Gello's retreat. They were bone-tired, exhausted by their long march, their run and their victory over the Tenochs. But the sight of a fleeing enemy put fresh life into their legs and they were not weighed down by shields and armour. Soon they began overtaking the slower runners, the men puffing and panting in their long mail shirts. But while those shirts slowed them down, they did not save them from a Derthal spear — or the Dragon Sword.

Gello, free of his armour, was the first to reach the horses, which had been left saddled, ready for a triumphal parade through the city. He clambered onto his horse and looked back over the field, to watch in horror as his men ran desperately, pursued by Derthals, Rallorans and Norstalines. Some tried to fight — and died — some were unable to run fast enough — and died — some tried to surrender and, if they were lucky enough, they lived. Many of their pursuers were in no mood for mercy.

Gello dared not wait — he spurred his horse away, only feeling a pang at the thought of having to leave Mother behind. But he had no time to get to his tent. He just had to escape. He was followed by Prent, Ezok and Onzalez's bodyguard. The Fearpriest had been lashed across a saddle, like a sack of turnips, and Ezok led his horse by the reins. Behind them came Livett and Feld and a mixture of infantry and cavalry, the strongest and fittest ones, and the ones who knew they could not surrender because their crimes would doom them.

Barely a thousand made it off the field; the last of them were dragged down from their horses and killed, even as their comrades galloped wildly away.

But even escaping from the battlefield was no guarantee of safety. The capital had almost emptied, with angry men determined to gain revenge for all they and their families suffered. Exhausted Tenochs and Berellians were caught and butchered. There was no mercy.

They pleaded with Gello and his frightened men for help, begged to be taken along, saved from the very people they had planned to slaughter. Gello only chose Berellians and any surviving eagle and leopard warriors, until every man was riding double and he had to leave the rest behind to their deaths.

'They shall not catch us!' he declared. Thinking about escape enabled him to pretend the day's events had never happened. He had begun it thinking he had a plan to rule two countries and become an emperor. He had finished it by seeing the greatest army that had ever marched on this continent being beaten into bloody defeat and being forced to run for his life. But he was not dead — and they would regret that, he swore.

Merren did not join the rush to slaughter Gello's fleeing men, or the retreating Tenochs and Berellians. For a long moment she sat, eyes shut, coming to terms with the fact she had won. That her people and her country were safe, and could finally live in peace.

Then she stared over the battlefield, where thousands of men and hundreds of Derthals lay.

Where the ground heaved and sobbed as wounded men and Derthals tried to stop their lifeblood flowing into the soil, and held out their hands for help. Already the priests and priestesses from the city, as well as every healer and apothecary, were trying to save lives and staunch wounds. She looked carefully, burning the image forever into her mind. Then she signalled to Barrett and turned towards the capital, where thousands of women and children thronged the walls, and waited outside the gate.

'There are men and Derthals here who need your help! Quickly!' she cried, her voice echoing over the city walls.

As their menfolk had rushed out to chase and kill the fleeing Berellians and Tenochs, so the women hurried out to help the wounded. Merren watched in pride as they went to help the Derthals and Rallorans as swiftly as they rushed to help their own. But they needed more than just hands, they needed the healing powers of priests. With that in mind, she rode Tomon over to where Archbishop Nott stood, flanked by Milly and Kesbury.

'What now?' Hutter shouted, as the last of Gello's men either died choking on their own blood or stood miserably, hands high in the air.

Kay shrugged. 'I thought we were going to die. I hadn't planned for after the battle,' he admitted.

All around them, men and Derthals raised their weapons in the air and cheered, embraced each other, or slumped to the ground, exhausted. Some sobbed, almost unable to believe they had survived and overcome with the reality of what they had faced.

Martil did not have time to think. 'We'll take Gello's spare horses and chase the bastards down.

We can't let them escape again. If we had managed to catch Gello after Pilleth, none of this would have happened,' he declared. 'Nerrin! Get the men ready for a pursuit!' He found Hutter, Kettering, Kay and Ryder. 'The rest of you, there're wounded who need to be helped. Although Gello left plenty of horses here. We need to pick a company of men from your regiments to join.'

'With your permission, sir, we're out of arrows and my men aren't used to horses. I'd like to stay here and help the wounded,' Ryder said tiredly.

Hutter looked around. 'I'll call for volunteers. But I'll stay here also, to help our wounded.'

Martil looked to where a blood-spattered Kettering stood.

'I will hunt them down,' he said wolfishly. 'While a Berellian is alive, I shall not rest!'

Martil nodded, seeing the anger within the man, and recognising himself there.

'Whatever happens now, whatever else you do in your life, you will be able to look back on this day with pride,' he told them. 'You and your men have saved a country, and a people. Your King Riel, the heroes of the sagas the country loves so much — they are nothing. Not compared to a pair of peasant bowmen, a fat militia sergeant and the manager of an inn. I salute you all!'

Shocked, they watched as he raised the spotless Dragon Sword in the formal salute. Then he hurried off to where Nerrin was mustering the tired Rallorans, and where a mass of Derthals sat or lay on the ground, clutching bloodied spears.

They stared at each other, unable to quite believe what he had said.

'I pity the bard who has to get that line to rhyme properly,' Hutter finally said, with a grin.

'I always wanted a saga about me. But I wanted to get the princess at the end,' Ryder offered.

'Princesses are over-rated. Give me a barmaid any day.' Kay nudged him.

Kettering sighed as they looked at him. 'I cannot jest. Not while there is work to do. I shall return with Gello's head, to go with the Berellian King's.'

'Not much of a perfect ending,' Hutter complained.

'This is real life. Not a saga. It doesn't end, it goes on,' Kay told him.

Hutter smiled. 'Aye, you're right there.' He raised his voice. 'I want the best riders ready to go with Captain Kettering now! The rest of you — there're mates out there dying! Help them!'

'So what happens now?' Sacrax asked tiredly, sitting on the ground and massaging his spear arm.

'I shall chase our enemies, make sure they can never hurt us again. You help the wounded, then we celebrate. We won, my friend! We won, thanks to your warriors!' Martil held out his hand.

Sacrax looked at his tired and bloodied warriors. 'Glad it is over,' he admitted, pushing himself to his feet. 'Now I see why my fathers left our home rather than fight like this.'

'Well, you have your home back again. And you shall never have to leave there,' Martil promised. 'Anyone who doesn't want you there will answer to me, and every man who fought with you today.'

'And you also welcome. From today, you are a Derthal.' Sacrax ignored Martil's hand and embraced him instead. 'You saved my life — the lives of many of my warriors.'

'I must go, my friend,' Martil said finally, when he managed to extricate himself. 'I must not let Gello escape.'

'Perhaps you can do it from the dragon.' Sacrax pointed to where Argurium swooped towards them.

Martil felt a sudden chill. Something had gone wrong. He knew it. All thoughts of pursuing Gello vanished.

'Archbishop! You were magnificent! For a moment I thought that Fearpriest would turn the battle — and you defeated him!' Merren called.

'Your majesty, you too were magnificent. Your courage and vision have saved this country, this continent — perhaps the world — from the dark clutches of Zorva.' Nott smiled tiredly. 'As for me, I did what I was required to do. I was but a vessel for the power of Aroaril.'

'You sell yourself short, Archbishop.' Merren smiled, but trailed off when Nott toppled over.

Kesbury caught Nott in his arms and laid him gently on the ground.

Merren jumped down from Tomon's back and rushed over to where Milly held Nott's hand.

'Do not cry. I have fulfilled my purpose,' Nott said. 'Man is not supposed to hold so much power. Better that it be me, rather than one of you. Tell Karia I love her, she has my blessing and I will watch over her always.'

'But who will lead the Church back?' Milly asked, tears running down her face.

'You will, my dear. You and Kesbury. That is your purpose. Mine is finished.'

Merren stared down at the old man, who smiled back up at her. She thought of all the things she said about him in anger, the way she had accused him of manipulating her and tricking her.

'I am sorry,' she told him. 'This country will not forget what you did.'

Nott smiled once more, then his last breath whispered out and he was still.

Merren fought to compose herself as Milly sobbed and Kesbury sat, cradling Nott in his arms, tears running down his face. She looked up as Argurium swooped in to land, and the small girl leaped from the dragon's back and pounded across the ground. Merren raced towards her and caught Karia up in her arms.

'Let me go! Let me go! Father! I'm coming!' she screamed.

'He's gone. He's gone. But I'm still here for you, Martil's still here.' Merren hugged the sobbing girl close and pointed at Havell.

'Get Martil!'

By the time Argurium had returned with Martil, Karia was almost beside herself. She flung herself into Martil's arms and he held her close.

'Kesbury, can you carry the Archbishop into the city? We must honour what he did,' Milly asked.

Merren put her hand on Milly's shoulder.

'Archbishop,' she said. 'There are others who need your help first.'

'Don't call me that! I'm not fit to follow in his footsteps!' Milly turned a tear-stained face to Merren.

'You are the Archbishop, and you have a duty to your people! Would you let his sacrifice be in vain?' Merren snapped.

Milly's eyes blazed for a moment, then she wiped them, and nodded.

'There are men and Derthals who need us,' she agreed. 'We shall help them.'

Merren watched her go and felt exhausted. She knew she should feel elated. But she had lived with the pressure on her shoulders for so long, the burden of so many lives depending on her, that even victory left her feeling empty. The death of Nott, of so many others was also no reason to celebrate.

She looked back across the field, to where Rallorans, Derthals and Norstalines put down their weapons and worked, side by side, to save each other on the field where they had fought as one. That made her feel good, at least.

'Why did he have to die? Why?' Karia demanded.

Martil held her close. 'I don't know. But he would have done that because he knew it would save many other lives.' He did not add that Nott's insistence on spending time with Karia made sense now. He could not stop a flicker of fear at Nott's fate. The man had been forced to give up everything he loved — and his reward had been death. He had saved them but it was still a cruel end and, worse, Martil wondered if it also awaited him.

'I miss him! I want him back!'

'I know. But I'm here. I'll always be here. There will be no more battles. It is all finished,' Martil told her. He had taken a few moments to clean himself. But he could see he was still smearing her with blood. Barrett had released the magical protection, and the cut he had taken from a Tenoch spear along his side was bleeding, as were several other wounds on his arms, chest and legs, which he had barely noticed before but were now burning with pain.

'Just stay with me. Don't leave,' she begged.

'I will,' he promised, hugging her tight.

'I just wanted to say goodbye, tell him I love him,' she tried to wipe her eyes.

'He knew.' Martil held her until her sobs quietened down, and became aware that Merren was standing close.

'We did it, my Queen!' he said softly.

'We did, my Champion.' She smiled back, trailing her fingers across his cheek.

'So do you think the people will accept a Ralloran Prince Consort now?' he managed to ask.

Merren wanted to say yes, but hesitated. 'We shall see,' was all she said.

Gello and the Berellians had left behind nearly two thousand horses. Nerrin could not find riders for them all — but he still had five hundred Rallorans, and more than that again of Norstalines under Kettering. With them went Barrett, in case the Fearpriests tried to use magic. Milly believed they would not stop and fight, they would just run, that Nott's power had scared them but Merren insisted and Barrett was happy to show his strength.

The pursuers were tired, but angry. And every mile of countryside they went through made them angrier. Every burned farm, every ravaged village was a spur to them. Tenochs and Berellians, the men who had done this, fled before them. But against men on horseback, they had no chance. Some tried to fight — and died. Some tried to hide, but companies of men went through every cutting, house and village, everywhere there was a place where their enemies could lurk. Some tried to surrender, rushing out with hands held high. A few of these were killed — particularly if they tried to surrender anywhere near the bodies of dead Norstaline women and children. Most were just tied up, where they could do no harm. Although even these did not always survive, for following behind were ordinary Norstalines, men from the city, who had been driven out of this land by the Tenochs and Norstalines. They had no mercy, not even for a tied and cowering enemy. Kitchen knives, wood axes and clubs were used to finish them off.

But while they slaughtered thousands of Tenochs and Berellians, Gello and his riders drew further ahead. They halted as it grew dark.

'We need food to continue the pursuit,' Nerrin told Dunner. 'Take a company back to the capital and bring us supplies. They'll get tired and we'll catch them. We don't stop until we have the last one.'

It was a cold camp for Gello and the bedraggled survivors of what had been an army of conquest. Some saddlebags had a little food in them and a few men had something in a belt pouch — if they had not thrown it away in their desperate dash for life — but most went hungry. There was fire and there was water — but little else. And then there was the fear. They knew they were being chased and that they could expect little mercy, as they had promised none.

'What now?' was the common question being asked around the fires.

There was no answer. Only the fact that they had to stay together to survive kept men from running off. And where, in this country, could they run to?

'What now?' Gello asked Onzalez.

The Fearpriest had finally woken up after Prent had tried to heal him, and he was sitting away from the fire, for the heat was aggravating the burn on his face — the burn caused by Nott's blow.

'This is a valuable lesson for us,' Onzalez declared. 'We were arrogant, we thought we could achieve with strength of arms what Zorva wanted us to do through His power. But we are not defeated. Oh no. The foul Aroaril worshippers may rejoice tonight but their time is coming!'

Gello felt a flare of anger. He had placed himself and his men in the hands of this Fearpriest — and once more he had been left defeated at his moment of triumph. If he was ever going to achieve his destiny then he had to seize some control. 'How?' he demanded. 'Where can we go? All that is left of the Berellian army is with us. And this time Merren won't let us escape over the border. There's no-one to stop Martil coming after us now — and we all know what happened the last time he invaded Berellia! Then the Rallorans under Tolbert will want a slice of revenge and probably the Avish as well — there is nowhere to hide.'

There was a collective intake of breath around the fire as Prent, Khaliz and Ezok all looked at the Fearpriest. Just one day ago, nobody would have dared to speak to Onzalez like that. But everything had changed in that day. Not only was Gello the only monarch left but every man was dependent on him.

Onzalez said nothing for a long moment. He could not go back to Tenoch like this. The Ruling Council had been his. They had given him power, freedom and an army to wield. But he was under no illusions that they were loyal. They were like the wolf pack — if they smelled weakness they would turn on him, and tear him to pieces. If he returned with nothing, he would be first undermined, then eventually stretched out across the altar. He had to give them a prize, something to show for his years away from Tenoch. His first instinct had been to seek sanctuary in Berellia, where he had left thousands of worshippers. But Gello was right. There was no Berellian army any more and the Norstalines, Rallorans and Avish could parcel the country up between them. He glanced up to see Ezok looking at him and was struck by inspiration.

'Dragonara Isle,' he said instantly.

'What nonsense is that?' Gello snorted. 'Do you think the dragons will welcome us in?'

'No. But that is not why we go there. They have a magical object, so powerful it makes the Dragon Sword look like a child's toy! It is called the Dragon Egg and, with it, we cannot be stopped,' Onzalez declared, enthusiasm returning to his voice. 'With it in our hands, we shall have power over magic itself!'

'Why did you not tell us of this before? And why have we not heard of it ourselves?' Gello asked suspiciously.

'Ezok discovered it on his failed trip to the north to see the foul creatures of Aroaril!'

Everyone turned to look at Ezok and Khaliz.

'Yes, the trip that cost us victory! If the goblins had stayed in their mountains, we would even now be sitting in my palace!' Gello growled.

Ezok met his gaze. 'The fault lies with Cezar — and he is long dead,' he replied defiantly. 'And perhaps we were meant to go there to find out about the Dragon Egg. Perhaps this is all part of Zorva's plan for our eventual victory.'

Gello snorted with disgust. Having a massive army was the key to victory. Then he paused. Twice now he had had a massive army — and failed. Perhaps he needed something to counter the Dragon Sword ...

'Ezok is right,' Onzalez agreed. 'With the Egg in our control, we can bring down the thrones of the world!'

'And you are sure of this Egg's power?' Gello challenged Ezok. He had not trusted the man since Pilleth.

Ezok looked him in the eye. 'On my life. The dragon we all saw above the battlefield was there in the north and let slip the truth about it. They need Martil and the Dragon Sword to guard it. In exchange for his help, the dragon aided them in the battle. It is unbelievably powerful — it can control all magic!'

'What I could do with that!' Khaliz said reverently.

Gello hesitated. After all, if it was so powerful, surely the dragons would not give it up easily.

Onzalez levered himself to his feet. 'Walk with me, King Gello. You and I have much to discuss,' he invited.

Gello stood also, although he made sure he kept his hand on his sword. He followed Onzalez to a quiet area, away from the obvious interest of the other three.

'I want to see you crowned emperor, ruling over this entire continent,' Onzalez said simply.

Gello said nothing.

'But, as you rightly point out, there is no safe land here for us. We can sail back to Tenoch, to recover and build our strength there. But I will not lie to you — we shall not receive a warm welcome if we return there in defeat. The Ruling Council belongs to me — but they will rediscover their independence if they think I am weak. Besides, the best warriors Tenoch has are either here, or lying dead outside the Norstaline capital. To build an army big enough to retake Berellia, let alone Norstalos and the other countries, will take many years. But if we have the Dragon Egg, we shall be welcomed back in Tenoch. With it in our hands, we can build an army by magic. We can sail back here and destroy everything and everyone who tries to stop us! And then you can take your rightful place on the throne.'

'As your puppet?' Gello asked sourly. He knew Onzalez only wanted help because of weakness. Return his power and he could not be trusted.

'No. My life's work is to convert the Aroaril-lovers to the true God. It was my arrogance and lust for power that destroyed us today. I see it now. Only together can we secure the final victory.'

'And the Ruling Council? What is this?' Gello sniffed.

'The city, indeed the continent, is ruled by the Seventeen, also known as the Ruling Council or, simply, the Council. These are the seventeen most powerful priests of Zorva on the continent, nine from Tenoch, one each from the eight city-states that we rule. When I say the seventeen, I mean sixteen others and myself,' Onzalez said carefully. 'For years I have been the leader and they have done whatever I asked. But they are not loyal. If they see a chance, there are those among them who shall try to seize back power. That is why we need the Egg, so I can show them I am still as strong as ever.'

'So will we sail to our deaths there?' Gello asked sharply.

Onzalez did not hesitate. 'We shall tell them the army is back here, still fighting and we need more men to secure victory. To them, I can disguise lies with half-truths. And, when they see the power of the Dragon Egg, they will give us what we want. Everything will go on as before.'

Gello chewed his nail and wished he could talk to Mother — only he had been forced to leave her portrait behind. He did not much like the sound of this Ruling Council. But he knew men. Habits of obedience became ingrained. If they were used to agreeing with whatever Onzalez suggested, it was reasonable to expect they would continue to do so.

'But what about the dragons? Surely they will not hand over such a powerful magic item?'

'The dragons are rarely on their island. They will not expect anyone to dare what we shall. We have men, we have magic and we have the power of Zorva. But, most importantly, we have nothing to lose. We can go away and live in failure, or we can do something to snatch victory!'

Gello reluctantly agreed. What else could he do, where else could he go? He had no choice. He would go along with Onzalez's plan but if the Fearpriest or Ezok was lying, then he could take control. With two thousand swords at his back he could find a new land, carve himself out another kingdom. But Norstalos was the one he really wanted, so he would use the Fearpriest for as long as he could. Gello stared at the shadowy cowl. 'You ask a great deal. But how can I trust you?'

Onzalez hesitated only a moment before lowering his cowl, revealing his face.

Gello had not known what to expect — he was thinking an elderly man perhaps, one whose face was marked by all the blood he had spilled for Zorva. But Onzalez was young, no older than Gello himself. It was hard to see in the dim light from the nearby fires but his skin was swarthy, marked by several tattoos as well as the livid burn on his right cheek. He looked ... normal. Gello could barely believe he had seen the man parade around in the warm, bloody skin of a flayed victim little more than a day before. Onzalez looked as though he could be a diplomat, or prosperous merchant, not a bloody-handed priest of the Dark God.

'You are the first person not on the council to see my face — and live — in ten years,' Onzalez said simply. 'There is no greater trust for me. No words could equal that.'

Gello stared at him coolly.

'Nevertheless, I would like you to swear to Zorva that you will make me emperor — and let me rule alone — if I help you retrieve the Dragon Egg from Dragonara Isle.'

'I do swear by Zorva,' Onzalez agreed.

Gello chuckled. 'Then all we have to do is escape Martil's pursuit and sail strange craft from Worick to Dragonara Isle, where no man has sailed for decades.'

'Those are the least of our problems,' Onzalez told him, as he raised his cowl once more.

17

They worked on, by torchlight and lamplight, priests, priestesses, healers, the Magicians' Guild and ordinary people. There were so many wounded and dead.

By unspoken agreement, the Tenochs, Berellians and Gello's traitorous Norstalines were left. The priorities were the Norstalines, Rallorans and Derthals. Not only were they spread over a massive area, but they were also often buried under other bodies. Then there were the civilians, who had poured out of the capital to chase a beaten enemy. While they had slaughtered many fleeing soldiers, some of those had turned and fought back, like trapped rats. Dozens of wounded and dead had been brought back, some from miles away.

Merren was still on the field, determined to be there when the last man or Derthal was found.

The dead were being buried together — the hundreds of prisoners taken had been forced to dig a massive trench before being allowed back out to help their wounded comrades. Merren had decreed that all would lie together — Norstaline, Ralloran and Derthal. They had fought together, now they would lie together for eternity.

The huge number of people helping saved lives,

she was sure of that. Unlike Pilleth, where the only men available were the ones who had fought so hard to win the battle, thousands of women had rushed out to help, as well as dozens of priests. A grief-stricken Milly had worked to save all she could, healing the most grievously wounded men and Derthals, while those with minor wounds at least had their hurts bandaged and stitched.

'I think that is the last of them now, my Queen.' Hutter saluted as he escorted a dozen horses laden with dead Derthals back to the mass grave.

'Do we know how many?' Merren asked numbly.

'We won't know until the morning. We don't know how many went with Captain Nerrin to pursue Gello, your majesty,' Hutter apologised. 'But I'd say we lost about five hundred Norstalines and Rallorans and perhaps the same of Derthals. There are many more wounded, although most will eventually recover.'

Merren nodded. As numbers on parchment, it was not many. Not compared to the ten thousand or more Tenochs, Berellians and Gello's Norstalines who had been killed or wounded on the field, and the same number who were still dying as they tried to flee on foot or by horse. But they were still men and Derthals who had been walking, talking and smiling in the morning and who now lay in a grave together this night.

'Let the prisoners do what they can for their wounded. I cannot feel sympathy for those who would have killed us all. But those that they save — see if Archbishop Milly — I mean, Archbishop Sadlier, can help them. And get some rest.'

Hutter smiled. 'Strangely, I do not feel much like sleep. There are too many I know who are in an endless sleep.'

Merren nodded understandingly. 'Thank you for your report. Whatever you need, when you need it, ask it of me.'

She climbed wearily onto Tomon to ride back to the palace. She needed to see Martil, wanted to know how Karia was. But she could not do so when men who had died for her were still out there. As well as supervising the search for the wounded and the collection of the dead, she had made sure she spent time talking to High Chief Sacrax, emphasising how much Norstalos valued their help, their sacrifice — and how it would not only be remembered but the debt the Norstalines owed the Derthals would ensure his tribes' lives would be forever changed for the better.

She had expected the city to be almost silent when she rode back, escorted only by Jaret and Wilsen. After all, it was past midnight and the day just gone had probably been the most dramatic in the country's history, following from a night where most had not slept.

But the streets were still packed. It was a mirror image of the night before. But where that night's revelry had been marked by desperation and tinged with despair, this one was genuinely joyful. There was grief, too, there had to be grief when so many had died. But the overwhelming feeling was relief. People were embracing each other, talking, eating and drinking the previously hoarded stores — and as soon as she rode by, they stopped what they were doing to cheer and clap. And not just people. Derthals were also eating and drinking, especially with men in her surcoats. They did not speak each other's language but that did not seem to matter. Sign language, and the odd Derthal who spoke a few words of human seemed to suffice.

Even as she marvelled at the celebrations, people and Derthals rushed over, holding out their hands for her to touch; others held out children. Wounded men, even those unable to stand, still managed to salute.

'The Queen! The Queen!'

The chant began at the gate and followed her right through the city. Merren had to fight to hold back her emotions. They had trusted her, and she had managed to save them. Now they could actually have a normal life, a safe life, in a peaceful country. Everything would be right, now. Seeing them like this lifted her in a way that even the victory had not. She knew what she wanted to do and, although the reaction to the day's events, to the events of the past few weeks, was sweeping through her, she forced herself to keep going until she was standing outside Martil's rooms.

'You can leave me here,' she told the ever-present Wilsen and Jaret. 'Have a drink, have some fun, get some sleep. Whatever you want, you have earned it!'

The pair of them saluted, grinning, and hurried off.

This suite had lain empty for fifty years, as had Karia's rooms, next to it. These were part of the royal wing. There were suites for a dozen princes and princesses, although many had not been used for centuries. The old Royal Bedroom, the one she had used in her first reign, was still sealed off, after Gello and his troopers had fouled it following their defeat at Pilleth. She had moved back into her childhood room this time, which was much further down the hall. But after all that had happened, she did not want to lie in bed alone. Her head was telling her this was a bad idea but, after what she had seen that day, she was in no mood to listen.

She reached out and knocked lightly. She was beginning to think he had fallen asleep when the door opened.

Martil had washed and changed, and had his wounds stitched and bandaged. He looked tired but he smiled as soon as he saw her.

'How is she?' Merren asked.

'Sleeping now. Do you want to come in?'

Merren reflected that, a couple of days ago, such a question would have been loaded with meaning and she would have had to weigh its political ramifications before agreeing. Now she could just smile and step inside. As with all the royal suites, this had a sitting room, with a bedroom and bathroom leading off it. Through the open doorway of the bedroom, she could see a small shape curled up in the large bed.

Martil shut the main door carefully, tip-toed across the room to draw the bedroom door shut, then strode back and enfolded her in his arms, stifling a groan as she pressed against one of several wounds.

'I can barely believe it! We won! We were ready to give up, ready to die — and we won!' Merren clutched him tighter.

Martil gently shifted her left arm higher up his chest, to avoid the cut he had taken from a Tenoch spear, and held her back.

'They had no leadership and the three parts of their army would not work together. Each wanted to preserve themselves. Gello had at least three opportunities to win the battle — and took none of them. You saw your opening, took it and defeated him,' he explained in a whisper.

'I know what happened, I just wanted to share what I am feeling,' she told him, with a touch of asperity.

'There're plenty of people out there you could talk to, your majesty,' he offered, with a smile.

'But only one of them I love.'

He kissed her then, feeling the tension inside him begin to fade away. 'I cannot believe it, either. We should be overjoyed but I feel almost empty inside. So many dead, so many I knew — and then Nott's death, right at the end.'

'So you do know how I feel.'

'Just because I do not say the words, does not mean I do not feel,' he grunted. 'And I especially feel when your arm is right on the biggest cut I took today.'

She adjusted her arm around him but was not ready to let him go.

'After the way you squealed when I tugged on your chest hairs, it's probably too small to see,' she teased him gently.

'Nine stitches! And those were all hard won, to gain you your most famous victory!'

'It was not just my victory!' she protested quietly.

'That's not what the people and Derthals out there are singing — I was told Romon was composing the Saga of Merren. It's already eighteen verses, with a catchy chorus!'

'Then I shall order at least two verses to be about you,' she said, hiding her smile in his tunic.

'Two verses!' He looked down to see her grinning and could not help but smile back.

'So what do you want to do now? We can order some wine, if you like. Find Romon and get him to sing to you ...'

'Or we could just lie down on the couch over there,' she suggested.

Martil glanced over his shoulder. The couch was wide, well-padded and with a number of decorative cushions. 'Just lie down?' he asked.

'Just. Lie. Down,' she emphasised. 'I do not want to have you complaining every time I put my hand on your stitches — and I need to sleep.' She looked up at him and came to a sudden decision. What she had seen in the city had fired her blood, left her feeling inspired. Everything was going to work out now. They had been through their trial of blood and fire. 'Besides, there is no rush. We have the rest of our lives together.'

Martil stopped trying to hide his disappointment that they would only be sleeping and looked at her. 'Is that a jest?'

She hit him on the chest, then kissed him when he winced because her blow landed on a bandaged wound. 'That is no jest.' She laughed, sure she was making the right choice. 'You should see what is going on out in the city tonight! Rallorans, Norstalines, Derthals — all drinking, laughing and celebrating together. Rich merchants and poor farmers, westerners and easterners, goat herders and heads of guilds — they are all together. I think one thing this has taught us is that it does not matter where a person is born, or who their parents were. Their true worth is inside.'

'And that has convinced you it is safe to marry me?' Martil demanded.

'I always wanted to. But it was never about that. I had to put the country first, think about what the people wanted. I will feel guilty about being happy when so many are in mourning, but from what I saw tonight, I think the people will let me have a little happiness. So the only question is whether you want the marriage before or after you fly off to Dragonara Isle to open the Dragon Egg.'

'Aroaril! I'd forgotten about that!' Martil exclaimed. Then he stroked her hair back. 'Before, obviously. How does tomorrow sound?'

She laughed loudly until he silenced her with a kiss.

'Don't wake Karia!' he hissed.

'Sorry.' She yawned and walked over to the wide couch, where she sank down with relief. 'How will Karia be about this?'

Martil joined her on the couch. 'She needs a family — she has been going on about how she never had one. After losing Father Nott, this is the best thing for her.'

'A normal life — it's something we all need,' she said with feeling.

'Aye. Surely nothing else can happen now!'

But she was already asleep.

Count Sendric rode back into the capital feeling both elated and frustrated. Against all the odds, they had won! The goblins had fought better than he had imagined and had helped turn the day. Now they could rebuild Norstalos, turn it into a country everyone could be proud of. But, once again, Gello had escaped. It was a hot coal in his gut. His daughter's spirit cried out for revenge. Despite his sore shoulder, which had never really healed properly since the battle of Sendric, he had ridden down a score of Berellians and Tenochs, killing the evil bastards who had invaded his country. But he would have exchanged all of them for one chance at Gello. Killing the man was the only thing he wanted for himself. He still had ambitions for his country, of course. As Prince Consort, he wanted to help rebuild, and remake Norstalos. This was a unique opportunity to wipe out many of the mistakes made in the previous centuries. The spirit of the people, tested like never before, had shone through. The next few years would be hard but the results would be worth it, he was sure. Under Merren's rule, with his help, Norstalos would flourish. And not only flourish, but take its rightful place on the world stage. No more would countries watch on as others invaded. Sendric dreamed of a continent where the countries could work together, sorting out their disagreements amicably. A continent where the naked aggression of the Berellians would not be tolerated and rogue countries would be faced by nations united in peace.

The capital was still partying when he rode through the gate, and he smiled indulgently at the way the goblins — no, he corrected himself, the Derthals, were laughing and dancing with Rallorans and Norstalines alike. He had been wrong about them. He could admit that — he would admit that! In the morning, he planned to say as much to Martil. It had been the Ralloran warrior's plans — the use of the Derthals and the bowmen taking up the pikes — that had won the battle. That made three times Martil had won the day and he intended to make sure everyone knew what a debt the country owed Martil.

As for Merren, there were no accolades high enough for her. The way she had held the country together through sheer force of will — she deserved her place in history. Complimenting Martil could wait until the morning but he had to speak to Merren tonight. With all that needed doing, he was sure she would still be awake.

But he could not find her in the throne room, nor in her bedroom suite. He tried a few smaller offices then, because he was also hungry and thirsty, went into the kitchens. There was quite a party going on in there — dozens of servants eating, drinking and dancing on the tables used to prepare the food. On another night he would have bellowed at them, ordered them to stop this outrageous display. But he could not begrudge it, not on this night. He was about to turn away, to find somewhere quiet, when he spotted Jaret and Wilsen dancing on a table with a pair of serving girls. He knew the Queen never went anywhere without them, so he hurried over.

'Count Sendric!' Wilsen put down a giggling serving girl and snapped to attention. 'What can we do for you?'

Sendric gave them a smile. 'Don't let me spoil your fun. But I was looking for the Queen. Do you know where she is?'

Wilsen and Jaret exchanged a nervous look, then the big guardsman dropped to one knee, and lowered his voice.

'We escorted her to Captain Martil's rooms, sir. Then she dismissed us from duty.'

Sendric was able to control himself only because of his years of practise. 'Quite right, too. Enjoy yourselves,' he said stiffly, before turning and walking out.

Once the kitchen doors were shut behind him, he allowed himself the indulgence of swearing loudly and fluently.

How could they? Here he was, trying to think about the future of the country — and all they could think about was each other. It would not do! It simply would not do! He would not have his honour trampled and the country made a laughing stock because she could not control herself around that brutish Ralloran! He told himself it was not just his pride that was at risk, either. The country had suffered more than at any time in its history. The trials of King Riel were as nothing to what they had just gone through. Healing Norstalos would be an enormous effort. The people were going to face the hardest winter in history. And the thousands of people already unsure about having a Queen must also accept both thousands of goblins living within their borders and a female Archbishop. Adding a base-born Ralloran Prince Consort and a half-breed Ralloran Crown Prince could tear the country apart!

'I must put a stop to this,' he said aloud.

The more he thought about it, the more sure he was. There was no point in saving the country if Merren was going to throw it all away like this. He had to protect her from herself. It was probably tiredness that had affected her judgment, he decided. When she realised how she was risking the country, she would thank him for what he was about to do.

He had once thought of Merren as almost a surrogate daughter. Since she had become Queen that had been hard to sustain but he recognised he still felt that fatherly protectiveness towards her. Martil was not good enough for her. It was as simple as that. He was not her father, he could not forbid such a marriage. But he could still stop it.

Nodding to himself, Sendric hurried out into the night. There were many people he needed to see, and much he needed to organise.

Merren woke suddenly. Her eyes were gritty, she needed a drink of water and she could sense her hair was a tangled mess. But she felt happy, relaxed, for the first time in she did not know when. There would be many problems to be dealt with today. But, for the first time in weeks, she did not have to think about armies carving paths of destruction through the country. She was lying on her side and Martil's arm was across her shoulders. While he had obviously washed after the battle, she could smell that it had only been a quick wash. And she could see that his cuts had only been stitched quickly — probably because there had been a hundred other men to see to. One on his upper arm had opened again in the night and not only stained the bandage but dripped onto her clothes. Clothes that smelled like she had worn them for more than a day, and were stained by dirt, and worse. But none of those things bothered her. Not today.

Martil was still asleep so she turned her head to see what had woken her — and saw Karia's face almost right at hers.

'Hello, Merren. What are you doing here?' she asked.

Merren took the child's hand. 'I wanted to see how you were. I was worried about you,' she said gently.

Karia's face seemed to dissolve into tears and Merren reached out to her, drawing her in.

'I miss him,' Karia sobbed softly.

Martil came awake then, lifting Karia up with a grunt and depositing her in the middle of them both.

'I know you miss Father Nott. It's good to miss someone like that,' he told her.

'Good?'

'Aye. So they know how much they meant to you. But you have us both now to look after you.' He hugged her close.

'When you're not too busy,' Karia added.

'I won't be busy nearly as much now. We will be able to spend more time together. Even play some dolls again!' Merren told her, also hugging her.

They stayed like that for a while, until her tears dried up and she just lay there, enjoying being cuddled by them both. Then something occurred to her.

'Good! But why?'

Martil and Merren exchanged a look over the top of her head.

'Well, Merren and I are going to marry,' Martil said carefully.

But Karia only rolled her eyes.

'Well! About time!' she told them. 'Haven't I been saying that for ages? Finally, you decide to listen to me!'

'I know. I should have listened to you earlier,' Merren agreed with a smile.

'But there is one problem with you marrying Martil,' Karia admitted.

'And what's that?' Merren glanced up at Martil, whose face reflected her own concerns. Would Karia be angry about the new baby on the way?

'You realise you will have to sleep in the same bed as him every night? And, Aroaril, does he smell! Take a whiff now!'

Merren tried to keep a straight face as Martil tickled Karia. But she could not hold herself in and their laughter rang out, mixing and filling the room.

'Move!' Gello roared at the men.

He urged on the laggards with the flat of his sword. 'Anyone who falls gets left behind! We wait for nobody!' he yelled at them.

He had woken the battered remnants of the grand army of conquest before dawn and pushed them through the day. They were covering in turns of an hourglass the distance it had taken the Tenochs days to achieve. It was killing the horses but, as they planned to leave those at Worick, it did not matter, they just needed to last long enough to get the men onto the Tenoch ships.

He could have despaired, he could have given up. But he was utterly determined not to be beaten. As far as he was concerned, the massive defeat was the fault of Markuz and Onzalez. He had nothing to do with it. But, if he could get these men away, he still had a chance. And if Onzalez was able to unlock the power of the Dragon Egg then he had a good chance. The way he saw it, winning from a position of despair was the true path to greatness. Three times now he had had all the advantages, all the numbers, and each time Merren had beaten him. If she could do it, surely he could! And he imagined the saga that would follow! Gello, beaten twice, left with a pitiful, bedraggled force, somehow snatched victory from the jaws of defeat. It would be a wonderful story. And surely it would not be that difficult? True, she had defeated him, but her little army had been badly hurt in the battle and the last thing she would be thinking of was building up a new force. He could return within the year and Norstalos would still be ripe for the taking. Thoughts like this sustained him, drove him to push the stragglers onwards. He wanted to save every man he could — for when he returned.

Onzalez watched the way Gello inspired and pushed the men to greater limits, and he approved. He did not need the distraction. His mind was occupied by one thought. The Dragon Egg. The most powerful magical object in the world. The one thing that would not only guarantee him life on his return to Tenoch but allow him to return to victory. He would do whatever it took to get his hands on it. If that meant giving Gello a crown, handing over power to a man he did not trust, then so be it. What mattered was the victory.

* * *

Nerrin gazed out over the ruins of what had been the bustling port of Worick and spat in disgust. A dozen ships were slowly making their way out to sea, their decks packed with men.

'Bastards are getting away!' Kettering snarled.

'We couldn't have gone any faster,' Nerrin sighed. 'The horses are just about dead as it is. And the men wouldn't have been far behind.'

Kettering did not answer. They had caught a score of stragglers, most of them in the last few miles, men whose horses had fallen and who could not keep up with Gello's fleeing forces. Kettering's sword was still wet with the blood of the last.

'They won't be back. We won't see them again, sir,' Dunner offered.

Nerrin smiled. 'Aye. You're right there. But I'd have been happier returning with that bastard in chains — or at least his head.'

'You're right,' Barrett agreed. 'To think the Fearpriests will take him back to their land, where he can live out his life in luxury! After all he has put us through, after all he has done to the country, it's not fair that he escapes justice.'

'Life isn't fair,' Nerrin pointed out, and none disagreed with him.

'What do we do now?' Kettering asked disgustedly.

'I'll let the Queen know that Gello has escaped,' Barrett said tiredly.

'I hope we haven't missed all of the party — or the victory parades,' Dunner grumbled.

'I care nothing for any of those!' Kettering said harshly. He turned his horse. In some ways, he wished he had died on the battlefield. How could he go back to a normal life now?

The others watched him go, silently. Nerrin and Dunner exchanged looks, for they recognised in Kettering some of what they had felt after the Ralloran Wars.

'Maybe one day we can go and get Gello?' Dunner suggested hopefully.

Nerrin snorted. 'Sail across the sea? Are you mad? Come on, we'll let the men rest, then we'll start back to the capital.'

'We had a deal. Now is the time to fulfil it,' Havell declared.

'What, we need to go right now?' Martil protested. He had been playing with Karia, trying to keep her mind from Father Nott and her grief. Merren had joined in, but had left to go and see the wounded, as well as to supervise the collection of the dead Berellians and Tenochs. The bodies had to be buried. Apart from the threat of disease, thousands of birds already fought over the juiciest parts of the corpses, and more flew in every day. The noise alone reached into the palace. Seemingly every crow and raven across the continent — the ones who had grown fat and sleek on the southern battlefields — were on their way.

Havell sighed. 'We do not have to go immediately. But there is no sense in waiting. You have a task. A simple task, to be sure, but one with the utmost importance. You might as well be on the Isle as here. And it might be better for Karia, as well. I know she has been looking forward to Dragonara Isle. After what she has suffered, the trip might do her good.'

Martil leaned in close. 'I hear what you say,' he agreed. 'But you realise she has been looking forward to the Isle because she thinks she's going to meet fairies and pixies and talking bunny rabbits?'

Havell paused, looking over to where Karia had a dolly and a teddy bear talking to each other. 'Well, there won't be anything like that. But it is still a wonderful place. Warm, sandy beaches, the clearest blue waters and fish that will allow themselves to be fed by hand.'

Martil smiled. It did sound pleasant. But there would be no Merren there, which was a perfect reason to put off his trip for as long as possible, and ensure his stay was brief.

'I'll speak to Merren about when she thinks I might be spared here,' was all he would promise.

Havell looked at him. 'It is a beautiful place. Perhaps the ideal one for a honeymoon?'

Martil had to grin. 'I'll ask her, Elf.'

'Elfaran.'

'Whatever.'

'See you do it. Soon.'

18

It was a very different council meeting to the ones they had been holding for the past few weeks. Gone were the strained faces, the stress, the fear. Instead people were laughing and joking or, in the case of Conal, nursing a huge hangover. There were a few faces missing — Nott being the most noticeable.

Quiller, now Bishop Quiller, had finally arrived at the capital. Gratt, of course, was still in the far north, trying to organise the thousands of refugees who had arrived there, and help them return to their homes further south. Barrett was returning from the fruitless pursuit of Gello, along with Nerrin, Dunner and Kettering, while Rocus was still confined to bed. Almost everyone tried to talk to Karia, offer her sweet treats or drinks, which she was happy enough to accept. There were two seats near Merren left empty — one for Nott and one for Count Sendric, who was the other noticeable absentee.

'We cannot wait for Sendric,' Merren announced finally. 'There is too much to get through.'

'First, with your permission, your majesty, I would like to call for three cheers for Queen Merren, and a vote of thanks for how she has guided us through the darkest time in the country's history,' Conal stood and announced.

Before Merren could protest, the room had erupted with cheers, which took her several attempts to wave down.

'You may cheer me — but it is the rest of you who need thanks. Every one of you played a vital part in saving this country — and it is I who should applaud you.' She paused and looked around at them all. 'And I hope Romon here reflects that, in the saga I hear he is preparing.'

Romon stood and bowed, grinning. He thanked his lucky stars he had decided to go with the Queen in that desperate dash from the ranger barracks. The saga he was writing would become famous, more famous even than the Song of Bellic — for it had a happier ending.

'But we still have much to do. We are yet to find out the true extent of the damage to the southern part of the country, not to mention to the cities of Worick and Cessor. Thousands of people must return to their homes and our saviours, the Derthals, must be welcomed into the northern forest. Our borders must be made safe and we must continue the work we began before the invasion. But first, there will be a cause for celebration. You may remember I announced I would marry Count Sendric, the last surviving noble. That is no longer the case. Instead, I shall marry Captain Martil.'

Martil could not keep the grin off his face as people rushed to shake his hand. Unlike the announcement of her engagement to Sendric, the cheers and applause were genuine.

'The marriage will also include our formal adoption of Karia,' Merren continued and Karia laughed at the cheers for that.

'Naturally the ceremony will be performed by the Archbishop — and will have to happen soon, for

Martil needs to fly to Dragonara Isle, to perform a vital task for the dragons, which will take him away from us for we don't know how long. But I'm hopeful the dragons will allow me to visit now and again!'

She smiled at Martil and he felt his heart swell. Karia leaned in and hugged him and he wanted to preserve that moment forever. It could not get any better.

Then the door crashed open.

Everyone turned to see Sendric stride in, looking grim, followed by a dozen men Merren recognised as guild leaders and who were a mystery to everyone else. His entrance was so sudden, and dramatic, that Jaret and Wilsen, who had been laughing and clapping along with the rest, actually started forwards and had half-drawn their swords before they saw who it was.

'Sendric! Welcome!' Merren greeted. 'We were just dealing with a happy announcement before moving on to ...'

'Your majesty, I apologise, but what I have to say will change all plans you have made, or want to make,' Sendric warned.

Instantly the atmosphere in the throne room chilled, as if a bucket of cold water had been thrown over it. The last time such a statement had been made — coincidentally just after a wedding announcement — they had been told of the invasion threat.

'What is it?' Merren demanded.

'The country is on the brink of collapse and your relationship with Captain Martil will destroy it,' Sendric explained.

Martil started to rise but Merren held out a hand and he subsided.

Sendric gestured to the men behind him.

'As you suggested, I have been investigating the economic impact the invasions and the mass evacuation have had on the country. Here with me are the leaders of the biggest guilds in the country, men who keep the treasury full and the country moving. And the news from them is horrific. We must stop this celebration, this wanton waste of food now. Immediate food rationing must be brought in and harsh penalties imposed for anyone breaking these laws. I would also suggest martial law be imposed, with full authority resting with the crown, imposed by the captains around this table.'

He looked around the table to see most people gazing at him in shock, although from the expression on a couple of faces, there was also the strong suspicion this was some kind of jest.

'But Count Sendric, surely it can't be as bad as that!' Gia was the first one to protest.

'Actually, it is worse,' Sendric told her, with some satisfaction.

'That is an extraordinary statement, Count. Please explain it,' Merren said simply.

Sendric signalled to the men with him, who began moving around the table, handing out parchment lists.

'First, we are facing mass starvation this winter. Autumn crops have not been sown, while livestock losses have been near catastrophic. By the time our farmers return to their homes, and rebuild, we are not going to have anything worth harvesting until next summer, at the earliest. Add to that our promises of food and seeds for the Derthals and you are looking at the worst winter in our history. And that is even before we look at the prospect of bad weather. The magical storm that our enemies stirred up has had an effect on our weather patterns. We are

Merren had listened to his words with mounting horror and revulsion. She could see, without even looking, that Martil was ready to explode and she stood quickly.

'Count Sendric. Some of the things you said are disturbing. I do not doubt the damage to the country, and the threat of starvation for many of our people. I shall address that. But what you say about the people's feelings about the Derthals, about the Rallorans — I cannot believe that to be true. What we have seen in the last day or so here has proved that our people can look beyond someone's birthplace to judge their worth. The people are hurting but to think that the country will break apart over old prejudices is impossible!'

She stared at him carefully and he knew she was adding the unspoken question about ulterior motives and his oft-spoken demand that she not marry Martil, and marry him instead.

'Your majesty, I am saying this because I love this country and I do not want it harmed. I am only presenting what others have told me. Do not take my word for it. That is why I have brought so many guild leaders with me. And don't rely on their word, either. Ask Bishop Quiller what the people are saying about a woman Archbishop, a woman who has never held a parish before! Ask Gratt what is happening in the north — and what will happen when thousands of Derthal females and young march out of the mountains and into the northern forest! Every timber worker in the north will be out of work, every mill must shut! Talk to the surviving people of Worick and Cessor! They are our two main ports, remember — half of our imported goods come through there. Without them, you are looking at a long road trip through the eastern side of the continent, or sailing to Tetril and coming west from there. We cannot even make up our shortages that way. Talk to the people and you will find out how bad it is! Talk to the people and you will see that, far from exaggerating, I am stating the bitter truth.'

Merren looked at him closely. She suspected his motivations but, more than that, she feared what he said was true. All her old concerns about marrying Martil bubbled back up.

'I had hoped we could enjoy this victory, relax and luxuriate in what we have achieved. But it seems battles do not finish when the swords are laid down. The work begins after the victory. I want to see confirmation of everything Count Sendric has said.'

'You cannot be taking this seriously!' Martil could not sit and listen to this any longer. Sendric had avoided looking at him during his long speech but Martil had not taken his eyes off the old noble. The man was up to something. Martil had no doubt of it. Some of this might be true, but much of it had to be made up, or at least just threads of truth spun into a much larger garment. This must be his last, desperate attempt to stop a marriage he saw as unsuitable. But what worried him was that Merren had not dismissed him immediately.

'I must take this seriously — until it is proven wrong,' she told him.

Martil just stared at her in shock.

'I have not devoted so much time to saving this country only to throw it away now, in the moment of victory,' she added, speaking to all around the table but, Martil knew, especially for him.

'What I do not understand, Count, is what all this has to do with whether Merren marries or not,' Martil said coldly. 'Even if all this were true, why would having me as a Prince Consort be the final blow for the country? I could walk out of this room and down any street in the capital and every person would want to talk to me, to shake my hand or offer me a kiss.'

Sendric swivelled and looked at Martil. 'They would do so, to your face. But I think you would find, in private, they are thinking something else. Your reputation as a War Captain has earned you respect — but that would sour if you tried to pass yourself off as their ruler.'

'And you know this? You know the people's thoughts?' Martil said sarcastically.

Sendric smiled thinly. 'I do. I had thought to hand this out when you could not see it, for I did not want to hurt you. But, since you ask, you should read this. I know how much store the Queen puts in surveys — how she likes to see what the people are really thinking. So I arranged one through these guilds this morning.'

Again the guild leaders hurried around the table, giving each person a new piece of parchment. Martil snatched his and read it swiftly. It was scratched hastily in ink, so quickly that some of the ink had run and other words had spotted. He dropped it on the table from fingers gone suddenly cold.

'This is a pack of lies!' he snarled.

Sendric shrugged. 'We asked the people for their thoughts. You cannot blame us for reporting what they said. These surveys have always been accurate before. They have been a useful tool for the Queen — and I am afraid they have proved so again.'

'What is it?' Karia asked, picking it up before he could think of stopping her.

Nobody else said anything, they just looked at the parchment, not at Martil.

'What does this mean, Dad?' Karia tugged on Martil's sleeve.

He looked again at the parchment, a sick feeling sliding deep into his gut. 'They talked to all these people, asked them who they wanted to see as the Prince Consort, and what they would think about having me sitting beside Merren. Almost all of them wanted to see a noble-born Norstaline as Prince Consort and most of them said they would hate to have me as a Prince Consort.'

'I am afraid Gello's trick with the bards did its work rather too well,' Sendric said gently. 'The phrase Butcher of Bellic kept coming up when people were asked. The people are willing to let the Rallorans live among us after what they did to help the country — but they are not fully trusted. A more detailed report is being prepared by guild scribes, even now. One thing that comes up time and again is the fear that, once they have a Prince Consort, the Rallorans will take over the country — as Gello, the Tenochs and Berellians tried to do. This country has never been invaded before. After the trauma it has suffered, the people want reassurance. They want something and somebody they know and trust. They want familiarity, not something new.'

'Well, I don't believe it!'

Everyone looked as Karia climbed onto the table and stood, hands on hips.

'My daddy is kind and good and nice. People like him! If they knew him like me, they would love him! This can't be true. It's all made up. I bet if I asked people, they would say different to this paper!'

Sendric shook his head. 'These people gave their honest opinions. If you send armed Rallorans out to ask people the same questions, then of course you will get a different response, for the people will be too scared to talk to them!'

'Well, let's get those people in here and have them tell the Queen!' Karia cried. 'Then we shall hear the truth!'

Sendric laughed gently. 'My dear Karia, I am afraid we would not be able to do that. We do not know their names. They spoke only because they knew no angry Rallorans would be visiting them in the dead of the night …'

'Enough!' Merren interrupted.

Martil searched her face, looking for some hint that she would dismiss this out of hand.

'I want to see the detailed survey, as well as the raw reports made by every scribe in every guild that carried this out. And I want you all to investigate the truth of what Count Sendric has told us this morning. If it is true, then the fight to save this country has only just begun. Before I make any decisions, I need the full picture. Conal, I put you in charge of this. Nothing else is as important. Meanwhile, Louise and Gia must compile a full inventory of the food we have in the capital, as well as what we captured from the supplies of our enemies.' She looked around the table. 'What are you waiting for?'

Martil and Karia were the only ones not to hurry out. Martil deliberately sat at the table, looking at Merren. She waited until the room was empty before she stood and walked over to him.

'What did you want me to do?' she asked.

'Tell Sendric that this was not fit to wipe your … nose on.' Martil tossed Sendric's parchment onto the table, conscious that he had to be careful what he was saying in front of Karia. 'That you trust the spirit of the people. You've seen what is happening out in the city — the people have changed already!

The rest of the country will change with them, they just need time.'

Merren shook her head. 'Time is something we don't have. Either of us. I have to be married soon and you have to leave for Dragonara Isle.' Uppermost in her mind was the memory of the last time she had let her heart rule her head; when she had spent the night with Martil before the battle. If the Derthals had not arrived in time, her selfishness would have doomed thousands more people to death. She would not make the same mistake twice.

'By the time I get back, they will have grown used to the idea,' he argued.

'Or the country will be in turmoil. The people have suffered too much as it is. I cannot put them through months of civil unrest, on top of what they have to face in privation and hunger. My first duty is to the people, not to myself. If it was my choice, then we would marry today. But …'

'But nothing. You are the Queen! You can do what you like,' Martil almost howled.

Merren grabbed his arm. 'No. I cannot,' she said deliberately. 'That is the path that leads to Gello and even the Fearpriests. I must do what is right.'

'Even if it means marrying Sendric?' he demanded. 'How is that the right thing?'

'If it is what the people want, then it is the right thing,' she insisted. 'I am the Queen first. You knew that from the start.'

'So you have already decided to marry Sendric, and you believe this ridiculous lie that he has thought up!'

'No, I have decided to look into it further. I cannot dismiss it out of hand! If it is true, then I have to consider it. What sort of ruler would I be if

I ignored the people, after telling them I wanted to give them a voice?'

'I tell you, this is a plot by Sendric ...'

'And if I find out he has lied to me, then he will see the inside of a dungeon cell,' she assured him.

'And if not?'

'We'll talk about it then.' She turned away from him. 'And I am wasting time here.'

Martil watched her go with a rising sense of despair. How could this happen? He had been so sure his destiny was about to change, that all his dreams were about to come true — and now this. How could she listen to that concoction of half-truths and believe it? How could she turn her back on him?

Merren leaned against the wall and took several deep breaths. Sendric's report had been like a blow to the stomach. The choice it offered was her happiness or the country. But that was not a choice. The thought of hurting Martil was like a dagger in the heart. The thought of seeing him every day, of being so close yet so far away, was worse still. She hoped with all her heart that Sendric's words were false. But her head was telling her he was probably right. She sighed. Nothing for it but to get back to work — and pray there was still a chance for them both.

'What if the Queen finds out?'

Sendric shook his head. 'She won't find out. She knows what I'm saying is true, anyway. We just have to make it look convincing. Just because every man we spoke to was a guild member who was telling us what we wanted to hear, doesn't make this survey less real. Now finish those parchments and get them over to the Queen.'

Martil tried to get into the streets — but ran into Havell almost immediately.

'I must see the Queen. We cannot delay,' the Elfaran declared. 'More dragons are dying each day. The time for the Dragon Sword wielder is approaching and we must get to Dragonara Isle as soon as possible.'

Martil stared at him.

'You know, you have to thrust the Sword into the Egg to ensure the rebirth of the dragons, and the magic?'

'I remember! But why now? Can't it wait for a few more days?'

'No.'

'You don't understand what is happening …'

Havell grabbed Martil by the tunic. 'No, you don't understand! It is a simple duty, an easy task — but you have to be there to perform it! If you are not there, then all life on this world will end. You cannot take that risk!'

'Take your hands off me!' Martil growled.

Havell stepped away. 'Don't ignore this! Everything else must come second!' he warned.

'Easy for you to say!' Martil fired back.

'Yes, very easy, considering when the last dragon dies, I shall follow in the next breath! Believe me, I wish it were many years hence but we do not choose our future!'

Martil gave him a grudging nod. 'How long before we must go?'

'Tomorrow morning at the latest,' Havell said.

Martil threw up his hands. 'Go and find the Queen! I have work to do! I shall see you tomorrow.'

* * *

Gello looked out to sea. There was something about the water that appealed to him. Its power, its vastness, seemed to call to him. He could stare at it all day.

Usually there were few sea voyages undertaken at this time of year — too many storms. These Tenoch ships were large and powerful, propelled both by sail and oar — but there were waves that could turn them into kindling. Except they had Fearpriests with them, as well as the Berellian magician Khaliz. The power of Onzalez, Prent and Khaliz was ensuring this was a peaceful, easy voyage — as well as a swift one. Most of Gello's men had barely thrown up. After the desperate struggle to get the men away from the pursuing Rallorans, he had little enough to do on board. But he could not just sit and stare at the sea.

The biggest problem was the Berellians. They had families and friends at home. Naturally they wanted to know what was going to happen to them, fearing a Norstaline invasion led by Captain Martil and his Butchers of Bellic. Gello had pointed out the best way to save Berellia was to return to Norstalos with a massive army, created with the help of the Dragon Egg. And then he reminded them they owed him their lives and anyone who disagreed would go over the side.

That dealt with, he had decided to corner Ezok over the magical object they were all pinning their hopes on.

'And you are sure about this Dragon Egg?' he demanded.

'In what way, sire?' Ezok said carefully.

'I know you. You have a way with words. You twist them and all the time you are playing your own game. You did it to me before Pilleth. Are you doing it to Onzalez now? Is this Dragon Egg real?'

Ezok smiled naturally, keeping his fast-beating heart to himself. 'It is as real as you or I. As you will see when we reach the Isle. And if you think I can fool a Fearpriest such as Brother Onzalez, you overestimate me.'

Gello stared at him. He distrusted magic. But, after what the Dragon Sword had done to him, he was willing to try anything.

'Stay close to me when we reach the Isle. I want to keep a close watch on you. If you prove worthy of trust, then we shall talk again.'

'As you wish, sire.' Ezok bowed, keeping his face impassive. Behind the mask, he was thinking furiously. He had no doubt the Egg was real — but in describing its abilities, he did fear he had overegged the pudding — so to speak. There had to be a way to explain its abilities, which would also preserve his head for a few more days.

Merren listened in silence as Havell explained that he needed the Dragon Sword wielder by the next day.

'How long will he be away then, if the dragons are dying out?' she said, when Havell had finished talking.

'I cannot say. It could be days, it could be weeks, it could be months. It is better to err on the side of caution, however.'

She stared down at her desk, which was covered in parchment. Scroll after scroll had revealed scribbled comments that backed up everything Sendric had said. Along with that was the news from the others, from Gia, Louise, Milly, Quiller and even Conal.

None of it was good for Martil.

Gia and Louise had discovered the desperate escape from invading armies, as well as two nights of frantic celebration, had left the capital short of food and drink. And, as it had been the major storehouse, this was serious indeed. But both of them had insisted there were ways around this problem.

'Look, we've got thousands of extra horses in this country left from the invasion. If we have to, half the country will eat horsemeat soup for the winter. Aroaril knows we won't be using them for cavalry charges any time soon,' Louise pointed out.

'Do what is right for you. The country will follow you,' Gia offered.

'But can I really be happy, if marrying him throws the country into turmoil? I could not bear it if even one life was lost because I put myself first ...'

'You cannot think like that,' Louise implored.

But Merren could not stop thinking about the sobbing people in the park, who thought they were waiting to die on a Fearpriest altar, because she had chosen to spend time with Martil rather than work at saving them.

She had sought out Romon.

'There is no doubt the people respect the Rallorans and, to an extent, the Derthals. But there is a difference between respecting an ally and preparing to let your daughter marry one of them. And that is how the people see it. We know that you are the Queen, the true ruler of this country and that Martil has no desire to wield power. But many of the people still see the woman as subservient to the man. Marry a Ralloran and they will think their country has been taken over,' Romon admitted. 'But give them time. Already the tales of what happened here, of how Martil helped save this country, are spreading across the land. We are singing songs of

359

the Battle of Sendric, the Battle of Pilleth and now the Battle of Norstalos. Tales of how the Rallorans rescued a village from the Berellians, of how one Ralloran priest saved an entire village by himself, how the new Archbishop defeated a Fearpriest to save him, how the old Archbishop defeated the High Fearpriest on the field of battle to save us all. Of how you persuaded our ancient enemies, the goblins, to fight by our side and destroy those who sought to rule us through Zorva. The people are hearing the stories and they know them to be true. With time, they will come around. Ask me again in six months.'

'Six months? I do not have six weeks!' Merren had sighed.

Archbishop Sadlier had proved to be little comfort.

'Archbishop Nott's sacrifice has inspired the people here. They have seen what the Fearpriests had planned for them — men, women and children having their hearts ripped out of their bodies. And they saw Aroaril defeat Zorva. The church is facing an extraordinary upsurge. People are not just coming to services out of habit, or because they want to stay in the priest's good books, in case they might need healing one day. We have had hundreds inquiring about joining the priesthood — men and women. These people want to go out and tell the country the truth they have discovered — that there is evil out there and good people cannot just sit back and rely on others to fight it.'

'Well, that sounds wonderful!' Merren had smiled.

'But these people need months of training. The church is already in disarray, after what Prent did to it. I have two bishops to help me administer the whole country. One of them was a Ralloran sergeant a few moons ago and knows little more than the newest novice. Bishop Quiller, on the other hand, is an old man and the exertions of the past few weeks have taken their toll on him. I cannot ask him to do much of the actual work, although his advice is extremely valuable. Meanwhile, the rest of the country has not seen any of those things. All they know is that their familiar parish priest is gone, the Archbishop they knew, as well as the one they had heard about, are gone and a young woman wears the robes, for the first time. I shall win them over, but I need time. Within a year I shall have real priests in every town and village and the church will be strong again.'

Merren just shook her head.

'I know you don't have that time but I would still advise you to marry Martil,' Milly said softly.

'Why? Is it Aroaril's wishes, or is it merely because you think it will ease the way for you to marry your Ralloran lover?' Merren asked sharply.

Milly locked eyes with her.

'I shall marry Kesbury regardless of what you do or what the people think. I shall do it because I want to, and because it is the right thing for us. I expect you to be at the ceremony and give your blessing.'

'Do you know how that is going to look, politically?' Merren gasped.

'No. Nor do I care. It is up to us to lead, to do the right thing. The people may not like it but they will come to accept it.'

Merren smiled grimly. 'Easy for you to say, when you have Aroaril's power to wield!'

Milly leaned forwards. 'Trust the people. They are changing. I have been given no guidance on this but I would advise you to do what your heart tells you is right.'

Merren had waved her away. Her heart already knew what it wanted. It was her head that needed convincing, and it had heard nothing it liked so far.

The news from the north, delivered via Tiera, who was organising the new Magicians' Guild while Barrett returned from the fruitless attempt to capture Gello, was hardly better. The people had been delighted to hear they were safe and a night of celebrations had followed news of the great victory. But news the Derthals would be living in the northern forest — and that thousands of females and young were on their way now, while the remaining warriors were walking north to meet them — had been less well received. Apparently it had taken all of Gratt's authority to calm things down — and even then, he had asked for every man who had travelled south to fight for the Queen to return north immediately, both to give the people a sense of security and to preserve order.

Conal had returned, after trying to speak to as many people as possible in the streets — but had found it a difficult task.

'I cannot use soldiers or militia to talk to the people, because it may give a false result, and we cannot speak to anyone when there is a Ralloran or Derthal nearby, in case they are not honest — these conditions are impossible!' he had complained.

She could see there was no easy answer. Nobody was going to come in and hand her a piece of parchment that said it was safe to marry Martil. It was down to her. A choice between head and heart.

'Queen Merren?'

She looked up to see Havell still standing there, while she had been lost in thought. The decision had to be made now. There could be no waiting, for Aroaril knew when Martil would be back —

and the baby was not going to go away. Norstalos could not have a Bastard King. She had to choose now. Everything inside her wanted to reject Sendric's argument and embrace Martil. But, like a tree that bent but would not break, her training, the conditioning her father and her tutors had given her would not allow her to put herself before her country. She tried to push past it, tried to ignore what her father would have said. But she could not. She knew she simply could not find happiness that way. Especially after giving in once before and then seeing the result — thousands of weeping, terrified people facing death, families split apart because she had let them down. She could not risk it. She was a queen first, a woman second. It was a bitter truth to face but she told herself she had faced worse. A saga would not end like this. It would have a happy ending, a neat ending. But this was real life, she told herself.

She dismissed Havell and sent for Martil. She had to speak to him, face to face.

Martil had paced through the streets fruitlessly. People were happy to talk to him — at first. But when he said he was looking for people who had spoken to a guild scribe that morning, they became confused, and defensive. None seemed to know what he was talking about, and his obvious frustration, slipping towards anger, had them making excuses to get away.

'I don't think we're going to find any,' Karia told him.

'So what does that mean? That people are scared of me, or that Sendric lied?'

Karia shrugged. 'I don't know. But I am getting hungry.'

'Well, if Sendric's right, then everyone's going to get hungry,' Martil grunted, but he took her back to the palace anyway.

The guards on the gate waved them through — but Wilsen and Jaret intercepted them as they walked towards the kitchen.

'Captain! The Queen wants to see you!' Wilsen called.

'Can it wait until we get something to eat?'

'Perhaps we could take Karia for some food, while you see the Queen,' Jaret suggested.

Neither would meet his eyes, which was hardly comforting.

'I'll see you soon.' He kissed Karia on the head and strode towards the throne room. He clung to hope. Merren had looked into his eyes, told him she loved him. They had shared so much, experienced so much since he had helped rescue her from Gello. They were meant to be together, he was sure of it. He had never felt this way about another woman. Surely she would feel the same. The people would accept him — after all, he had the Dragon Sword. They must see him as a good man. They must!

The short walk to her office room seemed to take no time and forever. He hesitated at the door, squared his shoulders and strode in. It was empty but for Merren.

As soon as she saw him, her determination to put the country first wavered. A voice inside her told her to run to him. But she did not.

'Sit down,' she said.

Martil walked stiffly across the room, until he was beside her.

'So you've decided to believe Sendric. You think marrying me is too big a risk and will put the country in danger,' he stated, feeling dead inside and hoping against hope that she would deny it.

Merren surged to her feet.

'Do you think it was that easy?' she exclaimed.

Martil felt something inside him break. He wanted to grab Karia, find Havell and fly to Dragonara Isle, get as far away from here as possible. He wished with all his heart he had never come to Norstalos, never drawn the Dragon Sword, never fallen in love with a queen. He had actually begun to think that Aroaril, destiny, whatever was driving him, was finally rewarding him for all that he had done, all he had suffered. Peace was at hand, he had Karia, he had Merren, he would soon have another child. It was all within his grasp. And now it had been taken away. Martil had never been beaten before but he was beaten now. He tried to fight back but his heart was not in it.

'So you don't trust the people. Don't think they can change.'

'Yes, they can change — over time. Time that we don't have!' She moved into the speech she had rehearsed. The politician in her could see the sense in it, but her heart was not in it. 'You have to leave tomorrow and won't be back for perhaps months, and our son will never be accepted if he is not born within a marriage. I have to be married now, or there will forever be questions about his birth! I don't want to do this! If I could choose, you know I would choose you. But I don't have a choice. I cannot wait for the people to realise how wrong they are. If I marry you, on top of everything else the country has suffered, it will fall apart! You have seen the figures from Sendric ...'

'Sendric! He has tricked you — I know it!' Martil declared. 'I cannot find a single person who spoke to a guild scribe this morning.'

'Of course not. They are hardly going to admit to you, of all people, something like that, are they?' she pointed out. 'How could it be a trick? I have seen the interviews from the scribes. I agree he has done this to stop our marriage. But he believes it to be the best thing for the country and I cannot disagree with that ...'

'Well, I can!' Martil spat. 'Doesn't our child, our son, mean anything? How can questions about his parentage be worse than him never knowing his real father?'

'He will know his father. You will still be my Champion.'

'So you are saying we shall be married in deed, if not in name?'

'That was not what I said. I promised I would not humiliate Sendric. But he is an older man. When he is gone, perhaps then we can be together ...'

'And that's supposed to make me feel better?'

'That was not what I said,' she hissed. 'Don't think this is easy for me! You are not the only one hurting here!'

'Then ignore Sendric. Ignore his stupid reports. I have the Dragon Sword — the people will see that I am a worthy Prince Consort. Just give me a chance!'

He stared into her eyes, willing her to agree.

But she shook her head, tears spilling from her eyes.

'I am sorry,' she whispered.

He could feel his eyes threatening to betray him, as well. But he would not let them. He had to have some sort of victory here, even if it was a hollow one, over himself.

'I am going to Dragonara Isle now, with Karia. Don't expect to see me again,' he said stiffly.

'And where will you go?'

'High Chief Sacrax has made me a member of his tribe. I shall live up in the northern forest — buy a farm close to the Derthals that one of your stinking Norstalines wants to sell because they don't want to live near the people who saved their worthless lives,' he said bitterly.

'Don't be foolish! You both have a place here, at the palace. And you have duties here,' she fired back.

'I ask you to release me from my oaths to you,' he said coldly.

She slapped him then. It stung rather than hurt but he gazed at her in shock.

'Damn you! You act as if this is all about yourself. You knew what you were getting yourself into. You knew who I married would be a matter of politics, of statecraft! I was never going to be able to marry for love. Now you act as if I have betrayed you! I did not choose any of this. So don't you think you are the wronged one here. I am as much a victim as you!' she yelled at him. 'How do you think I feel?'

Martil could not find the words to answer her. He did not have them and, if he did, they would never have got past the lump in his throat.

Instead he leaned forwards and kissed her, shocking her as much as she had surprised him with a slap.

'Farewell, my Queen,' he managed to say, before turning and striding away. 'I shall always love you.'

Merren wanted to run after him, grab him, tell him it was all a mistake. But she did not. Although when the door shut behind him, she collapsed into a chair and cried as she never had before.

She wished Gello had been able to draw the Dragon Sword, all those years ago.

Martil thought about going in search of Sendric. For a wild moment, he even thought about killing the old noble. Then sense reasserted itself. No, the best thing was to get away from the scene of defeat.

In moments he was down at the kitchen, where Karia was being entertained by Jaret, Wilsen and a couple of serving girls.

'We are leaving! Now!' he cried.

Karia looked up. 'What is it?'

He could not answer her, not in front of other people.

'Upstairs! We pack now! Jaret! Wilsen! Find that bloody Elfaran and tell him to get the dragon ready. If they are not waiting by the time I get outside the palace, I shall hold you two responsible! Move!'

They moved.

Karia caught up with him and grabbed his hand as he strode back through the palace.

'Dad! What is it?' she cried, then saw that he was not looking at her because the tears were running down his cheeks.

'Is it Merren?'

He could only nod.

'She's not going to marry you or look after me, is she?'

Again, he could only shake his head; his voice was gone.

She ducked under his arm and hugged him tight around the waist.

'You still have me. I'll look after you,' she told him.

All he could do was pat her shoulder, and try to smile at her.

'We've both lost someone we love. But while we have each other, we'll be fine,' she told him.

Now he had to stop and hug her close, dropping

to his knees. The damned tears did not want to stop but she was there to hold him.

'We'll always be together,' she promised.

They were all there to see him off, to wave farewell to both him and Karia. All of them — except the one that really mattered.

Beyond them was a small crowd as well, mostly Rallorans but also Norstalines he had trained — and saved — since he had arrived in the country. The other notable absentee was Count Sendric but he knew when to keep a politic distance, especially after his victory.

Even Barrett was there, ostensibly to say goodbye to Karia but Martil swore he had caught the wizard smiling to himself, more than once.

And while Karia was happy to go around to hug everyone, Martil stood beside Argurium, glowering at them all. He still shook hands with anyone who came near him, from Conal to Wilsen and Jaret, embraced the likes of Louise and Gia and patted the shoulder of the still-sick Rocus, who had dragged himself out of his bed to be there.

He could feel the anger and hurt within him, struggling to get out, but he would not let it show — in case she was watching. So he exchanged a few platitudes with those who wanted to talk to him, forced his face to remain a mask and wished he was elsewhere.

'Come back to us, Captain,' Conal said softly. 'We need you.'

'Tell that to Merren,' Martil snorted.

'Look around here, at all the people whose lives you have changed. Look at me. I was scum, worse than scum, when you walked into my inn. Now I have a life again, thanks to you ...'

A life. Martil heard those words and his control cracked.

'I have to go,' he said roughly and turned to where Havell was chatting animatedly with Louise and Gia. 'Hey, Elf! I thought we had to rush?'

'Well, there's no ...' Havell caught sight of Martil's face and gulped. 'You are right. We must go! Clear the area, please!'

Martil immediately grabbed Karia from where she was giggling with Archbishop Sadlier and clambered onto Argurium's neck. There he sat, as Karia waved and the people below cheered him. It had happened again — he was running from a country where he should have been a hero. And all he could think was how much he wanted to get away. He did not look at the people below and around him as Argurium leaped into the air. Instead he gazed at the palace, until it swam before his eyes.

Merren watched the dragon circle the city once, before flying away, and felt as though her heart would break. It knew this was a terrible mistake and nothing, not even the most reasoned argument, could persuade it otherwise.

He was gone. Even if he did return, things would never be the same between them. She had made the choice, picking her country ahead of him and she could never go back. That knowledge burst upon her like a wave and she dropped to the floor. All the sense in the world could not change that.

She raced to the window as the dragon flew into the distance.

'Come back! I was wrong! I am sorry!' she screamed into the wind, but the dragon vanished into the distance and her eyes blurred too much.

'What have I done?' she whispered.

19

'This is a healing Isle. You can see why my people chose to stay, and serve the dragons,' Havell said, floating lazily in the water.

Martil had to agree with him. He had never swum before but, after some tuition from the grinning Havell, had managed to stay afloat, although Karia refused to go near him for all the splashing. The Elfarans had given them both strange, close fitting clothes to wear in the water; the cloth was oiled so that the water did not leave the garments soppy and sagging. Naturally, Karia had taken to swimming like everything else, gliding easily through the water 'like a mermaid', as Havell had put it. Martil had wished the Elfaran had not said that, for Karia then wanted to go looking for mermaids. Already disappointed not to find happy fairies and talking rabbits all over the island, her excitement at the thought of visiting mermaids was only matched by her disappointment when Martil and Havell explained there were no such things, that they too were figments of a saga-writer's imagination.

Martil ducked his head under the water. Swimming was not his favourite occupation but he enjoyed sitting here in the shallows, feeling the warm, saltwater wash over him. His half-healed wounds from the battle of Norstalos were much better. And he found he could forget about Merren, for a while, if he was making sand castles with Karia, looking through the rock pools with her or cooking a fish or crab fresh from the water on the beach with her.

He closed his eyes and thought back over the past few days.

Dragonara Isle had changed him, from its first impression. He had arrived feeling bitter and angry, wanting to get this over and done with as soon as possible, so he could hide himself away in the far north of Norstalos, try and forget all about Merren. Havell and Karia had let him travel in silence, although she had bombarded the Elfaran with endless questions about the Isle and where she might find talking animals. But Karia's cries of excitement at seeing the Isle had stirred Martil from his sullen mood and he had gazed at the Isle as Argurium circled around it. Unlike Norstalos, which had been wet and cold, a warm sun shone on Dragonara, while impossibly white sandy beaches and clear blue water surrounded it.

'The water and the weather are unique to this island, coming from the magic that resides here,' Havell had explained. 'Outside the island, it is winter on your continent; the sea is cold and rough and the wind howls. But here is an oasis of peace and calm. Do not try to explain it, just seek to enjoy it.'

Martil, his heart still raw, had said nothing.

There were no towns or villages, just the Dragon Hall. From above it looked incredible, resembling a giant dragon lying on its side. Martil could barely believe such a building was possible. It weaved in and out of trees and hills, as if it was part of the island, something living rather than a structure imposed on the land. Then, from the belly of the Dragon Hall, a score of other dragons had flown out into the air, soaring up and around Argurium, looping and circling in endless, dazzling patterns that made Karia cry out with delight. Even Martil could not hold back a gasp of amazement at the display.

They had landed near the head of the Dragon Hall, which faced a gentle bay. Martil inhaled deeply, the perfume of a score of flowering plants mingling to make a heady ambrosia. The sun was warm, the sand they walked over soft and everything seemed bright and colourful. It was as if he had stepped into another world, where every sensation was heightened, every sense indulged.

They had gazed around, Martil in wonder and Karia in the hopes of seeing a fairy or unicorn, then gates opened inside the 'mouth' and a hundred Elfarans rushed out to form a double line to welcome them.

They had cheered them both, reaching out to shake Martil's hand or bowing to Karia. She enjoyed it thoroughly, and accepted flowers from half-a-dozen Elfarans.

Martil had hesitated to plunge from the bright sunlight into the cool, dark hall. But the marvels did not stop inside. It was made out of wood and stone, but not as Martil recognised them. He was used to simple homes with little decoration, although he had seen many castles and churches with fantastic designs carved into the stone. But the Hall was something else again. Passageways twisted and turned, changing from Elfaran-size to dragon-size and back again, opening into cosy nooks or soaring halls or to the skies. Grass, trees and other plants grew in, around and on the structure, making it look as though it were one with the landscape. It seemed somehow organic, as if it were a living and breathing part of the island.

Much of the dragon part of it was empty, although through every other corridor they found smiling Elfarans.

'How was this built?' Martil had run his hand over the smooth wooden and stone walls in wonder. 'Do your people remember how it was done?'

'Remember?' Havell had laughed. 'Martil, we built it, with the help of the dragons and magic. I helped shape the walls myself.'

Martil looked at him. 'You built it? It looks like it has been here for centuries, the way the plants have grown around it ...'

Havell patted a wall gently. 'It has been a while.'

He had shown them to a pair of comfy little rooms, off one of the main corridors, which were connected by a common door. The table and chairs were part of the wall, while the bed was a raised tree root on which grasses formed a thick mattress. Martil had been highly dubious that such a thing would be comfortable — or dry — but was astonished to find it felt even better than the thick beds back at Norstalos' palace. Karia, predictably, loved it. A natural spring provided a shower and bath in one at the back of the rooms, while its run-off was topped by a wooden seat that Karia was highly amused to see was the privy.

'We don't get many guests here but I am sure you will be comfortable. If you need anything, just ask,' Havell had said. 'I will let you rest and relax. Someone will call you for a meal and then tomorrow I thought I could show you across the island?'

'Can we see the Dragon Egg?' Karia had asked immediately.

Havell hesitated, looking at Martil, who had shrugged.

'Might as well see what all the fuss is about,' was all he said.

Havell had directed them through more twisting, turning passages, until Martil felt lost, then opened a door into a large chamber. Around the edges were benches and seats and, in the centre, stood the Dragon Egg. He heard Karia cry with delight but felt vaguely disappointed. For something that was supposed to be the source of all new magic and on which the fate of the world rested, it looked like a normal, albeit giant, egg. It was large, probably up to his waist, and a glossy, pearly white. He had expected something massive, covered in gold or jewels. But it did have one amazing feature. Every so often, a burst of colour would ripple across its surface, reminding Martil of the shadow of a dragon.

'We had better not stay too long,' Havell had said nervously.

'Why not?' Karia had demanded, but Martil had tapped her shoulder and pointed towards the Dragon Sword.

It had been shaking in its scabbard, and a faint, yet piercing howl came from the dragon on its hilt — whose eyes were glowing ferociously.

In answer, the swirls of colour across the Egg had grown faster and more expansive.

'Probably best to go now — they sense each other,' Havell had suggested.

But Karia was only willing to go when Havell promised to bring her back for a better look, without Martil.

He had washed and changed back in their room, wincing a little as his wounds stung from the water.

But the pain of them seemed somehow lessened. And the hurt inside him felt less as well. He had been sure he could not laugh again but, sitting with Karia, reading sagas and playing games, he had been unable to stop his smile.

'You know, I don't miss Father Nott as much since we came here.' Karia had said what he'd been thinking, as they joined the Elfarans for a surprisingly delicious vegetable stew that night. The Elfarans ate no meat, for they did not like to kill living creatures. Martil had quietly decided to go fishing at the first opportunity.

He had thought being surrounded by Elfarans was going to be a nightmare, he was sure to pick a fight with one, the mood he was in. When he had left Norstalos he had felt as he did back at his darkest days, just after Bellic, when anger came easily and violence was never far away.

But he managed to sit through a saga performance they had put on for Karia's amusement without wanting to punch someone. It had to be magic, he thought. Or perhaps a magical little girl.

That night, she had walked over and sat on his bed, talked to him as he lay there, unable to sleep for the bitterness swirling around in his head.

'Why did she do it? Why didn't she want you and me?' she had asked. 'We were going to be a family, the three of us and then the new baby.'

Martil breathed out heavily. His first instinct had been to dismiss her words with a quick comment, say he had no idea. But she deserved more of an explanation than that.

'She's not an ordinary woman. She's not just a wife and mother. Or not just to the likes of you and me. Normally a mother looks after the children. But Merren has to look after the whole country.' He sat up then, for the next part of what he had to say he wanted to be sitting next to her. 'You know your mother gave her life for you?'

Karia nodded, biting her lip. 'Father Nott told me that,' she agreed.

'Mothers would do anything for their children.'

'What about fathers?'

He hugged her close. 'Fathers would do anything for their children too.'

'Good.' She hugged him back.

'So Merren has to do this for her country. It hurts her, but she thinks it is the best thing for the country — for all her children.'

'It's not fair, though,' Karia said seriously.

'No. And I don't agree that it is the best thing for the people, either.'

'Me either,' Karia agreed. 'But at least we've got each other.'

After talking to her like that, he had found things easier still.

Again, the island helped. Sometimes he would have sworn he could feel the island working on him. The hurt he felt, they both felt, seemed more distant here. Every time they walked though the cool forest or along the flat, white sands, or sank into the crystal-clear, warm waters, they could not help but feel better. It was impossible to explain unless, as Havell insisted, it really was a healing island.

It was the perfect place to relax. While there were no talking animals or fairies or other creatures from Karia's favourite sagas, the animals on the island were numerous, and all willing to come and speak with her, magically.

'The magic seems so easy here — it is no effort to do things,' she told Martil.

'You will find that,' Havell agreed. 'Magic flows so strongly here, especially now, with so many dragons having returned to the Egg.'

Martil had nodded. In the short space of time he had been here, the array of dragons who had greeted them so spectacularly had dwindled to just a handful.

He had thought he would never be happy again when he had walked out of the throne room without Merren — but he had not counted on Karia. They clung to each other and found, in each other, something to replace what they had lost. Perhaps back in Norstalos it would have been different, would have been much harder. But here, on the island, with its gentle sun and warm water, it was somehow easier.

He thought this, then raised his head back above the water and looked for her.

'Thank you,' he told her, as she splashed into the water and sat beside him, stretching out her toes towards a school of tiny, brightly coloured fish.

'What for?'

'For coming into my life, and saving it.' He shrugged.

'Someone had to look after you. It's a dirty job but someone has to do it,' she sighed, then splashed him, before running off laughing as he chased her through the shallows.

Havell watched them with a smile.

'I thought perhaps tomorrow I would take Karia to have a proper look at the Egg?' he suggested, as Martil piggy-backed Karia through some deeper water. She was holding her nose and trying to look underneath the water, just in case a mermaid swam by.

'Yes please!' Karia squealed, pulling her head out of the water and wiping her wet face on Martil's hair.

'Good! Then perhaps I can swim in peace!' Martil grunted.

'Only if you can't hear all the fishes laughing at the way you swim,' she warned.

'That's it! You're going under!' he mock-threatened her as she clung on tight around his neck, giggling.

Havell smiled too, as their laughter echoed around the deserted beach.

Merren sighed. Carefully she stood and stretched, feeling her back creak and her shoulders finally settle back into their normal position. She looked out the window to see the setting sun and guessed she had been at her desk for more than twelve turns of the hourglass. And the pile of work did not seem to be getting much smaller.

'You need to take a break, my Queen,' Louise told her, worriedly.

'You're a fine one to talk! You three have been here just as long as I!' Merren tried to smile at where Louise, Gia and Conal worked.

'You have to take a break anyway. The Royal Dressmaker is coming to do the final fitting,' Gia reminded her.

Merren's attempt at a smile faded instantly. 'Can't you put her off?' she complained. 'There is still so much to do ...'

'My Queen, the wedding is tomorrow,' Conal said gently.

Merren rubbed gritty eyes. 'It is all nonsense anyway,' she muttered.

They tried to ignore that.

'The people need this; they are all looking forward to it. They see it as a symbol of Norstalos being reborn,' Gia tried.

But Merren did not react, even though she knew the Norstalines needed something to cheer them. The country was still in an uproar, still dealing with the effects of the mass evacuations and the triple invasions.

Somehow, Merren had to get everyone back to their homes, rebuild every village and town that had been destroyed, resettle the Derthals, restart every industry that had ground to a halt and get the farming community back on its feet. And she had to do that while ensuring that the people did not starve to death. Just one of those tasks would have been enormous — to try and solve every one of them at the same time was proving near-impossible. But she had to do it.

Barrett and his Magicians' Guild was proving invaluable. Not only were the mages hard at work all over the country, helping with the rebuilding and, most importantly, with growing crops but thanks to Barrett, she had been able to get across the country almost as fast as when Argurium had flown her around. She had been driving herself hard, driving Barrett to exhaustion as she worked from dawn to dusk — and often deep into the night. This was the first day she had been back in the palace since Martil had left, which was why there was so much paperwork waiting for her. She had spent plenty of time up in the north, while also visiting Cessor, Worick, Wells and the ravaged south.

Luckily it seemed she could at least concentrate on Norstalos — for now. Berellia was in chaos — with King Markuz dead and Onzalez gone, the country had split into a score of small fiefs, run by the remaining nobles, as well as by Fearpriests. She did not want to leave that nest of vipers to her south but, realistically, it would need a major invasion to wipe out their evil — and her people were not ready for that. The northern border was deserted — Merren presumed the closest Berellians had fled south, fearing invasion. Without an immediate threat, nobody wanted to begin another war. She had heard from both the Avish and Ralloran ambassadors that those countries were preparing their own invasions, to secure their own borders — and no doubt extract a portion of revenge. With the Berellian army destroyed, there would be little resistance. It was a concern — but it was a problem for another day.

Besides, she had too much else to worry about.

Sendric had the various other guilds all at work — although their help was coming at the price of almost all the country's gold reserves.

The army was trying to help people rebuild, while the roads were filled with long columns of refugees returning home. The weather had improved a little, thanks in part to the work of Archbishop Sadlier, although the roads to the north were still difficult to traverse, especially with all the wagons and carts that had become bogged in the attempt to flee north.

Some of the invaders' supplies could be used — but they had obviously planned on living off the land, bringing only a few extra days of rations. It helped — every bit helped — but it was not the answer. Luckily, the thousands of horses left behind by the invaders were being used to help carry people — and then were being used as food. Horse would never be Merren's favourite dish but she had no need of thousands of warhorses — and the people desperately needed food. Of course a diet of horse would never get them safely through the winter and here the Magicians' Guild came into their own. Enough fruit and vegetables were being grown that, while belts would have to be tightened, the people would survive the winter.

The one thing she did not seem to worry about was the people. After reading Sendric's devastating survey, she had been scared that they would be taking out their anger and fear on her. But, even in the far north, they had been delighted to see her, cheering her even when she told them the Derthals would be given the northern forest as theirs forever.

Part of this she put down to the work of Romon and his bards. Again, thanks to Barrett, they had been sent out to every part of the country, where they were singing songs of Archbishop Sadlier, who had defeated a Fearpriest to save a village, of how the Derthals had saved the country — and how the Fearpriests had ripped out the hearts of a hundred men, women and children who had stayed behind to support Gello.

But it was more than that. It was as if the spirit she had seen in the capital, when Norstalines had rushed out to help wounded Derthals, Rallorans and their own countrymen, was spreading across Norstalos. The new town council of Cessor, led by a man named Fergus, was the embodiment of that. Fergus had offered homes to every one of Kettering's pardoned criminals who wanted to come and make a new life in the ruined city. Scores had agreed and two of them — Leigh and Hawke — had even become part of the new town council. Rich and poor alike were working together to get the city rebuilt. Meanwhile, the surviving Rallorans had all been offered homes in the south, in the villages they had saved as well as Wells, the town they had held. Some of the villages had almost been competing with each other to invite the most Rallorans into their midst. The once-hated Butchers of Bellic were now accepted, even welcomed and Merren felt, at last, they might get the chance for peace and the new start she had promised them months ago, at Sendric.

In fact, she was beginning to think Sendric's doom-laden predictions might not come true.

'Is it too late to call it off?' she muttered, then looked up in horror as she realised she had spoken aloud.

'It's never too late, my Queen,' Louise said boldly. 'Why not contact Martil? You can still have the marriage, just not to Sendric.'

Merren ran her fingers through hair that she was horribly aware was dirty and lank and needing both a wash and the attentions of a maid — possibly two. It was a thought, an intoxicating thought.

She understood what Sendric was saying: the country could still fall apart. The people were happy because she was about to marry the last Norstaline noble and protect the royal bloodline. A Ralloran Prince Consort and Crown Prince would be too much for them.

But against that was the utter certainty she had made the worst mistake of her life. She could not get Martil out of her thoughts. And every time she heard a child laugh, her heart leaped, thinking it was Karia.

Sometimes she thought about sending a message to Martil, imagined the reunion they would have — before she came to her senses again. Both of them had too much pride for that to work.

Besides, how could she go out and tell the people she had made a mistake? That the wedding to Count Sendric, the event that was taking people's minds away from their loss and grief, was off? That she was to marry a Ralloran War Captain instead?

All the scandal, the rumours and the gossip she had tried to stop by marrying Sendric would return in full force. People would suspect — rightly, as it happened — she was pregnant and had to marry in haste to hide something.

Then there was the fear Martil would simply refuse to return. She had made it clear she did not love him enough to put him before the country. Imagine if she were to cancel the marriage to Sendric and then Martil refused to return! What would she do then?

'You know, your majesty, there has been some talk about your marriage,' Conal said carefully.

'Oh yes?' Merren replied absently, her mind still far away.

'There has been a growing feeling that you deserve more than Sendric. After all, in the sagas they love so much, the Princess always marries a young, handsome Prince. Even the kindest of his supporters would not say Sendric was one of those ...'

'This is not a saga! Real life does not end happily and neatly!' Merren almost snarled.

'But —' Louise began.

'It is too late. My decision stands. I shall marry Sendric tomorrow. I shall go and bathe — send the dressmaker to me,' Merren announced, before striding out.

'I can't believe she's really going to marry Sendric!' Gia sighed.

'Aye. After all she has done for the country, the least she deserves is a little happiness ...'

'After all they have both done for the country,' Conal interrupted.

Louise acknowledged it with a nod. 'Aye. But none of that matters. As she said, this is not a saga and tomorrow afternoon we shall see the ending.'

                        * * *

'Dragonara Isle!'

The lookout's call brought Gello up from the cabin where he had been eating fish for breakfast. There had not been much food on the ships but there were plenty of fish in the sea and, thanks to Khaliz, they were easy to catch. Gello was a little sick of them by now but had high hopes of richer fare that day. He had been eating in his cabin, trying in vain to draw a picture of Mother. Since he had been forced to leave her portrait behind in his tent, in the flight from Norstalos, he had missed her terribly. He still tried to talk to her, but it wasn't the same.

When he heard the call, he put down his crude sketch and, along with every other man on board, rushed out on deck, pushing aside a pair of Tenochs to make room for himself.

'Has anyone ever been there?' he demanded of Onzalez.

'None here. But Khaliz will be able to sense the Egg. Its magic will make it stand out. We shall follow him there. Any that try to stop us must die,' the Fearpriest declared.

'And what of the dragons?' Gello demanded. This was the one thing he had feared. Yes, they had no alternative and yes, Onzalez was supremely confident, but Norstaline history was rich with stories of the power of the dragons. Certainly, if mere goblins could capture one and almost kill it, they could not be all-powerful but still …

'The dragons will do nothing. They spread tales of their ability but they never do anything. How many times did the dragon swoop on our men during the invasion of Norstalos? And not once did it actually kill a man! Besides, I can only sense one dragon on the island. The rest must be away,' Khaliz reported.

'They will not be expecting us,' Onzalez said confidently. 'And anyway, we must have that Egg. Better to die taking it than waste away, doing nothing.'

Gello paused at that, but even the thought of seizing some barbarian kingdom somewhere was a pittance compared to Norstalos. He would always be complaining about the throne he should have had. He had to do everything in his power to get it back. 'So we take the Egg and any food and women we can find!'

'We shall make land within a few turns of the hourglass,' Khaliz predicted.

'What? Why don't we set sail?' Gello snorted.

'The wind and current are against us. The men are having to work hard on the oars to get there,' Khaliz explained. 'I can do nothing against either — the power that propels them is far beyond me. Luckily these Tenoch ships have those oars, or I doubt we could ever get there.'

'Well, I want two companies of men spared the oars. We shall need them for the assault.'

Martil carefully lay the Dragon Sword down on his clothes. With no Karia or Havell around, he planned to leave off the Elfarans' swimming outfit and swim as Aroaril intended. The sun felt good on his skin — and the water felt even better. His skin had begun to turn a darker colour from being out so much, although that just highlighted the many scars criss-crossing his arms, legs and body. So many that he had forgotten how he had come by some of them. But the warm water seemed to help the fresher ones and he planned to laze in the water before strolling back to the hall and joining Karia for the noon meal.

Karia liked the Elfarans, even though they weren't like the elves she had read about in the sagas, and they still stubbornly insisted there were no fairies or talking rabbits on this island. She knew there were magical animals here — they must be shy. As for the Elfarans, they looked young enough but they acted funny, like the oldest people she had ever known, very quiet, reserved and gentle. There were no women or children — apparently they had lived without women or children here for a thousand years or more! Karia found that hard to believe, but Martil had told her it was probably true — and he had not even laughed when he did so, to tell her it was just a joke.

'How come more people don't visit?' she asked Havell.

'We don't encourage visitors.' The Elfaran had smiled. 'You are the first in centuries.'

'Why not? It's lovely here!'

Havell chuckled. 'That is the problem. Half the people of the world would live here, if they could. So the dragons set a natural protection for the island, to stop any ships that try to come near here. Uninvited people soon find that a mysterious wind and current is pushing them away from the island. Those who try to get past there receive a polite visit from a dragon and a rider. Once, we were a warrior race. We still have the old armour and swords, kept safe in a chamber at the back of the hall. We can look pretty impressive, dressed up and riding a dragon. We explain that the ship must turn around and leave — or there will be a hundred of us returning with fire and sword and none shall survive. At that point, they decide they have business elsewhere!'

'Ooh! Can I go for a fly this afternoon? Karia asked.

Havell sighed. 'I am sorry. But not today — or indeed, for a few days. Argurium is the last dragon.'

'Oh no!' Karia gasped, her eyes brimming.

'It is all right! It is natural, a part of the circle of life. But Argurium cannot leave here — now she is the last, the end cannot be far away. That is why everyone is in their rooms, preparing themselves for the end. And there will be no more dragon flights until the rebirth. I just wish I could see that!'

Karia was feeling miserable, but she heard the sadness in Havell's voice and reached out to pat his arm.

'You will be able to see it, if you led a good life. Father Nott always said that death was not the end, that there was more afterwards. He said you didn't have to be afraid.'

Havell smiled. 'Thank you. Although I am afraid. I have lived for such a long time. So many years, far, far beyond the span of normal men. It has been wonderful — but now the end draws near, I am scared.'

'You can be brave,' Karia told him.

'It is the not knowing that is the worst thing,' Havell confessed. 'But I should not talk of such things with you.'

'Oh, don't worry. Dad always says I know far more than I should do,' Karia said breezily.

Havell could not help but smile. 'Well, the good news is that the Egg looks better than ever today. The swirls of colour are endless!'

She gasped as he opened the door to its chamber and she saw the lights sparkling over the walls and ceiling.

'It's so beautiful!'

Merren woke up, and groaned. Her neck was stiff, her eyes ached and her fingers were ink-spotted after a long day of paperwork.

'I am sorry to wake you, my Queen. But it is time to get dressed. The maids are ready to do your hair and the kitchen has sent up something to eat,' Louise said gently.

'They can go away for at least another turn of the hourglass,' Merren yawned. 'Aroaril knows what time I went to bed last night.'

'Me either, my Queen. But you have to get up. You cannot be late for the wedding.'

Merren opened her eyes wide and rolled over to stare at Louise. Just the words made her heart sink.

'Or you could postpone it. It is not too late …'

'It is too late. I must go ahead. It is what the people want,' Merren said dully. 'Send in my maids. I must look my best on this day.'

'As you wish, my Queen.'

Gello had been merciless with the men on the oars. He had held back a mixed company of men — the best Berellians, all veterans of the Ralloran Wars, the biggest eagle and leopard Tenochs and his own picked soldiers. The rest had sweated and worked to drive the ships against the wind and current.

It had soon become obvious that not all the ships could make it to the island — so Gello had transferred most of the men onto two ships, leaving the rest with a skeleton crew. Then, with three men to each oar and his hand-picked soldiers on deck, those two had been chosen to push through to the island. Already dozens of exhausted men had collapsed — but enough remained. Gello could see a large settlement that seemed to weave in and out of the hills and trees of the island. He struggled to see where it began and finished but noticed one structure that stretched out towards a small bay, so he ordered the steersman to aim for that.

'We're through the current!' Khaliz reported, excitedly.

Gello felt the ship lurch, as though an anchor had been cast away — and then they were sailing straight for the bay.

'Back oars! All men ready!' he roared, before turning to Feld. 'Stay on board and turn the ships around. We might need to leave in a hurry.'

'At least the current will be with us on the way out,' Feld grunted.

Gello nodded, then strode up to the bow. He could feel the warmth of the sun — as strong as the hottest Norstaline summer day — that set the sweat trickling down his back. But he ignored such things as the ship eased into the bay, its bow nudging into the soft, white sand.

'Follow me!' he called, drawing his sword and leading the surge of men over the side of the ship. But there was nobody around to stop him, so he led the men up towards the settlement. The sand coated his boots and the effort of walking up the beach to what was unmistakeably the entrance made his calves burn.

'Sire, does it not look familiar to you?' Ezok pointed at the entrance.

Gello glanced over it. The beautiful carvings around the doors, the way the doorway seemed to be part of the hillside — none of that interested him.

'It looks to me like a dragon's mouth,' Ezok continued.

Gello looked again and grimaced as he saw the resemblance.

Word passed swiftly around the men, and they began to draw back, muttering among themselves.

'The Egg is inside!' Khaliz announced. 'I can feel its magic!'

That was enough for Gello. Who cared what it looked like? 'Break the doors down!'

Two axemen smashed down the doors and Gello followed the first rush inside.

The coolness of the hall was in stark contrast to the hot sun outside, and Gello paused for a moment to let his eyes adjust, and to enjoy the cool air.

'Who are you? What are you doing here?'

Gello turned to see a strange-looking man, his eyes and ears and cheekbones seemingly stretched back. He was wearing a light tunic and sandals and his arms and legs were bronzed by the sun. Gello decided he must be one of those elves, that legend said lived here on the Isle.

'Do you know where you are?' the elf continued, advancing towards the armed men. 'You shall leave now, or I shall summon a dragon!'

Gello leaped forwards and rammed his sword into the elf's neck. Blood sprayed high across the wall and the elf, his strange eyes wide from the pain and shock, collapsed to the floor.

'Quick now!' Gello waved the others forwards.

Karia was marvelling at the Egg, enjoying playing with it. She would pass her hand close to its surface and laugh as colours sparkled and tried to chase her fingers around its curves. She imagined she could see the dragons inside it, although Havell assured her that was impossible.

'You must love coming in here to watch it.' She grinned at Havell.

The Elfaran sighed. 'It has sat here for so many years without doing anything — you see its beauty and its wonder but all I see are the remnants of the dragons who were my friends for centuries — and my own impending doom.'

Karia thought about asking him more about that, then decided she did not really want to know.

'Can I touch it?'

'Well, perhaps. You need to be careful. It is a storehouse not just of magic but of the dragons themselves. Like the Dragon Sword, it can choose who it wants to hold it.'

Karia stretched out a hand and saw the colours flash invitingly, pulsing for her. Carefully she lay her hand on the Egg and gasped with pleasure as its warmth rippled up her arm. The Egg flashed gently and she stroked it lovingly.

Then the door burst open and a rush of Elfarans pushed inside, dozens of them, all wide-eyed and scared, some with wounds, others being helped along by their companions.

'Invaders! They're inside the hall, killing everyone they find!' one yelled.

'We must get Argurium! She can save us!' another shouted.

'Are you mad?' another bellowed. 'Argurium is the last dragon! She is too valuable to risk for our lives! We must flee instead!'

The others seemed to agree with this.

'But what of the Egg?' Havell shouted.

'If we take it, they will catch us! Worse, we could lead them to Argurium and lose her as well!'

'We cannot lose the Egg, we must defend it!' Havell shouted. 'The world depends on its safety!'

'Defend it how? There are hundreds of them, all

with swords and axes! We are all that are left!' a wounded Elfaran cried.

Havell looked around wildly, while the rest of the Elfarans kept moving, hurrying towards a door at the back of the chamber, a dragon-sized door this time.

Karia climbed on top of a seat, put her fingers in her mouth and let out a piercing whistle. Conal had taught her how, and she was delighted to see it got their attention instantly. She knew what had to be done here, even if nobody else seemed to. The Egg needed her and Martil and Merren had told her often enough that you had to do dangerous and scary things sometimes to save others.

'Barricade that door! Use the benches and chairs!' she snapped. 'Havell, get Argurium and go and get Martil. He'll save us. The rest of you need to get your rider armour and swords out.'

The Elfarans just looked at her, dumbfounded.

'Hurry!' she shouted at them, trying to use the tone of voice Martil had when he was shouting at people.

'But what will happen to the Egg?' Havell whimpered.

'I shall defend it until you get back.' She stared at him calmly. It was the obvious solution. These elves were less use than a handful of talking rabbits but she was utterly confident that Martil would be able to defeat these attackers and get there in time to save her. She could feel the power of the Egg — with its help, she would be able to hold off anyone.

Havell just gaped at her, while several of his fellow Elfarans laughed in disbelief.

'Hurry! We do not have much time!' Karia told them, then pointed towards the door, while keeping her free hand on the top of the warm, pulsating

Dragon Egg. Instantly every chair and bench in the room flew across to pile up at the door the Elfarans had run through.

The laughter died in a moment and the Elfarans stared at her in shock until someone began hammering at the blocked door with what sounded like the hilts of swords.

'Move!' she yelled at the Elfarans — and they ran, or limped, for safety.

'I shall stay with you,' Havell said shakily.

'Thank you.' She patted his arm. 'But do you think you will do any good? Getting Martil back here will be far more useful.'

'But —'

'Martil will save me. So get him!'

Havell nodded jerkily and joined the rush for the other door.

Karia ignored them, instead breathing deeply and carefully, calming her mind as Barrett had taught her. She was a little afraid but she knew what she could do. There was almost unlimited power in that Egg and, while touching it, she could use it without fear of exhausting herself. Nobody could fight against that. And she only needed to hold them back for a little while, then Martil would be here — and then they would run.

She let herself sink into the magic, feeling for the plant life that made up part of the structure of the room, as well as for any insects that were nearby, as axes began to carve chunks out of the wooden door and her barricade of chairs and benches began to shake.

'Get in there! Don't give them time to escape or find a dragon!' Gello directed men forwards. There were plenty of these strange-looking elves running around this rabbit's warren of a place. But they died easily and fought not at all. Far from the creatures of legend, they seemed to be ridiculously weak. Not one of his men had even been hurt so far. But he was still wary — after all, this was the home of the dragons, and who knew what surprises awaited them? The dragon-sized doors and hallways were eerie, although there was no sign of the magical creatures. Gello had no intention of being at the front of the men when they did find one, however.

'The Egg is in there! I can feel it!' Khaliz cried.

The door surrendered to one last blow, then the axemen began attacking chairs and benches that blocked the way into the hall. There were three of them, big men in mail shirts and helms, with the large double-bladed axes that the Berellians loved to use. They made short work of the chairs — and then went flying backwards as something large and barely seen swatted them aside.

'What is that? Get in there and destroy it!' Gello shoved men at the doorway.

Some were struck by flying chairs and knocked down, others were knocked aside by what Gello could see were tree roots. Others screamed as armour became unbearably hot, thrashing around on the floor as they struggled to pull it from their bodies. Some slapped and scratched as insects attacked them — but none seemed able to get inside the room. Gello peered through the chaos and saw the giant Egg, as well as a small child standing beside it. As he locked eyes with her, she flicked her fingers and he dropped to the floor — as a broken chair whistled above him and smashed into the wall behind.

'Khaliz! This is magic! Get in there and stop it!'

The mage stepped over unconscious men and writhing bodies and into the room.

Merren stared at herself in the mirror without any pleasure.

'You look beautiful, your majesty.' Her maid, Anna, curtseyed.

Merren had never seen that about herself but this wedding was all about show, a display of confidence to give heart to a battered country. It would not work if she did not look the part. She could not even take a glass of wine to help her get through it.

'Thank you, Anna. You may go now,' she said absently.

Anna curtseyed again, then headed for the door, leaving Merren to try and look into her own eyes.

'You had to do this! It is for the country!' she told her reflection — but it did not seem to believe her.

'My Queen, there's a man here to see you,' Anna called.

Merren whipped around, her heart leaping, despite herself. Had Martil returned?

'Show him in!' she ordered, and Anna leaped to obey.

Merren tried to control her breathing — and then exhaled in disappointment when she saw it was Sendric.

'What are you doing here, Count?' she demanded. 'Don't you remember that it is bad luck for the groom to see the bride before the church? Aroaril knows what will happen to you now!'

Sendric ignored her poor attempt at a jest.

'It is worse luck, your majesty, for this groom to not see his bride when he is waiting in the plaza outside, in front of thousands of people!' he said stiffly. 'I came to make sure you have not had any second thoughts about this marriage. For it will have a disastrous effect on the country if they do not see you wed today. It is all many people have been talking about. It has given new heart to the country — the people have really responded to this good news.'

'Was it to this good news? Or just that your prediction of chaos and anarchy was false?' she asked archly.

'It was not my prediction! I merely told you what others feared! If you are unable to face the truth from an adviser —' he began hotly, but she held up her hand.

'Go and wait outside. I am not ready yet, but I shall be there at the appointed time. You have my word,' she said tiredly.

'Thank you, your majesty. It is the right thing, for the country.' He bowed rigidly before walking away.

'Don't say a word,' Merren told her reflection.

Khaliz stopped the flailing tree roots that had been causing so many problems, and despatched the insects that had been plaguing the men. He almost ignored the little girl. There was no way a child could best him!

'It's safe now!' he called out — a moment before the tree came back to life and knocked him across the room.

Cursing, he managed to stop himself before he crunched into the wall, and reached into the magic, picking up a chair to hurl at the child. But it stopped in mid-air, and even began to inch back towards him. Sweating now, he doubled his efforts to send it back at her. But she did not even appear to be troubled as a second chair, then a third and fourth rose into the air and pressed in at him.

Grimly he tried to keep them under control, but he could feel his energy slipping away. How was she able to do this? It was impossible! His breath was sawing harshly in his throat and spots were beginning to dance in front of his eyes.

Gello watched in astonishment as the wizard was unable to vanquish a small child. He knew Khaliz had been bested by Barrett in the far northern mountains, but by a little girl? Then the four chairs, which hung in the air between the two, smashed into the Berellian wizard, sending him crumpling to the floor.

Gello looked around to see the men behind him cowering away from the doorway, where the tree roots were whipping back and forth once more.

'This squad, get in there! The rest of you, find some other way in!' he said in frustration. 'We did not come all this way to be stopped by a child!'

Martil had enjoyed a relaxing swim and was lying on a large rock, allowing the sun to dry the water from his skin, when Havell and Argurium swooped down from the sky, skimming the water before landing on the sand with impossible grace. Martil had half-closed his eyes, expecting a spray of sand and water — but there was barely a breath of wind. He grabbed some clothing, expecting to see Karia leap down from the dragon's back and impress him.

'Martil! We need you!' Havell screamed down from Argurium's back.

Martil had a pair of the Elfaran swimming shorts halfway up his legs when the Elfaran's words hit him and cold suddenly sliced through him.

'What is it? Where's Karia?' he shouted back.

'We're under attack! I'll explain on the way!'

Martil hauled the shorts on, grabbed the Dragon Sword and ran up Argurium's extended foreleg, jumped to her shoulder and onto the neck, where

Havell sat. Almost before he was there, the dragon had taken off and zoomed across the treetops.

'Attackers burst in and started killing everyone! Karia stayed to protect the Egg! She's using magic to hold them back!' Havell gabbled.

'What?' Fury and fear mingled within Martil. 'You left a child to protect it, while you ran? What about the rest of your people?'

'We're not warriors! She told us to go, showed us how she can use the magic within the Egg! I said I'd stay with her but she told me to get you!'

Martil restrained himself from hurling the Elfaran into the trees below only with the greatest of difficulty, then an icy calm seemed to descend on him.

'How many attackers? Who are they?' he asked.

'We don't know. But my people said they're killing everyone and that there's hundreds of them!'

As much as he wanted to rush to Karia's side, Martil knew he might need some help. 'Where are the rest of you?'

'Karia sent them to the old armoury, where we keep our dragon rider costumes, for when we need to scare off ships.'

'Playing dress-ups, while a child protects them. Take us there now,' Martil ordered coldly, ice within his veins, fire in his heart.

Merren could see the crowds gathering. It was like the evening when she had been prepared to sacrifice herself to save people's lives, and Martil had gathered everyone in the plaza. She had been willing to offer her life — and yet, somehow, this seemed harder. But, she told herself, when you have offered your life for your people, sacrificing your happiness for theirs should be an easy bargain.

She swirled her long dress and sighed. Karia had wanted so much to carry a basket of rose petals on this day, not just scatter them but make them dance as she threw them.

'I've been practising!' she had said.

She would never get to do that now.

'Not long now, my Queen,' Louise said softly. 'We cannot keep the people.'

'The traditional feast — is it simple? I do not want excess when so many go hungry.' Merren turned swiftly. 'Perhaps I should go and see …'

'We have already supervised it, my Queen,' Gia replied. 'There will be horsemeat soup, as you requested. The only concession is some fresh bread, and of course the cake.'

'Yes, of course,' Merren said absently, turning back to stare out the window.

'This is the only way through! And that child is blocking it!' Heath reported.

'That is not a normal child!' Gello spat. 'We have to get past! We are wasting time here!'

'At last we have not seen any more of those elves. They are probably still running,' Heath grunted.

'That does not solve this problem! Has anyone got a crossbow?'

Ezok had been close by Gello at all times, as ordered, and had seen attack after attack literally swept aside as the child used the very walls of the chamber to strike at all who tried to get inside. But it had given him an idea. He had spent the last few days terrified that Gello would kill him, or that Onzalez would kill him. They had invested so much hope in the Dragon Egg, on his recommendation. If it did not live up to their dreams then he would be the one to pay. Only now he could see his salvation. Thanks to this child, everyone could see just how much power was in the Egg. The limp body of Khaliz, along with two score of others, was simple testimony to that. If the girl could make the Egg work, bring her along. Make her the focus of Onzalez's anger if the Egg did not work. And if she was killed, place the blame on her killer for why the Egg would not work.

'We must not kill the child!' he announced dramatically.

Everyone turned.

'What? Is it some kind of magical guardian that we can only defeat by reading it a bedtime saga and offering it a glass of milk?' Gello snarled.

'It is some kind of guardian of the Egg. I remember now! It's the Radiant Child!'

He pointed and they all turned to look inside the room, past the tree roots that waved menacingly at them, to where the child stood, her skin glowing in all the colours of the rainbow, reflected by the Egg that she stood beside, protectively.

'What?' Gello hissed.

'It is the only thing that can use the power of the Egg! We must capture it, bring it with us, force it to tell us how to use the Egg!'

Gello looked back in the room. It certainly knew how to use the Egg's power. 'And without it ...'

'The Egg might prove useless. We might never learn how to unlock its power!'

Gello swore. He looked at Khaliz. He would have liked the wizard's advice on this one. But it did not look as if Khaliz would be able to speak for a while — if ever again.

'How do we capture it?' he growled finally.

'I used to be a slinger,' an eagle warrior said into the silence. 'I still carry my sling with me, for luck. If you can keep it occupied, I think I can hit it with a piece of wood, perhaps knock it out.'

'And what if you crack its skull?' Gello snorted.

'Do you have any other suggestions — sire?' The eagle warrior met his gaze.

Gello was tempted to kill the man for insolence, but he had no other ideas.

'I want a huge rush of men in there. Keep that child occupied and give this man a clear shot. He is to be protected at all costs, understand? We have wasted too much time here already.'

Gello massed men in the corridor, then waved his arm.

'Charge!' he signalled.

20

Argurium brought them to an abrupt stop by the tip of the hall's tail, half-hidden by trees. Martil had seen a pair of ships in the bay beyond, and more on the horizon. While he doubted there would be hundreds of men in the Hall, there would certainly be too many, even for the Dragon Sword to handle. He needed men — and the Elfarans were the only option. Almost before Argurium had stopped, he had run down her leg and into the open door.

It took his eyes a few moments to adjust to the gloom, although his nose told him he was surrounded by armour. More than fifty Elfarans stood there, most of them now wearing armour and clutching swords, some of them arguing, all of them doing nothing about going back and saving Karia. They fell silent when they saw him.

He drew the Dragon Sword, and could almost hear it humming. Behind him, Havell rushed over to a rack and began hauling down the armour that was there.

'You ran away, left a little girl behind to protect you!' Martil accused, struggling to keep a lid on his anger and fear.

'We are not warriors!' someone cried.

'And is she?' Martil spun, his voice dangerously quiet. Havell was fussing around him, strapping on armour as he spoke. But he ignored the Elfaran as the man worked around him.

'You say you are not warriors. But that little girl is protecting the essence of almost every dragon you swore to serve until death. I understand you are afraid. But if you let the girl die and the Egg be taken, everything you have done will be wasted! You think you are elves, you believe you are the creatures children read about. You have forgotten that you are men. But men you are. And you shall follow me now. And you will fight like men while there is breath in your bodies!'

His eyes bored into theirs — none could look away.

Havell adjusted a pair of straps and stepped back. Martil looked down to see he wore strange-looking armour, carved and worked from steel. A solid breastplate, a leather kilt with strips of steel and forearm bracers in the same worked metal. It looked strange and barely fitted him, but did not seem as heavy as his trusty mail shirt.

'Magic.' Havell shrugged, as he handed Martil an unusual helm, full-faced, with merely a wide-open strip for his eyes.

Martil slipped it on and raised the Dragon Sword, its eyes gleaming and its blade glowing in this dim chamber, the light making his own eyes glow redly in the gloom. The Elfarans, who had watched this man playing happily with a child and applauding their songs and dances, shuddered.

'Follow me!' Martil led the way at a run, the Dragon Sword lighting the way, propelled by massive anger. He had to get to Karia. Nothing else mattered. The Elfarans followed him with a shout.

Karia was unaware of the passing of time. She was lost in the magic, feeling the pulsing power of the

Egg beside her. Barrett had taught her to focus her mind, to concentrate on what she was doing, excluding outside distractions. So when more men burst through the shattered doorway, leaping and running over the bodies of those who had already failed, she was ready for them. Tree roots detached from the walls, swung and slashed at men who tried to block them, or who tried to grab them and hold them. But she focused on those who tried to get close to her, ignoring the man who crept around the back of the chamber.

With Louise and Gia by her side, Merren stepped out of her rooms. She took a deep breath and stood there for a long moment, the other two women behind her. It seemed so unreal that she was doing this. What was Martil doing at this moment?

'My Queen?' Louise prompted.

'Let us go,' Merren sighed, and began the long walk that would lead her outside and to the makeshift altar, where Archbishop Sadlier and Count Sendric waited.

Screaming men were hurled across the chamber, or knocked back into the hallway as Gello, cursing, yelled instructions from the safety of the corridor.

'Distract it! Throw things!' he roared.

In response, the surviving men threw remnants of chairs — which were returned to them at double the force. They suffered — but not in vain. The slinger chose his moment well, sending a small chunk of polished wood whistling across the chamber to strike the child on the forehead.

Instantly she crumpled to the ground and the chamber's defences stopped in the same moment, the tree roots hanging limp. Men who had been held by the walls themselves were suddenly free — although those who had been battered unconscious, or impaled by flying chairs, still writhed and screamed or moaned.

Cautiously, Gello eased into the room. When nothing seemed to be happening, he waved men over to the Egg, and the fallen child.

Ezok was the first there.

'She's alive!' he reported. 'Help me bind and gag her, just in case.'

'Are you sure she is the key to this Dragon Egg?' Gello asked, doubtfully.

Ezok gestured around the chaos in the room, where the likes of the unconscious Khaliz were being hoisted up.

'Do you know of another small girl who could do such a thing?'

Gello looked down at the small blonde child, a lump of a bruise already swelling on her forehead, where the wood had struck her. Something stirred in his memory, something about a child in one of the reports he had read. But he could not remember in what context. He had dismissed it as unimportant then, thinking that a child was worthless. He shrugged. Surely it was nothing.

'Bring her along, as well as the Egg. We shall let Onzalez sort out this mystery,' Gello decided. 'We have tarried here too long. You two — get the Egg.'

A pair of Berellians reached out to lift up the large Egg — only for it to flash out bright colours, almost too fast to distinguish. They drew back uncertainly.

'That was an order!' Gello barked.

The pair bent down again — only to drop to the ground, screaming, as their hands blistered and burned.

Gello cursed. 'Build a cradle for it!'

Using tunics ripped from dead men, as well as broken benches and chairs, a cradle for the Egg was hastily constructed and four men, grunting with the effort, picked up the Egg and led the way back to the ships. Ezok carried the unconscious girl over his shoulder.

'Hurry! Who knows what else waits for us in this place!' Gello urged them onwards.

Martil ran swiftly. Fatigue was not going to be a problem. There was but one thought in his head. Save Karia. Anyone who got in his way would die. The Dragon Sword seemed to have caught his mood — or perhaps it could sense the Egg nearby. Not only was it beginning to glow, but it was also emitting a steady hum, a low, insistent noise that echoed the pounding blood in Martil's ears.

'They're in there!' an Elfaran shouted. 'The door to your left!'

Martil saw it: a dragon-sized door that was just ajar. Barely slowing, he slammed his left shoulder into the door and pivoted into the room, Sword at the ready — to see it empty of Karia and the Egg. A scatter of bodies lay across the floor, as well as a number of men too badly hurt to be rescued by their comrades. Martil strode across to one, a man with a chair leg through his chest, who was propped against the wall, his breathing painful and blood on his lips.

'Where is the girl? Tell me now,' Martil ordered.

'Why?' the man gasped.

Martil reached out and grabbed the chair leg, twisting it around in the man's chest. The man howled in pain and coughed up a spray of blood onto Martil's breastplate, which he ignored utterly.

'The child and the Egg are going back to the ships,' he moaned.

Martil stood and inspected the Elfarans, who stood in a group, looking in disbelief at the stand where the Egg had sat for centuries.

'We must cut them off! Half of you follow me, the rest take to the corridors — you know this Hall better than they do. Hunt them! They cannot get away!' Martil held up the Sword, before sprinting after the invaders. The Elfarans waited but a heartbeat before obeying him.

Gello chafed at the slow progress back to the ships. Not only were the men struggling with the Egg, which none wanted to touch, but with the dozens of wounded men being carried or helped along. He was tempted to leave them behind but trained men were too valuable.

'Heath! Take a squad forwards and warn the ships we are on our way! Tell Onzalez to be ready!' he ordered. He watched them run off and wondered if he should go too — but thought it better if he ensured the Egg was safe.

'More men on that cradle! Move faster! And I want a rearguard! Livett, take two squads and wait here for a count of a hundred, then follow us slowly,' he ordered. 'The rest of you, get a move on!'

Martil sensed there were men ahead in the corridor. But he did not slow his pace. The passage here was only wide enough for perhaps three men abreast — and he had the Dragon Sword. He did not care how many men he had to carve through to get to Karia. He had to believe she was all right. After all, they had taken her with them. He would not think of her dead. He lengthened his stride and noted, absently, that the Elfarans were right behind him.

Around a bend and there they were — a pack of

nervous men waiting in the dim corridor, swords ready.

Martil let out a shout, releasing his fear for Karia and his anger at the danger she was in, turning it into a wordless war cry. Then he was upon them, the Dragon Sword lashing out in a deadly pattern. He remembered his race through the troopers to reach Karia at Sendric. But that was as nothing to what he felt now. Tiredness, caution, pity — none of those things touched him as he ripped into the men facing him. None could stop the Sword or block it and men fell screaming as it sliced them apart. Behind him, the Elfarans threw themselves into the fight, swinging their swords with more enthusiasm than skill. But to a group of men terrified of the bloodied demon in the strange armour, whose sword cut through steel as easily as paper, it was enough. They fled, screaming, with Martil right behind, cutting down anyone he could catch.

Merren stepped out into the square and waited as the people erupted into cheers, waving and clapping. She waved back and the cheers redoubled. Two companies of men lined the long aisle; behind them, people pressed as close as they could, waving and shouting her name. Her heart was telling her to turn around but all her training, everything she had put into this country to save it, made her stay.

Inside, she felt dead. Regret almost swamped her and it was a real effort to begin to walk towards her doom. The euphoria of those first days after saving the country from Gello and the Fearpriests were long gone. And it was all her own fault. It was a bitter pill to swallow but there was nothing for it but to gulp it down.

Slowly, she started down the aisle.

Gello and his men heard the screams first. Cries of pain, followed by shrieks of terror.

'What's going on?' someone yelled.

'It's more of those magical guardians! They are after us, seeking to regain the Egg and its magic child!' another shouted.

'The first man to run gets cut down!' Gello roared at them. 'Keep together! There's more safety in numbers!'

Those men who were already eyeing their escape saw Gello's drawn sword — and the look in his eyes — and thought again.

Then Livett and a handful of men raced out of the darkness.

'Elves! Led by a demon! They're right behind us!' Livett screamed. 'They'll kill anyone they catch!'

'Stay where you are!' Gello boomed.

Too late. Many of the Tenochs bolted.

'Leave the wounded! They're no good to us! And let's run!' Gello ordered.

The men had no qualms about dumping the wounded and unconscious men, such as Khaliz, although the ones who were awake begged and pleaded to be taken along. With as many hands on the makeshift cradle as could reach, the Egg was carried at a run down the corridor.

'Give me the girl! You command the rearguard!' Gello told Ezok, who wordlessly handed the child over and drew his sword.

'Of course, sire,' Ezok agreed. But he had no intention of making a desperate last stand. He would do whatever was necessary to save his life.

The forty men who stood with him nervously did not have long to wait. A blood-spattered demon with red eyes, in strange armour and carrying a glowing sword, descended on them, followed by warrior elves. The bravest of Gello's men tried to stop him — and were swept aside.

Ezok did not wait any longer. He turned and ran, followed by most of the other men a moment later.

The corridor led to a large hall, one of the many that was big enough for dragons to use. The fleeing Tenochs had got this far, Gello saw, until they ran into more warrior elves — and been slaughtered. Now that blood-spattered band barred the way.

'We're trapped! We're all going to die!' Livett moaned.

Gello turned and back-handed him, sending his captain staggering back.

'Hold this child and I shall clear the way!' He turned to his visibly frightened force and stared at them hard. 'Those of you carrying the Egg, keep going. As for the rest of you, any man who wants to live, follow me!' he shouted.

With mingled cries of defiance and nervousness, they followed him in a rush.

The Elfarans howled in return and sprinted to meet them, the two sides coming together with a crash.

Gello dodged a wild slash of a sword, then cursed as his return bounced off the elf's armour. He had never fought for his life before, and fear touched him.

'Give us the Egg!' his attacker challenged, cutting wildly at Gello.

But Gello had trained with the sword for years, and been tutored by some of the finest bladesmen money could buy. He found time seemed to be slowing for him — the elf's blows were easy to avoid — and he could feel his confidence growing.

He stepped to one side and thrust his sword into the elf's throat. The elf choked, his blood spraying out, then slipped limply off Gello's sword.

The former King felt a surge of exultation the likes of which he had not experienced since the first time a crown was put on his head.

'They die like any man! Come on!' he waved, shoulder-charging another to the ground and stabbing down.

But then Ezok and the remnants of the rearguard ran into the chamber.

'They're right behind us! None can stop the demon!' Ezok gibbered.

'Hold here! We can face them here!' Gello yelled in reply.

Still, he could see his men looking nervously towards the various doors leading out of the hall — but before they could do more than look, Martil burst out of the darkness and was upon them.

Gello stared in shock and horror as the demon fell on his men. The demon's sword was humming, its eyes were glowing and its strange armour was drenched in blood — and more was being added by the moment. One stroke of the sword and it cut through everything — swords, armour and flesh. It seemed to dance through his men, every movement creating death. It was as if the others were wading through thick mud, while he skimmed across the surface. None could get near him. Meanwhile, the warrior elves who followed it were slaughtering his terrified men. But Gello could see he still had the advantage of numbers. And here was the place to use it. All it required was a little bravery on his part.

'Come on!' Gello led a charge. 'There's hardly any of them!'

Martil heard the call and recognised the voice. He beheaded the man in front of him and pivoted smoothly, seeking out Gello. When he saw him he raised the glistening, pristine Sword and pointed it at him, letting out a bellow.

Gello saw the challenge, heard the inhuman cry of rage from the demon and felt his legs go to water.

'Run!' he yelled, and led the rush for the doors.

The men scattered, and the remaining elves chased them, hacking and cutting at all they could reach.

But Martil had no intention of letting Gello escape, and raced after him, men either scattering before him, or dying by the Sword.

Livett led the way through the corridors, the band of Egg-carriers close behind. These men were puffing and grunting with the effort of carrying the heavy Egg in its unwieldy cradle — but the sounds of fighting and the screams of the dying drifting through the air lent speed to their feet and strength to their arms. Ahead they could see daylight, and a way out of this mysterious and terrifying maze.

'Hurry! They're right behind us!'

Gello's shout made them almost drop the Egg. Somehow they recovered and hurried out into the sunlight, closely followed by Gello. Outside the shattered door, Gello stumbled, fell and whimpered, fearing a blow from the demon. But Ezok, close behind him, hauled him to his feet.

Frightened men pounded past them, racing for the ships, leaving just a handful around the Egg.

'We'll never make it back!' Livett whimpered.

Gello was about to hit him when he realised how few men stood close. His shoulders slumped for a moment, then he straightened.

'Whining won't save us! Move!' he ordered. 'Get the Egg and the girl onto the ships and you shall all be rewarded beyond your dreams!'

This Egg was his way back, he would not abandon it for anything. Then he looked over his shoulder, saw the demon running towards him and quailed.

'Don't worry, I am here!' Onzalez shouted in the next moment.

The shattered entrance to the hall closed up in an instant, sealing itself and blocking them off from the demon and his elven warriors.

Gello could not keep the smile of relief from his face. Not only was Onzalez there, but Heath as well, along with a squad of his best men, the ones he had sent to warn the ships.

'Where is Khaliz?' Onzalez demanded. 'And the rest of the men?'

'Dead. All dead. First we had to defeat the magical guardian of the Egg, then came a demon and these vicious elves. Men ran or died.'

'The guardian of the Egg?'

'The girl. She defeated Khaliz in a magical duel. Ezok knows all about her,' Gello explained. 'She cost us time, and men, gave the elves the chance to summon this demon.'

'Numbers are unimportant. Not now we have the Egg!'

'We still have to get it back to the ships,' Ezok muttered.

Martil slammed into the door, cursing. It would not move.

'Another way out!' he barked.

'This way!' Havell, who had caught up after arming himself in time to help slaughter some of the slower runners, led them off to the right, down an infuriatingly long passage and up stone steps to a second door, which was not barred. They came out higher on the hill and Martil led the remaining Elfarans, now just a few dozen, in a desperate run down to the bay. The fighting had grown confused in the hall; the slower runners among the invaders, as well as those who had taken a wrong turn, had been found and massacred — but it had all taken time. Now he could see the effect of that, as well as the blocked doorway. The Egg and Karia were almost down at the ships. Desperation gave strength to his legs and he increased his strides, out-running even the fastest Elfarans. He could see the ships clearly, see the party slowly hefting the Egg on board. He almost did not care about the Egg. That could be retrieved later. But Karia … he had to rescue her. Everything was concentrated on getting to her. He could see her being carried limply in the arms of a Berellian. The sight sent a fresh surge of anger washing through him. Nothing could stop him.

Then the Fearpriest with them saw him pounding down the hillside. He thrust his hands into the sand before him.

Martil knew what was going to happen, so hurled himself forwards as the wave of power rippled through the ground. He hoped to get over it but it still caught him in its radius, sent him tumbling. He lost the Dragon Sword and lay winded for a moment.

The Elfarans were running at full pace now, catching up to him, but again the Fearpriest used his hands to make the earth quake and knock them down. Martil staggered to his feet, grabbed the Dragon Sword and charged at the last few men pushing the ship out into the water. Already the oars were digging into the water but he knew if he could only get on the ship, he could at least get to Karia. Nothing mattered but that.

The Dragon Sword cut down the last man then Martil leaped to grab a trailing rope with his left hand. He bobbed up to the surface and was pulled along, as he tried to haul himself up the rope while keeping hold of the Dragon Sword.

On board, Livett pointed back at where Martil clung grimly to the rope, dragging himself along it one hand at a time.

'Look at that!' Livett pointed.

Gello, Ezok and a dozen others rushed to the rail, to see the armoured demon moving ever closer. It saw them and let loose a chilling shout of rage. Its eyes still seemed to glow, while blood crusted the faceplate of its helm.

'If that thing gets aboard, we're all dead men!' Livett bleated.

Gello shouldered Livett aside and hacked at the rope with his sword, heedless of the damage he was doing to the wooden rail or the blade. Livett and Heath joined him and, next moment, the rope was cut.

They stared overboard fearfully as the demon floundered in the water for a moment, then seemed to raise itself up, roaring once more. Livett trembled at the sight, then the weight of the demon's armour dragged it under the surface.

Merren could see Milly and Sendric now, at the end of the long aisle. She had taken her time with the walk, stopping to speak to people she recognised, or to take flowers from small children. Every time a girl held out a bunch, her heart leaped, thinking it was Karia. She could not help but think back to the day when she had ridden across this square in a carriage, stuck in the depths of despair, only to be told by the girl that her father was the greatest warrior in the world, and here to rescue her.

Milly was smiling at her but Sendric looked impatient, no doubt the result of the long wait he had endured. In response, she slowed even further, and made a point of talking to a young woman with two small children, who was standing near a grim-faced Kettering.

Karia woke up slowly, unaware of where she was. Her head hurt and she opened her mouth to ask Martil what was going on — only to discover there was a strip of cloth in her mouth. She tried to reach up and remove it, only to find her hands and feet were tied together. Panicking now, fully awake, she tried to escape, the beginnings of a scream in her throat.

'Shh! It's all right!' a strange voice said.

She looked around, frightened, to see a tall, blond man, in rich but dirty clothes holding his finger to his lips.

'Please listen to me,' he whispered. 'Both our lives depend on it!'

Karia looked at him and could see the pleading in his eyes. Slowly, she nodded.

'We only have a little time. They are securing the Egg in the ship's hold, and then they are going to come and talk to us both. This is what you need to say, if you want to live. Get it wrong, and we shall both die. Understand?'

Again, Karia nodded. She remembered the exercises Barrett had taught her to calm her mind and used one of those.

She did not know where she was but she was sure of one thing. Martil would come for her. Somehow he would come for her. She just had to stay alive long enough for that.

Merren nodded to Archbishop Sadlier, who in turn nodded to Barrett. Thanks to the mage, everyone in the square would be able to hear the service.

'People of Norstalos! We have come through the darkest period in our history into the light! This ceremony today marks a new beginning, a way forward ...'

Merren sighed as Milly began her speech. This was also an important symbol for the new head of the church and the new Archbishop's chance to speak to a major part of the population. It looked like it would go for some time. But it had to come to an end eventually. She hoped it would not be soon.

Martil came to the surface gasping and spitting water.

'Karia!' he bellowed, his voice echoing across the water, as the ships rapidly receded, the oars and the current pushing them along swiftly.

Despite the armour and the Dragon Sword, he tried to swim after them.

'Get him to the shore!' Havell gasped.

'Let go of me! They're getting away!' Martil protested, nearly going under again.

Several Elfarans had thrown off their armour to come and rescue him, and they struggled to keep him above water. He thrashed and struck out at them, knocking all but one away from him.

'Damn you! Let me go! I can catch them!' he insisted.

'Martil! You can't do it that way! We have to use Argurium!' Havell yelled into his ear.

The words penetrated the red haze in Martil's

brain, and he allowed himself to be dragged to the shore, where he ripped off the helmet and vomited up bile and seawater in equal measures. His exertions, the running and fighting, caught up with him and it was all he could do to force himself to his knees, where he looked at the rapidly diminishing ships through a veil of tears.

'We shall take Argurium, get her to land on the ship with the Egg and Karia, then tear them apart and bring the ship back,' he vowed.

'Listen to me,' Havell appealed.

Martil wiped his mouth and eyes and stared at the Elfaran. 'What's the matter? Afraid?'

'Of failing, yes. There are too few of us. We cannot risk Argurium. The last dragon, man! And we cannot risk you! If you were to die, then the magic, the world could end.'

'If you think I will let —'

Havell grabbed his arm. 'No! But use your head. They have to land. We need to find out where, so we can take back Karia and the Egg then!'

'But what if they —'

'They went to a lot of trouble to get her onto the ship. They took her when they left their own men. They must think she's linked with the Egg somehow,' Havell said urgently.

Martil gazed at him before finally nodding. He would follow them — and destroy them. 'We must find where they are going. And when we arrive, they will pay!'

There were plenty of wounded men, most slowly dying from their wounds, although a few were merely insensible. Martil inspected them quickly, looking for someone who would have useful information. The wizard, although unconscious, seemed by far the most promising.

'Tie him and then bring some water to revive him,' Martil instructed Havell. 'The rest of you better help these wounded.'

The Elfarans nodded agreement and several drew their swords and began finishing off the wounded.

Martil, who had seen these men almost in tears when he cut up a fish, stared in surprise.

'They came here to bring death to us and the dragons and, by their actions, may have doomed the entire world. They do not deserve our pity,' an Elfaran, bloodied to the elbows, stated.

Martil shrugged. He had much bigger worries.

The wizard was tied down, while Elfarans stood around him with swords poised.

'I have seen wizards in action and ...' Martil began.

'We have been around magic since before your great-great-great-grandfather drew breath. If he seeks to try something, we will know before he does,' Havell said grimly.

Martil almost smiled, then threw a bucket of seawater over the wizard. Nothing happened.

'Try this,' an Elfaran offered, holding out a small pouch of herbs. 'Hold a pinch under his nose. Just try not to breathe it yourself.'

Martil gingerly held a pinch of the powdered herb under the wizard's nose, then jumped as the man convulsed.

'Who? What? Where am I? Did we get the Egg?' The wizard's eyes were open but unfocused. He tried to stretch and groaned. 'I think my leg is broken — and some ribs too. Why can't I move?'

Martil waited until the wizard's eyes seemed to clear, then grabbed the man's beard.

'Do you know who I am?' he demanded.

The wizard's eyes widened. 'Captain Martil, the Butcher of Bellic,' he croaked.

Martil nodded grimly. 'Then you know what I am prepared to do. I need answers. If you are to live, then you will give them to me. Try to use magic and pain will break your concentration. Understand?'

The wizard looked up at the grim-faced, bloody elves, and shuddered.

'What do you want to know?'

'Who are you and why did you come here?'

'I am Khaliz, once King's Magician to Markuz of Berellia, now serving King Gello. We are here because we were defeated on the plains of Norstalos. The Fearpriest Onzalez learned of a powerful magical item, the Dragon Egg and ...'

'Who told him of that?' Havell interrupted.

Khaliz's eyes flickered up. 'I know you, also. The elf who rode the dragon that so impressed the goblins.'

'Talk to me!' Martil said sharply.

Khaliz's eyes jerked back to Martil. 'A man called Ezok. Once Berellia's ambassador to Norstalos. He and I accompanied Cezar to the far north, to win over the goblins. Ezok was talking to several of the goblin chiefs, and had bribed some of the goblins who served the priest of Aroaril there. Through them he found out about this amazing object, the Dragon Egg, which was even more powerful than the Dragon Sword and could control magic itself. When our mission ended in failure, we knew our lives would be at risk from Onzalez. Ezok talked to Onzalez, did a deal for his life, telling him about this Egg. In return for this knowledge, Ezok and I lived.'

Martil glanced up at Havell, who looked ashen.

'Go on.'

'So when we were defeated before the Norstaline capital, Onzalez decided this was our last hope. With so much magic, he could not be stopped.'

'That is not what it is for! You fool! That Egg is the only chance the dragons have of being reborn. If it is not returned, all life will end!' Havell grabbed the wizard by the front of his robe.

'What? Dragons reborn?' Khaliz gasped.

'Did you not wonder why there were no dragons on the island?' Havell shook the mage before letting him drop back to the floor.

'We thought they were away! If I had known ...'

'That Fearpriest would still want it for himself. He craves power, does he not?' Martil said harshly. 'Where is he going and what does he plan to do with it?'

'Tenoch. He is going back to Tenoch,' Khaliz gabbled. 'He hopes to use the Egg's guardian to unlock its power.'

'Egg's guardian? What nonsense is this?' Martil now grabbed Khaliz.

'The strange child with magic powers, who used the Egg against us, who defeated me. We knew she could not be a normal girl! Ezok told us she was its guardian, a creature called the Radiant Child and the only way we could unlock the Egg's power!'

Martil shifted his grip to Khaliz's throat.

'That's my daughter! What will he do with her?'

Khaliz choked and gasped, unable to talk.

'Martil!' Havell struck at his arm.

Reluctantly, Martil let go of the wizard, who gasped for air.

'I do not know what he will do to her. But if she can use the Egg, then he will seek to use her to unlock its power ...'

'How many men does he have with him?' Martil

interrupted. 'How strong is his power base at Tenoch?'

'I have never been there. But his army is gone — destroyed at the Norstaline capital. Gello has perhaps two thousand men with him, and they will seek to use the magic of the Egg to turn the people of Tenoch into a fresh army of conquest.'

'And how big is Tenoch?'

'It is rumoured that our continent of Albiona could fit inside it half-a-dozen times,' Khaliz coughed.

Martil stood, his mind awhirl. His first instinct was to rush there himself, take back Karia and the Egg with the Dragon Sword. But he was not going to be enough. He needed an army, both to win them back and for his vengeance. He would not make the same mistake thrice. He was going to go there and destroy everything, make sure that Gello was dead, that the Fearpriests were dead and these Tenochs would never dare to cross the sea again.

'We must fly back to Norstalos, gather the army, follow them to Tenoch, take back the Egg and Karia and teach them a lesson they shall never forget,' he vowed.

'But how long will that take?' Havell asked.

Martil rounded on him, trying desperately not to think about whether Karia could stay alive that long without angering a Fearpriest. But the Fearpriest should hope that he let her live, for Martil's vengeance would make Bellic look like a minor disagreement if anything happened to Karia.

'Do you have any better ideas? Besides, we can use magic to speed ourselves along.'

Havell looked at him for a moment, then nodded.

'Agreed. What do we do with this one?'

'I promised him life,' Martil shrugged.

'I did not,' Havell said fiercely, and stabbed down once.

Martil looked on dispassionately as the wizard died.

'Find Argurium. Every moment is vital,' he said.

21

Merren found her mind wandering as Milly's long sermon came to an end, to thunderous applause from the assembled people.

She felt her heart beat a little faster, when she saw Bishop Quiller hand Milly the thick Book of Aroaril. Until then she had been able to imagine she was merely listening to a church sermon, albeit one that had gone on for more than a turn of the hourglass. But now it was real. Now she was about to marry — for all the wrong reasons.

'And now, before I begin the traditional vows, I ask the traditional question: is there anyone here in this congregation who knows of some reason why these two people should not be joined in marriage? For when a couple is brought together before Aroaril, it is a partnership for life.'

There was the usual expectant pause followed by a few laughs as a half-drunk man raised his arm, then had it pulled down again swiftly by his wife.

Merren could not help but glance around, and felt her heart fall when there was nothing.

You are doing this for your people. Be strong. Be brave. You have faced worse, she told herself.

Milly smiled gently at Merren, as if she knew what was going through her mind, then opened the Book of Aroaril.

She went through the vows for Sendric first but Merren could not hear them. A tiny part of her had hoped, had believed, that something would happen to stop this. But her last hope was gone.

Then Milly turned to Merren who had to stop herself from throwing up.

'So, Merren, do you promise —' she began.

The bellowing challenge of a dragon drowned the rest of the sentence.

Everyone looked up and around to see a dragon swoop down from the sky. Merren recognised Argurium and could see a score of figures on her back. She just knew one of the riders was Martil — and was sure he was not here to offer a wedding toast. Was he going to do something crazy, fall on one knee and declare his love for her, or demand that she marry him? She hoped he was.

The dragon roared again, a deafening sound that caused the cheering crowd to fall silent. The packed people edged away, creating space as the dragon hovered impossibly overhead, then landed close to the altar. Almost before its claws had touched the cobbles, Martil had slid down and was running to where the shocked wedding party waited.

Martil saw Merren in her wedding dress, and the sight of it went through him like a knife — but he had more to worry about.

'What is the meaning of this?' Sendric shouted, but Martil ignored him, as well.

'Merren! I need every man you can get together! Gello and the Fearpriests have kidnapped Karia!' he announced. 'We have to get her back before it's too late!'

Merren stared at him. He looked terrible. Blood, sweat, vomit and seawater had soaked him, then been dried to a crust by the rapid flight over the water. But she still wanted to hold him. This was her chance to make everything right, to fix the mistake she had so nearly made.

'Merren, they took the Dragon Egg!'

His words snapped her back into focus. Her stomach rebelled and it took a moment to get past the sheer horror of it — the Egg, the future of the world, in the hands of Gello and his Fearpriests. Then the other thing came back to her. They had Karia. Unbidden, the image of the poor sacrificed people the Fearpriest had slaughtered before the gates of the capital swam into her mind. Her heart went out to him. She wanted to hold him close, tell him everything would be fine, that they would get Karia back. Except she worried she could not be seen to do that in front of the people — and especially in front of Sendric. Then she thrust all that aside. Personal feelings had to be put away.

'How did this happen?'

'There are no dragons left. Argurium is the last. Gello landed on Dragonara with two companies of men and got inside the Hall. Karia was using the magic of the Egg to hold them off while Havell went to fetch me. I nearly got her and the Egg back but there weren't enough Elfarans, and Gello escaped on the Tenoch ships. They're heading for Tenoch with about two thousand men. We need to load up the rest of the ships they left behind, get there and take back Karia and the Egg, then destroy Gello and his Fearpriests once and for all. Argurium will help us get there much, much faster but we have to go now!' he gasped out.

'We understand the importance of what you are saying if not the words themselves — and we all know how you must feel about Karia. But do you have to interrupt the ceremony?' Sendric growled.

Martil turned on him instantly, his rage in check by the finest of threads. 'There is no time to lose! The difference between life and death could be these moments that we are wasting now!'

'This is the last dragon. If she dies and we are not able to reach the Egg before sunrise the next day, all life will end!' Havell added.

'We must act now,' Merren agreed. 'I want all soldiers to meet outside the city gates. We shall leave immediately.'

'Immediately?' Sendric protested.

'Now! I want everyone here! Every captain, High Chief Sacrax and his chiefs — everyone! Someone get some quills and parchment!'

'But,' Sendric tried one more time.

'This is the priority. There will be time for ceremonies later,' she said crisply.

The crowd gazed on as the altar was used as an impromptu table, presided over by Merren.

They also stared at the surviving Elfarans, who stood in a small group aside from the council. All were wearing blood-spattered armour and looked like the elves of the saga tales, rather than the gentle Elfarans they were. The strange armour and, above all, the signs of battle, had people talking, whispering and wondering.

'Does Gello know what he has done? Does he realise this Egg holds the key to life itself?' Merren asked.

Havell shrugged. 'I doubt it. He thinks it a magical object, similar to the Dragon Sword, that will provide him with the means to seize back Norstalos.'

'Would he listen to an appeal? I could contact him, explain to him about the Egg ...' Milly suggested.

'I doubt he would believe us,' Merren sighed. 'He would think it a trick.'

'Surely we must try anyway?' Sendric offered.

'And what will happen to Karia then?' Martil demanded.

'With respect, that is the lesser of two evils. Returning the Egg must be the priority,' Sendric pointed out.

'The lesser of ...!' Martil stepped forwards, snarling, but Merren held out her arm.

'Stop! If I thought Gello would listen to reason, I would try that. But he would not believe us if we told him the sun rose in the morning. We must go there and take it back. What forces have we got around Worick and Cessor?' she asked.

'Plenty.' Rocus, wearing a surcoat but no armour, was the only one seated, because his leg was not strong enough to stand for long periods of time. 'Most of Kettering's regiment have moved there, while almost all of the rangers and archers are helping with the rebuilding. The Rallorans are helping rebuild the south of the country. They're in and around Wells ...'

'They all have horses. They can be at Cessor swiftly,' Nerrin agreed.

'Why not Worick?'

'Gello took almost all of the ships from there. It will be simpler if we go to Cessor,' Nerrin explained.

'What have we got here that can get there fast?'

'The Royal Guard, of course, and High Chief Sacrax brought an honour guard of two hundred warriors with him as well.'

'We can outrun a horse,' Sacrax agreed with a grin.

'And we shall fight. Our lives are running out anyway — better we die and take our enemies with us than some of your men die,' Havell stated.

'Then we need to feed them on the voyage to Tenoch. Aroaril knows how long that will take ...'

'The Magicians' Guild will ensure that you have plenty of fish to eat,' Barrett declared. 'We can also turn seawater into drinking water.'

'Good, because we shall need every wizard,' Merren said grimly. 'Going against the Fearpriests, we shall need every drop of magic we have. It means they will have to leave the valuable work they have been doing here but our need is greater.'

'The Guild shall be with you,' Barrett promised. 'I shall gather as many as I can. We will do whatever it takes.'

'It will be a fast trip,' Havell offered. 'And a calm one. There is no need to hold back on the magic. Argurium will have us across the sea in days.'

'We shall need Archbishop Sadlier, as well, if we are to face the Fearpriests in their lair,' Merren decided. 'She has defeated one already.'

'Aye, and once inside their city, we do not stop until the last Fearpriest, Berellian and traitor of Gello's is dead,' Martil snarled.

Silence greeted his words.

'We have let them get away twice now, and each time Gello has returned with more evil. He shall not escape a third time — and all who stand with him must fall,' Martil went on.

All eyes swivelled to Merren, whose face was impassive at Martil's words. But inside her stomach was churning anew. She did not like the look in Martil's eyes, nor the tone of his voice. This was how she expected the Butcher of Bellic to look and sound.

She cleared her throat. 'Bishop Quiller shall look after the church. I shall lead this expedition, as well ...'

'My Queen!' Sendric protested.

Merren adjusted her wedding dress train to turn and face him. It gave her time to think. She had to be careful here. Martil needed to be kept under control, as did Sendric.

'I trust Captain Martil implicitly. But, as he said, they have Karia. I am sorry to say this, I love Karia, but rescuing her is secondary to the real mission, as Sendric said. We must retrieve the Egg first of all. Also, as Dragon Sword wielder, Martil cannot risk his life. It will avail us little if we retrieve the Egg, only to have no Dragon Sword wielder to finish the ceremony.'

Martil bristled but was not willing to waste time on arguing. Merren, meanwhile, lowered her voice and signalled them in close.

'But perhaps we should not tell the people that the world might end. Better, instead, to say that we are going to rescue the Captain's daughter. After all he has done for the country, I think the people will understand ...'

'Of course they will, my Queen! And Karia is more famous than most of us!' Louise declared. 'There's not a parent in this country who wouldn't agree with what we are doing!'

Merren smiled thinly. 'But let us remember that returning the Egg and saving the world is our priority. It has to be. So I shall command. Sendric will stand in as regent in my absence.'

'With respect, your majesty, that would not be a good idea,' Sendric said stiffly. 'Might I have a word in private?'

Merren glanced around the packed square, then sighed and beckoned to Sendric to follow her.

'Merren, the sand is running out of the hourglass,' he whispered. 'There is only a small window of time for the wedding to take place at an acceptable distance from the birth. If you take too long with this expedition to Tenoch ...'

Merren gritted her teeth.

'Alternatively, we could finish the ceremony now.'

'There is no time! We shall be back swiftly, within a few days. And you shall watch over the country in my absence. After all, you were the one who told me the country was about to descend into anarchy. Who better to keep a lid on any trouble?'

'Conal can do that. I must come along! There will be more than enough spare time for the marriage ceremony to be finished on board the ships.'

She stared at him. 'Is that what you are concerned about? Or are you thinking to chaperone me on board a ship with Martil? This will not be a pleasure cruise, Sendric! We are rushing across the sea to save the world! And do you imagine Martil will be thinking of anything other than Karia?'

'Nevertheless, I should still come along,' Sendric insisted.

Merren was inclined to forbid him but thought it might be better to keep him close to her, rather than leave him behind, where he could foment trouble. Already he seemed too close to many of the guild leaders and badly needed gold seemed to be getting diverted from rebuilding the towns and feeding the people to restarting industries. While she appreciated the country needed its business community back at work, feeding the people was a greater priority.

'You shall come along — but I will not marry anywhere but here. The people must see it,' she warned.

Sendric bowed his head. 'As ever, your majesty is wise,' he said.

She spun around and walked back to the altar. Her

head said this was foolish, it would be easy to finish the wedding now, then ride hard to catch up with everyone else. But, deep inside, she knew she would never marry Sendric. Part of her said it was because she was worried about Martil, the thought he might fall to pieces if she were married. But the truth was, seeing Martil again, even like this, just reminded her of all she had so nearly lost. She would not make the same mistake again. She would explain it to him, he would understand and they would marry on their return. Simple.

'Conal, Louise and Gia shall lead the Royal Council in my absence, the rest of us must get to Cessor as fast as possible — and from there to Tenoch,' she told them. 'What are you waiting for? Time is trickling away! Hurry!'

With help from Louise and Gia, she picked up her skirts and hurried back towards the palace.

A moment later, everyone began bellowing orders, in human and Derthal.

Sacrax walked across to Martil and embraced him.

'Karia is part of our tribe. Let the Norstalines worry about this Egg. My warriors go with one thought — to get back Karia,' he said simply.

Martil nodded grimly. 'Like a Derthal, I shall not rest until their tribe is destroyed.'

Sacrax clapped Martil on the shoulder and then began shouting again at his warriors, pointing them towards the gates.

'Come on, you need a wash and to change.' Conal put a fatherly arm around Martil's shoulders.

Martil ignored the angry stare he was getting from Sendric and shrugged off Conal's arm.

'I suppose the people will hate me for this. Ruining their happy day and risking the lives of their men for a little girl,' he said bitterly. 'Well, they don't have to like me — they just have to follow me.'

'Not just any little girl,' Conal pointed out. 'But I think you might be surprised at what the people do. Sendric's little survey predictions haven't come true.'

Martil was not really listening. The reaction to the day's events was sinking in and he felt hollow inside, but the burning knowledge of Karia's kidnapping and the warmth of his anger kept him going. He allowed himself to be led towards the palace. The only way to get through this was to think only about what was happening in front of him — and to always believe he was going to get her back, he decided.

Around him was chaos. The shocked crowd had watched as soldiers, in full surcoat and armour, tried to find families to say goodbye, and find horses for the ride south. Derthals had pushed through the streets, while Barrett, Milly and Kesbury, all in traditional flowing robes, also hurried off to change. The sight of the Queen rushing back towards the palace was the last straw — many people seemed close to panic.

'What's going on?'

'Your majesty, what is it?'

The cries of the people forced Merren to stop. She could see the concern on the faces all around her. The last time they had been here, a massive army had been grinding towards them, ready to destroy them. It was natural for them to imagine something similar. She could not tell them the truth — she had to tell them a version of the truth, the cover story they had agreed upon.

'Gello and his Fearpriest allies have attacked Dragonara Isle. Captain Martil drove them off but they captured his daughter. She used her magic to help the dragons and Elfarans escape, so they think her a powerful creature of the island. We are going to get her back,' Merren shouted.

She almost held her breath. Would they think this a good enough reason to abandon the wedding, to disrupt the country and take most of the army across the sea on a desperate expedition?

'The girl that rides dragons? The one that saved you from Gello's trap in Gerrin?' someone shouted.

'That is the one!' Merren agreed, silently thanking Romon and his bards for spreading such tales so fast and so far.

'Aroaril speed you, your majesty! We must rescue her!'

The confusion in the crowd changed swiftly, as news spread. People turned to each other, called out the news.

By the time Martil got there, the story had not only spread but changed.

'I hear Gello has killed almost all of the dragons and this last one only escaped because of your daughter, Captain!' someone shouted.

'Don't worry, Captain! We'll help! Norstalos won't forget what you did!' another roared.

'We want to help sir! Take us with you! We'll get her back for you!'

Martil looked around, shocked, to see men and women and children surrounding him. They were not cheering or clapping, they were not shouting abuse or hurling rotten fruit. They looked … sympathetic.

A woman embraced him.

'I know how you must feel, sir,' she said simply. 'I thought my children were lost. It was only you and the Rallorans who saved them.'

Martil stood there numbly until she let him go.

'Gello won't get away with this! We'll help you get her back and sing songs about it for a hundred years!' someone yelled.

'We'll all stand with you, Captain! Anything you need, you say!'

'Three cheers for the captain!'

Martil stared around him as the people called his name.

A small girl left her mother's side and offered him something. He dropped to one knee to see she was holding up a small doll.

'This is my favourite. Take it with you. Your daughter's prob'ly scared. This will make her feel better,' the girl stated.

Martil looked at the small cloth doll, which had been lovingly stitched in a blue dress. It had yellow wool for hair, black wool for its nose and mouth and small horn buttons for eyes. He gazed at it and suddenly it seemed to be swimming before his eyes. He saw himself taking it, breaking down and being comforted by the people around him. Perhaps even Merren would rush to him. But while that would help him, how would it aid Karia? She needed him to be an unstoppable force, driving ever onwards, no matter what it took, until she was safe. No, he could not take the doll. Anger and hatred were the only things that would keep him going. He did not need anything else.

'Thank you. But this is all I shall need,' he told the crowd, patting the Dragon Sword. 'And I shall make sure Gello never dreams of touching this land again!'

Above, Merren heard the calls, heard the cheers. She left her wedding dress lying on the floor and stood on the balcony, a cloak around her. She saw Conal guiding Martil, saw the people reaching out to pat him on the back or to try to shake his hand, saw the women and children offering him a hug. It was a desperate situation but it was also a chance to make everything right. Looking at the reaction of the people, she knew it was safe to do so. She turned away from the balcony. When he came up to see her, she would tell him how much she regretted her choice, that she would ignore Sendric and marry him, if he still wanted it. And, hopefully, she could take some of the bitterness and anger away from him. She was sure he would come up soon. With Karia gone, he would want to be with her. It was perverse almost, but her overwhelming sense was of relief. Of course she was fearful for Karia, and worried what Gello and his Fearpriests would do with the Dragon Egg but the wedding to Sendric had been looming over her like an execution. Avoiding that had her feeling like a prisoner granted a last-moment reprieve. She had nearly made a huge mistake — but now was a second chance. And she knew Martil would jump at that.

Down below, Martil almost had to push through the crowd. Women and children were in tears, coming up to him sobbing, swearing that they would be praying to Aroaril to protect Karia, men were offering whatever they had to help get her back.

He heard them all but it washed over him. All he wanted to do was release the Dragon Sword on the bastards who had taken Karia. It was all he could do not to shout at the crush of people around him, not strike out at them for slowing him down. He pushed into the palace with the cheers of the people, the promises to help Karia and the prayers for her safety echoing around the square.

'We are a sentimental people. And we do love our sagas,' Conal tried to explain. 'Rushing off to rescue a little girl … probably in Rallora they would think it foolish — here, it makes perfect sense.'

'It doesn't matter. They can think what they like of me. All I care about is getting her back and punishing Gello,' Martil grunted. 'I have to save her. Aroaril knows what she is going through!'

'Well, I can tell you one thing. That little girl is a survivor. And she has her magic. Plus she knows you'll be coming for her.' Conal considered Martil doubtfully. The man looked as though he was going to fly apart at any moment. 'I think you need to change. You'll scare the horses, looking like that!' He tried to grin but his heart was not in it. He had never seen Martil like this before and he dreaded to think what would happen to the man if anything happened to the girl.

'Oh, I'll be ready,' Martil promised coldly.

Conal tried once more to break through. 'Well, you had better hurry back. I need you to stand in as the best man at my wedding on your return!'

Martil was barely listening. 'Best man?'

'Aye, well, Louise wants me to make an honest woman of her. And the kids would like it …' Conal trailed off as he realised what he was saying. 'Are you going to see the Queen?' he asked hurriedly, to change the subject.

Martil paused. 'There's nothing more I need to say to her,' he said grimly.

Karia had listened patiently as Ezok explained to her that she had to pretend to be the Radiant Child, the wielder of the Egg — and that both their lives depended on it.

When she had first woken up, she had panicked, but had forced herself to stay calm, using some of the exercises Barrett had taught her to relax and focus the mind.

'The mind is a muscle like the one in your arm. Remember it has to do what you want. Never let fear or uncertainty stop what you are trying to do,' Barrett had told her, then taught her ways to keep herself in control. Never had they come in more useful.

Martil was coming for her. She had to cling to that thought. Do whatever it takes to survive. She reminded herself she had survived life with Da and her brothers for six months. She reckoned six days would be more than enough for Martil to get her out. Six days. That was nothing! So she listened when Ezok talked.

'They will want you to tell them how to use this Egg. You have to think of something to delay them,' he had said. 'Say that you need food, and warmth, and plenty of rest and you will consider their request. Just don't tell them the truth. I remember you from Norstalos — you were the young girl with the priest who tried to stop Prent and me then. Prent's not on this ship, none of the others know you and you need to keep it that way. Now, can I trust you to talk to me, and not scream or anything if I remove your gag?'

Karia nodded slowly and sighed with relief when Ezok removed the cloth covering her mouth.

'Do you know what this Egg is? Do you realise that all life will end if we don't return it?' she hissed.

Ezok gulped. 'Listen, you can't tell them that. They will kill you — and me. You can try to persuade them to return it …'

'As if they're going to do that,' Karia told him scornfully.

Ezok looked around desperately. He was horribly aware his life could be measured in hourglasses unless he came up with something.

'How about we do a deal? They'll be coming after this Egg, won't they?'

'My dad will come after me,' Karia said loftily. 'And he's the greatest warrior in the world.'

Ezok rubbed his chin. 'He's the one with the sword that can cut through anything, even armour?'

'And he'll be chasing after you.'

'Don't tell them he's your father. They think him a demon, summoned by the Egg to protect it.'

'But he's not ...'

'It doesn't matter. Look, here's my deal. You tell them you are going to train me to use the Egg.' He held up his hand. 'I know that's not possible, but it will help keep us both alive.'

'But why would the Egg's wielder do that?' Karia demanded.

Ezok grimaced. Why did she have to make this so difficult? He sighed. At least having her point out the flaws in his plan was better than Onzalez discovering them.

Karia cleared her throat. 'You have to tell them you are tricking me. You have sworn an oath to me to betray them and return me and the Egg. As the oath was sworn to Aroaril, it does not bind you. But, I think it is binding, so I have agreed to begin showing you how to use the Egg to fool them into giving me more freedom, enough that eventually I can escape. You tell them that I will reveal the secrets of the Egg to you this way.'

He had to think about it for a while before he saw what she was getting at. 'How did a small girl think of that?' he demanded.

Karia shrugged. 'It's the sort of thing you find in sagas all the time. Princes who have lost their thrones to their evil uncles and cousins always do things like that.'

'I was never a fan of the sagas,' he admitted.

'Well, you are silly then. Just think of all the useful things you would have learned from them.'

'You are a very unusual little girl,' he sighed.

She rolled her eyes. 'Why does everyone say that?'

Ezok decided to change the subject. 'So I shall do what you said. Meanwhile, I'll do everything I can to help and protect you. All I ask in return is that, if your father catches us, you protect me.'

'If you help me stay alive, I'll make sure he does not kill you. But we have to get this Egg back to him quickly, or all life will end.'

He grimaced. 'Well, wish me luck when I tell them your plan.'

Karia could not disagree with that.

Merren had been surprised when Martil did not come to see her but, as usual, had little time to think about it. Organising a rescue expedition across the seas was going to take plenty of work, especially as they had no time to plan. She rushed around the palace, issuing orders and meeting with Conal and Hutter, trying to leave everything in place while she was away. She sent Wilsen and Jaret to find Martil but they had returned empty-handed. She knew Martil had to be devastated by Karia's capture and decided he was too upset to talk to anyone. At least she hoped that was the case. The other reason was he was still furious with her, after their last meeting. Naturally she hoped what she had to say would make him think again, make things right between them. She would give him time, then try again. Meanwhile, she held a dozen meetings, trying to organise a hundred different things — though her mind was elsewhere.

* * *

'The Radiant Child is the only way you can access the enormous power of the Egg,' Ezok said confidently. *When you are going to tell a lie, it is always better to make it a big lie*, he told himself. Confidence was also vital in selling the story. Luckily there was plenty of evidence to support his lies — and no Khaliz to refute them. The wizard was the last expert on natural magic they had, but he had been left for dead on the island.

'So this child defeated Khaliz?' Onzalez asked sceptically.

'As easily as I would defeat a woman in battle,' Gello confirmed.

'And none of the men could touch it?'

'Well, the two who tried both had their hands burned. None wanted to try after that,' Gello admitted.

They were all sitting around the Egg, which sat on its makeshift cradle in the main cabin of the Tenoch ship. Gello and Onzalez were the unquestioned leaders of the rabble that had been an army — Prent was on another ship and, anyway, Onzalez did not like sharing power.

Onzalez stretched out his hand towards the Egg, which began to flash its colours warningly. The Fearpriest, whose face still needed regular applications of a soothing salve, eased his hand back, unwilling to put his own flesh to the test.

'But the Child was able to touch it without fear or damage,' Ezok added.

'Will this Radiant Child help us? After all, it did not greet us warmly in the hall!' Gello growled. 'Why bother with this magical child anyway? If the Egg has power, why do we not use it?'

Ezok sighed. 'Do you know how? Brother Onzalez is the most powerful of us, the only one who understands magic. Brother, do you know?'

Onzalez shook his head. 'I can sense the power within ... but I do not know how to get at it! If only we had Khaliz ...'

'Surely there are wizards in Tenoch ...' Gello began.

'No, there are none!' Onzalez interrupted. 'None have the ability!'

Ezok and Gello exchanged a look. Unspoken was the thought that the Fearpriests wanted to be the only ones who could use magic. Anyone with magical power was a threat to their authority, and therefore to be stamped out.

'Search for someone with undiscovered magic power. Perhaps we can find some when we return there, trick the child into training them ...' Gello suggested.

'This will take too long!' Onzalez snapped.

'And why will they come forwards, if they think it will mean their death?' Ezok pointed out. 'But I believe I have the solution.'

'Then let us hear it!'

'I have spoken to this Radiant Child. She is a powerful creature, but not wise to the ways of men. She is used to only dealing with elves and dragons. She asked me to help her to escape and I agreed, swearing an oath to help return her to Dragonara Isle.'

'I presume there is more to it than that, if you're telling us this,' Onzalez said dryly.

'Indeed. I swore the oath to Aroaril!' Ezok chuckled. 'It is an oath that has no power over me! In exchange for helping her, she is going to teach me how to use the Egg. She thinks she is doing this to lull you into a false sense of security, so you will allow her enough freedom that she might escape with my help. She thinks she has my loyalty and that I am fooling you to help her — when she will be the one who is fooled, for she will give away her secrets and never be allowed to escape.'

'It sounds unnecessarily complicated. Why do we not just force this child to help us?' Onzalez grunted.

'You did not see her in action. She scattered our men in all directions, swatted away Khaliz as if he were a fly! We cannot use force — Ezok is right, we need to use cunning,' Gello agreed.

Onzalez sat silently. 'I need to talk to this Radiant Child myself. Bring her here.'

'Should we not go to her? It might not be wise to let her too near to the Egg,' Ezok pointed out.

'Then we go to her! Now,' Onzalez snarled.

Karia had thought hard about how she should act when the Fearpriest and the others came to talk to her. Ezok seemed harmless enough, although a little silly. But she had seen what the Fearpriest could do from her vantage point on Argurium during the battle of Norstalos. And, of course, she had heard much about Gello during all the war councils she had attended over the past few months.

She had experienced a wave of panic while in the cabin by herself. She wanted to see Martil. She wanted to see Merren. She wanted them both to hold her. Part of her wanted to scream and cry and beg for them to let her go. But then she had calmed herself. These were evil men and they would have no sympathy for her, nor mercy. Thanks to Barrett, she was able to use her mind carefully, logically, think the problem through. Looking at it, she was almost grateful she had spent that time on the farm with her da, and in the woods with her half-brothers. It had taught her how to survive a situation like this. And, with a little saga-style acting, she would stay safe until Martil got there.

Breathing deeply, she controlled her thoughts and planned what she was going to do, what she was going to say, as Barrett had taught her. She had read, and been read to, about many strange beings in the sagas. So she knew how they were supposed to behave. Hopefully Gello and the Fearpriest had not read the same sagas.

So when the three of them ducked into the cabin in which she was kept, she made sure she was sitting cross-legged on the bunk, the ropes that had pinioned her piled up neatly on the deck. Altering the ropes, so they slipped off her wrists and ankles had been easy enough and would create the right impression, she felt.

She had also learned from Ezok that they had described her as the 'Radiant Child', whatever that was, so she used a trick of Barrett's to make it appear as if she was surrounded by a golden light.

The intake of breath from the trio almost made her smile but she kept her face calm.

'Why is she not tied up? Ezok, did you release her?' Gello growled.

'I am free of my bonds because I chose to be. If you want my help, I would advise you not to anger me,' Karia said smoothly.

She saw the three of them stare at her.

'This is no normal child,' Ezok whispered.

'You are right. I am the Radiant Child, Wielder of the Dragon Egg and you have made a grave mistake in removing me and the Egg from our rightful place on Dragonara Isle,' she said. 'When you attacked me, I summoned my Guardian. The demon warrior with the sword that cannot be stopped. He is coming for you. And he will not rest until you are all dead. Return me to Dragonara or you shall all die.'

For a heartbeat she thought she had them. Ezok looked terrified, while Gello was plainly alarmed. But the Fearpriest merely chuckled.

'Your demon might have frightened my allies in your own hall. But, on Tenoch soil, he shall be no match for me,' Onzalez boasted.

Ezok could feel the sweat trickling down his back. This was a dangerous game he was playing. In truth he did not quite know just who he would betray. Whoever it looked like was going to lose, he guessed. He had embraced Zorva for power — now he would do whatever it took to survive.

'So you think,' Karia told the Fearpriest. 'But I must warn you that the Egg was not designed to leave Dragonara Isle. Taking it away could doom everyone on this world.'

Onzalez did not move. 'I do not believe you,' he said calmly. 'You are a creature of the dragons and not to be trusted.'

'What of the Egg? Will you show us how to use it?' Gello demanded.

Karia turned to him. 'Why should I do that?'

'Because we shall kill you otherwise!' Onzalez said.

'And then you will have nobody to tell you how to use the Egg. And my Guardian will wreak a terrible revenge,' Karia forced herself to say, trying not to look afraid. She took a deep breath. Time to show her power. 'Touch me and you shall scream in pain.'

Onzalez laughed. 'I have the magical protection of a God! Zorva has promised to keep me safe — and you say I cannot even touch you?'

He stepped forwards and, lightning-fast, grabbed

at her hand. Karia had been trying to think how she could use the magic to make her skin hot while not hurting herself, and did not react quickly enough. But she did not need to. As soon as his fingers touched hers, Onzalez shrieked with pain and jerked his hand away.

'What? What is it?' Gello cried.

Onzalez stared at Karia as if he were seeing her for the first time.

'She has power,' he whispered. 'Touching her was like putting my hand into flames.'

'So how were we able to carry her off the island?' Gello grunted.

'We never touched her skin — just her clothes. Besides, she was unconscious. Perhaps the power only works when she is awake ...' Ezok suggested.

'We should not touch her again,' Onzalez decided. 'We must discover the source of her power.' He turned back to Karia. 'What if we do you honour, worship you as a God? Would you grant us power then?' he offered.

Karia looked at him blankly. This was something she had not considered. Besides, she was still trying to work out what had just happened. Certainly she had done nothing to stop the Fearpriest. Or had she? She was not sure now.

'You should do me honour,' she told him. 'Provided you treat me well, I will begin to reveal certain secrets of the Egg to — him.' And she pointed at Ezok.

She saw the three of them exchange looks, but kept her face blank.

'Agreed,' Onzalez said finally. 'Food will be brought to you, as well as water.'

'And you will let me see the Egg?' Karia asked, a little too eagerly. Once she had her hands on the

Egg, she was sure she could seal herself off and turn this ship around, have it back at Dragonara by the end of the day.

Onzalez looked towards Ezok before turning back.

'Not immediately. But perhaps, if you can show Ezok how it works, so we can understand it better,' he said carefully.

Karia bowed her head in agreement, thinking they had fallen for her ruse and wondering if she would ever find out what she had done to scare Onzalez, how he had been affected when touching her.

Gello looked over to Onzalez, and smiled.

Ezok watched them all, and sweated.

The ride down to Cessor had been a blur to Martil. People kept trying to talk to him, when all he wanted was more speed, to be on the ships and after Karia already.

It had been the same back in the capital.

Conal had found him fresh clothes and helped clean the blood that had survived his swim in the sea from his face and hair and hands. Louise had embraced him, told him she would be praying for him, while seemingly every Norstaline wanted to shake his hand or touch his boot as he rode past, out of the capital. He ignored them — these were the same people that had told Merren that they did not want him as a Prince Consort. So the fact they lined the walls to cheer everyone, human and Derthal, heading south was of no consequence to him — although Merren was pleased to get such a send-off.

She had sent Wilsen and Jaret over to him, several times with a request to speak. But he just ignored them and, after a while, they gave up and went away. He was glad of that. He did not want to hurt them. He could not let himself go near Merren. He wanted nothing to distract him.

If Archbishop Nott had been there, perhaps he could have spoken to him. But he could not confide in Kesbury and Milly, although the new Archbishop had told him that Aroaril, and Father Nott, were watching over Karia.

'One of the last things he did was to bless her. At the last, he was more a servant of Aroaril than a man. The power of that blessing would be extraordinary, especially against a Fearpriest. Should one of them try to lay hands on her, it will burn him like the hottest fire imaginable,' Milly had said.

Martil had nodded. That was a little comfort to him.

Strangely, Barrett was one of those to seek him out.

'We have had our differences,' the wizard said. 'That is putting it mildly. But we both care about Karia. And the lessons I gave her will stand her in good stead. She has been trained to focus her mind, to banish fear and worry and concentrate on her magic. And her powers are extraordinary. There is much she can do to protect herself. She will not be helpless.'

Martil ignored that. 'I just want to know if you will help me destroy Gello and all who harbour him.'

Barrett hesitated. 'I shall obey Queen Merren's orders,' he said finally.

Martil stared at him. 'That will be all then.'

He greeted Nerrin and Dunner, listened to them swear they would bring Karia back and talk happily about the way the Norstalines had truly accepted the Rallorans. He was pleased to hear that villages and towns were welcoming Rallorans into their midst but still stayed apart. He preferred to stay with the Derthals, where Sacrax told him about their new home, in the northern forest.

'The caves of my ancestors are much bigger than my people remember. So much better than the north. My people can wander, as they were meant to. Follow the game through the forest, make camp where they want. It is everything we wanted. I think if you tried to take it back, I would stay and fight!' Sacrax chuckled.

'How have the Norstalines been? Has there been any trouble?'

Sacrax shrugged. 'Many do not like us, still. They do not come near. But some do. Ones who fought with us against your enemies, they trade with us, they will visit.'

Martil thought with a pang of those men, the ones he had trained all those months ago, when it was just a handful of them in the northern forest where Sacrax's people now roamed. But they were too far away to join this expedition.

'So your chiefs are happy? They are pleased that you allied yourself to Norstalos, came south and helped us?'

Sacrax laughed. 'Oh yes! I have even had some of Rath's old followers beg to join my tribe, so they can leave the mountains! Especially when I showed them the plants growing around the caves. There is one fruit plant that blooms in winter!'

Martil thought then of all the walks he had taken with Karia, of the magic she had learned there and used on the surrounding plants — and he could not talk any more. The memories were too painful.

Merren watched him, and worried.

If it had been anyone else who had refused to

speak to her, she would have been furious with them for disobeying her orders. But she told herself he was still upset, though she hoped he was not harbouring a grudge against her. Normally she was willing to face any problem head on but she was scared of what might happen if she confronted him. She could not bear the thought of losing him once more, removing all hope from her life. She resolved to make him talk to her once they were on the ships, when there was more time.

And, in truth, there was more than enough to keep her busy.

For instance, many homesteads and villages had been damaged or destroyed in the Tenoch advance, and each wanted to show her the pace of rebuilding, as well as talk about the problems they still faced. Word seemed to be spreading faster than they could ride, with people coming out of villages and farms to cheer them on. Although the people were hard at work rebuilding, they still stopped to wave, or to offer something, even if it was only water, as well as talk.

Apart from that, many of those helping rebuild were prisoners taken after the battle, Tenochs, Berellians and Norstalines who had surrendered rather than run or die. Now they laboured to show they could be trusted, although some were still being identified as criminals and needed to be taken away to face punishment for their crimes. Three times Merren was asked to look into a case where a prisoner had been identified as having burned down Norstaline buildings but the village that he worked for thought he was repentant and should be forgiven his crime. With the example of the Rallorans in the back of her mind, she promised to hold any sentence until she had looked at the case.

The country was getting back on its feet, she could see that. There were still signs of the invasion everywhere, from farms that had been burned out and not yet rebuilt, to the raw wood and fresh thatch and sound of building, to the graves of Norstalines who had died at the hands of the invaders and the graves of the invaders themselves, slaughtered as they fled in panic.

Food was a major concern but Barrett's Magicians' Guild had been travelling around to many villages, helping grow just a few fresh vegetables to keep them going through the winter.

And while Martil did not want to talk to her, she could barely get Sendric to shut up. Every time they paused, either to speak to villagers or for the night, he was there. Always pushing for her to complete the marriage, cautioning against this expedition.

'We do not know what we face! We are taking the best of our army into a strange country. What if it is all a trap? What if they are waiting for us? Norstalos will be defenceless if we are defeated!' he cried.

'If the Dragon Egg is lost, then it will not matter if Norstalos is helpless, for the whole world is doomed,' Merren told him finally. 'Let that be an end to the discussion!'

While there was plenty to occupy her, like Martil, she chafed at the journey and just wanted to be on the ships.

But once at Cessor, there were tasks waiting. The city had been almost destroyed by fire and although thousands of men had been hard at work rebuilding, there were still vast areas that were blackened and ruined. Yet the people turned out to welcome them, to promise their support and to cheer her, giving her the first reason to smile in days. And she was relieved to find the allied army waiting for them at Cessor, having assembled swiftly. In the little more than two days of hard riding it took to get down from the capital, the Rallorans and bowmen had made it to Cessor, while several hundred of Kettering's men were already there. Between Norstalines, Rallorans, Derthals and Elfarans, there were more than three thousand in this allied army. But while this was a powerful force, every man tested in more than one battle, they were heading off to an unknown country. They had to do it — but she did not want to go in blind. Knowing what she would face was vital. If they failed, then not only would these men die, but the world would end. In terms of pressure on her shoulders, it made the Berellian invasion look like a playground fight. With that in mind, she had ordered the few Tenoch prisoners taken after the battle to be questioned by Nerrin and Kettering, so all could learn more about this mysterious continent they were about to invade.

Then she could tackle the other problems.

For instance, the Tenoch ships had been used as temporary accommodation by the citizens of Cessor without houses and many of these were unhappy at having to leave what they thought of as home but Fergus and his fellow councillors helped her soothe them. That was a relief, having the support of the city's council, for Fergus could not do enough for her.

'My Queen, your men stayed behind to save my life and the lives of my family and friends, after we had insulted them and spat upon them. They had no reason to stay — in fact good military sense says they should have left before those Tenochs arrived. I have much to be grateful for, and much to make up for. I am eager to do what I can,' he told her.

She talked with him about what the city needed and wrote out orders for Conal to send more aid.

That all took time but, at the end, it meant she could leave the loading of the ships to Fergus and his councillors, so she could summon the leaders of this allied army, as well as the few ships' captains in the area, who would transport the army in the morning. These men also sat in on the council, albeit at the fringes, for they were going to be vital to the success of the expedition. Already they had been looking over the various ships, selecting the ones that were the most seaworthy.

Despite her dismissal of Sendric's words earlier, she was very conscious of not sailing into the unknown. Yes, the fate of the world rested on this. But at the moment she was more worried about the men and women who would follow her across the sea.

'So, before we sail let us learn about Tenoch,' she announced. 'Captain Nerrin. What did you discover?'

Nerrin laughed. 'Plenty. The prisoners could not do enough to help us.' He took out a piece of parchment and used a dagger to hold it down. 'They even helped draw us a rough map.'

'And what will we face in Tenoch?' she asked them.

Nerrin cleared his throat.

'Tenoch is not like Norstalos. It is not even one country — it is many. Or, at least, it was. This is a bit of a confused story but, from what I can piece together, it seems Tenoch has a massive river that runs through much of the continent. As well as providing water for crops, high up in the mountains its tributaries wash down gold — so much gold that they pick it out of streams. The continent took its name from the river but now the river itself has been overshadowed by the city that took its name. Rather than defined countries, as we have on this continent, there was a series of city-states. Tenoch was the first, was always the largest and most powerful of those and, when the Fearpriests took over, every other city-state was either crushed or forced to swear obedience to Tenoch. Soon it had control of the entire continent, which is far bigger than Albiona. At first it had used its army to control its conquests but then had the problem of too many cities to hold and not enough men. There was also the thought that the army's leaders would want more power than the Fearpriests were prepared to share. So while they kept one army to crush any rebellions, they changed tactics. The ruling classes of each city were basically kidnapped and brought to Tenoch. Fearpriests rule each city, aided by a small guard but, with every nobleman and their families hostage, there is nothing and nobody for a rebellion of the common people to rally around. And, of course, Fearpriests keep a tight rein on the people. Anyone who speaks out ends up with their heart cut out. Fear rules the continent. But now they have no army. It was destroyed by High Chief Sacrax outside the capital. They have a company or two in each city but they will be unable to concentrate them at Tenoch before we get there. All we shall face is Gello's men and the few hundred they have in the city. And even those are likely to be the old, or inexperienced men. Their best warriors are dead.'

'And if they try to raise a city against us, we shall slaughter them. A shield wall, backed by archers, will destroy a rabble,' Martil said harshly. 'This is the heart of the evil. We must cut it out.'

That brought no response, so Nerrin continued.

'The River Tenoch opens to the sea, so we can sail most of the way up to the city. It should help our surprise. By the time they realise we are there, we shall be only ten miles from the city.'

'So far so good. But there must be some bad news in this,' Merren commented.

Nerrin sighed. 'Aye. The city walls are said to be massive. More than sixty feet high, with towers every one hundred paces, and walls wide enough that wagons can run along the inside. They can move men rapidly from one point to another. Your majesty, if the walls are as big as the prisoners claimed — and I do not think they lied — I do not know how we can get into such a city with the men we have.'

'We shall find a way!' Martil vowed. 'There is no choice! There is always a way inside!'

Again, nobody had anything to say to that.

'Does anyone know anything else about Tenoch? Havell?'

'We have not gone there in centuries. Since the Fearpriests came to power, they do not use natural magic. They have no mages. The only magic used is the one Zorva gives them in exchange for blood sacrifice.'

'So there is a difference — the magic from the gods and the magic we use from the world around us are not the same?' Barrett asked thoughtfully. 'For centuries great wizards have wondered about that.'

'Not only wizards,' Milly added. 'The Church has struggled with this question. We are taught that everything comes from Aroaril, that the magic was created by Him. It is a fundamental question of the Church. What came first? Were the dragons and the magic created by Aroaril or did the magic come first? Did life begin then and the Gods grow out of people's need for spirituality, a reflection of the good and evil within us all? Are wizards just unusually gifted people, able to use the magic Aroaril put into the world? Do we use the power of a God, or is it just natural magic, somehow changed by Aroaril into a form we can use, when we cannot access the natural magic?'

'It is a fascinating question that has consumed even the dragons,' Havell agreed. 'But I cannot answer it. Perhaps at the end, when the magic goes with the last dragon, the answer will reveal itself. If you and the Fearpriests can still use magic, then we know that Aroaril was the one who created everything, and the natural magic is a device of the Gods. If not ...'

'I think we have more pressing concerns now,' Merren said firmly. 'What of our ships' captains? Do they know anything of Tenoch?'

One man stood up, a man who looked vaguely familiar to Martil, although when he had met a Norstaline ship's captain, he did not know.

'I am Lavrick, your majesty,' he said in a deep voice. 'I have been to Tenoch, once, on the orders of Duke Gello. I received good prices for my goods but dared not go back there again — I felt I was lucky to escape with my life. I can guide you up the river, past the defences they will have there.'

Merren opened her mouth to demand more information, only for Martil to interrupt.

'Do I know you?' he asked harshly.

Lavrick looked at him. 'We have never met,' he said coolly. 'But I believe you knew my younger brother, Havrick.'

Martil was on his feet, Dragon Sword in hand in an instant.

'I knew him — and killed him with this! If you are here for revenge, then you will find more than you bargained for!'

Lavrick shook his head. 'My brother was a fool. And he destroyed my family's honour with his behaviour in the north. I am here because I am a loyal Norstaline and because I do not believe in kidnapping children. I am here to help you.'

Martil turned to Merren. 'This man has been to Tenoch on Gello's orders. And he's the brother of a murderer! It's obvious this is a trap! I say we either kill him now, or at least leave him behind!'

'Without me, you'll never find your way up the River Tenoch! I understand you are upset but …'

Kesbury managed to get to Martil in mid-leap.

'You dare to tell me I am upset!' Martil raged as Kesbury had to use all his considerable strength to hold his former captain back.

'Captain! Sit down! This is not helping! Do you want to rescue Karia or not?' Merren shouted.

Martil stared at her. 'What sort of question is that?'

'Then you need to take whatever help is offered! Captain Lavrick, you shall command the ship carrying myself and Captain Martil. Is that going to be a problem?'

'Not at all,' Lavrick replied. 'I shall show you I can be trusted.'

'And what was your order from Gello?'

'It was near ten years ago. Gello had heard Berellian ships were returning from there laden with gold. He wanted me to find out why, because I had the best ship in his Duchy. The Tenochs bought my goods but told me never to come back if I valued my life. I believed them, so never returned but I made secret charts. I can get you in there, when no others can.'

Martil said nothing, but knew he would be keeping a very close eye on the man. If he was planning some sort of trap, he would not survive it.

22

Merren made sure both Sendric and Martil were on board her ship. Ideally she would have liked to split them up but she felt it was better to have them both where she could keep an eye on them.

The men had been loaded as fast as possible, bringing with them just weapons, armour and a little food. Merren had used the time to quickly tour the rebuilding work under way at Cessor, as well as talk to the many people who packed the jetties and surrounds to wave them off.

Work was proceeding well and, better yet, the people were eager to meet and cheer Merren. What they had seen and gone through in their town, and at the capital, had forever changed this place.

She would have almost liked to stay longer but the ships were ready and, with the dragon Argurium circling overhead, they quickly eased out of Cessor's wrecked harbour and into the open water. Sailing with magic seemed to be an easy business — the sails were put up and, next moment, the ship was moving rapidly through the water, waves foaming at the bow. The oars were not even needed.

With Barrett's Magicians' Guild turning barrels of seawater into fresh water or making schools of fish leap out of the ocean and onto the deck, food and drink did not seem to be a problem. But she worried about how they would manage to take Tenoch. Even though it sounded as though the city was stuffed with captives who would be highly reluctant to fight for the Fearpriests, even a few hundred defenders armed with clubs and rocks would make it almost impossible to take its walls. And then there was Martil. The mood he was in, the mood he had many of the men and Derthals in, she could see another Bellic happening if they got inside the walls. She had to act before then.

So she sent for Sendric once they were out of sight of land, which took less than a turn of the hourglass thanks to the work of Argurium, who flew lazily overhead.

'Have you reconsidered your plan to wait until we have returned to Norstalos to marry?' Sendric asked, as soon as he sat down.

'Quite the opposite,' Merren said grimly. 'I am not only doubting the need for it at all but I am questioning the nature of the reports, and the information you brought before me.'

Sendric stiffened in his chair. 'I have done nothing but my best for the country! You have toured the south, seen the scale of destruction, the task waiting for us even now. It will take years, if not generations, to heal the scars left by the Berellian and Tenoch invasions. It needs gold, far more gold than we can hope to mine in ten years! Cessor and Worick may never fully recover. Did I overstate the way in which our industries are reduced, the way our farmland is slighted, the livestock scattered? Have I somehow —'

'No, that was all correct. But I cannot help but contrast what you said with the way the people reacted to Martil's return, and the way the entire country seems willing to do anything to help Karia's rescue …'

'With respect, your majesty, there is a big difference between feeling sympathy for a man's missing child, and embracing him as their Prince Consort! If you had married Martil, as you planned, who knew what would have happened?'

Merren locked eyes with him. 'I would have been happy,' she said simply.

Sendric's eyes widened in horror.

'He is a base-born Ralloran! No matter what state the country is in, the people deserve better than him! He is not good enough for you! And to think of a half-Ralloran as a future king! Your majesty, the people are grateful for everything Martil has done to save this country. But you can be grateful to a dog for scaring away thieves. It does not mean you want to see it marry your daughter and bow to its pups!'

'That is enough!' she stormed, jumping to her feet. 'I warn you, Count, you go too far!'

He glared at her, breathing just as hard.

'My country is always uppermost in my thoughts. I had hoped it was also in yours. I would remind you that I never asked for this — you ordered me to marry you to cover up the scandal that you created —'

'I was wrong,' she interrupted him. 'And you are right in one respect — this is my problem and it is up to me to solve it. If I can do so, I shall no longer need you to marry me. If you are unable to accept this, I suggest you renounce your position and retire to your country estate.'

Sendric's mouth sagged open. He gazed at her for long moments before slowly rising.

'I have always been a loyal servant of the crown. I will do everything possible to see Gello dead and my daughter avenged. But if you persist in marrying that Ralloran, I shall spend my remaining years protecting the people from the ill effects of your foolish decision.'

'Then you shall have little to do, for there will be no ill effects, as you call them,' she said coolly. 'That will be all.'

Sendric bowed stiffly. 'As your majesty wishes.'

Merren sighed when he had left. The Count had been her fervent supporter and she had as good as turned him into an opponent. But she had made her choices — now she would have to live with the consequences. Perhaps it would be better if he did not return from Tenoch ... She stopped that thought and went to find Martil. She knew sending Jaret and Wilsen to bring him to her would not do any good.

Martil just sat at the bow of the ship, looking into the distance as the ships surged forwards. The wind of their passage did not seem to bother him, nor did the spray coming from the waves they skipped across.

She walked across the deck, holding carefully to the various ropes and rails placed for that purpose. Even though the dragon was using magic to aid and smooth the ships' passage, there was still a fair bit of movement. She let go of the last rail and staggered a few steps before sinking gratefully onto a coil of rope next to Martil.

'Why don't you come back, get something to eat?' she asked gently.

'No. I shall wait here,' he replied, staring out across the sea.

'There are things we need to say. It would be better to say them in private,' she tried again.

Martil did not want to look at her. He wanted to keep his focus on Karia. Merren had made her choice. Karia was everything now. Besides, she obviously had something she wanted to say. After what she had done to him before, he was happy to let her suffer now. It was petty but the memory of that walk out of her office, and the flight to Dragonara Isle was still raw. If he could hurt her now, then he might feel a little better.

'You said all you needed to say before. I have nothing more to add,' he replied harshly.

She felt the stab of those words but kept her voice gentle. 'I thought you might like to talk to someone about what happened, and how you are coping.'

'I just want to get there fast, and then kill them until they give Karia back.'

Merren sighed. He was still not looking at her. There was nothing for it but the truth.

'I made a mistake when I sent you away —'

'Don't tell me that! Not now!' He whipped around.

'You don't think I can admit to a mistake?'

'I can't deal with this now, I have to concentrate on Karia. We are on different paths now, you and I.'

'You don't think we could —'

'No!' Martil felt the temptation there. It would be so easy to look at her, to hold her, to kiss her, to … He shook himself. How could he even think of such things, when Karia was in the hands of Fearpriests? He had promised never to leave her — everything else had to be put aside.

'If you care for me, you will leave me alone,' he managed to say.

Merren stared at him, seeing the rigid set to his jaw. In the past she had used physical contact to break the walls that he put up — but, with a pang, she worried that would not work here. He was like a spring, wound up to the point of breaking. What could she do?

'Well if you do ever need anyone to speak to …' she offered. There was a burning sensation in the pit of her stomach. Had she turned away both men? What would she do if they both refused to marry her?

She hesitated, torn between leaving him alone and trying one more time to talk to him, when a shout made her look up.

Barrett was rushing towards them both.

'Your majesty! Martil! We have a bird from Karia!'

Onzalez had called upon his God to ensure fair winds and fast sailing. As well as the sails, the men were working hard on the oars, driving the ships forwards at a great speed. Magic was also needed to keep all the ships together, especially at night. When Gello had been saving Tenochs, he had chosen the best warriors, rather than the ones that knew how to sail these ships. Keeping them together was no easy task.

But the various soldiers, while initially distrustful of the ships, were growing used to their demands now. Hands were growing calloused working on the oars, while most crews seemed able to set sails without knocking their fellows into the water or falling from the rigging.

'We are making far better time than on the trip over,' one of the surviving Tenochs declared.

'We shall be back in Tenoch swiftly,' Onzalez agreed. 'The sooner the better. We must understand how this Egg works, and use its power.'

'The sooner we are off these ships, the better,' Gello grunted. There was no entertainment on board, no way of relieving the boredom of seeing the same piece of ship, the same monotonous sky and waves. All his pleasure at watching the sea was over — he just wanted to get back to Tenoch and begin using the Dragon Egg to gain his revenge on Merren. He had been working on his sketch of Mother, been trying to talk to her but she was no help. She had not come up with one useful idea to get him out of this mess. Sometimes he felt himself seized by melancholy, unable to get out of his bunk. How could it all have gone so wrong? He'd had everything — three times now his dream was within reach and each time it had slipped away. At times like this he almost felt like giving up, killing Onzalez, throwing the Dragon Egg and child overboard and going away, far from Norstalos, finding a place where he could carve out a new legend for himself. But each time that happened, his eyes were drawn back to his crude portrait of Mother, and how he had promised her she would see him as King. He could not let her down — and he could not give up. Victory could still be his.

'Let's see what Ezok has learned so far. Feld, fetch him!'

Ezok sat with Karia in her cabin.

'There must be something I can do to impress them! We need them to think we are making progress,' Ezok complained.

Karia sighed. How silly was this man? She had explained things to him so many times, and still he did not understand! Honestly, sometimes she wondered why she bothered with grown-ups like this. He seemed nice enough compared to the others, but that was not saying much. She missed Martil terribly. She had managed to attract a seabird to her small cabin window, and sent it off in search of Barrett. By now she was sure Martil would have got

Barrett, and Merren, and all the others and found some way to be chasing after her. She was sure of it — but she still needed to know where they were. Barrett's exercises to control the mind and calm fears were fine up to a point but the nights were getting very hard. She wanted a bedtime story, she wanted her dolls — she wanted a hug. At least during the day Ezok sat with her and talked. He had even told her a couple of traditional Berellian sagas, which weren't nearly as fun as the Norstaline ones, but at least they were better than nothing.

'It is a source of natural magic. If you do not know how to use magic, you will never be able to use it,' she told him tiredly.

'Can you perhaps make it look as though I am using it?'

She considered that one carefully. It was going to be difficult. Then a tapping at the window distracted her. She slid open the horn panel that allowed light and air into the small cabin and a gull squeezed its way through and sat on her shoulder proudly.

'What is that doing here?' Ezok gasped, edging away from the bird's glittering eyes and sharp beak.

'He's my friend!'

Ezok shook his head. 'He's a bird. I am your only friend here — trust me.'

Karia smiled. 'I know, you're the only one who's been kind. But this bird is more than that. He's brought news from my father. He's got the Norstaline army and they're using the dragon to chase after us in the Tenoch ships you left. He's got Derthals, Rallorans, Norstalines and the Elfarans! They'll be right behind us when we land!'

Ezok nodded absently, worrying what would happen when they reached Tenoch.

'Derthals?'

'You might know them as goblins,' she offered, stroking the gull's neck gently.

Ezok wondered what to do with the information. A knock on the door did not give him time to decide.

'Ezok! King Gello wants to see you!'

Ezok gulped, trying to think what he could say, then looked at the gull and inspiration struck him.

'Tell me, could the Egg let you see across long distances?'

'No, your magic does that. But you could use the Egg's magic instead of your own energy to do so ...'

'Excellent!'

Ezok opened the door and almost bolted up the steps to the deck.

'Well Ezok, do you have any progress for us?' Gello demanded.

'Indeed I do!' Ezok almost gabbled. 'The Radiant Child has shown me how the Egg can be used to see across great distances!'

'Very useful, I am sure,' Onzalez said dryly.

'It could save us all!' Ezok said hotly. 'For I have seen her guardian and the others who are pursuing us!'

'Tell us,' Gello commanded.

'They have gone to the Norstalines. These have gathered the ships we left behind and filled them with Norstalines, Rallorans, the goblins, and her guardian and his warrior elves. The dragon has given them magic and they are flying across the waves to catch us. They will arrive at Tenoch barely a day behind us!'

Gello felt his heart lurch and guessed that, had Onzalez's face been visible, he would have shown his shock also.

'They'll have perhaps a thousand archers, as well as the damned Rallorans, Merren's Norstaline traitors and the goblins — how many goblins did they bring, Ezok?'

'It's hard to see,' Ezok hedged, 'but there are plenty of ships. And we know you can fit two hundred warriors onto one ship alone.'

'There could be thousands of those damned goblins! And even if they only brought a few, there's no way we can defeat a Ralloran shield wall backed by that many archers! Markuz couldn't crack them with eight thousand men, and we have barely a quarter of that!' Gello gasped. What was going to happen? He had thought himself safe …

'This is a valuable gift, Ezok!' Onzalez said solemnly. 'Go back and work more with this Radiant Child. Seek ways of destroying our enemies, while we consider what we can do.'

Gello waited until Feld and Ezok had left, before taking the Fearpriest's arm.

'How many warriors have you got back at Tenoch?' he demanded.

'We have a few thousand scattered across our empire. But there would only be about five hundred in the capital. Most left with us and died at the hands of the goblins,' Onzalez said coolly. 'The others are too far away to be able to help us. But there are tens of thousands of people living in Tenoch. We shall arm them and swamp our enemies with numbers! I can raise a massive army, easily enough to replace what we lost!'

Gello paused. 'But they will not be trained warriors. And what will they be armed with?'

'Whatever they can bring. Spears, clubs, knives. If there are forty to fifty thousand of them, our enemies will not stand a chance!'

Gello scratched his chin. He would have preferred thousands of veteran warriors. But surely even

Martil and the demon guardian could not defeat that many men! They could stiffen the ranks with their trained soldiers and they would just roll over the top of whatever Merren had brought! Still, it never hurt to be prepared ...

'And if they brought ten thousand goblins with them?'

'Then we will have lost a few peasants and thus we have lost nothing. We shall withdraw behind the walls of Tenoch and laugh at their attempts to get inside. Tenoch is the mightiest city in the world! Its walls cannot be scaled, its gates cannot be broken. They are a long way from home and will find no friends there. And we shall have learned how to use the power of the Egg by then — and we shall destroy them. With their army lost, Norstalos will be ripe for the picking!'

Gello liked the sound of that. His heart began to slow down, and he could take a deep breath and gaze across the water without fear. It might turn out well, after all.

'Make sense of this!' Martil snarled at Barrett.

'I am anxious to see her rescued too! Don't think that you are the only one worried about her,' the wizard fired back.

'We are wasting time —' Martil began hotly, only for Merren to interrupt.

'We are all concerned. Barrett, just explain what the gull has told you.'

The wizard sighed. 'It seems strange but perhaps she has found a way to win their trust long enough for us to get there. They think she is the Egg's magical guardian, after what she did to them back at Dragonara Isle ...'

'Yes, we have been over this! But can she do it, can she make them believe ...'

Barrett rubbed his eyes. 'I don't know,' he admitted. 'They have a mistaken belief that the Egg is a magical weapon, not unlike the Dragon Sword. But, unlike the Sword, the Egg was not designed to be used. Only an experienced mage, sure of their power and with the blessing of the dragons, would be able to try it. For it is aware, as is the Dragon Sword. If Karia had not ridden on a dragon, if she had not been shown the Egg by an Elfaran, its power would have burned her. Teaching someone who has no magical ability to use it is like teaching archery to this ship.'

'Oh, so pretty easy then,' Dunner muttered, just loud enough for a few people to smile and for Barrett to glare at him.

'Our best hope is to be so close behind them that they do not have time to learn their error,' Merren declared.

Martil could not restrain himself. 'This is all too risky. That bird knows where to find her. Let's follow it on Argurium. We can smash our way in there and have her back safe before they even know what is going on.'

'But what about the Egg?' Barrett pointed out.

'We still go after them and take it back. But we shall have Karia back with us first,' Martil pointed out.

'We cannot risk the last dragon and the Dragon Sword wielder!' Havell insisted. 'If one or both of you falls, there is no hope left! Besides, without Argurium, the ships will not be able to sail as fast.'

'We can help them a little,' Barrett offered. 'My mages and I. Give you the time to get to Karia.'

Everyone's eyes swivelled to Merren.

'If we can get there without them knowing, it could be done,' she judged. 'But I shall go too, along with Havell. We do not go in without my permission, no matter what Martil says or does.'

'My Queen! Do you think that is wise, to risk yourself ...' Barrett began.

'I will not be risking myself. That is the point. We shall only attempt a rescue if it is safe,' Merren told him.

Havell reluctantly nodded. 'I trust your judgment, Queen Merren,' he agreed.

'But it will be on my judgment. Martil, you understand you must accept my decision, whatever it is.' Merren stared hard at Martil.

Martil gritted his teeth. Once he was on that dragon, he was not coming back unless he had Karia with him. But he knew her well enough to realise he was not going to get on the dragon unless he said the right thing.

'Mark my words, Captain, I shall not let the rescue attempt go ahead if it looks too dangerous. Don't think that your arm and the Sword give you the power to defy me,' she warned.

Martil forced himself to look as though he was resigned. 'I understand,' he lied.

'I'll let Karia know to expect us after dark. It will be harder to see the dragon then,' Barrett suggested. 'Besides, even with a little magical help, this bird is going to be exhausted, the distance it has covered.'

'Do so,' Merren agreed.

'They're coming to get me tonight!' Karia could not restrain her joy as she stroked the exhausted gull. Even magic to strengthen and speed its wings for the trip had barely been enough for the bird to make the return.

'What was that?' Ezok gasped in horror.

Without the girl, his story about the Egg was going to look foolish and his life would be forfeit. Either he would be killed by Onzalez or by the Egg itself, when the Fearpriest ordered him to use what he had 'learned' from the Radiant Child.

'They're coming to get me on the dragon! You can come too!' Karia offered. 'You said they had forced you to do bad things, that you hated them and wanted to get away, so you'd be safer with us than here.'

Ezok masked his face. He might have fooled her into thinking he was willing to help her but both Martil and the remaining priests of Aroaril had seen him kill their old Archbishop with the help of Prent. That was even before he catalogued what he had seen and helped do in the invasion of southern Norstalos. He would not survive a trial.

'That's a wonderful idea! I'll just go and get a few things to bring with me.' He smiled.

Karia grinned back, cradling the gull gently. Martil was coming to get her! She would be back with him tonight!

Ezok slipped out carefully, shut the door gently and then raced to find Onzalez and Gello.

Argurium shot across the waves at an incredible speed, an impossible speed. This was a risk, in more ways than one. Without the dragon to escort them, the fleet of ships was without the magic that helped speed its progress. Barrett and his mages were doing their best to keep the ships safe and moving swiftly but the speed had dropped away dramatically. The time they were away would mean they were not closing the gap on Gello and his ships nearly as fast. Also, the longer they were away, the greater the chance of a storm or a freak wave striking one or more of the ships. It was just one more thing for Merren to worry about.

The dragon's wings beat only irregularly but that did not seem to affect her progress. If Martil thought about it, it was to wish the dragon could go faster. All he could think about was how he could get Karia out and away. Then he could tell her he had lived up to his promise, he had come for her.

Merren could see what Martil was thinking. It was obvious from the way he gazed hungrily ahead. While she hoped it was possible to bring Karia out of there, she was prepared for anything. Her feelings for Karia could not stop her duty. Not just a few people, not just a country, but a whole world rested on her shoulders. If either the dragon or Martil died, there was no hope for any of them.

She had tried again to talk to him, but received only one-word answers in reply.

Now they were both alone with their thoughts.

'Not far,' Havell said.

The moon shining on the waves was the only light that night, and often it would disappear behind clouds, though that did not seem to worry Argurium. But ahead was a strange glow, lighting the sky.

'What is that?' Martil asked.

'It is the ships,' Havell sighed.

The glow grew brighter and brighter until Argurium flared her wings and their speed dropped right away. Now they were hovering above the waves, looking at a small fleet of ships, every one of them lit by a sea of torches and lanterns around the decks. The ships were clustered around one in the centre, which was lit even more brightly. On the deck of every ship were scores of men.

'Which one is Karia's?' Martil asked desperately.

'The one in the middle,' Havell said sadly.

Argurium slowly looped around the fleet, keeping her distance, keeping to the shadows. Merren could see many of the men on deck had crossbows or those strange spear-hurling devices the Tenochs had used. Wherever they went, eyes were looking for them. Merren knew all the torches on the decks would have destroyed the watchers' night vision and they would be unable to see far from their ship. But they did not need to. To get to Karia, Argurium would have to fly over at least two of the others.

'What are we waiting for? Let's go in there!' Martil demanded.

'They knew we were coming. It's too risky,' Merren said, a sick sense of despair sliding into her chest. She did not want to fight with Martil but there was no choice here — they could not risk a rescue attempt now. If she had been able to speak to Martil earlier … but there was no sense in what-ifs. She had to deal with this now, whatever the consequences.

'They're just on guard! That's nothing! The dragon's magic can protect us!' he insisted.

'They have a Fearpriest down there! He will be able to pierce Argurium's magic!' Havell snarled. 'We cannot do this! Queen Merren, we must leave.'

'No!' Martil let out a howl of anger and despair that echoed across the waves. Instantly men rushed to the rails of the ship, crossbows in hand.

'We cannot just leave her! It's worth the risk!'

'Martil,' Merren warned.

'She's just down there! Take us in!' he ordered Havell.

Merren slipped her dagger out of its sheath. Anger, frustration and fear lent strength to her arm. As Martil reached out to grab Havell, she struck Martil hard on the back of the head with the heavy pommel. Instantly he slumped forwards.

'Hold him,' Merren snapped, slipping her dagger back into its sheath. 'Don't let him fall!'

'What did you do?' Havell gasped, as he reached back to hold the dazed warrior.

'Saved his life, and ours also. Now get us back to our ships,' Merren said grimly.

Argurium gave a shrieking roar of challenge into the night, then beat her wings rapidly and went back the way she came.

'They were out there all right,' Gello said with satisfaction. 'Good work, Ezok!'

They had waited nervously on deck, wondering what was going to come out of the darkness. The men had almost been helpless with fright, for word of the demon with the unstoppable sword had managed to spread across all ships. It had taken all of Gello's authority, as well as a few threats, to get them ready to defend the ships and not just try to save themselves. Onzalez had been praying all night, and had sacrificed a pair of wounded men to make sure he was ready for whatever the night would bring, which had done little to improve morale.

After the debacle in the Dragon Hall, Gello had been half afraid the dragon and its riders would prove too much to handle but, evidently, a show of force had been enough to scare it off. Although, judging by the noise it had made, perhaps scare was too strong a word.

'Your work with that magical child is beginning to bear fruit, Ezok,' Onzalez judged. 'How soon do you think it will be before all its secrets have been revealed?'

Ezok controlled his face, glad of the semi-darkness that helped hide the nervous sweat.

'There is much work. We have barely scratched the surface of what it can do,' he said carefully. 'We were most lucky tonight. For without the child, the Egg will be useless to us.'

Onzalez grunted. 'You need to hurry. That creature down below is summoning pursuers after us. Who knows what else it might call up from Aroaril's deepest pits? The sooner we can sacrifice it to Zorva, the better.'

'What happened?' Martil felt himself reviving. 'Were we attacked?'

'Keep quiet! You need to rest until Milly has had a chance to see you,' Merren told him.

Martil reached up and felt a huge lump on the back of his head.

'What was it? Slingshot?' he asked. 'I didn't think they had seen us properly.'

'Don't touch it!' Merren ordered. 'And it wasn't a slingshot. It was the pommel of my dagger. I hit you.'

'What?' Martil tried to turn around. 'Why did you —'

'It was the only way to save your life. This was a good idea, but they were ready for us. We could not risk Argurium — or you.'

'But Karia!'

'We shall get there as fast as we can, land right behind them. After all, we are able to cut the corner on them by not sailing past Dragonara Isle.'

'We could have got her! It was worth the risk!'

'Don't you understand?' she snapped. 'It is not just about you! Inside that Egg is the future of this entire world! And it is on my shoulders to see it saved! I love Karia, if anything happened to her I would be devastated but, if it comes down to a choice between her and every other child on this world, I have to be able to make the right decision.'

The vehemence in her voice penetrated Martil's daze. He could barely believe she had hit him, from behind, to stop him from saving Karia.

'I cannot think that way,' he said, finally.

'Well, I have to. And I will do it again if I must,' she told him.

'Well, I know only too well how ruthless you are. How willing to sacrifice anything and everything for what you see as the greater good …'

'Oh, so now you want to talk to me? Perhaps I should have struck you on the head earlier!' she declared.

'Why not? You already stuck a dagger in my heart,' he fired back.

'And still it is all about you! You think you are the only person to suffer, the only one who was hurt by my decision!'

'Well, it doesn't seem to have bothered you!' he yelled at her.

'That shows just how little you know!' she shouted back. 'I have regretted it every moment since you flew away on Argurium and I regret it still. If you had talked to me, I would have told you that. I never wanted to marry Sendric but I had no choice then. Now I do and I choose you!'

Martil tried to look at her in the eye, but it was too dark. A few weeks ago he would have shouted with delight to hear those words. But they had been down this path before and it just led to more pain for him. She had promised him everything — and gone back on her word. What was to say this time would be different?

'It is too late. All I care about is getting Karia back,' he said, deliberately hardening his voice. She had rejected him before, now she had stopped him from rescuing Karia. Although every part of him ached to hold her, he also wanted to hurt her like she had hurt him.

'You don't really mean that!' she accused.

'But I do,' he said coldly, wishing it were true.

Merren looked out to sea, bile in her mouth. This was a bad idea, and it had got even worse.

'We're almost back at the ships,' Havell said into the sudden silence.

'We'll get more men and try again tomorrow night, come back with Barrett and Milly, to counter the Fearpriest,' Martil said harshly.

'No, we shall not. If we take them, then the ships will be left without magical protection. And this is too much of a gamble as it is. We cannot risk it again,' Merren said regretfully. She did not want to think of Karia being left behind but what could she do? Karia was not the only life in her hands.

Martil fumed in silence as Argurium circled the ships below, nursing the pain in his head and the one in his heart.

Karia had opened the small window so she could see when Martil arrived. The noise from the deck above, the lights, they did not bother her at first. But when it did not die down, she wondered what was happening.

The hours seemed to trickle past — without an hourglass, she had no idea of the time. Only the ringing of the ship's bell to signify the change gave her some idea of passing time.

Surely he had to be coming soon. Surely! He said he would.

Then she heard a dragon's roaring challenge and her heart leaped. At last! She peered through the tiny opening, trying to see what was going on. It was almost impossible but she thought she could make out the shape of a dragon, silhouetted against the moon. Then it turned away and disappeared.

She stared and stared, hoping to catch another glimpse, but the cheers from above made her scared. She reached out with the magic, searching for the dragon — but she could feel it moving away.

She slumped down on the bed and tried to stop her tears. But all of Barrett's training and all of his tricks to keep control were useless against how she felt. She was back at the farm, locked in a dark room while her da and brothers were out. She was left alone in a dark forest while they waited in ambush for hapless travellers. She felt so lost. How could this have happened? Why had Martil not charged in? She had felt sure nothing would stop him. Her tears began to slow as she wondered why the ships had been lit up, why there had been so much activity on deck. Normally it was quiet at night ...

A gentle knock on the cabin door made her instinctively sit up and rub her face dry. She would not give them the satisfaction of knowing how she felt.

Ezok popped his head around the door.

'I am sorry,' he said simply. 'But I could not let you go. While you are here though, I shall see that you come to no harm ...'

'Get away from me!' Karia screamed at him. 'I won't help you ever again! Go!'

'Now that's not going —' Ezok began, but she reached out with the magic and shoved him backwards, then slammed the door shut, making the wood shriek and groan as she sealed it tight against the rest of the wall.

Let them try and come in. I'll make them wish they had never seen me, she vowed.

Everyone was waiting when Argurium flew over the ships. But sighs of disappointment went up when they saw there were still only three on the dragon's back.

Martil slid down to the deck, refusing Merren and Havell's help.

'Milly! See to him! He's hurt,' Merren commanded.

Martil tried to slip past Milly and go below but the Archbishop held his arm and then everyone caught up to him.

'What happened?' Barrett demanded.

'We were betrayed!' Martil hissed. 'It was that Lavrick, I know it was!'

Everyone turned back to the quarterdeck, where the ship's captain stood by the wheel.

'How in Aroaril's name could he do that? With myself and Barrett on board? One or both of us would have detected it,' Milly pointed out. 'More likely they thought we might try something like this.'

'How do I know? Perhaps the Fearpriest gave him something to let him communicate with them, like that Berellian bard we had in Sendric's dungeon,' Martil argued. 'But his brother was an evil little bastard and I can't believe any relative of Havrick could be good.'

'We cannot do anything without proof. I want Norstalos to be all about judging a person by what they do, not by who their relatives are. That applies just as much to Lavrick as it does to me leaving the country in the hands of Conal, Louise and Gia,' Merren told him briskly.

Milly laid her hand on the lump on the back of his head.

'What happened here?' she asked.

'Ask the Queen,' Martil replied shortly.

'Well, luckily there was nothing valuable in there to damage,' Milly said coolly. She took her hand away and the pain, and the lump on his head, were gone.

'Thanks,' Martil grunted.

'So what happened, my Queen?' Barrett asked.

'They knew we were coming. They had all their ships formed up around the one with Karia, every deck was lit and there were men ready to fight us. It was too risky.' She sighed.

'So if they knew we were coming, who told them?' Martil growled. His frustration and anger were bubbling over and he wanted an outlet for it.

'It could have been the Fearpriest. If he offered blood sacrifice, he could have received guidance from the Dark One,' Milly said.

'I still think we should question Lavrick,' Martil declared.

'Like you did the Berellian bard?' Merren snapped, the memory of the man's bruised face and broken hands swimming into her mind.

'He was a Fearpriest spy and tried to lure you into a trap!' Martil protested. 'He deserved everything he got!'

'A trap that you wanted us to plunge headlong into, if I remember rightly,' Merren pointed out.

'That was not how it was!' Martil began, but she brushed him aside.

'You shall not question Lavrick. Archbishop Sadlier shall speak to him. If she deems there is a problem, then we shall take action. Meanwhile, we must increase our speed, if possible. We need to be landing right behind our enemies, if not catching them at sea. We must all work together.' But even as she finished speaking, she saw Martil stalking towards his place at the bow.

Their passage across the sea was incredibly swift. Without the magical help of the dragon, they would never be able to cover these distances in so short a time. Travelling at such a speed put a huge strain on all the ships just to stay together. If one fell behind, or drifted off-course and out of the range of Argurium's magic, they would be left behind. The ships' captains virtually slept at the wheels. Lavrick ate there, lashing himself to the rail so he could sleep upright, holding on to the wheel, when he slept at all. Milly was kept busy, going from ship to ship, helping all of them.

Most of all she was needed by the Derthals. The effect of the waves seemed to be far more dramatic on them. Most could be found heaving the contents of their stomachs over the ship's rail each morning, while others just lay on the decks, as if dead. Merren was worried they would not be able to fight when they finally reached Tenoch but Sacrax, when he was not sick, insisted they would recover in no time.

But for everyone else, there was a certain rhythm about the days on board.

There was enough for all to eat, although all were muttering about never wanting to see another fish again after just a couple of days.

There was little enough to do, except polish armour that threatened to rust in the sea air, sharpen swords and pikes that were already sharp, and watch the sea slip past. Merren tried to distract them by dreaming up games and competitions, races across the deck, up the rigging and back again, while the officers and sergeants drilled the men until their sweat ran down to the deck. Romon and several of the other bards travelled from ship to ship, performing sagas on request but still there were many long hours where men just gazed out to sea, looking in vain for their enemy.

But at the back of every mind, at the edge of vision, was Martil.

He either sat at the bow or in the crow's nest at the top of the mast, watching. He ate the fish he was brought, drank the water he was given and ignored any messages from Merren.

A delegation went to see Merren about him.

'My Queen, should we not try to talk to him? It is affecting the men, seeing him like that,' Nerrin asked stiffly.

'Thank you. But I do not think that will work,' Merren told them gently. 'He needs to be left alone. Once we have reached Tenoch, things will improve. Tell your men that the Captain is just focused on getting Karia back but he will be his old self once we are there.'

They went away, slightly happier, but Merren could take no comfort from her own words.

She was spending her days reading about Tenoch, both the city-state itself and the continent it ruled. Much of what the prisoners had said was fascinating. It seemed the continent had found different ways of doing many things that Norstalines — indeed all on Albiona — took for granted. For instance, they had not developed techniques for metal-working. It may have been that the metal ores were simply not there, or perhaps they had found a solution that seemed easier. A volcanic rock, black and incredibly hard, which the Tenochs called obsidian, had been found and proved to be almost as efficient at cutting, although not as easy to work into shapes and designs. But it had proved sufficient for them to develop their skills in stone-working, if the prisoners were to be believed. They also had an even more rigid social structure than Norstalos — and slavery. Even without the blood sacrifice they practised, it would have been abhorrent to Merren. But it was all important information, and she tried to absorb everything.

Of most interest was how they had exercised their rule over the continent by effectively kidnapping the ruling classes of every other city and bringing them back to Tenoch, where they could do little harm — and certainly never inspire rebellion in their old homes. She was sure this could be the key to defeating the hold the Fearpriests had over the continent.

And at least it stopped her thinking about Karia, and Martil.

Gello recognised that his future was bound with Onzalez. No other Fearpriest was going to help him regain his throne and his destiny. Previously he had tried to avoid the Fearpriest but now he saw himself not just as the man's equal but even his master. To this end, he frequently called for Onzalez and they sat and discussed what they needed to do. Onzalez removed his cowl for these meetings, to show Gello he could be trusted. Gello even showed him his picture of Mother, and formally introduced him to her.

There was little else to keep them amused. The men were kept busy on the oars, trying to extract the last bit of speed from the ships — but Gello and Onzalez were not going to subject themselves to that. Ezok had locked himself away in his cabin, claiming to be studying the Dragon Egg. Since the news of the pursuit, they had lost some interest in this magic object.

'They cannot have more than a few thousand men and goblins with them — there was not enough time for more to assemble,' Gello pointed out.

'Indeed. And if we can get back to Tenoch before they catch us at sea, all the advantage swings to us. They have no hope of taking my city with so few men,' Onzalez hissed with pleasure. 'We can go through the city and summon a horde to sweep them back into the sea.'

'And once we have crushed her force, Norstalos shall be defenceless before us,' Gello exulted. 'As long as your Ruling Council still supports us.'

This was the question that dominated their discussion.

'They will be happy to see me. And they shall still do my bidding,' Onzalez told him with a smile. 'Do not underestimate me, as our enemies have. Far from being defenceless, I have an enormous amount of power — as well as agents everywhere. With their help I shall lead us to victory!'

Gello grimaced at Onzalez's boastfulness. Onzalez was obviously using it to cover up for his failure in Norstalos and he knew it annoyed Mother, because she was always quiet afterwards. Still, he was intrigued by the thought of Onzalez's agents. 'Even aboard my bitch of a cousin's ships?'

Onzalez smiled enigmatically. 'Perhaps. I cannot tell you all my secrets!'

Martil had been trying to stay awake at night, so he could watch Lavrick. There were plenty of eyes on the man during the day but, if he was going to try anything, it would be at night. So Martil was trying to sleep during the day and keeping watch at night. That was most of the reason, anyway. He was being haunted by dreams again — nowhere near as bad as the ones of Bellic, but a warning nonetheless. Sometimes they were of Karia, sometimes of Merren, always of death and blood in Tenoch. He tried to ignore them, tried to tell the Dragon Sword he would change once Karia was back. All he wanted to do was to get her and then he would forget about revenge. But it was not working. The dreams kept coming. He could sleep — but he would wake with their images burned into his brain. On top of everything else, it left him itching for a fight. So far Lavrick had not done anything suspicious — but he could not trust him. Any brother of Havrick had to be watched. From an uncomfortable position in the crow's nest, he peered down at the stern of the ship, where Lavrick had lashed himself to the tiller. The man was eating something and Martil watched him sourly, his own belly grumbling. Then he forgot all about food and sat up, staring down to where Lavrick stood, lit by half-a-dozen lanterns. A large seabird had landed by the rail and was watching the ship's captain intently. Lavrick glanced around, then held out his hand to the bird. Martil held his breath. No wild bird would sit there like that! Surely it had to be magicked! He watched as the bird took something then flew away.

'Seize him! Traitor!' Martil bellowed, then swung clumsily down onto the ropes and clambered to the deck, heedless of the rope burns he was picking up.

By the time he reached the deck, people were rushing up from everywhere, while Lavrick was looking around wildly.

'What is going on?' Merren shouted.

'He's a traitor! I saw him passing a message about us to a magicked bird!' Martil accused, pushing his way towards the wheel, where Lavrick stood.

All swivelled to look at the ship's captain.

'This is ridiculous!' Lavrick called. 'I merely offered a scrap of fish to a hungry bird! You can't accuse a man without proof!'

Martil shook his head. 'We are wasting time! Our secrets are even now flying on their way to Gello! Barrett, get the bird back and we shall have our proof!'

All looked at Merren, who gestured tiredly at Barrett.

The wizard walked across to the rail and held out his hand. All watched him silently until the bird flew down to his hand.

'There is no message attached to it,' Barrett reported. 'And it has not been magicked — until now, of course.'

'Then why was it sitting there? No wild bird would do that!' Martil cried.

'It has been around us all day — many people have been feeding it!' Lavrick protested.

'A likely story!' Martil sneered. 'So why did I not see it?'

'Perhaps because you were asleep for most of the day?' Milly offered.

'I think that is enough,' Merren declared. 'We all need to sleep!'

'What? We are going to let him get away with this?' Martil exlaimed.

'Get away with what? Lavrick did nothing! Now I suggest we all return to our bunks and hammocks!' Merren ordered. 'Captain Martil, I need to see you in my cabin. Now.'

Martil, who was about to protest some more, followed her grimly.

She stood behind her small table in the cabin, making sure there was a discreet distance between them, although he stood closer to the door than to her.

'I know how you feel about Karia and how much you want to rescue her. But, at the moment, you are a danger to yourself and to the rest of us! Give me one reason why I should not order Argurium to dump you on Dragonara Isle until we have retrieved the Dragon Egg!'

'Because you need me, and the Dragon Sword, both to defeat the Fearpriests and to finish the job the dragons wanted me to do. If Argurium dies, then we have to get the Egg and the Sword together before the next sunrise.'

She sighed. 'I know that. But the danger of Argurium dying is less than the danger you pose. You would kill the one man who can get us upriver at Tenoch. And you would have killed yourself trying to get to Karia. How does that help us, you — or her? How would I begin to tell her that you threw your life away foolishly? That she lost you because you lost your head and rushed in? Or how would I tell the families of the men and Derthals on these ships that their husbands and fathers are dead because Captain Martil did not think? Are you having trouble sleeping? Is it dreams again?'

'No!' Martil lied unconvincingly.

'Surely that is enough of a warning! Do you really want to go back to how you were before the battle of Pilleth?'

Martil glanced away. 'I hear you,' he said sullenly.

'Good! Aroaril, we are trying to invade a country and take a massive city — and do it in days! We need every man we have and I need all the help I can get! Added to that, I want to get Karia back — you are not the only one afraid for her, the only one who loves her! So do you think I really want to send you away?'

'Well, you did before,' he said coldly.

She paused for a moment before exploding. 'Yes, I did. And it was a mistake. But it seems keeping you here might be just as big a mistake!' she shouted. 'I can see where you are going — and it is not a good place! If we get into this city and, Aroaril forbid, Karia is dead, will you be able to control yourself — or will we have a massacre to make Bellic look like a skirmish?'

Martil stepped closer. 'Those bastards took her, after everything else they have done. They deserve everything they get! And yes, I want to make sure they never threaten us again!'

'Even if it means another Bellic? The nightmares from that, the agony you went through with the Dragon Sword — do you want that again? Do you want to destroy your future?'

'Without Karia, I have no life worth living,' he said simply.

'And what about us? What about our child?' she challenged.

'How can I think about that now? And what would be the point? You promised we would marry, you spun me a tale of a rosy future — then as soon as you saw a piece of paper from Sendric, you threw that future away!'

'Well, I was wrong! Perhaps I want to change things now. Perhaps seeing you fly away showed me how foolish I was.' She stepped around the desk and walked closer to him.

He glared at her, breathing harshly. But as she drew closer, she sensed the conflict within him. The air in the cabin seemed suddenly thick, like the heaviness before a summer storm, as she reached out and put her hand on his chest.

Instantly he jerked backwards, as if stung.

'How can I believe that now? How can I know this is not another of your tricks, your ways to manipulate me? Ever since I met you, you have been in my thoughts. But a man can only take so much. You twist things around, twist me around, make me confused. I cannot think of anything but getting Karia back. Everything else is just a distraction!'

With that he stormed over to the cabin door, yanked it open and slammed it behind him.

Merren buried her face in her hands. How could she have played this so wrong?

Onzalez was having trouble sleeping. Not from guilt or regret — although he did wish he had taken more control of the army outside the Norstaline capital. No, what kept him lying sleepless on his bunk was the thought of what waited back at Tenoch. The Seventeen had been servants to his will but there was a faction that desperately wanted him to fail, headed by a Fearpriest called Horna, who had been the nominal leader of the Seventeen until Onzalez had supplanted him. Horna's supporters had been enthusiastically behind him until now — because they wanted him to make a mistake and then they could destroy him.

Now they had their chance, did they but know it. The trick was not letting them know.

The Dragon Egg would be vital in helping him fool them, Gello and his small army nearly as important. Once he would have been confident. But that had been before that damned priest of Aroaril had defeated him. He had never been thwarted before, never even been seriously challenged. But now a worm of doubt had crept inside him — and he lay awake at nights, worrying about what would happen.

'What should I do?' Merren asked.

Barrett shook his head. He was barely able to believe what Merren wanted from him. Even a few weeks ago, the thought of discussing Merren's relationship with Martil would have had him incandescent with rage. If Tiera had not been here on board with him, he would have already exploded. But she had told him to keep his hatred for Martil hidden better. There was no benefit in it. Attacking Martil was not the way to impress Merren. Barrett wondered what he would have done without Tiera. Then he put that aside. It was not worth thinking about. Instead he concentrated on his reply to Merren.

'You need to leave him alone. Give him time and space,' he managed to say, finally.

Merren sighed. 'I suppose you are right. But it feels so wrong to sit here and do nothing! As it is, he is affecting morale. He just sits there, glowering at Sendric and Lavrick. Look at what happened with that bird!'

'We just have to get to land — and to Karia in time. But I think you should consider alternatives to Martil. He has proved he is not worthy ...'

Merren grimaced and held up her hand. Obviously this was a mistake. She had not meant to speak of her fears to Barrett, of all people, but it had just slipped out.

Time hung heavily; there was a constant dread of waking up to find Argurium gone and the world doomed. The stress was getting to her — was getting to all of them — but she had nobody to talk to, with Louise and Gia back in the capital. Martil's outburst at Lavrick, then at her, had been the final straw.

'I know you don't want to hear this, especially from me, but you must face the truth. Martil is turning back into the Butcher of Bellic and is not fit to be the wielder of the Dragon Sword, let alone a Queen's consort —'

'Enough!' Merren snapped and he fell silent. 'Barrett, I am sorry. I should not have begun this conversation. Please leave me,' she said heavily.

He bowed jerkily and hurried out of the cabin, keeping his dark thoughts to himself. In the fresh air, he took a deep breath. How could Merren be so foolish? He could not help but think she was not the same Queen he had served faithfully for years. Now he knew he was not in love with her, he saw her in a completely different light. Sighing, he went in search of Tiera. Lately, only she seemed able to calm the anger within him.

Back at her da's farm, then later in the woods with her half-brothers, Karia had learned several ways to try to make time pass. They used to leave her alone in the dark farmhouse, with its strange smells and noises, as well as at the camp, often without fire, in the dark forest, with its even stranger noises and cries. Many was the night when she had sat hunched in a corner of a room, or against a tree, crying and wishing only for the darkness to lift and the light to come again.

She had prayed never to feel that way again — but here she was, alone on the Fearpriest ship. And the darkness never seemed to end, even when it was light.

She did everything she could not to think about it. She counted the wooden nails in the timber beams and planks, the beams themselves and tried to sing every song she knew, retell every saga she had read, so as not to think of where she was. She had no intention of opening the door — except to Martil. She knew he was coming for her — she just had to hold on. She had a small barrel of water already in her room and, for food, she had called on some of the ship's rats, who were happy to help. They brought her what they could find, from hard cheese to dried fruit. There wasn't much of it but it kept her going and playing with them was entertaining, as well. She concentrated on that, rather than think about what might happen. Martil would come for her. She knew he would.

'I think you should leave the Queen's service when we return,' Tiera said.

'Leave? Why?' Barrett asked.

They lay together in the small cabin. More and more, Tiera was bringing Barrett down here, trying to stop him from exploding at Martil.

'This is not good for you. I know how you feel about Martil but it is obvious Merren loves him. How would it be, every day watching them together?'

Barrett's silence said more than any words could.

'If you left, we could find another country, far away from here. Your abilities would be prized wherever you went. And you would be happier, I know you would.'

'I am happy as long as I am with you,' he said with a smile.

She grinned back. 'That sounds like a line from a saga! Will you think about it, at least? It hurts me to see what is happening to you, how it is eating you up inside.'

'I do not need to leave — but I shall think about it, for you,' he promised.

'Captain!'

The cry startled Martil from sleep and he looked around wildly. The call had come from the masthead and he wondered if the lookout had spotted Lavrick betraying them. He had been ordered not to go up the mast after the last incident but it had not entirely stopped him watching the ship's captain.

'Sails! Sails on the horizon!'

Martil ignored Merren's orders and led the race for the mast. He scrambled into the crow's nest and nodded to the lookout, the Ralloran sergeant Redder, who had helped Kesbury escape the Berellians.

'There, sir! Against the sky!'

Martil peered forwards, adjusting against the pitching of the ship against the waves. Up here, the movement was far more pronounced. For the past day or so, the sky had been grey and forbidding, the wind whipping the waves into whitecaps. Argurium's magic had kept them all safe but it made it difficult to see what lay before them. This morning the sky was blue and clear — and outlined against it, at the very curve of the horizon, was a collection of tiny white sails.

Martil grinned and clapped Redder on the back before clambering back down, to where Merren, Barrett and the others were clustered around the mainmast.

'They're in sight! We're catching them!' he cried, and the men aboard let out a roar of triumph. 'Havell, tell Argurium we need to go faster still!'

The Elfaran shook his head. 'I cannot. We are driving the ships as fast as we can already. Any more and they will break apart. We are going faster than they were designed to — the timbers cannot take any more strain.'

Martil's face darkened but Merren grabbed his arm.

'We are catching them up. In another day or two we shall be beside them. Hold to that,' she urged.

Martil managed to nod his head. 'I shall,' he vowed. 'I will be ready at the bow.'

The lookouts spotted the sails behind them not long after dawn, but Gello had ordered they keep any sightings quiet and bring their news to him, not shout it out. Their pursuers could not be seen from the deck and he did not want panic sweeping through his force.

'Tenoch will be in sight soon,' Onzalez promised.

'But will it be soon enough?' Gello worried. 'It will help us little if we are caught before we can reach the safety of the city!'

'Perhaps I need to make a few sacrifices. I could choose some of the men, use their deaths to help me speed us up,' Onzalez offered.

'We need all the trained men we can get,' Gello disagreed. 'What about the Radiant Child? Surely she's powerful enough to ensure you get us to safety —'

'No!' Ezok gasped. 'You cannot!'

'You dare to forbid me?' Gello thundered.

Ezok bowed his head. 'Forgive me, sire, but you cannot harm her! Without her, the Egg is useless to us!'

'It is useless to us now. None of us know how to make it work — and its purpose is to get the Ruling Council of Fearpriests to accept us. That it can do with or without its wielder,' Gello said viciously. 'Our victory will not come through it, but through destroying my slut of a cousin when she lands behind us! I say she dies!'

'Brother Onzalez, who knows what will happen to the Egg without the Child? We cannot risk it! The Ruling Council will be amazed by what they can see in the Egg now — none can doubt its power. But if we gave them reason to —'

'Nonsense! I say she dies. Now!' Gello ordered.

'Brother!' Ezok pleaded.

Onzalez wanted to give in to Gello. He wanted to secure the man's trust, his loyalty. But the night-time fears came back and he licked dry lips. The Egg had to be at its most spectacular to impress Horna and his supporters.

'No,' he said finally. 'Ezok is right. I shall not sacrifice the Radiant Child now. We need her to show the Council. Besides, they may want to send such a powerful being to Zorva. We should not waste this opportunity.'

Gello stepped closer. 'Have a care, priest,' he warned. 'I do not like to have my orders questioned!'

'Then give me two men who have displeased you — and it shall have the same effect. Do you want to reach land, only to be slain by the very people we thought would save us?' Onzalez asked bitingly.

Gello glowered. 'Do it then, priest. But do not cross me again.'

The sight of Gello's fleet had cheered everyone. There was a new spirit about the men and Derthals, a fresh enthusiasm both for their duties and for their training. Many men and Derthals liked to join Martil at the bow, where he was talking to people for the first time in days.

'We shall aim straight at Gello's flagship, use the dragon's magic to lay us alongside. I want you all to have specific tasks. There must be men to kill Gello, men to kill the Fearpriests and men to kill any of Gello's officers. We will soak the decks in their blood so they can never come back to haunt us again. No more mistakes — we shall leave not one enemy alive to trouble us. If just one of them lives, then we and our families are not truly safe,' he was telling them.

Merren wandered down, both to look at Gello's fleet and hear Martil's words. They chilled her, but not as much as the cheers of the men and Derthals did.

'We must take Gello alive. Bring him back to Norstalos for trial!' she called. 'And that goes for any man who surrenders to us.'

The men and Derthals fell silent at her words, although Martil stared challengingly back at her.

'Gello will never stand trial. He shall die on this!' he promised, holding the Dragon Sword aloft.

The men and Derthals around him bellowed their approval.

Merren just stared at Martil until he looked away, but she was no longer worrying about winning him back. She was more concerned about him turning into the Butcher of Bellic.

'Land!'

The cry from the masthead brought everyone out on deck.

Gello had ordered the lookouts to call out the moment they saw land. Despite his best efforts, the men knew they were being pursued, for all could see their pursuers. They were far behind, but coming on fast. Another day and they would be fighting for their lives. The tale of the demon with the unstoppable sword had been told and retold on every ship in the fleet until even the bravest among them were quaking.

But not now. Now they would reach land safely — and spring a trap on their hunters. Even those who had never seen Tenoch and never wanted to come to this strange land across the sea were grinning with delight.

'There it is! Tenoch!' Onzalez crowed. 'Now let our enemies despair! If they follow us up the river, they will be wrecked! They shall land behind us and be swept into the sea! Then we shall be able to return and take everything!'

Gello watched the smear on the horizon grow until it resembled a rocky coast, thickly covered in trees. But not trees as he was used to. They towered impossibly high, were strung with vines and reverberated with the strange calls of stranger animals. Even though it was almost winter back in Norstalos, he could feel it was warmer here. But he was more interested in thinking about snatching victory from the jaws of defeat than about the trees and animals of Tenoch. He had been chased out of his country not once but twice. To return now, having destroyed Merren and her army far from their home, would be sweet indeed. That was the way to start a legend! The defeated hero comes back from across the seas to rule the world. He liked the sound of that. The only concern was Onzalez. They were joint commanders but the business over sacrificing the Radiant Child had disturbed him. He had thought Onzalez would obey his every suggestion before then. So would things change further once they were in Tenoch?

'What do we do about the Radiant Child? Do we present her to the Seventeen?' he asked, just to see what Onzalez would say.

'Zorva willing, the Seventeen will be satisfied with the Egg. But we should keep her in reserve, just in case we need more,' Onzalez decided. He left unspoken the thought the Seventeen would be more interested in a powerful magical object than in knowing a vengeful army was about to land on their shores. 'Ezok, she is your charge. Any trouble and you will both pay the penalty, understand?'

Ezok wiped a sweating brow.

'She is too valuable to discard. The power she possesses, and can unleash through that Egg, is vast. We went to so much trouble to steal it. It would be an affront to Zorva to waste that now,' he said.

Onzalez turned away. Not being able to use the power himself had diminished its value to him. He disliked the thought of having to be dependent on some capricious spirit or, worse, Ezok. If he could destroy the Witch Queen and her minions here, he would not need it. It could be put aside for later study. All he needed for now was for it to show some worth, to save his life.

'It shall be our last resort. But make sure it is no trouble. And for Zorva's sake, be ready to show my fellow Fearpriests some of its powers — they might need to see something! Understand?'

Ezok bowed and hurried away, his heart thumping painfully. He feared that might be too much to ask.

Karia lay listlessly on her bunk. She had not eaten anything for almost a day now. The rats had been unable to find any more food and, anyway, she did not have the energy to call them. Even the water barrel was empty but still she kept the door sealed. She did not want to see any of them. She did not want to do anything. She had heard activity on the ship, heard the cries that meant they were close to land. Even that did not stir her out of her despair.

Someone knocked on her door but she ignored it, as she had before. But, this time, the knocking did not go away.

'You must let me in!'

She recognised the sound of Ezok's voice but, after he had betrayed her, she just rolled over on the bunk, so she was facing the wall.

'Break down the door!'

She heard the order but did not stir until the axes began slicing through the timbers of her door. The sound gave her fresh life and she jumped up, eyes blazing, ready to punish whoever came through that door.

The axes cut through the warped timbers, opening a hole big enough for a man to walk through — then next moment the axemen dropped them with a cry as the weapons became too hot to hold. Karia prepared to give them another surprise but her legs suddenly felt wobbly and she had to sit down. Too late she remembered Barrett's training and his orders to eat and drink well.

'I'm going in there,' Ezok told the men with him. 'Leave us.'

'You are a brave man, sir,' one of the axemen said, as they gratefully hurried away.

Ezok inclined his head in acknowledgment, although he knew it was not bravery. It was fear of the alternative. He stepped through the wreckage of the door, a tray of delicacies held before him, like a shield. Food supplies were running low but he had been able to scrounge and steal these.

'We have reached Tenoch. You need to eat and drink,' he told her gently.

'Why?' Karia glared at him. She wanted to lie down and sleep but she was ready to do something nasty to him.

'You need to be strong. Your friends are in sight. They are not far behind us now,' he offered her the tray.

Despite herself, Karia inspected it. Fresh fried fish, some sort of roast seabird and some fruit in honey.

'You're lying to me,' she told him.

'Get your strength back and come up on deck and see. They are closing fast and will probably land no more than half a day behind us,' he wheedled.

She stared at him and he kept a light smile fixed.

'I don't trust you, but I shall do it,' she declared finally.

'Good.' Ezok exhaled in relief. 'Just keep quiet, and healthy, so you can do magic if you need to. The other Fearpriests need to see what you can do, so they will leave you alone. And who knows? By this time tomorrow you could be back with your family.'

Karia nodded, then began stuffing her face with the food he had brought.

Ezok smiled in encouragement.

'And can you get me a quill and parchment? I want to leave a message,' she mumbled through a mouthful of food.

'Of course,' he agreed. He would tell her whatever she wanted to hear to keep her happy. What he had no intention of telling her was that she would be rushed ahead to Tenoch, along with the Egg, and placed in the Temple of Zorva, right in the middle of the city. Ezok's future health depended on her being there. The only time he wanted her to see her family was when they were dragged into the Temple to be sacrificed to Zorva to give thanks for a historic victory.

23

Gello had been fascinated by the way they had sailed up the River Tenoch. Personally, he would have been happier if the early inhabitants had showed a little more imagination with their place names. Having the continent, its pre-eminent city and the main river all called the same thing was annoying, and a little confusing. He had not seen the city, while little of the continent had revealed itself as yet. But the river was fascinating. It stank — the detritus of a major city saw to that — and strange reptilian monsters lurked on the banks. When one opened its mouth to show long lines of sharp teeth, he eased himself back from the ship's rail.

'Crocodiles. They can take a man as easily as we would wring a chicken's neck,' Onzalez said with relish. 'They grow fat on those who dare to oppose us.'

'Foul creatures!' Gello spat.

'They shall help us,' Onzalez promised. 'This river has many hidden shallows and rocks. Only someone who knows it well can hope to make their way up its length to the city's docks. Others strike the shallows and then have to struggle past the crocodiles just to get to the bank. They are likely to be forced to abandon their ships miles away and then try and march through the jungle. Wild animals and quicksands shall take a toll of their numbers and they will take days to reach the safety of the docks.'

'It does not look dangerous to me,' Gello protested mildly.

'Watch and learn, my friend,' Onzalez said with relish.

And so it proved. Using the oars, with Tenochs in the bows of every ship, they rowed carefully up the river, avoiding what seemed like endless hazards.

'We have diverted much of the river's flow for our crops — as a result, the river is not strong enough to scour out the silt and sewage from the city,' Onzalez pointed out. 'But it is also an effective defence.'

Gello could only agree. On either side of them, jungle pressed in tight on the riverbank, tree branches brushing the masts at times if they swung wide at a bend, although it was easily a quarter-mile across, even at its narrowest. The heat was oppressive and he caught glimpses of strange animals high in the trees. Trying to march through this would be a near-impossible task.

With a last effort, the ships came around a final bend.

'Behold, Tenoch!' Onzalez said with a flourish.

Gello inspected the collection of ramshackle wooden jetties and huts with dismay.

'Is that it?' he gasped.

'No! These are the docks — the city is over there, past the trees!'

Gello looked up and saw, towering over the trees, the golden towers of a magnificent city. It was still some miles away.

'The river is not navigable further up,' Onzalez explained. 'But it is another ten miles our enemies must march and we can make those a misery.'

The ships were tied up at the jetties, an army of men in mere loincloths rushing to catch the ropes and make fast the ships.

'Bring every wagon you have!' Onzalez ordered from the side of the ship. The sight of his rust-red robe brought an instant reaction.

The dockmaster — or so Gello judged by his more impressive clothing — fell to his knees, as did every man in sight.

'Up! We have no time to waste! We must empty these ships and then get everyone to the safety of Tenoch!' Onzalez clapped his hands.

'At once, High One!'

The docks burst into frenzied activity, which Gello watched with pleasure.

'Come, my friend. We must move quickly. I need to reach the city before word of our arrival is brought to the Ruling Council. We must not give them the time to prepare for us.'

Martil watched the Tenoch coast appear with badly concealed impatience. Day after day he had worried about Karia, while his sleep was tormented by fresh nightmares in which he was forced to watch Karia being sacrificed to Zorva, helpless to stop the Fearpriests. In this dream, he fought his way to her side across a mountain of corpses and when he reached her, it was to find her with just enough breath to tell him he had let her down, betrayed her and broken his promises. He would wake, sweating, and pray they reached Tenoch quickly. He did not know whether this dream was coming from the Dragon Sword or his own imagination. He did not want to know. But now they could see Gello's fleet clearly and, better yet, see how fast they were gaining. Gello's ships, even powered as they were by sail, oar and Fearpriest magic, could not hope to compete against the dragon's magic. They were just entering the wide river mouth that broke up the coastline — but that did not mean safety. He estimated they could catch them a few miles upriver. It would make it more difficult to get to Gello's ship, the Egg and Karia, but he relished the thought of carving his way to her. He could see it now. His ships would speed upriver, powered by magic, to catch Gello's tired rowers one by one. He would leave each ship piled high with corpses until they begged for the chance to give Karia back to him.

Then his ship slowed right down, gently yet quickly, so that Martil could hear timbers creaking in protest while the bow wave, that had foamed high for days, dropped away to a trickle. He glanced around to see every ship in the fleet doing the same thing, and was shocked to see the sails being furled.

'What's going on? Why are we stopping?' he roared, storming back towards the stern.

'I ordered it!' Lavrick shouted back.

Martil drew the Dragon Sword. 'So you admit it! You want them to get away! You are in league with Gello and his Fearpriests!'

'No! But we have to stop here!' Lavrick protested.

'Why? Afraid we might catch your masters and prove you are a traitor?' Martil snarled.

'It is not safe I tell you! The ships will be wrecked on the river's hazards!' Lavrick realised that he was still tied to the wheel as he tried to back away from Martil.

'It's not safe for you! Now order the sails put back up and follow those ships! We can catch them in a few miles!'

'In a few miles we shall all be wrecked, and probably dead if we go in there too fast,' Lavrick declared. 'For Aroaril's sake, put down your sword! Without me, you have no hope of getting upriver safely and making it to the city!'

'If I was to listen to you, we'd never get upriver!' Martil retorted, then turned away. 'I don't have time to waste on you. I want those sails back up and I want this bastard taken below and chained up!'

'Captain! What are you doing?' Merren raced on deck, as did almost everyone else.

'This traitor tried to stop our pursuit, delay us so Gello can reach the city safely. I am getting us under way again,' Martil explained.

'No, he was following my orders. We cannot just sail up that river without preparing for it, or we shall never reach Tenoch. If you had bothered to come along to one of a dozen meetings, you would know that!'

Martil stared at her. 'But they're getting away!'

'We shall catch them,' she promised. 'Captain Lavrick, tell Captain Martil why we have slowed down. And Martil, sheathe your sword this instant!'

Martil reluctantly slid the Dragon Sword back into its sheath and glared at Lavrick, who met his gaze evenly.

'We must be careful when we enter the River Tenoch. It has many hazards that can destroy a ship. We cannot use the sails in there, we have to use oars to move upriver. You must listen to me, listen to my warnings, or the ships will become stuck, and we shall have to march through thick jungle to get to Tenoch,' Lavrick explained. 'Even this close to the city, the jungle is dangerous, filled with wild animals and pits of water and sand that can swallow a man whole. We do not want to become mired in there.'

506

'So we put all our trust in you?' Martil asked sarcastically.

'If you want to reach the city quickly, then you will,' Lavrick said calmly.

'He has not done anything to arouse our suspicion,' Merren pointed out. 'Beyond your wild accusations, that is.'

'We can't trust him! He's Havrick's brother! This could be the chance he is waiting for! We put ourselves in his hands and we'll end up in a trap!'

'Listen, I know you fear for your daughter but I have a wife and children waiting back in Worick. I know what is at stake here. If we fail, they will die. I want to get that Egg back as much as you!' Lavrick snarled.

Martil started forwards but Merren stepped in front of him. 'We all know what you are going through but there is plainly no landing site close by. If we do not go up the river, then we face a long delay — perhaps a fatal delay,' she said softly. 'Captain Lavrick is our best hope.'

At last Martil nodded. 'But I'll be watching him,' he said ominously.

'Agreed. But you'll also be apologising to him if he brings us in safely,' she warned.

'Apologise? For what?'

Merren lowered her voice. 'I need you. But not the man you are now, I need the one who's calm and controlled and ready to lead this army to victory. We are about to land a small army in a hostile land. We shall be surrounded by enemies. If we are to live, let alone rescue Karia and save the Dragon Egg, we need Captain Martil. Karia needs Captain Martil.'

Martil glanced over to the thick jungle, which seemed to steam a little in the heat of the day. The wide river mouth stained the seawater, a thick brown discharge of soil, leaves and the detritus of a huge city upriver issuing into the clear seawater and turning it a strange, murky colour. The smell of it, thick and rank, wafting across the water to where the ships waited, seemed to fill his head. His anger, his fear for her swelled with it. Up there was Karia. Up there were the bastards who had taken her. He tried to harness his anger, to direct it towards getting her back, but it felt as if it would get out of control at any moment. Still, he had to give Merren something.

'You shall have him. I will do whatever it takes to get her back,' he managed to say.

Merren looked at him critically but decided not to push the point. Seeing him like this was ripping her up inside. She could not shake the thought there was something she could do to help but, try as she might, she could not think what. If only she had never rejected him, sent him away, they could have helped each other. The thought of losing Karia terrified her also but she had to pretend she was in control. There was nothing for it now, no way to change the past. All she could do was press forwards and hope there would be a future — for all of them. Hiding what she was feeling, she turned to Lavrick. 'Take us in, Captain Lavrick. As quick as you can!'

But, before he would agree to bring them into the river mouth, Lavrick insisted on making the men practise with the oars. He had them working together, then had them pull against each other, which allowed the ship to pivot one way or the other, almost on the spot. Around the sea he took the fleet of ships, until he was satisfied all could handle them as he wished and respond to his orders. Only when the men were sweating and Martil swearing with frustration did he signal the other ships to follow him into the river mouth.

'You must obey my orders the instant they are given,' he told the rowers, while ordering the other ships to follow him precisely. 'Make a mistake and you shall beach your craft, or possibly sink her. So don't make a mistake.'

As they eased up the river, working against the current, he had men at the bows taking soundings of the river bottom constantly.

'This is not good country,' Sacrax muttered to Martil. 'Too hot, and trees too tall. Smells funny. And look at that!' He pointed out a large reptile that lay on the bank, mouth open to reveal serried ranks of teeth. 'It would swallow me whole!'

Martil just grunted. The smell was the worst thing. The water was brown, filth staining the banks, making it almost impossible to see what was below the surface. He did not want to think about what had made the water that colour.

He looked over at Lavrick, who alone of those on the ships did not seem to be bothered by the stench of this new land. But the sea captain ignored the stare that Martil was giving him, instead watching closely the river surface, as well as the bends ahead. The ships sailed past the first bend, keeping to the middle of the wide river and away from the forbidding jungle to either side. But as they came to the second bend, Lavrick ordered them to swing wide, to go as close as possible to the right bank.

Martil did not question it, but made sure he was watching the jungle on that side, just in case. His hand was close to his sword, to use first on any attacker, second on Lavrick.

'Look at that!' Merren pointed and he whirled — to see the ship glide past several huge underwater rocks, whose presence were only revealed when the wash from the ship's bow rippled across them.

He turned again, to see Lavrick looking at him.

'Keep your eyes on the river,' was all he said.

At first, every strange noise in the jungle, every manoeuvre Lavrick ordered, every sight of an unfamiliar animal had him reaching for the Dragon Sword. The slow pace had him grinding his teeth in frustration. But as each new hazard of the river was revealed, and Lavrick guided the fleet expertly further upriver, he could not stay on edge. He even joined the men on the oars for a spell, helping pull the ship past a sandbank.

And, four turns of the hourglass later, he had to admit Lavrick had done a good job. He had directed the ships past a score of obstacles, any of which could have ripped the bottom out of a vessel, at times forcing the ships to almost turn in a circle to get past them. And only when they were level with, or past, the obstacle could it be properly discerned.

One final bend was dealt with, and then they were easing towards a ramshackle settlement, where ten ships were already tied up and, in the distance, the towers of a city loomed above the forbidding trees.

'Here are the docks. The river is navigable no further. They told me once you could sail up to the gates but the Tenochs diverted much of the flow for their crops, and what remains is not enough to float a ship. Once the river was twice this wide, with many side channels and tributaries but the jungle has reclaimed the rest as the flow diminished. The city is about ten miles away. The path is well marked, but the first couple of miles will be through jungle, before it opens up into the farmlands and plains around the city of Tenoch,' Lavrick announced, wiping sweat from his brow.

'Captain, I applaud your efforts,' Merren congratulated him. 'I don't know how we would have made it this far without you!'

Martil walked over to face Lavrick, who stared him down.

'My thanks.' Martil held out his hand, but Lavrick ignored it.

'I did what needed to be done. Now you had better earn it,' Lavrick told him.

'I intend to.' Martil took his hand back.

'Remember to agree with whatever I say and to show not the slightest hint of doubt or uncertainty,' Onzalez instructed.

Gello sucked in a breath. He, Onzalez and Prent, along with a company of his men and the Dragon Egg, had rushed ahead of the others, so that they reached the city before the spies that the Council undoubtedly had working at the docks had a chance to send a warning.

They had climbed aboard the Tenochs' strange carts, pulled not by horses or donkeys but by something similar, a strange furred creature with a long neck that Onzalez called 'alpaca', which he said came from the continent's mountainous interior. These may not look like horses but they propelled the carts at a good pace through thick jungle, past woodcutters and vast fields, until they reached the city. Gello had little time to sightsee — he was more interested in the city itself, as well as the reception he expected to get.

They were met outside the huge city gates by a detachment of soldiers, as well as a tall Fearpriest and six acolytes. Before Gello could ask who this was, the Fearpriest spoke.

'Brother Onzalez, welcome back to Tenoch! But may I ask why you arrive with such haste, and with strangers from across the sea?' he grated.

Onzalez took a moment to compose himself. 'Brother Horna. I return with momentous news. This is King Gello of Norstalos. He and I bring not only great fortune, but great danger. We have captured an amazing magical treasure. With it in our grasp, the whole world will be at our mercy. The days of Aroaril shall be numbered and the Great God triumphant! But, in desperation, the Aroaril-lovers have sent an army to try and take back this precious magical object, an army that will land on our shores by nightfall. We need to talk to the Council, while the forces our new ally King Gello has brought help secure the city against the army that has pursued us.'

'What is this? An army of Aroaril-lovers, here? I thought you took our army to defeat them? What has happened?' Brother Horna asked slowly.

'The army, along with Nobles Yertlaan and Itlan, and our other ally, King Markuz of Berellia, remains in Norstalos,' Onzalez said blandly. 'The army that has dared to sail here is a pitiful force, no more than a few thousand. It was all the Aroaril-lovers could muster and, once they are destroyed, total victory will be ours. All this, and more, I need to explain to the Council. We cannot waste time here.'

Horna looked over at Gello, who stared back impassively, horribly aware that he had been wearing the same clothes for more than a week and, despite his best efforts to wash them in saltwater, he did not look like a king.

'My men and I are all sworn to Zorva's service. And we shall lead you to victory over the Aroaril-lovers,' Gello stated.

512

'But only if we hurry. Time is against us, Brother,' Onzalez added. 'I must address the Seventeen and we must begin organising the city, gathering our warriors and the people, so that we have a force capable of crushing our foes.'

Horna and the guard officer exchanged looks.

'What is this? Has there been some change since I left? Are my instructions to be ignored now?' Onzalez hissed, taking a step closer.

The guard officer, sweating lightly, bowed deeply. 'Of course not, High One. All shall be ready for you.'

Horna bowed also, although not as deeply. 'Let me escort you to the Seventeen,' he rumbled.

'That is more like it!' Onzalez declared, although Gello could hear the slight tremor in his voice — and wondered if Horna picked it up also.

At Horna's orders more carts were brought out, these ones smaller and more ornate than the carts Gello and Onzalez had arrived in from the docks. More worthy of a king and a Fearpriest, Gello thought.

Horna and his acolytes climbed into a larger cart and led the way into the city.

Onzalez sighed with relief as they rattled through the huge gates. 'All is well,' he told Gello. 'The Seventeen will do whatever I tell them. And our victory shall secure them, once and for all.'

Gello only half listened. Instead he watched the city greedily as he rode through its wide streets. He was fascinated with the amount of gold he could see in the markets, and on both men and women. All but the poorest workers wore something gold as a decoration and some wore as much gold as an average Norstaline worker expected to see in a year.

'Further up the river, the gold flows down from the mountains. The people up there can pick it out of the water, as if the pieces were common stones,' Onzalez explained. 'It is a sign that Zorva favours us. It has little value here but we have been stockpiling it, for use in lesser countries, such as yours.'

Gello bridled at this but the sights passing before his eyes allowed him to forget the insult, a little. The size of the city, the number of people filling its streets was awe-inspiring. To a man raised in Norstalos City, who had been taught that was the world's greatest capital, in the world's greatest country, it was a strange experience seeing something that was both bigger and better. Every house, even the poorest and smallest, was made of stone and lime washed in different colours — although blood-red seemed to be the most popular choice. Some of the carvings, in both wood and stone, were also stunning. They were intricate, featuring both the practical, such as fish over shops that sold fish, as well as decorative. Of the latter, these tended to be strange faces, contorted and agonised.

'They are both a reminder and a celebration of Zorva,' Onzalez explained, as he followed Gello's gaze.

One thing intrigued Gello — the lack of metal. Knives, spears and the axe-clubs the guards all carried featured not familiar steel or even the bronze that Gello's ancestors had used. Instead they had a strange black rock.

'Obsidian. It is found in the mountains, as is the gold, and is another gift from Zorva. It can cut through anything, even be used to shape stone,' Onzalez said expansively. He was enjoying Gello's awe at the sights of the city.

'Why do you not use metal as we do? You have the ability to work with gold, fashion it into shapes. Why do you continue to use this obsidian when steel cuts better and makes better armour than those padded jerkins you use?'

'We do not have the red rocks necessary for iron. I have sent men searching for them, ever since I saw the steel your people use,' Onzalez admitted. 'We may have the ability but we lack the raw materials. Although obsidian does everything a steel blade can.'

'Still, you have to admit steel has uses that rock cannot hope to,' Gello pointed out. 'Perhaps the lesser countries can provide some of the tools for your people?'

Onzalez whipped around but Gello kept his face impassive. That would teach the man to insult Norstalos! 'After we conquer them, of course,' he added blandly.

'Indeed,' Onzalez said after a long moment.

Gello smiled to himself. But the smile did not last long. The city saw to that. Swiftly he found himself both humbled as well as relieved the Tenochs were on his side. His foolish cousin did not know what she would be getting into! The size of the city was astonishing, while he could appreciate why the surrounding countryside was cultivated for many miles around, with a network of intricate irrigation channels and a series of small villages where the workers lived.

He tried to remember it all, so he could tell Mother later. He knew she would be interested.

As he passed endless markets filled with crowds, he felt the stares of thousands of people on him. With his — albeit dirty — tunic and trews, as well as his blond hair and lack of tattoos and piercing, he stood out immediately. But he noticed that all looked down quickly if they caught his eye, and many bowed deeply as the cart went past. As for Onzalez, he seemed to take that as no more than his due.

The bowing became more pronounced as they came closer to the huge Temple, which dominated the skyline. He marvelled at how much effort must have gone into its construction.

'One life for every stone that was laid,' Onzalez told him. 'It was the first, and still is the greatest pyramid in the world.'

The sides and back were smooth, washed white with more lime, while the front was stepped — and stained a rust-brown. Gello did not need to be told why that was.

The carts rumbled around to the back of the Temple, where a walled courtyard was guarded by a dozen warriors.

'We shall take the Egg inside, up to the Council chambers. It is in the middle of the Temple. I'll speak to the Seventeen and then send for you, to introduce you as our valuable ally.'

Gello liked Onzalez's confidence, as his own was ebbing at the sight of the imposing Temple. Still, once past the walled courtyard and the solid gate, the interior of the Temple proved to be luxurious, and the servants almost fell over themselves to offer him food and fresh clothes.

'We do not believe in hardship bringing you closer to your God, like the weaklings of Aroaril,' Onzalez said simply.

Gello surveyed the richly appointed rooms and merely laughed.

'If you need anything, you have but to ask. And I do mean anything,' the Fearpriest told him. 'I shall go now to meet the Seventeen. Do not worry. Zorva is on our side. Nothing can go wrong.'

The docks were not like the ones at Cessor, with wide jetties and large warehouses. These seemed much less permanent, as if the Tenochs could pack them up and move them down the bank if the river's flow was reduced. Lavrick and the other captains tied their ships to the Tenoch craft, then to each other, until the ships stretched across half the river and men had to walk from one to the next to reach the bank.

On the other side of the bank a crude shipyard waited, with a half-completed ship sitting on a slipway down to the river. Piles of timber lay to one side, while the skeleton of the ship seemed an ominous warning to them all.

Unloading the men and supplies took some time as a result, particularly as they all waited while Kay and his rangers searched the other ships and the nearby small settlement to make sure it was no trap. They reported everyone gone and everything useful taken.

Merren watched them search through the small huts, each built on a platform so they were above the ground. All were made of wood, not stone, and seemed somehow insubstantial. They were no cruder than the wood and thatch huts most of the Norstalines lived in but while the roofing was thick and well made, the walls were much simpler and seemed to be more supports for the roof than something to keep out wind and rain. Although, given this was supposed to be their winter, perhaps the cold was not a problem, she mused.

Even though it took a while to empty the ships, the pile of supplies looked small when assembled by the dockside. The bowmen had a few spare sheaves of arrows and a poleaxe each but there was little extra food.

Many of the men were struggling to stand without swaying after being at sea for days, while most of the Derthals just lay down, looking mightily relieved to be back on ground that did not move.

'We shall have to hurry. Even if we had the time, we do not have the provisions for a siege. We shall have to rely on Barrett to help provide, as well as live off the land.' Merren sighed.

Martil pointed to where the biggest of the Tenoch ships was tied up to a special dock further upriver. 'While the men are marshalling, I want to have a look on there,' he declared.

Merren just looked at him

'It's the one that carried Karia. Since I saw it at Dragonara, then again from Argurium's back, I know it. I have to look over there. I have to know that she arrived here safely, see where she slept. It is eating me up,' he admitted.

Merren hesitated for a moment, before nodding. 'Don't take too long,' was all she said.

He ran up the gangplank swiftly, sword in hand. He doubted anyone would be around. And woe betide them, if they had stayed.

But, like all the others, the ship was empty. He went aft, to where most of the cabins waited. He did not even hesitate at the doorway, just went down swiftly, the Sword held before him. The sight of the ripped cabin door, obviously torn with axes, made his heart miss a beat, and he could feel the fear squirting through his body as he pushed through its tattered remnants and into her cabin. It only took a moment to see that she was gone, that there was no other sign of a struggle and no blood or anything that might indicate her death. He looked around carefully, his eyes drawn quickly to a piece of parchment on the bed. He rushed over to it and snatched it up, seeing at once the letters on the front in her familiar crude handwriting: 'Dad'. There was a second one underneath, with a large 'M' on the front. After looking at that for a moment, he put it in his belt pouch and turned to the one with his name on it. He unfolded it with trembling hands and read it swiftly.

Dad, I know you will get this. I know you will come for me. I will make sure I stay safe until then. They think I am the, here she had tried to write 'wielder' but after two attempts had crossed it out and continued, *user of the Dragon Egg. See you soon, love Karia.* And underneath was a crude drawing of the two of them, holding hands, with a large heart shape drawn around them.

He stared at it for a long moment, until it blurred from the tears.

'Hold on. I am coming,' he told her softly, tracing the outline of her head where it had indented the pillow.

He was filled with a terrible purpose. He would get her back, no matter what it took. He tucked the piece of parchment inside his tunic, where it could sit over his heart, then strode away without another look.

He walked back to the docks, where the last men were still crossing from ship to ship and then to dry land. On the shore, the Derthals were getting to their feet now, although they still looked shaky.

'What did you find?' Merren asked nervously as he strode up to her.

'Karia left me a message. She's alive, she's healthy and they are not going to hurt her — yet,' he said softly.

'Thank Aroaril!' Merren smiled and restrained herself from embracing him, not because she could see Sendric watching them, but because of what she saw in his eyes.

'And she left one for you.' Martil held out the second piece of parchment.

Merren took it and read swiftly. *Dear M, look after Dad. Don't let him do anything silly. Miss you. We shall be a family. Love, Karia.*

Merren took a deep breath. She knew she had to focus on the big picture, worry about the Egg before the girl but reading that made it hard. For a moment only her control wavered. *We shall be a family ...*

'I'm ready to lead the men now,' Martil stated.

She looked at him and was reminded of the way he had been just before they had gone to see Count Sendric, when he had slaughtered soldiers who had tried to arrest her. She wished she could hold him back, wished even more she could break through the defences he had put around himself. But she had no choice, they had no time. They had to get the Egg back as soon as possible and she needed him for that.

She pointed to where the various Norstaline, Ralloran and Derthal warriors were slowly forming up. 'What about the order of march? I thought perhaps the rangers first ...'

Martil shook his head. 'Their bows are all wrong for this sort of country. Too big and unwieldy. If I was Gello, I would have a few companies of men in that jungle, ready to ambush us as we march. If they know the country, they could slow us down and hurt us badly before we can get out of there. I think we should send the Derthals in there. There is none better for moving through rough country. I'll lead them myself.'

'Wait!' Merren commanded. 'We need to rest here and begin in the morning. The men — and especially the Derthals — need to regain some strength and we do not want to make a night camp in the jungle.'

'We are right behind them! We cannot give them time to organise,' Martil snarled.

'What good will it do if our men are not ready to fight? That is my order and you will obey it or stay on the ships!' Merren hissed.

Martil struggled for control. 'Right. I'll go and talk to Sacrax.'

Merren watched him go and wracked her brain to think of a way to get through to him. But none came to her.

Sacrax was delighted to be given the chance to lead the way but was happier to hear they could rest and begin the following morning.

'Ground is still moving,' he grumbled. 'My warriors need a night to be better.'

'They'll need to be ready. Gello will have men waiting for you, probably hidden,' Martil warned. 'They have had time to plan for our arrival.'

Sacrax patted the butt of his own spear. 'Good. I like a challenge.'

Despite her fears, Karia had been fascinated by the journey from the docks to the city. The Tenoch docks had plenty of carts and sledges, used to carry goods to and from the city itself. She was sitting in one of these, pulled by an animal she did not recognise but she longed to pat. The cart was hardly comfortable but was high enough to give her a good view of what was going on. The strange forest they had passed through had been like nothing she had seen before. The trees and plants were completely different from the ones she had grown used to, living in the woods with Edil. She had seen small animals with long tails swinging through the trees, which seemed impossibly high, while strange insects swooped through shafts of sunlight. Everywhere she looked there were amazing things to see, while the smell and sound of the jungle was something far out of her experience. Then the jungle had ended abruptly, going from enormous trees to huge stumps in an instant. Forest giants lay where they had fallen, chunks carved off them, while men with strange axe-clubs hurried away, joining a rush back to the city. Beyond them, the remains of a hill, now an open-faced quarry, swarmed with activity. Sledges piled high with blocks of stone waited at the side of the road while hundreds of workers were trudging wearily back to the road, tools over their shoulders.

Beyond were more timber workers, then endless fields. She gasped as she saw the range of them, stretching into the distance as far as she could see. Like the quarry and timber workers, thousands of field workers were streaming back towards the city, dragging carts full of strange food with them. Many of the fields seemed to be filled with tall green plants producing some sort of husk-covered fruit or vegetables. She could see carts full of them, stripped of their leaves to reveal strange, golden-coloured cylinders. Other fields had bushy green plants, which the workers had obviously been digging up before being told to leave, and flee for the city. She passed sledges filled with the roots of these plants, thick purple and brown lumps, twisted and covered in dirt, and stared in wonder. How could people eat such things? On the opposite side of the river, more fields stretched off into the distance, filled with other plants she did not recognise.

All the workers she passed turned dull eyes towards the armed men, before looking away. Some averted their eyes completely, although Karia knew the sight of the renegade Norstalines and Berellians must have been strange. Worse, some of the stone workers stopped to cough, a rasping noise that always seemed to end with them spitting out blood. Karia turned away in horror at the sight of it cutting channels through the stone dust on men's chests.

She focused on the city. It loomed over the plains and the river that wound through the fields. She could remember when the market town of Wollin had seemed huge and mysterious to her. She had grown used to the splendour of Norstalos City but Tenoch made the Norstaline capital look like a provincial town.

The walls were huge, a beautiful golden stone that seemed to catch the sun, the same stone that had been dug out of the quarry. Its towers were huge and square, jutting out every one hundred paces, while the gates were enormous, seemingly made from entire trunks of trees. The problem was, the walls were so huge that she could not see the buildings inside. The only thing that was visible was a stone pyramid. It was a long way away, deep into the city, but still easy to see. A thin trail of smoke rose from the top and, although she did not know why, it filled her with dread. So much so that she called out to Ezok, who rode on the same cart.

'What is that?' she asked, pointing it out

'The Temple of Zorva,' he replied absently.

Karia looked again, then realised what the smoke must be. She decided she did not want to look any more. She closed her eyes, praying softly that Martil would reach her soon.

The trip through the city seemed to take forever. The streets were wide and paved with stone, the houses likewise of the same material. There were markets everywhere, each one selling just one thing. One just had fish, another just meat, one more vegetables and fruit, while others had clothes or jewellery and one even sold men, women and children. She gaped at that, as well as the people dressed in many different ways. Some wore nothing but simple loincloths, some wore plain-coloured tunics, while others wore robes in bright colours. Many of the women, and the men also, had strange tattoos etched into their faces, arms and legs, while others had their faces, ears, eyebrows, cheeks and noses pierced with gold and bone. Some looked away from the strangers, while others stared at them boldly, almost in challenge.

She watched it all, intrigued. Were they all bad people? She watched them and wondered. It seemed to her that the more richly dressed they were, the more gold they wore, the nastier they looked. As for the men, women and children with rope collars around their necks, who followed the rich ones dumbly, she pitied them — and feared what it meant.

But the biggest horror waited at the Temple of Zorva.

It sat alone in the middle of a square, much like the palace at Norstalos City. But it was bare of shops and people, all except a crowd of cheering, chanting men, clustered around the front of the pyramid.

Karia wondered what they were cheering. They all seemed to be looking up towards the top of the tall Temple. The front of it seemed to be stained a strange brown colour. She wondered why, then gasped in shock. Someone had fallen from the top! She watched, horrified, as a body bounced down the rough stone steps. Why was everyone laughing, pointing and cheering? The cart rattled closer and she saw the body land at the bottom. It was picked up by men and thrown onto a pile of others. They were all dead, she saw. At least twenty of them.

She stared, unable to turn away, then looked up to the top of the Temple, where red-robed Fearpriests stood, waving at the crowd.

The lessons of Father Nott, as well as what she had overheard Martil and Merren talking about came back to her then. They were killing people!

She felt sick, and had to look away, or she would surely vomit. She wished she could get her hands on the Egg, so she could bring that whole Temple tumbling to the ground.

Onzalez prepared himself for the Ruling Council of Seventeen meeting and for an expected battle with Brother Horna. From the look he and the guard at the gate had exchanged, it was apparent Horna had been doing some plotting in his absence. It was no surprise. He knew Horna was one of the few that had thought the Albiona expedition a waste of time and effort. The others, even Horna's erstwhile supporters, had listened, spellbound, as Onzalez outlined the tens of thousands of new souls that would bow to Zorva, the power and plunder that would flow into Tenoch. Only Horna had disagreed, before being forced to go along with the majority.

Until Onzalez had made his move, Horna had been the Council's nominal leader — not that there was an official leader — but he was the most influential, used to the Seventeen agreeing with his plans, his ideas. But Onzalez's passion and ambition had been too much for Horna to fight against and had allowed Onzalez to bring the Seventeen under his control. Onzalez's dreams of conquest and expansion had overwhelmed Horna's desire for things to stay unchanged.

But he had to be careful. Horna was always waiting for a chance to seize back control. And, if he did but realise it, this was his perfect opportunity. Just one of Gello's soldiers or an eagle or leopard warrior could let slip that the army was not still fighting in Norstalos — but was dead.

Still, he had a few surprises up his sleeve. The Dragon Egg was one. Gello and his soldiers were another, for the presence of the Norstaline Queen and her lackeys of Aroaril was the most pressing danger to the Seventeen. With no Tenoch army, Gello — and by extension Onzalez — was the power in the city. As long as the rest of the Seventeen thought Gello was under Onzalez's control, he was safe. And he had another plan as well, which he planned only to reveal at the meeting.

He took a little longer to prepare himself, to make sure his face gave nothing away. For the Council room was the only place, apart from the bedchamber, where the Seventeen removed their cowls. Here their faces could be revealed, must be revealed. Secrets were harder to keep then.

Onzalez stepped into the chamber and slipped his cowl from his head, feeling the rare sensation of a breeze on his hair. He nodded and smiled to the other sixteen, who took their places around the circular stone table, designed so that none were seen to be above the others.

He could feel their eyes on his face, especially on the livid scar on his cheek, the memento from his duel with the foul Archbishop of Norstalos. He held his head high.

Servants had placed food and drink on the table, made sure the lanterns were all lit and the table and chairs spotless, then left through a hidden door before the first of the Seventeen entered. All was as it had been before he left, he reflected as he took his seat.

'Brother Onzalez has returned to us after more than a year on the southern continent of Albiona, bringing with him strange warriors and stranger tidings. I think we should hear from him now,' Brother Horna said and, almost before he had finished, Onzalez had pushed back his chair to stand.

With a mild smile, he began with his best news, that virtually the entire country of Berellia had been converted to worship of Zorva and the acolytes he had taken with him were even now finishing that job, while a second country, Norstalos, was almost within their grasp. He went on to tell them about the Dragon Egg and how its power had drawn the Aroaril-lovers across the sea.

'They have brought all the leaders of Aroaril's resistance with them,' Onzalez explained, 'in a desperate attempt to seize back this Egg, their last hope to destroy us. They thought us at a disadvantage but all we need to do is defeat this pitiably small force and the entire continent is ours. Without their Witch Queen, they will fall apart. We just need to raise the city against the invaders and everything I predicted will come to pass.'

'Witch Queen?' Horna asked sharply.

'How she is known by true followers of Zorva on the other continent. She is strong with Aroaril and while she has no magic herself, she commands men who use magic, priests of Aroaril with power and a warrior with a magic sword. But once she is gone, they are nothing and we shall rule!'

He expected to see nods and smiles of agreement — but felt a moment's terror grip his heart when the other Fearpriests turned to Horna.

'Why have the leaders brought their best soldiers all the way here, when they are locked in a war back in their homeland? And an egg? How can that be more powerful than we are? I warn you Onzalez, the Seventeen are not your unthinking lackeys. There are things you are not telling us!' Horna thundered.

Onzalez met his gaze calmly. 'It is not "an egg". It is the most powerful magical object in the entire world. It is a creation of the dragons, that we took from them and the last hope of the Aroaril-worshippers. Once you see it in action, you shall believe me! As to the ways of the Aroaril-lovers, who can say what madness drives them? But we can be sure of one thing. They have put themselves at our mercy by coming here. We must take immediate action to give victory to Zorva. Trust me as you always have, support me as you should and, with my ally King Gello, we shall destroy these impudent Aroaril-worshippers and then you may join us in returning to the southern continent in triumph!'

'Brothers, we have spoken about this. The Council is not hostage to the whims and ambitions of Brother Onzalez! We do not have to do whatever he tells us to. I propose we investigate this further, speak to the soldiers who have returned —'

'Brothers, your choice is simple,' Onzalez interrupted. 'All I want to do is crush this army of Aroaril-lovers and see glory come to Zorva! All you have to do is give me permission to win this last battle. Give me the power and authority to crush the Aroaril-lovers and give us the final victory. If I fail, then I shall present myself to the Seventeen for their judgment —'

'Let us vote on it,' Horna fired back.

Onzalez smiled coldly. 'Of course. But, before we vote, I should also point out that we need an extra chair in here.'

'What nonsense is this?' Horna protested. 'No new member of the Council has been appointed! Or do you see yourself above the Seventeen, given a new position perhaps?'

'No. But, with our success in Norstalos, I introduce you to the representative from that country, Brother Prent!'

With that, the door opened and Prent strode in, pulling the cowl from his face as he did so.

The room erupted immediately, with Fearpriests shouting at each other, and it was some time before calm was restored.

'We cannot add another to the Council!' Horna summed up the opposition.

'We can and we must. It is a law of the Council that every new city added to the Tenoch empire will have a priest to represent it on the Ruling Council,' Onzalez said triumphantly.

'Brother Onzalez is right,' croaked the oldest Fearpriest. 'I can still remember when we were the Sixteen. Now we must be the Eighteen.'

A quick vote showed twelve of the Seventeen agreed with him.

Onzalez acknowledged his victory with a smile at Horna, although inside he worried how Horna had managed to tie four other Fearpriests to his side so well.

'And now to the real question — will you allow me to crush this army of Aroaril-lovers and ensure final victory for Zorva?' Onzalez offered.

This time the vote was closer, with seven of the eighteen against him. Onzalez had won — but the extent of the opposition was disconcerting.

'You have your wish, Brother,' Horna said through gritted teeth. 'But do not let us down.'

'You may rely on me,' Onzalez assured him.

24

'How is this possible?' Onzalez screamed.

The two scouts pressed themselves into the ground, trembling.

'We do not know, High One. But we have seen it with our own eyes. Their ships have sailed up the entire river and are moored at the docks. They slept there last night and are now marching towards us,' the scout cried.

'We still have time,' Gello said confidently. 'The march through the jungle will take them most of the day, thanks to the men we have hidden there. And they will suffer for every pace they take.'

Onzalez let out his breath with a hiss.

'Go back to the jungle. Find my warriors and report to me on the progress of our enemies,' he ordered.

'At once, High One!' The two scouts crawled backwards on their bellies, then got up and ran.

'This is nothing to be concerned about,' Gello repeated complacently.

Yesterday he had waited nervously in his rooms, begging his sketch of Mother to comfort him. But there was nothing. To sit in a room, no matter how comfortable, without a glimpse of sun, hearing faint screams as another sacrifice was dragged up the stairs to their doom ... it was hard not to feel fear there, in the heart of the Fearpriest empire and he even had a moment when he wondered what would have happened had he accepted Merren's offer and joined his men to hers to defeat the Tenochs and Berellians. But then he had looked again at Mother's picture. He was destined to rule! He would never share power with anyone, let alone a woman! To do otherwise would betray everything Mother had taught him. Of late, he had been relying more and more on Mother's picture, telling it all his woes, all his hopes and plans. But, sitting there in that room, he realised he could put it aside. He could stand on his own feet. He did not need her.

So he had walked into the Ruling Council's chamber proudly and been welcomed warmly. But despite the pledges of allegiance and a vote of thanks for his aid, he had sensed the hatred for Onzalez radiating from several of the Fearpriests around the table.

'King Gello, I am pleased to announce that the Eighteen has decided you are a valued ally. We expect you to lead this city to victory over the rabble of Aroaril-lovers who have followed us here,' Onzalez had said gravely.

'My men, who are all sworn to Zorva's service, will be happy to give you this victory,' Gello bowed slightly.

'You must return to your men now, to prepare for the arrival of the Aroaril-lovers,' Onzalez continued.

Gello inclined his head, his eyes on the rest of the Fearpriests. Onzalez was playing a dangerous game here. If they beat Merren and her rabble, all would be fine but if they failed …

He had led his men back to the gates to be ready for what the next day would bring — and after he had arranged with Onzalez for wine, food and women to be sent to entertain them.

Gello had slept late, after a night of drink and debauchery, but had been pleasantly surprised by the sheer mass waiting for him outside the front gate, along with an impatient Onzalez. The Fearpriests and their soldiers had been through the city during the night and made sure every man had made his way to the gates at dawn. There were stoneworkers, with dust still caking their hair, clutching stone picks, hammers and chisels, farm workers with wooden spades, hoes and rakes, as well as shopkeepers and labourers with obsidian knives and clubs. As far as warriors went, there were only a few hundred of those, as well as Gello's own Norstalines and the Berellians he had rescued. But he had climbed one of the tall gate towers to gaze down on the men assembled and been unable to count them. Fifty thousand perhaps. Even more! They would be unstoppable. Merren and her pack of dogs would be outnumbered more than fifteen to one. True, only about one in twenty had armour or a weapon but not even those damned Rallorans could stand against so many!

'We'll send a few thousand of your true believers out in front, let Merren's bowmen use up their arrows on them. Then we'll send in our trained men, with endless thousands behind them. We'll drive them into the river, kill every last one of them ...'

'No!' Onzalez interrupted.

'No?' Gello stared at him in astonishment.

'We need sacrifices! As many as we can get!'

Gello grinned. It would be that easy! No army could stand against such a multitude as they had assembled! And then all that remained was to sail back to Norstalos and snap it up.

* * *

The jungle was silent as the grave. The birds and animals had melted away. Only the insects remained, eager to sting and bite at the men who crept through the undergrowth.

Martil led the armoured and sweating Elfarans forwards. They were the bait. And they had volunteered for the task, for all knew their time left in the world was limited. Martil would not let them go alone — or at least that was what he had told Merren. In truth, he wanted to let the Dragon Sword loose on those he knew were waiting for them. The warm, damp smell of the jungle filled their noses, while it was impossible not to glance at the tall trees and strange undergrowth, so unlike the forests they knew at home. But while small trees and strange bushes lined the wide trail through the jungle, beyond that it was relatively open and easy to see through. Sweat was pouring off them, both from the effect of wearing all that leather and steel on a hot day — and from the thought of what waited for them. Although they had not faced more than a few spears thrown from the trees. With Barrett using birds to spot Tenochs, it was easy for the Derthals to spring an ambush on those in hiding. Merren had been concerned about how the Derthals would recover from the sea voyage but it seemed a night on the land was all they needed. They had been awake at first light, looking as though they had just walked out of their mountains. Sacrax and his warriors were circling around a band now. They did not need Martil, although he would sprint forwards to join the fight nevertheless. And the way the Dragon Sword cut apart even the best and bravest Tenochs was making others run.

A safe distance behind, Merren wiped sweat off her brow that was only partly due to the heat.

They had avoided the traps in the river, while Barrett, Martil and Sacrax were ensuring their passage through to the city was relatively safe. But looming over them, occasionally visible through the trees, was the city of Tenoch. The sheer size of the towers alone had men talking. And what would be waiting for them on the walls — or even outside the gate? They were making such good progress — or were they just walking into the biggest trap of all? But there could be no slowing down. The dragon Argurium had been left behind at the docks. The magical passage across the ocean had exhausted her, Havell said — or perhaps it was just her end was near. Merren had not really wanted to know. She had enough worries on her mind as it was. But one thing was clear — they had little time left and Merren felt acutely the weight of responsibility on her shoulders.

And she worried about Martil, who would have to complete the ceremony but seemed to be slipping further away from her every day.

Karia knew something was going on — but nobody was telling her anything and nobody had been to see her, either. Which was fine by her — she did not want to meet any of the Fearpriests. She had been placed in a comfortable room, given food and drink — and then forgotten about.

She was a little frightened but she was mainly bored. She just hoped all the rushing around in the Temple and the trumpets and gongs meant that Martil was coming to get her.

'Say that again,' Gello demanded.

The remaining eagle and leopard warriors stood resignedly, knowing their fate.

'Every ambush we tried has failed,' one reported. 'Each time we prepared a trap, the demons of Aroaril who defeated us before the Norstaline capital struck and killed our brothers. We could not see them, or hear them. But they fell on us and we could not stop them, nor the warrior with the sword-that-cuts-through-everything.'

Gello saw their eyes darting towards where a fuming Onzalez waited.

'You did all you could. Now rejoin the rest of the city's warriors. We shall need every man we have,' he told them.

Astonished, the warriors just stood there.

'Now!' Gello barked. 'Our enemies shall be upon us soon!'

They almost ran away.

'Why?' Onzalez asked.

'Every man in this army saw the city's best warriors running away in fear of their lives,' Gello replied. 'They need to think it was all part of our plan, that we are merely luring our enemies out, so they can be destroyed. Having confident men is worth far more than the satisfaction in killing two score of fools who could not even spring an ambush!'

Onzalez sighed. 'You are right. But we cannot fail again!' The thought of what Brother Horna was saying and planning was always in the back of his mind.

'I know. But we still have all the advantages. They will march upon us and be destroyed, as simple as that.'

The march from the docks to the city had left the men tired and sweaty. That could have been a problem, for the river water was not safe to drink. Tainted by the sewage and detritus of a major city, it was more deadly than the failed ambushes. But the Magicians' Guild was purifying the water as fast as it could be brought up from the river, so men drank greedily as the waterskins were passed around.

First had come the ambushes from the trees, although those had been dealt with easily by the Derthals. Then they had seen the camp of the woodcutters, with the huge trees lying where they had fallen, leaves and sawdust thick on the ground. That had made them curious, as had the stone quarry. Merren had worked out they were using fire to heat the rock, then water to cool it, forcing the rocks to crack, where they could be cut out with the Tenochs' tools. The sight of several dead workers, dragged off to one side, showed it was not without risk.

But that was nothing compared to the huge pit that Sacrax had found, almost filled with bodies, all with the tell-tale slash below the ribs that showed they had had their hearts cut out. The Derthals scared off the animals who had been feasting on the dead, while a flock of birds took off to reveal the ghastly discovery. Men, women and children all lay in that pit — Merren did not want to think about how deep it went. It seemed to heave and move as they watched, as ants and other insects, who did not care about the presence of armed men, went about their meal. The smell, in the heat, was indescribable, and even men who had walked across entrail-strewn battlefields with a smile had to hurry past, trying not to vomit.

There was nothing they could do for those poor people, beyond what they were trying to do now, although it affected them all. There were more bodies in that pit than there were in Merren's little army and it was hard not to contrast that with the size of Tenoch, which was getting closer with every pace.

Without Argurium, Barrett had sent forwards several birds — not the ones they had found tearing at the corpses of the sacrifices, but brightly coloured ones with strange beaks.

'Once the jungle finishes, we shall walk into fields before we reach the city. If we reach the city. They have a massive army waiting for us,' he had reported. 'They do not wait on the walls but outside. They must think they can crush us.'

Merren decided to let the men wait and rest, eat and drink in the shade of the trees before going further. The march had already left many of the men nervous and what they had seen had left them feeling small and insignificant. So she did not want to march out until she had talked to them and boosted their confidence — starting with the officers and sergeants.

'As soon as we go out there, they will attack us,' she stated. 'We must be ready for that. I am worried that seeing such a large force, outside that massive city, will affect the men ...'

'They will not be able to stop us. Trust me, we shall slice through them,' Martil said immediately. 'They have barely two thousand warriors. The rest are like sheep — easily scattered and put to fright. We shall slaughter them!'

The answering roar from the men around him was both heartening and frightening to Merren, and she stepped forwards to gain control once more.

'The river shall protect our right flank, so they shall have to come at us from the front and left. Most likely they will send a few thousand men out to be slaughtered, thinking that we will use up our arrows on them, then they will send in their warriors to lead the rest. But we shall keep our bowmen in reserve. Our shield wall shall deal with the first attack, then we shall have arrows to destroy the trained men and put the rest to flight. As long as we keep our ranks and our discipline, we shall be in little danger,' she finished, with a confidence she did not entirely feel.

'Aye. A mob does not stand a chance against trained men, as I have said many a time. Now you shall see what I mean,' Martil added grimly.

Merren looked around the circle of officers and sergeants.

'We shall be facing the largest army any of us has seen. But we shall defeat it. Trust in me, trust in each other and we shall win!'

'We'll kill them all!' Martil shouted.

To Merren's delight and concern, they answered him with a bloodthirsty roar.

She, Martil and her officers went around to the various companies, spreading the message of hope and defiance. Finally, Merren felt they were as ready as they could be. Any longer and they would lose their edge.

She took a deep breath. Sendric, Pilleth, the capital and now this. The build-up to each had been very different but all had been gut-wrenching. She prayed this would be the last battle — for all the right reasons.

The small army poured out of the shade of the jungle and into the bright sun. Still several miles away, the huge city of Tenoch dominated the farmland around but they marched across the fields, ignoring the fallen farming tools and crops that the Tenochs had left when they had fled for the city. Merren did not like pushing on like this, charging at a massive force — but they had little choice. Time was against them — and besides, she did not think she would be able to hold Martil back any longer, not when Karia was so close. She suspected that many of the men facing them did not want to be there and might even be on their side, if they only had the chance. But she would have to defeat them before that would become a possibility.

As for Martil, his only thought was to smash through the men facing them and get to Karia. If the other men were picking up his mood, then that was fine by him. He did not care about the dreams, about what they might mean for him. He couldn't. Nothing could stop him now. Nothing.

Gello watched the advance from the safety of one of the gate towers. Onzalez stood with him, as did a score of trumpeters and men with huge coloured flags, ready to relay instructions to Feld, Livett and Heath. These three would direct the battle for Gello and had been drilled as to what each trumpet call and flag colour meant. They all knew what must be done anyway — the flags and trumpets would just tell them when. The one drawback with having so many men was that the army was unwieldy. Orders took an age to reach the different parts of the army and half of the Tenoch warriors had been forced to act as sergeants to the mass of conscripts, for otherwise Gello could not trust them to follow his orders. Fear would make them obey him, as well as the pack mentality. When others advanced, most would follow.

It had been a nervous wait, wondering what trickery Merren and Martil might be cooking up in the tree line. Would there be thousands of goblins pouring out, as the ambushed warriors had fearfully warned? Onzalez could feel the pressure acutely. Win this battle and his position was secure. Lose, and he was dead.

As for Gello, his imagination had too much time to work. Time and again, at his moment of triumph, he had been thwarted. Once again he had a chance to utterly destroy his cousin — surely he could not fail again?

At least the mystery of the demon from Dragonara Isle had been revealed: from the description of the warrior with the sword that cuts through anything, he had deduced it was Martil. Still, it was not much comfort.

He chewed his nails as he paced up and down the battlement, refusing food and wine, drinking only water.

'Sire! High One! Here they are!'

The cry went up immediately and Gello rushed to the wall, peering across the wide fields, to the small army that advanced boldly out of the trees.

'They have the Rallorans up front, followed by Norstalines, with the bowmen behind and then the goblins and elves,' Gello declared, after looking at the flags they held high.

'Is that all there are?' Onzalez asked.

Gello looked again, then glanced at Onzalez and grinned. The grin became a laugh, one echoed by the Fearpriest. Her army was so small it was laughable! Looking from her pitiable ranks to the mass of men waiting for them was ridiculous. Both men could feel their fear and doubt melt away, like ice under the warm Tenoch sun.

'Send out the sacrifices! Let them waste their arrows!' Gello ordered.

Onzalez and his Fearpriests had found several thousand men, sons of the city's ruling families, who embraced the chance to serve Zorva. Once told of the joys that awaited them in Zorva's realm, they had been eager to throw themselves at the foreign demons. With them, too, went a company of Tenoch warriors, to lead the way. Most of these would die, slaughtered by the Norstaline bowmen. But their deaths would open the way for the Berellian and Norstaline shield wall, led by Feld, that waited behind them. Still, they outnumbered Merren's little army all by themselves — and Onzalez had even suggested they alone could win the battle.

The trumpets sounded and red flags were lifted by a score of men, the bright colours easily visible from down below.

It took a while, and it was a frustrating wait, but the advance of the first wave showed Gello his orders had been received.

'Now feel terror, my dear cousin,' Gello muttered.

Merren watched her men form the battleline and thought her heart might break with pride. They were massively outnumbered — but none hesitated or turned away. There was fear — there had to be when faced with such odds. But beyond a few men breaking ranks to relieve themselves, and too many laughing too hard at bad jokes, she could see little sign of it.

The flags and calls from the city walls warned them there was going to be an attack, but it seemed to take an age to form up.

'They have learned nothing from their mistakes,' Martil laughed. 'That is not an army — it is a rabble!' He prowled up and down the front of the lines, encouraging the men, while Merren rode behind the line, doing the same thing, and Milly and Kesbury offered blessings and prayers to any who wanted them.

'Hold hard! You know why we fight, what we seek to save!' she told them, time and again.

'Here they come!' Nerrin's shout made her turn, to see Gello's massive army finally stir itself into motion, thousands of men running towards them. She could not restrain a swallow of fear as she saw it, as well as what waited behind, but she forced herself to look not just impassive, but uncaring. They had to take heart from her, she decided.

'Make ready!' Martil roared, pushing into the lines as the wave of attackers raced at them. 'Brace! Hold hard!'

Merren had been concerned about such a number of men striking her small force and had suggested Kay and his bowmen loose two volleys of arrows, to break up and slow down the attack. Although every arrow was precious, Martil had agreed.

So now Merren signalled to Kay, who led his bowmen in releasing just two arrows apiece. But that was still thousands of arrows, which now arched down out of the sky.

Martil watched the first ranks of the charge just disappear as men fell, snatched down in mid-stride by the strike of the arrows. None of these men wore armour, and had no protection against the steel-tipped shafts.

Disorganised now, as faster runners and survivors drew ahead of the others, the charge crashed into the shield wall — and was thrown back like a wave striking a stone wall. Nerrin and the Rallorans in the front two ranks used their shields as weapons, smashing men off their feet, while Hutter and Kettering marshalled the Norstalines in the third rank, using their spears to great effect in the gaps between shields, the heavy iron heads punching into men. In an instant a pile of bodies obstructed the rest of the attackers, slowed their charge and made it much easier to deal with.

Martil, in the third rank, saw there was little he had to do. Their attackers were using clubs, knives and other crude weapons. Hitting men armoured with mail and shields with these was pointless — the few that managed to land blows watched them bounce off Ralloran shields and armour. It was all too easy. His men had been hardened by years of warfare, while their attackers had never fought before. They would have been a waste of arrows — which was why they had been sent out. Merren had said many of these men had been tricked or forced by the Fearpriests into fighting but they were still the men behind Karia's abduction. It was time to make them pay.

He pushed himself into the front rank, as usual without a shield, and dared the Tenochs to come close. Any that did were cut down mercilessly. The slaughter went on, until the pressure on the front line slackened — Martil could see the remnants were hanging back, reluctant to cross the barrier of dead and wounded in front of them. He did not want to let them off so easily.

'Forwards!' he ordered instantly. 'Wedge formation!'

The Ralloran line slipped into its distinctive wedges, led by its best warriors, and pushed forwards, men using their shields as weapons to smash through the Tenochs once more. The Norstalines in the ranks behind added their weight to the advance, finishing off any wounded they stepped across. The Tenochs were helpless against such an attack, which sent them reeling backwards. Fanatic Tenochs tried to attack the armoured lines but it was like a small child beating at a wall with a stick. Martil could see them beginning to glance over their shoulders and pushed back until he could signal to his standard bearer, Sergeant Redder.

Merren saw the standard dip thrice and waved to where Sacrax and Havell waited.

The Derthal High Chief waved in return and then led his warriors around the open flank.

Howling and screaming, the Derthals and Elfarans smashed into the wavering Tenochs.

It was the final straw. The Tenochs turned tail and ran, throwing away their crude weapons, anything that would slow them down.

Martil wanted to chase them down but knew there would be far more to come. He was looking forward to it.

'Let them go! Back to our positions!' Martil ordered. 'Get some water up here!'

Men were already sweating from the warmth of the sun and the weight of the mail. Again the Magician's Guild had to refill the waterskins.

'Good work, lads! We'll let Kay and his bowmen deal with the next one!' Martil encouraged them. Only four men were dead, a dozen wounded, while the rest grinned back as they sharpened swords and spears and waited for the next attack.

'Cowards! They deserve to die!' Gello spat as he saw the men running back towards the city. He had not expected that first attack to win but it had still been a blow to see it beaten off so easily. The confidence that had filled him drained away, just a little.

'They were always going to die,' Onzalez said calmly. 'Ignore them. We have many more men. It is early yet. Our only concern is they defeated them without using up their arrows.'

'Agreed. We need to change the plan!' Gello growled.

'We cannot change the plan!' Onzalez exclaimed. 'Look down there! How long will it take to reorganise them all?'

Gello did not have to look at the seething mass below to know the Fearpriest was right. It was beyond organisation. All they could do was point it at their enemies and set them loose.

'Then we attack with everything we have!' he snarled, waving to the flag bearers.

Merren had the men sit, sheathe swords and lay down spears and shields. There was no point in wasting energy they would need later. Some men tried the strange cylindrical vegetable being grown in the next field, trying to chew the golden segments — and pronouncing them too hard to stomach. Others tried the green leaves of the plant underfoot — the ones not stained by blood and gore — and spat them out again, declaring they were revolting.

'How do they eat this stuff?' Dunner held up one of the plants, complete with swollen brown tubers underneath, for the men to laugh at, picked off a leaf, chewed it then made a face.

Merren let them enjoy themselves, while secretly asking Barrett about them.

'The golden cylinder needs to be boiled, or ground into a powder, like wheat into flour,' he announced, after studying them both. 'As to the other plant, you don't eat the leaves, you wash the tubers and cook them.'

They had plenty of time to talk, for it took the best part of a turn of the hourglass before the swirling mass of men outside the city resolved itself into an attack.

She had spoken with Havell, tried to reassure the Elfaran they would be able to break into the city — and that she would be able to control Martil. And she had tried to avoid Sendric, who only wanted to talk about the danger Martil posed.

'There's so many!' Merren gasped, as they came on, trampling down crops in a wide swathe.

'This is the one. As long as we kill off their trained men, we'll send the rest running, like we did with the others,' Martil declared. 'Then we won't stop until we're in the city!'

Merren did not like the sound of that but, equally, did not want to begin an argument just before a battle.

'We're ready,' Kay said into the silence. 'We'll drive them back.'

'Then Aroaril go with you.' Merren nodded. 'You know what to do.'

While Martil rejoined the line, Kay led his bowmen out to the left of the shield wall, arranging them in two ranks.

'First line aim at their front, second line drop them down from above. Let them get close!' he told them, not particularly raising his voice. 'Pick your targets and don't waste a shaft!'

On and on the horde came, bunching behind a tight line of trained men in armour — the Berellians and renegade Norstalines. But many of these did not have shields and their armour would not save them against Kay's bowmen with their bodkin arrows. The traditional broad heads would be saved for the shieldless ranks behind.

Kay watched the advance dispassionately. The Tenochs were shouting something, while drums and horns were sounding a ragged beat. It sounded and looked frightening, but looks were deceiving. Each of his bowmen had a full sheaf of arrows pushed into the soft earth at their feet, ready to be snatched up and used in an instant, while another sheaf was at their belt. A company of Hutter's men stood ready as well, spare sheaves slung over their shoulders, ready to bring them wherever they were needed.

Martil watched Kay almost as much as he

watched the Tenoch advance. He wanted to see those armoured men falling and he was almost ready to issue an order himself when Kay finally moved.

'Nock and draw!' he yelled.

The noise of more than fifteen hundred longbow strings being drawn back to the ears was like the first warning rumble of thunder.

'Loose!'

The thrum of the bows' release, followed by the hiss of the arrows in flight seemed to silence the Tenoch advance.

'Draw and loose! Fast as you can!' Kay shouted, in the instant before the arrows struck home with devastating effect.

Men fell screaming, or cowered under the arrow storm. Behind them, the rest of the Tenoch advance continued onwards, pushing the Berellians and renegade Norstalines forwards, into the arrows. With hundreds of shafts falling every moment, either coming down steeply from the sky, or snapping in fast and straight, it was impossible to defend against. There were just not enough shields. But there was no escape. All the time they were being pushed forwards by the solid block of men behind. And the wounded were being trampled by the following ranks.

And as more and more of the Berellians and Norstalines fell, those ranks, men without armour or shields or proper weapons, were exposed to the merciless arrows. Many of the Berellians and Norstalines were trying to push their way back to safety. Those on the right side of the advance, away from the river, ran into the open fields rather than go to their deaths.

'Pick your targets!' Kay bellowed, and the two lines of bowmen merged into one.

Most had already used up their first sheaf, and the men with the spare sheaves were kept busy, racing up and down the line.

Merren gazed in awe at the mass of men pushing forwards. But the pace of the advance had slowed dramatically. Nobody wanted to be in the front line. The bowmen aimed and sighted coolly, sending shaft after shaft whipping into that mass. Each one punched a man from his feet; some even pierced a second man behind. At barely seventy paces, it was almost too easy for the bowmen to hit. And the Tenochs were packed so tight, that even if they missed one target, they almost certainly hit another. The sheer number of bodies, of moaning, bleeding, screaming wounded, was making an advance impossible. The Tenochs tried to push around to their right, away from the river, towards the open fields — but not to outflank the Queen's army. Instead, men who found themselves no longer a target of the bowmen began edging back towards the city.

Some Tenochs, obviously the city's warriors, were screaming at men, pushing them forwards. But such actions instantly made them a prime target. Riddled with arrows, they inevitably fell. As for the remainder of the Berellians and renegade Norstalines — they were either dead, wounded or pretending to be dead.

It was slaughter, but Martil knew it could not last. Already the pile of spare arrow sheaves was almost gone. He pushed forwards to where Kay was sending shaft after shaft into the Tenochs.

'Switch your aim to those behind! The ones behind cannot see what is happening!' he pointed.

Kay loosed one more shaft, then lowered his bow.

'And the ones close to us?'

'We shall deal with them,' Martil promised.

'Yes, sir!' He began to pace along the line. 'Raise your aim! Target the ones at the back!'

Again arrows began to darken the sky, falling on the mass of Tenochs still blindly marching forwards. Martil could see most of the archers were now down to their last few arrows and many were grimacing with the effort of drawing the huge bows now.

The Tenochs at the front of the advance had been hunched over like men avoiding a fierce storm, which it was, with steel-tipped rain. Now the ones further back ducked and tried to cover their head with their arms — which was futile, for the arrows fell with enough force to drive the arrowheads through flesh and bone and into the heads beneath.

'Shield wall forwards!' Martil roared. 'Let them hear you coming!'

With a bellow, they charged into the mass of men milling around aimlessly. The Tenochs tried to attack the solid line of metal and wood advancing towards them and were brushed aside. Martil cut and slashed furiously, dealing death and wounds with every sweep of the Dragon Sword. Beside him Rallorans and Norstalines pushed forwards, shields punching men off their feet, where the rear ranks could finish off the fallen. Anger raced through Martil. These men were stopping him from getting to Karia — and they paid the penalty for it.

Assaulted from above, unable to face the implacable advance of the shield wall, the Tenochs wavered. Many looked at the crude weapons they had — picks and spades — threw them down and turned to run, pushing through the men behind.

'Back! Back! Flee! Run for your lives!'

Martil could hear the cries of terror, even over the shouts of his men and the screams of the wounded Tenochs. But he could not feel pity. Instead he pushed onwards, leading his men over the piles of sobbing, screaming wounded and the silent dead.

The Tenochs closest to the Ralloran-led line were now near to panic, actually fighting their fellows in an attempt to get away. For those behind, already afraid because of the arrows that still fell from the sky, hearing and seeing the men around them going down dead and wounded, it was too much.

One moment there was a solid mass of men, a seemingly unstoppable force that would roll right over the small allied army. Next instant, it dissolved. Men threw away what weapons they had and ran for the gate, trampling each other in the rush, pushing, shoving and fighting to get past their fellows and be the first to safety. The few remaining Tenoch warriors who tried to stop the panic were trampled down — most simply joined the rush to the gates, along with the handful of Berellians and Norstalines who had survived the massacre.

'Keep going!' Martil bellowed. The first inclination for the men was to stop, for the battle was won. But beyond the mob, the open gates of the city beckoned. This was the full strength of the Tenochs. If he could drive his armoured wedges through that panicked mass, he would be inside the city and surely Karia and the Egg would not be far away.

'Push through them!' Martil waved his men on.

In front of them, thousands of men lay dead or dying, weeping, screaming and pleading, with arrows deep in their flesh. They lay in piles, atop each other, in a thick carpet that stretched back towards the city. The struggling, pulsating mass of Tenochs, fighting to get into the safety of the city, was adding more to the pile every moment, as men were trampled or crushed.

'Hold!'

Martil turned, to see Merren galloping forwards.

'Hold your positions!' she ordered.

Instantly the men stopped.

Martil raced over to where Tomon was picking his way past the dead.

'What are you doing?' he cried. 'The city is at our mercy! Karia and the Egg will be just inside …'

She looked down at him sternly. 'Bellic,' she said simply.

'This is different! This is Karia,' he snarled at her.

'You go in there and it will be Bellic all over again. We slaughtered shopkeepers, labourers and slaves just then. We had no choice, because they sent them against us. But to pursue them will be murder. And while they run now, if you break into that city, they will try to protect their families. What if there are hundreds of women and children in a crowd of men between you and Karia? Will you kill them to get to her?'

Martil, covered in blood and gore, just stared at her. 'These are the men who took Karia, who took the Egg and brought us here. These are the men who rampaged through your country, killing men, women and children! How can you care what happens to them?'

'Because I am not like my cousin! And because I also care about what it will do to you and the other men I led here!'

'I will do whatever it takes to get Karia back,' he vowed. 'And if you try and stop me, I will order my Rallorans to follow me. You will have to fight us to keep me from saving Karia.'

'Listen to me!' Merren jumped down, so she could face him. Up close he looked even worse, wild eyes glaring out of a mask of other men's blood.

'This is it,' she told him. 'The decision that will forever define you. You can take men into that city and you might even be able to carve your way to

Karia. But you will be as good as dead and she will hate you for it.'

'What?'

'If the Dragon Sword does not kill you, your conscience will. You will wake up one day and realise what you have done is far worse than Bellic. For most of the people in that city hate the Fearpriests as much as we do and will welcome us as liberators if only we let them. At least the Berellians of Bellic were fighting back. These poor people only fight because the Fearpriests will kill their families if they don't! Do this and you doom yourself. Do you think Karia will thank you when you leave her alone? When the Sword takes your life because you wanted to slaughter innocent people?'

'She will be alive, that is enough!'

'No it is not!' Merren blazed. 'This is your choice. Life or death. Life with Karia, the baby and me or a lonely, bitter death, drowned in blood and nightmares.'

He stared coldly at her. 'I have to get Karia. I promised her,' he stated.

'We can still get her out! Just not like this.'

He shook his head, prepared to push past her.

She reached out once more, putting everything she felt about him into her words.

'You can have everything you want — a wife and family who love you — or every death you want. But you can't have both. Martil, I love you! I had to turn you away to realise how much. I made the worst mistake of my life letting you go. I know that and I'm trying to make up for it. I don't want to live without you! Take my hand, stay with me!'

Martil's rage, that had served him so well in the past, told him to carve his way into Tenoch. The gates were open, the city was at his mercy. But her words touched something within him. They were an echo of what she had said in his dream, when he had escaped from the nightmare of Bellic. The dream that hovered round him still, since he had vowed to get back Karia, no matter what. In that instant, he saw the two paths his life could go down. The two futures were crystal clear. There was the Martil-he-had-been, the angry man who killed without remorse, for no good reason and the Martil-as-he-could-be, who had learned from Karia and Merren that there was more to life. The screams and howls of the fleeing Tenochs bit into his brain and he knew instinctively they would never leave him if he gave in to his anger and put Tenoch to the Sword. Karia would not want him to do that. He had to rescue her and would happily sacrifice himself to do that but he did not want to save her only to leave her orphaned again. And then there was Merren. Despite his earlier words to her, he wanted Merren, he wanted their child, he wanted peace. He did not move but he turned his back on the old Martil. He dropped his swords, one covered in blood, one spotlessly clean and fell into her arms.

'Promise me. Promise me we'll get her back!'

She kissed him then, heedless of the blood that smeared over her face.

'We will get her back,' she told him.

Then he was crying, for the first time since Karia had gone, the anger and fear draining out of him with his tears.

She held him close until he opened his eyes and she could see the Martil that she loved was back again.

'What now?' he asked, finally.

'We help the wounded. We bring them back up to the gates and invite the city to surrender.'

'And if they do not?'

'Then we shall find another way in. But first we need to collect the wounded and show the city that we are not the monsters their evil masters claim we are.'

Gello gazed open-mouthed with horror as his grand army dissolved and raced back to the city, men fighting each other to reach safety first.

'How can this be possible?' Onzalez howled.

Gello could not answer. He had no idea. He looked across the field, to where Merren's soldiers had stopped their advance. His men had been massacred — he could see only a handful of men in armour joining the rush for the gate. Feld, Livett, Heath — they must all be dead as well. It had happened yet again and this time his mind was numb with the horror of it. There was nowhere to run to.

'You're the warrior King! Think of something! Aroaril's minions will be here soon and we cannot stop them!' Onzalez grabbed Gello's tunic and screamed into his face.

It snapped Gello out of his trance and he freed himself with a snarl, feeling his mind come back into focus. Everyone who could help him was dead, or useless. It was down to him. Time to see if he really could stand alone, without Mother.

'Seal the gates. We will have a few warriors still. With the gates shut, they will not be able to get inside. They have too few men, and no siege equipment,' he declared. 'And I thought you Fearpriests were strong enough to defeat any enemy by yourself?'

'I cannot risk it! Not after what happened outside the Norstaline capital! If the people of Tenoch were to see me defeated by one of Aroaril's foul priests ...'

Gello nodded as he saw where Onzalez was going. 'Your slaves would begin to think you are not so fearsome after all! You rule through fear — without fear, the people might turn on you.'

'And you also,' Onzalez pointed out.

'Fair enough. But we can keep them out of the city. These walls will prove impossible to assault.'

Onzalez, breathing heavily, stepped back a pace. With a visible effort, he regained control of himself.

'Yes! And we can easily sweep away attempts to climb the walls. But what then? They will just wait us out. We have water aplenty but our city needs massive amounts of food to keep going. And all the farm workers are within the walls — the ones not dead in the field, that is. Our enemies came upon us so swiftly, we did not have time to stock up on food. If the people are starving, they will not be able to defend the walls.'

Gello glanced below, to where the panicked mass was streaming through the gates and vanishing into the streets beyond. Outside, broken and bleeding men, crushed and trampled in the rush for safety, lay thickly on the ground, hundreds of them.

'The Dragon Egg! It is our last hope!' he exclaimed. 'Ezok must unlock the secret of its power. I saw what it did to our men back on Dragonara — it could crush every soldier out there!'

Onzalez clapped his hands together. 'The Egg! Of course! It is as Zorva intended. It was given to us by His plan, and I have been a fool to ignore it. Today's disaster was a result of me not following His wishes!'

Gello nodded doubtfully. He did not want to rely on magic but it seemed there was no choice. Still, no matter what happened, these walls were impressive. No army was going to get over them without months of careful siege work.

'You hold these gates, I shall return to the Temple. The Radiant Child shall show us how to use the

Dragon Egg or she shall die on the altar. If nothing else, the sacrifice of such a powerful being will result in Zorva giving me so much power that not even the foul priests of Aroaril will be able to stop me!'

Gello let him go. He had no wish to be anywhere near the Temple after this disaster. He needed to show not just Onzalez but the other Fearpriests that he was the only man capable of defending their city.

Merren ordered the bowmen to collect what arrows they could from the battlefield and for the rest of the men to begin collecting the thousands of wounded. The way the terrified Tenochs had run from the battlefield, leaving behind thousands of dead and wounded had raised her hopes. Surely Gello and his Fearpriests would surrender Karia and the Egg now their warriors were dead and the people panicked.

But she was shocked to see the gates swing shut behind the last, desperate fugitives.

'What now?' Martil asked, his voice calm.

She looked at him carefully but it was a reasonable question.

'First I want to thank the men — and Elfarans and Derthals. The scale of this victory is almost beyond belief. Then we proceed as I planned. Let the people on the walls see Kesbury and Milly help as many of the Tenoch wounded as possible ...'

'We shall do our best, your majesty, but you must remember that all these men have been raised to worship Zorva,' Kesbury warned.

'Nevertheless, you must try. They need to see evidence of Aroaril's power.'

'Indeed,' Milly agreed. 'They have been forced to worship the Dark One. Perhaps our healing can show them there is an alternative.'

Merren smiled. 'Then we shall see if the city wants

to defend itself against those who help wounded, rather than ripping out hearts on stone altars.'

'They do not need many defenders. Those walls are massive — there is no way we would be able to attack them. It would be useless,' Martil pointed out.

'Then perhaps one of the wounded that we help can provide us with information. Look for the ones who seem to be different from the Tenochs we already saw. Remember they hold hostage thousands of people from other cities, to prevent rebellion there. There will be those who have no reason to love the Tenochs and their Fearpriests.'

'And if not?' Martil had to say. The anger was gone but the fear for Karia remained. He had to get inside!

'Havell, contact Argurium. I need to have a look at the city and its surrounds.'

The Elfaran blanched. 'Your majesty, I do not think that is advisable. Argurium is weak and near death. If something were to happen while you were high above the ground —'

'My Queen! Let me go instead! What if something were to happen?' Barrett interrupted.

'I cannot send someone up there knowing they could die at any moment. Besides, I need to see it for myself, to understand how we can get inside.'

'What about birds —' Barrett began.

'They cannot find something we do not know is there. I have made my decision. You have your orders!'

Gello felt his pounding heart begin to slow down. Onzalez had returned to the Temple, along with the company of guards they had kept on the wall during the disastrous attack. But Prent was still there, along with plenty of junior Fearpriests. They had been scouring the streets, finding warriors and getting them into companies, as well as ordering ordinary men onto the walls.

'They don't need to be armed with anything much. Even a stone dropped from up there can kill. And, anyway, our enemies just have to think the wall is well guarded,' he had instructed.

Almost one hundred of his men had been found, the ones who had survived both the arrow storm and the terrified sprint back to the city. But one company, from almost two thousand men, was useless. He really needed more defenders. He had another three companies of Tenoch warriors, as well as perhaps a thousand Tenochs who had been dragged up onto the wall. But they just watched in silence — he did not trust them to fight with the ferocity needed to turn back Merren and her army. He had urged Onzalez to leave him the other company of guards but the Fearpriest had refused, saying he needed to secure the Temple. Gello suspected Onzalez wanted them as protection for himself against the other Fearpriests. He had seen the Temple and reckoned it almost impregnable. There were but two ways inside — the stone door at the base and an opening at the top, which led to the bloodstained altar. A score of men could hold the place forever and a day.

He had once been afraid of Onzalez, fearing the power the man boasted and the silken menace he projected. But, since Onzalez had been defeated outside Norstalos City, the man had changed. It was as if the Fearpriest had tasted fear for the first time — and it had tainted him. Not only was he unwilling to test himself against Merren's priests and wizards, he was obviously afraid that the Tenochs and the other people he had ruled would turn on him. Still, even if the Seventeen — or Eighteen — turned on Onzalez, there was still hope for him. With Merren's army at their front gates, the Fearpriests needed a captain for their men.

And if he could save the city now, the other Fearpriests would have to look favourably at him. With Merren destroyed and Norstalos at his mercy again, no doubt they would let him lead a new expedition to Albiona. He tried to discuss this with Mother but, without her picture, the only image he could remember was her last, when she was covered in blood and choking at his hands ... so instead he walked the walls, taking reassurance from their sheer size. He had little fear that Merren's men would be able to breach the wall or gates. There were only two gates, each as massive as the other. And the size of the walls meant he could move men swiftly from one end of the city to the other before an attack could be launched. Best of all, they had plenty of the strange spear launchers the Tenochs had developed.

But then shouts from up and down the massive battlements made his heart race.

'Are they attacking?' he shouted.

'No, they are bringing back our wounded!' someone yelled back.

Gello walked across the wide battlement to peer over. Not only was Merren there, her standard bearer holding a flag of truce, but her soldiers were dragging and carrying over hundreds of wounded Tenochs. He noted they were only Tenochs, not Berellians or his own men.

'Gello! We need to talk!' Merren's voice, magically amplified, echoed over the battlements.

Gello looked down the wall, where every ordinary man pressed into service was watching nervously. They would not stand for an order to hurl spears at their own men. It looked as if he would have to talk to the bitch.

Onzalez banished his doubts as he neared the Temple. The Council would want to know what had happened — he had to act before Horna could rally opposition against him. The Dragon Egg was his only hope. He had to get to it, get it working for him if he was to have any hope of keeping his hold on the Ruling Council — to say nothing of stopping the Aroaril-lovers.

Confidence was everything, he told himself. They are used to obeying you — do not give them a reason to change. The guards on the gate waved him through, as he had expected, and he hurried inside, a company of guards with him, hoping to reach the Dragon Egg before word of his return reached the rest of the Council upstairs. If confronted, he planned to blame Gello for the loss and try to buy himself more time with the death of his co-conspirator. Still, the presence of so many guards around him was comforting. None of the other Council would dare to stop him with so many men protecting him.

Except Horna was waiting for him outside the room where the Dragon Egg was held securely.

'What are you doing here, Brother?' Horna asked coldly.

'I need to reach that Egg,' Onzalez said casually, fighting to keep his voice steady.

'You need to come and talk to the Council,' Horna corrected.

'What is this nonsense?' Onzalez blustered. 'Out of my way or I shall have these guards remove you!'

Horna merely gestured to the guards behind Onzalez.

'Seize him and bring him up to the Chamber,' he ordered.

Before Onzalez could move, hands grabbed him and the guards he thought of as his were pointing spears at his face.

'How dare you? This is an outrage! I'll have your hearts for this!' he screamed but they ignored him.

'They obey only me,' Horna said coldly. 'Things have changed since you went away. Try to escape, try to use your power and you shall be killed.'

Merren could see hundreds of heads peering over the wall. If they had been warriors, they would have marched against her a few turns of the hourglass ago. Which meant Gello needed ordinary citizens just to defend the walls. They would not want to hurt their friends and family that her men were piling up before the city, where all could see Kesbury and Milly begin to heal their wounds. But she did not trust Gello, and Barrett stood ready to protect her in the face of treachery. Still, those people behind the walls needed to hear what she would say. It was a strange situation, almost the reverse of the one she had faced back at Norstalos City. There Gello had been the attacker and she the desperate defender. She was curious to hear what he had to say now.

The giant gates slowly creaked open, just part of the way, but enough for Gello and a score of his men to walk out. From the state of their armour, it was apparent they had narrowly escaped death on the battlefield earlier. And now they had to walk over the bodies of those who had been crushed and trampled in the rush to escape. These lay thickly near the gates. Some still moved, some even tried to drag themselves inside when they heard the gates open — for Merren had not wanted to send her men that close to the walls, where they could be attacked by the defenders.

Merren, with Barrett, Martil, Havell and his Elfarans, walked to meet them.

'I hope you are not going to do something foolish,' she warned Martil. 'We raised the flag of truce and must show these people we can be trusted.'

Martil merely shook his head. 'I will not break a flag of truce. And I am in control of myself,' he promised.

She smiled at him. 'I trust you.'

But inside she was churning. The stakes were so high here. The lives not just of her men but of every man, woman and child depended on them regaining the Egg. But after what she had so nearly done at the Derthal village, after managing to turn Martil back, she was determined not to let the end justify the means.

Gello walked to within ten yards before stopping.

'What do you want here, Witch Queen?' he roared, trying to be heard up on the walls above.

Merren smiled. She could do better than that.

'We could be here to arrest you, for the crimes you have committed against men, women and children. You are guilty of treason, murder and worse. But we are here to free this city from its grip of fear. We are here to show the people that the Dark God is not the only one, and that they can live without the terror of being sacrificed, or seeing their loved ones killed,' she replied, her voice, thanks to Barrett, booming out over the city.

She watched Gello's face twist in anger and he strode forwards the rest of the way, until they were only a few feet apart.

'No more games. What do you want?' he hissed.

'Two things. You stole a magical Egg and its

protector from Dragonara Isle. Return them and we walk away,' Merren said instantly. 'You will not see us again. You can live here in peace. Only if you try to cross the ocean shall I see you dead.'

Gello's eyes narrowed. 'You want the Egg and the girl? That is it? Why?'

Merren stared at him. 'Gello, put aside what has happened over the past year. You know I am not one for making up stories. That Egg and girl are vital not just to Tenoch or Norstalos but to every country and every person on this world. Without it, magic will die — and every living thing with it.'

Gello said nothing for a long moment and Merren felt a small stir of hope.

'Do you think me a fool?' he sneered.

She felt her heart sink. 'I am telling the truth,' she said wearily, knowing it was too late, he had made up his mind.

'You fear the Egg, fear what it could do to you! I give it up and you shall turn it against us! The girl will work for you — in an instant you would destroy me and this city. Walk away? As if you would just walk away when you would have us at your mercy!'

'Gello!' Merren barked. 'Listen to me. This is no tale — all our lives depend on this —'

'I have heard enough,' Gello snorted. 'You think to outwit me! Well, it shall not work. Is that all you have to say or do I return to these impregnable walls?'

Merren sighed. 'Only that you are welcome to take back your wounded. We shall save the worst of them, but you should have the city's healers ready to help those with arrows in their arms and legs.'

'Why?' Gello sniffed. 'I leave the gates open and your Ralloran monsters will soon be inside the city, raping and killing. It is all they live for.'

Martil just stared at Gello. One day he was going to face the man with sword in hand. He just knew it. It would be the right way to finish it.

'We shall not attack the city until your wounded are inside,' she replied. 'Whether you choose to believe that or not is up to you. But I give you this last warning. Unless the Egg and the girl are given back to us, we shall not rest until you are dead.'

Gello laughed shortly. 'I shall enjoy watching you eat your words,' he promised, before turning and walking back to the city.

They watched him go.

'Your orders, my Queen?' Martil asked stolidly.

'As I planned. I want you to march around the city, calling out that we are here to free the people from Zorva and the Fearpriests. That they can live in their own lands, their own cities once more, worship Aroaril again, live how they wish. Meanwhile we shall send all their wounded back, telling them the same message.'

'And you, my Queen?' Barrett asked.

'I shall be using Argurium to look at the surrounding land, and at the city itself. It must have a weakness,' she said determinedly.

'And if it does not?' Martil could not help but say.

'Then Barrett and his Magicians' Guild will need to bring down those gates. Havell and his Elfarans shall lead the assault. They are living on borrowed time as it is. Once inside the city we shall keep the men in hand, stay together and only fight when we have to. But we shall get the Egg, and Karia, back.'

They contemplated that for a long moment.

'To work,' Merren chided finally.

'What did they want?' Prent asked nervously. He had been waiting beside the gates, along with dozens of

Fearpriests, ready to spring an ambush on Merren, should she try to get inside while the gates were open.

Gello waved irritably for him to come closer. What he had to say was not for the ears of ordinary men. They stood in the shadow of the gate, near the huge mechanism, while a dozen men slowly wound the winches that closed the enormous gates, slabs of wood that were too heavy for men to move by hand.

'I must go and speak to the Council. They want the Egg. It must be as powerful as they say!'

'And what of the wounded?' Prent gestured towards where crushed and injured men still tried to drag themselves inside. Some were wailing, as they heard the gates winching shut once more.

Gello stared at them for a moment. 'Let them in. If they are so foolish as to give us back men to fill the walls, then we shall use them. But if any Ralloran comes within fifty paces of the gates, hit them with everything we have. I won't be long.'

Merren moved among the piles of wounded, to where Kesbury and Archibishop Sadlier laboured. Jaret and Wilsen were a step behind, and had their blades out, although she had insisted she would be safe.

'Captain Martil will have our guts ripped out if anything happens to you,' Jaret had told her.

'Are they responding?' she asked Milly.

The Archbishop wiped her sweating brow and smiled.

'They are terrified of us — of Kesbury more than me — but pathetically grateful when we heal them.' She gestured down at the man who clutched her hand, sobbing as he wiped away the still-wet blood that had caked his chest from an arrow wound she had healed.

'So they are not fervent worshippers of Zorva?'

'Not at all. They were forced to it and worship only out of fear.'

Merren smiled down at the healed man.

'You may return to your family. And when you go back, tell them and your friends we are not here to hurt you. Our quarrel is not with the people, only with the priests of Zorva. We are here to set you free. We will see to it that there are no more sacrifices, that you can return to your home cities if you wish and rule yourselves,' she told him.

The man stared up at her, eyes wide and mouth open.

'It is perhaps too much for them to take in,' Milly suggested.

Merren straightened up, hiding her frustration.

'Are there any that you have healed that I could talk to?' she asked.

'Forgive me, High One, but I am such a one,' the man croaked.

Milly and Merren looked at him.

'I am Garas. My family was one of the ruling clans of the city of Ayan, on the far west of this land,' he continued. 'We were brought here nearly thirty years ago, when Ayan fell to the Tenochs and became part of the Tenoch Empire. My father was one of thousands of Ayans made to live here, where we could cause no trouble for our Tenoch overlords. All the ruling clans, the heads of merchant guilds, every rich man and their family was brought here, to work like dogs for the Tenochs, while they took our houses and our treasures for themselves.'

'Then, Garas, you and your people should rejoice, for we are here to break the rule of the Tenochs. You shall return to your city, and rule yourselves once more,' Merren told him.

'Who are you?' Garas gasped.

'I am Queen Merren and I rule a country far to the east of here, called Norstalos.' She smiled.

'I would not believe such words, for they sound like madness, had I not seen the weapon that nearly killed me pulled out of my flesh and that same flesh healed by this lady,' Garas admitted.

'Will you help us defeat the Tenochs? Could you open the gates for us?' Merren asked quickly.

Garas stared at her for a long moment. 'I can talk to my people. My family's name carries much respect among the Ayans living in Tenoch. But we cannot fight for you. We have no weapons. Besides, all those who have fought the Tenochs have lost. And the Tenochs are not merciful. If we fail, it is not just us but our families who will pay. All I can offer is our promise not to help our Tenoch overlords defeat you.'

Merren sighed. It was about what she had expected, although less than she had hoped.

'One more thing: do you know the layout of the Temple, what we might find inside?'

Garas's eyes widened with fear.

'No! None who enter there ever come out again,' he breathed. 'My father, my sister, many of my friends — all have gone in the back. All that comes out the other end is flesh.'

Merren nodded, feeling a little sick. She would have liked to talk longer with him, but she was afraid Gello or a Fearpriest might see their conversation and single Garas out for punishment.

'Good luck,' she merely told him, while Milly moved on to the next moaning man who needed her help.

'Your majesty,' Jaret said warningly.

She swivelled — to see Argurium soar across the field and land gently near the river.

'Our last chance,' she said softly.

Gello sent half his Tenoch warriors around to the other gate to make sure that was secure, leaving barely two companies of Tenochs and his own men to hold the main gate. Still, with an extra thousand ordinary Tenochs on the walls he was confident Prent could look after things for a turn or two of the hourglass, especially as Merren had no siege equipment. He used one of the carts to head back to the Temple as swiftly as possible. With an army outside, and the workers unable to go to work, the streets were quiet. The Fearpriests had ordered all to stay inside — and nobody was foolish enough to break that command. Still, Gello felt eyes watching him as he travelled through the city. The quiet also allowed him to hear the shouts and calls from outside the wall. He swore as he listened to the magically amplified voices that told all within earshot that ordinary people were safe, this army was here to free the people from the Fearpriests, that afterwards they could go back to their home cities, could live and worship who they wanted — and need no longer fear their children being sacrificed.

Just when he was sick of hearing that, he heard shouts and screams echo across the city — and looked up, to see a dragon swooping lazily around overhead. From the reaction it was getting, Gello guessed most of the people had never even heard of a dragon before.

'Can't this thing go any faster?' he shouted at the cart driver. The frightened man plied his whip and the cart rattled along towards where the Temple still smoked.

Martil could not take his eyes off the city walls. He and the Rallorans were marching around the city, accompanying Barrett, who was shouting out Merren's message to the people. The words meant nothing to him — all he could think about was Karia, inside those walls somewhere. What was she thinking? What had happened to her? Since he had broken down in Merren's arms, the anger and guilt that had possessed him was gone. In its place was a fierce determination to not only rescue her but complete the task the dragons had given him — and win Merren, as well.

As yet he did not know how — but he knew he would do it, or die in the attempt.

Merren flew over the city, hoping to see some weakness. But she could not fail to notice the size of the walls, the huge towers and the gates, which looked just as formidable from the air as they did from the ground and equally impressive on the other side of the city. The size of Tenoch, with its endless streets, markets and houses, was stunning.

The two most obvious features were the river that snaked through it — and the huge pyramid that was the Temple of Zorva. She could not help but circle around it, horrified and fascinated all at once. The work that had gone into building it! It was flat-topped, the roof of it a platform marked with ornate carvings, with a huge burning brazier that smoked lazily, torches — and what she recognised was the sacrificial altar. From up here, the front of the Temple, stained rust brown by the blood of thousands, looked horrifying. She remembered the giant pit of bodies they had discovered and shuddered. She was conscious of not staying here too long — partly because the people were obviously terrified of the dragon but mainly because Argurium had warned her the end was near. Against the need to be back on solid ground was the more pressing need to find some way into the city that did not involve fighting in the streets, not just for Martil's sake but for every man she commanded and the poor people the Fearpriests would use against them. She turned away from the Temple and flew along the river — and realised there was another way into the city.

The wide Tenoch river ran into the city under an archway, through the middle of the city, bypassing the Temple, then out via another archway in the wall. The river flowed swiftly and the archway was low, the wall almost skimming the top of the water. Argurium took her in for a closer look and she saw stone spikes projecting out from the bottom of the wall into the water itself — the ones by the exit had rubbish caught on them.

'Where to now?' Argurium asked.

Merren was about to suggest a quick look across the north of the city, where the river entered, when she felt Argurium jerk a little in the air. The dragon, who had been soaring effortlessly, now began using her wings rapidly and was obviously fighting to stay in the air.

'Are you all right? What is wrong?' Merren cried.

But Argurium did not answer.

Gello rocketed into the courtyard behind the Temple while gripping the sides of the cart for dear life.

The guards rushed forwards — but stopped and saluted when they saw who it was.

'I must see Brother Onzalez immediately,' he instructed.

He had to admit, the Tenochs were trained well. Men leaped to obey and he was rushed inside and up to a waiting room outside what was obviously the main chamber.

'The Seven— the Eighteen are sitting now. We must not go in until they are ready,' a frightened guard told him.

Gello was about to shove the man aside and force his way in when the door swung open.

Ignoring the guard, Gello straightened his back and strode inside.

'Welcome, King Gello. The Council was just talking about you,' a deep voice said.

Gello looked around slowly. The sixteen Fearpriests around the huge stone circular table all had their cowls over their heads, so he did not know which one was talking. But he guessed it was not Onzalez. He alone was standing. And he alone was tied to the wall. On the floor was an eagle warrior, who looked familiar to Gello. He thought for a moment then placed the man — he was the one who had brought down the Radiant Child with a slingshot.

'What is going on?' Gello demanded.

'We have been finding out the truth.' A Fearpriest stood. Gello recognised him after a moment — Brother Horna, the leader of the faction that hated Onzalez. 'The truth, not the tales that Brother Onzalez told. Not only were we defeated before the city walls but this warrior explained our army is not still fighting in Norstalos but is destroyed! We have rewarded him for his help.'

'Rewarded?' Gello asked, looking at the dead man.

'He died swiftly,' Horna said coldly. 'A death that Brother Onzalez can only pray for! After lying to us, losing our army, now we find his plan to destroy the army of Aroaril-lovers has also failed and this city is under siege. So, *King* Gello, what can you tell us?'

'We are holding the walls,' Gello said immediately. If Onzalez was about to die, he had no intention of joining the man. 'But if you want to save this city you need someone to command them. The officers you have are useless ...'

'You are in no danger from us for now,' Horna said dryly. 'Now tell us what is happening.'

'My cousin commands the army facing us. At the moment they are marching around the city, using magic to tell the people that this army is not here to sack Tenoch, but merely end the Council's rule. That afterwards all people from other cities on the continent may return to their homes, no more human sacrifice —'

'Outrageous!' a Fearpriest on the far side of the table snorted.

'Meanwhile they are healing your men wounded in the battle. These wounded are returning to the city, after no doubt being given the same message to spread.'

'The people will not believe this!' one Fearpriest stated.

'They might. It would not be a problem if we still had our army to maintain control but, thanks to the mistakes of Brother Onzalez, that is not possible,' Horna said ominously.

'So what do we do, Brother Horna?' someone asked.

Horna stood.

'It is time to end this foolishness. We must show the people our true power. No longer shall we rely on others to do our bidding. We must meet the Aroaril-lovers ourselves and destroy them, so all can see that the power of Zorva cannot be challenged!'

Gello hesitated at that. If the Fearpriests saved themselves, then where did he fit into their future?

'High One, that is not a good idea,' he said loudly.

Horna swivelled. 'You dare to contradict me?' he asked coldly.

'No, I am merely warning you. The Aroaril-lovers have as much power as you — if you go out there, your people will see you defeated, they'll watch some, if not all, of the Council perish.'

There was silence in the chamber.

'What nonsense is this? Zorva is stronger than Aroaril — we cannot be defeated by mere priests of that weakling religion!' Horna snorted.

'Brother Onzalez was humbled by a priest of Aroaril. That was why we lost the battle in Norstalos and why your army was destroyed,' Gello replied coolly.

'What?' In an instant, the focus switched from Gello to Onzalez.

'He lies! I was not defeated!' Onzalez shouted furiously, glaring at Gello but Gello felt no loyalty to him.

'Look at the mark on his face. Left there by an old priest, not long for this world, who was barely able to control his bladder, let alone his God's power,' Gello sneered, knowing he had to embroider the truth if he was to swing the Council around to his side.

Onzalez snarled with rage, straining at his bonds, but Horna was at his side in a moment and reached out, grasping Onzalez's temples. Onzalez tried to struggle, tried to squirm away, but the ropes and Horna's strong hands held him. Gello felt his heart pounding as he realised Horna was about to wrest the truth from Onzalez's own mind. Was this what the legends meant when they said Fearpriests could read minds? He shuddered at what might happen if they ever tried to do that to him.

Then Horna released Onzalez and turned back. 'It is true,' he confirmed bitterly. 'Onzalez was humbled by a priest before the walls of the Norstaline capital. He fears the Aroaril-lovers now, thinks they have too much power for him to defeat.'

'See!' Gello cried, partly in triumph, partly in relief. 'It is not safe for you to go out there and face the priests and priestesses of Aroaril! You must rely on me to protect you!'

Fifteen cowled heads turned towards Horna, who slammed his fist into Onzalez's midriff in an explosion of anger.

'I warned you. I warned you all. Onzalez's lust for power has brought us to this!' he howled. 'Now see what he has done!' He struck Onzalez again, leaving the Fearpriest gasping, before turning back to the table. 'King Gello,' he said heavily. 'Hold the walls for us. The people cannot see us defeated — it would be the beginning of the end.'

'Agreed!' the rest rumbled.

'What is it they want?' Horna asked, leaving a moaning Onzalez hanging in his bonds.

'They want the Egg back, as well as the Radiant Child that protected it. They obviously fear the Egg, otherwise they would not have tried to trick us into giving it to them. They offered to walk away and leave us alone in exchange for the Egg and the girl, which means they think it has the power to destroy them.'

Horna nodded. 'That could be our way out of the mess Onzalez has created. King Gello needs to get back to the walls and give us the time we need to stop our enemies. Do you need our help?'

Gello only hesitated for a moment. 'I can do it alone, with help from Brother Prent and the fellow priests already there,' he said confidently.

'Acceptable,' Horna rumbled. 'But we shall send orders to the other priests. If you look like failing, we shall arrive, to take control ourselves. Meanwhile we need to get the Egg in here, as well as the girl. If she can show us how to use it to destroy the army that threatens us, then she may live. Otherwise, she and Brother Onzalez shall die on the altar at dawn.'

'Agreed!' The Council spoke as one voice.

Argurium flew over the city wall so low that her tail almost brushed the top. She fought for height, circling over the fields to the far side of the city, where livestock ran in fear from the dragon overhead. Merren desperately tried to see what was below, and also to hang on. Seemingly, the magic that kept her safe and protected on the dragon's neck was gone, for the wind was buffeting her and only the harness was keeping her in place.

Argurium swooped, towards where Merren could see Martil and his Rallorans making their way around the city wall. The dragon seemed to be fading as they flew towards the Rallorans, who were running to meet her.

'Forgive me,' Argurium's voice echoed sadly within Merren's head.

Karia had to use every trick Barrett had taught her to maintain control as she was escorted by Ezok into the Council chamber. To see so many hooded Fearpriests was almost more than she could bear. She had spent the day by herself, eating, playing and singing. It was comfortable enough but she knew where she was — and at night she could hear faint cries echoing up from below. She knew what went on here. But amid the fear there was a ray of hope. She could see the Dragon Egg. If she could just get her hands on it, she would destroy every filthy Fearpriest in this room.

'Radiant Child, as spokesman for the Council of Eighteen, I order you to serve us,' a deep-voiced

Fearpriest rumbled. 'Show us how we can use the Egg to destroy our foes.'

Karia had no intention of doing so but she did want to get her hands on the Egg, so she began to walk towards it.

'Do not let her near the Egg,' Ezok warned, grabbing Karia's hand.

For a moment she was too afraid to move or think but then her mind cleared.

'Do not listen to this liar,' she said softly, trying to make her voice sound mystical, the way Barrett had said clients expected it to be. 'He claims he knows how to use the Egg but he has fooled you. He does not know its true purpose. It was I who used it every time. He pretends to know what it does in order to save his miserable life.'

'You little ...!' Ezok shrieked, but he did not have time to finish his sentence before a pair of Fearpriests were next to him. At a gesture from them, he was frozen into immobility.

'Show us where the truth is, Ezok,' Brother Horna intoned. 'Show us how you can harness the Egg's power.'

Ezok's eyes darted around desperately, but there was no escape. At a gesture from the Fearpriests flanking him, he floated gently across the room until he was next to the Egg. Immediately it began flashing at him, pulsing a deep, angry red, an unmistakeable warning.

'Show us!' Horna repeated.

Ezok was released from his magical bonds a moment later. The sudden freedom made him stumble, almost fall into the Egg. He reached out his hands instinctively — and screamed in agony as the Egg flared up, burning his hands where it touched the surface. Howling with pain, Ezok reeled away, clutching his hands under his armpits. A faint smell of burning flesh wafted across the room and Karia looked away in revulsion.

The Fearpriests did not look away, however, and used magic to shackle Ezok to the wall next to Onzalez, using ropes there for just that purpose. Ezok hung there, moaning at his blackened hands until, at a gesture from Horna, he slumped silently in his bonds.

'I think that tells us where the truth is,' Horna observed. 'Now, child. Will you use the Egg for our purpose?'

Karia forced herself to stay calm and look at the Fearpriest. 'Let me show you what I can do,' she declared, walking slowly across the room to where the Egg waited.

The Fearpriests parted before her and she struggled to keep her steps slow, her pace measured. She wanted to run to the Egg, use its power to crush these bad men. But she had seen what had happened to Ezok, how they had held him immobile. She did not want to give away what she was about to do. Still, as the Egg began to flash gold, blue, green and yellow, pulsing out a greeting to her, it was hard not to smile. She could feel its power, could almost imagine what she could do once she had her hands on it.

The room was silent as she reached the Egg. She held her hands just above the surface of the Egg and felt its gentle warmth reach out to her. Colours flashed across the Egg, lighting up her face and making the room sparkle.

'The Radiant Child!' one Fearpriest muttered.

One final surge of colour seemed to almost explode from the Egg, making several of the Fearpriests instinctively cover their faces, then it settled down, glowing a pale golden colour.

She turned to face the assembled Fearpriests, then pressed her hands onto the Egg.

Merren could see the ground through Argurium now. If that was not bad enough, she could glance to her left and right and see the dragon's wings, still beating hard, were no longer thick with scales, but seemed to be made up of golden points of light. And these were moving, going down the dragon's body, transforming the seemingly solid scales and body into light everywhere they touched.

Merren did not want to look down. She was scared of what she might see. She could not die! She had to tell them what she had seen, how they could get into the city. But the wind was hammering at her now and she forced herself to look down.

She was no longer riding on a dragon's neck, she was in mid-air, sitting atop what seemed to be a cluster of golden lights. Below her, Barrett and Martil were racing towards her.

Thank Aroaril, Barrett can use his magic to get me down safely, she thought with a surge of relief.

Barrett skidded to a stop, below where Argurium used to be, and now merely a dragon shape etched in golden light was fading.

'Do something, wizard!' Martil roared at him.

Barrett did not even dignify that with a reply. Instead he reached into the magic, ready to slow Merren's fall and ensure she landed safely.

But nothing happened.

'Hurry!' Martil bellowed.

'It doesn't work! There is no more magic!' Barrett screamed back at him.

'What?'

'You bloody heard me! The magic doesn't work!'

Martil stared at Barrett in horror for a moment,

then looked up to where Merren was almost falling now, still fifty feet in the air. Desperately he pointed the Dragon Sword at her, wished with all his heart that she was safe.

The remaining golden lights that had been Argurium the dragon stopped fading; instead they seemed to thicken, cushioned Merren as she fell, brought her to the ground safely.

She landed next to Martil and Barrett and stared at them in shock and wonder as the lights flared around them, bathing them in a golden glow, before vanishing.

'Does that mean what I think it does?' Merren said into the silence that followed.

Karia imagined the stone table rising up and crushing the Fearpriests beneath it.

'Take this, you murbeling bustards!' she shouted at them in her own voice.

But nothing happened.

She thought about it again, reached into the magic to make it happen — but nothing was there. Desperate now, she tried again and again, with the same result. Why wasn't it working? Then she realised. She released the Egg and stepped back, feeling sick to the stomach. Argurium, the last dragon, must have died. She knew what would happen, Havell had told her often enough. There would be no more magic until the Dragon Sword pierced the Dragon Egg.

The Fearpriests were now advancing on her and she realised where she was, stopped grieving for the dragon who had been her friend and started fearing for herself.

'Grab her!' Horna barked.

Several Fearpriests pointed at her, but she dodged backwards, to a nearby table loaded with food.

'There is no magic!' one Fearpriest cried.

'Then use your hands! She is just a child!'

Karia grabbed a spiky round fruit from a nearby table and hurled it at the nearest Fearpriest. Her days of playing catch and throw with Martil had trained her arm and the fruit vanished into the darkened space beneath the cowl. The Fearpriest howled and reeled away.

Another made a grab at her but she ducked beneath his arm and swung with all her strength, burying her small fist in his groin. With a shriek of pain, the Fearpriest grabbed at himself and fell to the floor. Karia leaped over his body and ran for the door. She did not know where she was going — just as long as it was away from here.

But Horna stuck out a foot as she raced past and she tripped, sprawling on the floor. Before she could regain her feet, a pair of guards burst through the door and grabbed her, although she struggled and kicked at them.

'Let me go! Let me go!' she screamed but they ignored her. 'I want my dad!'

Horna looked around the room.

'Brothers, I have no power. Do any of you?'

All looked around, all shook their heads.

'What does this mean?' one cried.

'I do not know,' Horna admitted. 'But perhaps, after we sacrifice these three, the Great God will give us answers. Take them away. They shall go to the altar at sunrise.'

'So we have until sunrise,' Merren said. She was still shocked by her near-brush with death and what this meant for them. They had destroyed the Tenoch army but they still had to get into the city somehow — and they had less than a day to do so. 'Nerrin, you have to get your men busy as soon as it gets dark enough that the Tenochs will be unable to see what you are doing. For if they work out what we plan, there is no hope for us — and no hope for anyone.'

Nerrin nodded sombrely. Merren had hurriedly explained her plan to get in through the river gates, by diverting the river and lowering the flow to the point where they could slip under the spikes put there to guard against such an attack. The Tenochs had created a maze of irrigation channels and reservoirs to divert the water for their crops and livestock. By diverting the river into those, as well as opening every sluice gate they could find, she hoped to halve the river's flow into the city within a few turns of the hourglass.

'Captain Martil and I shall return to lead the attack into the city. In the meanwhile, do what you can on the river,' she told him.

As Nerrin hurried off to organise the men, Martil caught Merren's arm.

'Is this going to work? We have to get in there!' he asked desperately.

She recognised the worry in his voice, for it reflected what she felt.

'It has to. We have no choice,' she replied bleakly. 'Come on. We have a long walk ahead of us — and no prospect of magic to help us.'

They found the rest of the small army, minus the Elfarans, gathered at the main gates of Tenoch. 'The Elfarans fell to the ground and vanished into dust in an instant,' Sendric reported. 'It was one of the strangest sights I have seen. It was how we realised the last dragon must have died.'

'Time caught up to them,' Barrett said.

'Well, it's catching up to us all, so we need to focus on the plan,' Merren said tartly. 'Our Magicians'

Guild which we brought across the sea because we thought they would help us get inside the city, is useless without magic. As are Milly and Kesbury.'

'Well, the fact they cannot use magic proves one thing,' Barrett said into the silence. 'Natural magic and the magic from the Gods are linked somehow. While they are different in method and effect, they must come from the same source. It seems the magic came first, then the Gods, who are able to somehow appropriate the natural magic, convert it for use by their priests who are otherwise ordinary people, not like wizards such as myself, who are in tune with the magic that flows within our world.'

'While I agree there must be a link between the magics, there is another explanation,' Milly was quick to add. 'That the magic, the world itself was still created by Aroaril. It is the dragons who are the key. Their presence allows people to use the world's magic. And by people I mean wizards and priests. Without the dragons, there is no way for humans to access the magic — which is why we have no power now.'

'But if Aroaril is the Creator, surely He would allow His priests to still use magic, dragons or no dragons ...' Barrett argued.

'Although the plan was for Martil to use the Dragon Sword on the Egg right away. Perhaps there was not supposed to be this pause. Or perhaps we were supposed to use this time to reflect on the magic in our lives, and how lucky we are to have such a gift,' Milly snapped back.

'Enough! We can worry about this if we survive this next day,' Merren silenced them.

She looked around and while it looked as though everyone had an opinion they would like to offer, none were prepared to interrupt her. So she explained how they would use the river to get inside. 'We must hope that our work this morning, healing those Tenochs and telling as much of the city as we could reach that we were here to free them, will mean the ordinary people will stay in their homes. If so, all we have to do is seize the gates and the Temple.' She paused then and looked around. 'But if they fight against us, then we can show no mercy. The fate of the world rests on our shoulders. We cannot fail. Captain Martil, High Chief Sacrax and I shall lead the Derthals into the city to seize the Temple. A company of Rallorans, under Lieutenant Dunner, will open the gates from the inside, to allow Captain Nerrin and the other Rallorans to seize the northern gate. Meanwhile, Captain Kettering and a company of men will go in through this archway here and open the main gate for Captain Kay and the rest of the men to take. Almost as important is taking Gello. Alive or dead, I want him. Once the gates are secure, send as many men as you can spare towards the Temple. Taking the gates will mean nothing if we cannot seize the Temple and take back the Egg.'

'What about Bishop Kesbury and myself?' Milly asked.

'And me and my wizards,' Barrett pointed out.

'Magic does not work. You would be safer staying out here,' Martil suggested.

'But what if you succeed? If you restore the dragons, magic will work again. If you have not dealt with every Fearpriest by then, you shall need help,' Milly pointed out.

Merren nodded. 'Agreed. You three shall come with us, given that we shall be trying to wipe out the nest of Fearpriests. Fernal, Tiera and the rest of the wizards will help Kay with any Fearpriests that may remain by the main gates.'

'And I?' Sendric asked.

'You shall stay here. You shall hold the gates while Kay and Kettering bring the men to the Temple.'

'And what about you?' Sendric rumbled. 'Surely it would be better for you to stay here, in safety, rather than heading into the very heart of the evil?'

Merren shook her head. 'It is my responsibility to see the Egg returned and the world saved.' She glanced towards Martil. She hoped he would control himself but neither really knew how he would react once in the city — especially if something had happened to Karia. 'And there is another responsibility as well. None of us want another Bellic but neither can we fail. If we have to fight our way to the Temple I want none to mistake it was by my orders. Now, we have no more time for discussion. Kettering — yours will be the hardest task of all. The river level will drop here later than at the north gate. We shall leave it as long as we dare but it may be that the guards on your gate are alerted by fighting from within the city.'

'Whatever happens, we can handle it, your majesty,' Kettering said grimly.

Merren smiled. 'I know. And, if the worst should happen, know that I could not be more proud of every man and woman here. We have been sneered at and spat on, called butchers, drunkards, criminals, chocolate soldiers, peasants and goblins — but the fate of the world rests with us. It could not be in better hands. I want you all to know that.'

She looked round their faces and felt a shock of horror at the thought that they might fail. After all they had been through, after all they had suffered, it would not be fair. But life was not fair.

'Aroaril be with all of us,' she said.

'What is happening?' Prent demanded, when Gello returned to the main gate of the city.

'Onzalez is done for but we are safe,' Gello said with a wink. 'After all, you are one of them, on their Council. They do not fully trust us and have set the other Fearpriests here to keep an eye on us. But with the magic gone, they need us. All we have to do is wait. My cousin can do nothing. If she tries to get over these walls we shall slaughter them!'

'But what of the magic disappearing?' Prent whispered. 'Do you think that means the Witch Queen was right, it is somehow connected to the Egg we took?'

Gello paused for a moment, then shook his head. 'She was trying to trick us. Besides, Brother Horna will get all the answers for us at sunrise.'

They had to walk around half the city to reach the north gates, where the Rallorans waited. And they had to do it without the defenders on the wall seeing what they were up to. Martil had not liked the idea of stumbling around in the dark but they had Sacrax and his Derthals with them, who could find their way easily.

'Sacrax is delighted his warriors have been chosen to take the Temple.' Martil smiled as they followed behind the Derthals.

'It was not to find favour with him,' she replied. 'In the dark, it will be easy to confuse friend from foe. But the Derthals will not make that mistake. Anyone who is not a Derthal must be an enemy. It could be a decisive advantage.'

Martil nodded. 'What about you? You gave a fine speech but is it also that you think I shall abandon everything to rescue Karia?'

'There is a little of that,' she admitted, then caught his arm as he turned away. 'But the real reason is because I am afraid that something might go wrong.

And, if the world is about to end, I want to spend my last moments with you.'

He was silent for a moment. 'I am in control of my anger,' he said slowly. 'I thank you for that. It makes it twice you have saved me from myself. But perhaps we should wait until the night is over before talking about such things. You have to keep your mind clear of distractions.'

'Well, you are a distraction right now!' She poked him.

He grinned. 'And to think, a moment ago you wanted to spend the rest of your life with me!'

She laughed then.

'Sssh!' a nearby Derthal hissed.

That was it. It was all she could do not to double over and keep laughing.

'Why is that so funny?' she wanted to know, almost hiccuping with the effort of keeping her laughter in.

'Close to battle. Everything is funny then, when it could be the last time you laugh,' Martil whispered.

'I can't stop giggling though! What can you do?'

'I could kiss you to keep you quiet,' he offered.

She was tempted but managed to regain control. 'Save that for later,' she suggested.

'As long as there is a later.'

That stopped her laughter.

'There will be. I cannot believe it can end badly,' she murmured.

'This is not a saga. This is real life. It could end very badly,' he warned.

She did not feel like laughing after that.

25

Karia was given a small stone cell in the depths of the Temple, one of a whole row. She knew Ezok and Onzalez were there somewhere, mainly because she could hear Ezok whimpering and weeping. He was not the only one. At least half-a-dozen other men were either crying or begging for mercy.

There was little light in these cells, but she did not feel like sleeping. She knew Martil was out there, knew he was coming for her, but she was afraid. So afraid. None of Barrett's exercises were of use in this cold, damp stone prison that stank of fear and worse.

All she could do was wipe away the tears.

Dunner and a squad of Rallorans, who were all slightly damp, met them with a grin.

'It's working, your majesty.' He saluted.

'Show me,' she ordered.

They did not want to go too close to the gates, which were lit by a score of torches. Their lights showed there were plenty of defenders over the gate itself, although the walls to either side seemed undefended.

'Fools! They're destroying their night vision. They'll be lucky to see the ground in front of the gates,' Martil said scornfully.

'Good,' Merren said grimly.

But the light from the torches did show the spikes that served as a barrier under the river archway. Normally they stretched the height of a man under the surface but they were clearly visible now.

'As the river level drops, we are able to block its flow, divert it even better into the reservoirs and irrigation channels the Tenochs prepared for us,' Nerrin reported. 'Just a little longer.'

Merren looked up at the night sky.

'We all have to go soon,' she warned. 'We only have until sunrise.'

Kettering and his company of men stripped off armour and clothes, all bar a loincloth, and went down to the riverbank, where they covered themselves in mud, trying to disguise their pale skin and shape by stuffing long reeds in their hair, or down their loincloths. They had been concerned about the strange, giant reptiles with the teeth they had seen further down the river, but obviously those had learned to stay away from the city.

'Just make sure it's a reed, not a snake,' Hawke told Leigh, who was particularly enthusiastic about stuffing plants into his loincloth. 'The snakes here, if they bite part of you, that part falls off.'

'No!' Leigh stared at him in horror.

'Don't worry, man.' Hawke grinned. 'It's only a concern if you've got something worth keeping, like me.'

'Well, obviously it's not your wit,' Leigh told him.

'Quiet! And hurry!' Kettering told them.

'I shall lead the men into the city, Captain,' Sendric announced.

'Are you sure, Count? It could be dangerous to be the first inside,' Kay tried to warn him politely.

'Captain Kay, on the other side of that gate is the man who had my daughter raped and murdered. You knew my daughter, did you not? Would you stand by or would you want revenge?'

'Well, of course …'

'Good. Let that be an end to the discussion.'

'I think we are ready,' Dunner reported. 'I sent two men into the river to test it — you can stand now, and wade beneath those spikes.'

'And on the other side of the wall?' Martil had to ask.

'The river bank has been strengthened by stones and bricks. You can climb out easily enough.'

'Then we should go,' Merren agreed. She did not want to wait any longer, because it was almost too much to bear.

Martil led them into the river. As Dunner reported, the flow was slow, the water only reaching their thighs. Dunner's Rallorans were without armour, as was Martil, while Sacrax's Derthals never wore armour.

'Stay close to me,' Martil whispered to Merren, as he helped her into the water.

With Martil in front and a cluster of Rallorans clustered protectively close, she waded through the river and under the archway. Huge stone spikes, jagged and threatening, stained by the water and with weed hanging off them, hung over her head. It seemed almost unbelievable that nobody had noticed the river flow had almost stopped but the huge city was dark and quiet — the only lights were at the gate and around the giant Temple pyramid. Everyone was locked up tight for the night — whether this was usual or because of the Fearpriests' orders, she knew not.

The mud along the river bottom was thick and clinging and twice she had to grab hold of Martil to stop herself falling.

'Up here!'

The river bank had been strengthened and reinforced with stone over the years, the Tenochs thoughtfully adding a step pattern, to give people access to the water. It meant even Merren could climb out without too much trouble, after being helped up to the first step by Martil. As for the Derthals, they scrambled out in moments, going up the sides of the bank like mountain goats up a path. At the top they all paused, counting numbers.

'All here,' Dunner reported.

'Good luck. See you at the Temple.' Martil clasped his hand then watched the Rallorans fade into the darkness, using the shadowed alleyways and darkened corners to ease their way towards the massive gates, which alone of this part of the city stood in torchlight.

'Lead the way,' Merren told Sacrax, who grinned and waved to his warriors.

The Derthals flowed through the city silently, padding along on bare feet, the only sign of their passing the mud from the river that had caked their legs.

Merren, Martil, Barrett, Milly and Kesbury were much slower, their trousers waterlogged, water and mud dripping and squelching into the boots they had replaced once back on dry land. But nobody came out, no dogs barked and no lights went on in the endless houses they sneaked past.

'They do what they're told here,' Martil murmured.

'Or the word of what we are trying to do has gone around,' Merren whispered back.

None of them knew the way, but that did not seem to be a problem. All streets led to the giant pyramid that obviously dominated Tenoch life the way it dominated the skyline.

Kettering ordered his men into the river.

'I thought you said there were snakes in here that could bite your manhood off!' Leigh complained.

'Don't worry. They're not interested in river worms.' Hawke grinned.

Kettering stared at them, and they shrugged sheepishly. In truth, Kettering did not mind their foolishness too much. It helped distract the other men from what they were about to do.

'Come on,' he ordered, leading them down the bank and into the river.

The flow pushed against them, the water reaching to their waists and the river bottom was slick with mud, so that men kept slipping over.

'Form chains! Hold your mates!' Kettering ordered. 'If you go under, don't make a sound. You get us all killed and I'll see you dead!

'And don't think about what you're walking over,' Hawke added. To every man, whose toes were squelching deep into Aroaril-knew-what, that was the comment they remembered.

The archway, with its hooked spikes, festooned with the filth of an entire city, loomed above them, stinking and dripping loathsome liquid on the men as they squeezed below. But they were able to slip underneath and into the city.

'How in Aroaril's name do we get up?' Leigh murmured, as they stared up the bank.

Here, the Tenochs had strengthened the riverbank with stone — but made it sheer, so as not to impede the flow of the water. It reared high above them.

Men fought to stay on their feet, hung onto each other as the water pushed against them and the river bottom gave no purchase even to bare feet.

Kettering looked around desperately. 'There!' he exclaimed. 'Quick now!'

One single stairway had been cut into the bank, to give access to the water.

The men tried to force their way over there but one file went down, men clutching each other and cursing.

'Grab them!' Kettering urged.

But one man was swept past them and into the spikes. He cried out as he crashed against them and was swept downstream.

'What was that?' a strange voice challenged.

'Up those stairs! Now!' Kettering waved.

Dunner finished off the last gate guard then signalled wordlessly at the gate mechanism.

A score of willing hands began to turn it, the gates creaking and groaning as they opened inwards. Shouts of alarm echoed down from the wall, and men peered over the edge, shouting down questions.

Dunner waved cheerfully back at them and it took them precious moments to realise the men below were not Tenochs but the barbarians from across the sea. The Tenochs rushed down the stairs, where Dunner and his best swordsmen met them. The Rallorans had no shields or armour but they were all veterans of a score of battles. The Tenoch warriors were used to fighting against unarmed men and swaggering around the city — they were cut down as they threw themselves at the Rallorans.

Meanwhile the gates inched open, and a bellow from outside told Dunner that Nerrin and the rest of the Rallorans were coming through the gates.

The remaining Tenochs realised the same thing, because they started shouting at each other to run — and then Dunner was not being attacked any more, he was watching men run away from him. He sheathed his sword, breathing hard, a score of bodies on the stairs before him.

'Help your wounded mates,' he told the men with him, then went to find Nerrin.

These gates were theirs. The defenders were running away along the walls in both directions. He ignored them as Nerrin waved him over.

'I'll leave you two companies. Hold the gates,' he instructed.

They paused for a moment, as horns sounded distantly across the city.

'Make that one company. If we haven't taken the other gate, the Captain will need a way out of here. I'll go and help him,' Nerrin decided, then shouted to the rest of the men. 'To the Temple!'

'What is going on?' Sendric asked nervously.

There was shouting and horn calls up on the walls, while torches were being thrown down before the gate. It looked like an ant's nest that had been prodded with a stick.

'Ryder! Two of our best men to call back Kettering and his force!' Kay shouted. 'If they don't get out now, they'll be slaughtered. Without surprise, they don't stand a chance.'

Sendric waved his arms. 'Hold that order!'

'Your grace?' Kay turned.

'Lives do not matter. We have to get inside that city and get to that Egg, Captain! If we fail to take this gate, Queen Merren, the Derthals and Rallorans could be cut off inside the city. We have to get in there, no matter the cost.'

Kay hesitated for a moment, then nodded.

'Take your bowmen and land every arrow you have on that battlement. I will lead the rest of the men and act as a decoy — they do not have enough men to stop Kettering if they have us to worry about.'

Kay saw his point, knew there was no time for discussion, so waved his men forwards.

'Bowmen! I don't want any bastard alive on those ramparts! Draw and loose!' he shouted.

Sendric drew his sword, with some difficulty because the wound he had taken at the Battle of Sendric still pained him, then faced the rest of the soldiers.

'Norstalines! For your Queen! For your country! For your families! Follow me!' he bellowed.

With a huge roar, they followed him at the run towards the gates, which were still shut tight, and were lit by a score of torches and straw bundles the defenders had thrown over the wall.

Martil and Sacrax left the others in the shadow of houses and went to look at the Temple. It sat in the open, surrounded by a square that looked large enough to hold most of the population of Tenoch.

'We'll be easier to see than a black bear on a snow-covered field,' Sacrax grunted.

'They won't expect us,' Martil said automatically, trying to see the best way in. 'Looks like the main entrance is at the back, behind that wall. Or we can go up the top. There must be a way in there, some hidden entrance the Fearpriests use to drag the sacrifices out. They wouldn't climb up it themselves.'

'Covered in blood. Not a good way, that,' Sacrax grumbled.

'Still, that's the way. I need ten of your best warriors, your picked guard, to follow me up there.

You assault the main gate, keep them occupied. I'll meet you in the middle.'

'Thought we would fight together again?' Sacrax muttered.

Martil glanced up at the sky. It was still dark but he guessed dawn was not far away.

'No time,' he said shortly. 'Let's get the others.'

As he had predicted, they were able to creep across the open square without any sign or sound of alarm. The city slumbered around them and, while the pyramid was bathed in light, it was concentrated around its gate and wall.

And then the horns sounded.

Kettering led the way up the stairs, his boots flapping around his neck, bare feet slipping on the moss-covered stones. But his sword was in his hand and anger was in his heart.

The startled guard, who had raised the alarm, only had a glimpse of a noisome, foul creature coming out of the river with bright steel in its hand and teeth bared before Kettering's blade slashed home and blood spurted high. But his dying scream was drowned by warning horns, as well as shouts and cries.

'The barbarians are inside! The demons are loose in the city!' someone screamed.

The ordinary Tenochs on the walls immediately began running along the walls, seeking only escape but Tenoch warriors raced down the stairs and towards where Kettering and only a handful of his men had made it up out of the river.

'Follow me! We must reach that gate or we all die!' Kettering shouted, just before the Tenoch guards reached him.

The two sides met with a crash, Kettering shoulder-charging one man down and slashing out at another pair, driving them back with vicious cuts of his sword. But there were two score of the Tenochs and only a handful of his men. More Tenochs were appearing from where they had been sleeping or resting and joining the battle at a much faster rate than Kettering's men were making it up the stairway.

Snarling and spitting hatred, Kettering tried to drive them back but even the size and strength of Hawke was useless against the number facing them. They were only able to hold a patch of ground at the head of the stairway, with no way for more men to get up.

Then shouts and screams from the battlement above the gates was followed by more horn calls.

'They are attacking the gate! Everyone to the walls!' someone yelled into the night.

Instantly the Tenoch reinforcements turned and raced to the walls. Still, the dozen or so left poked spears at Kettering and Hawke, who teetered on the edge of the stairway. Once they were down, there was no way back up, Kettering saw in an instant. And there was no normal way of beating them.

'Throw me!' he roared at Hawke, holding out his hand.

The big man hesitated for a moment, then saw the look in Kettering's eyes. He grabbed Kettering and hurled him like a missile, his body smashing into the Tenochs and knocking them backwards. Instantly the pressure was gone and a rush of Norstalines could finally get up the stairway to finish off the fallen Tenochs.

Meanwhile Hawke and Leigh fell to their knees beside Kettering, who lay on his side with a spear jutting out of his chest and another in his leg.

'Killer! Why?' Leigh moaned.

Kettering glared at them, blood on his face. 'Because I won't lose! Now get those gates!'

'Come on.' Hawke grabbed Leigh by the shoulder and hauled him to his feet.

'The gate!' Leigh pointed, and led the men across the cobbles to the unattended opening mechanism.

Sendric could see men dying to his left and right, but he seemed to have a charmed life. Spears and rocks were falling from above — but not as many as he had feared. The arrows Kay and his bowmen were landing on the wall above made it unsafe for a defender to show himself for more than a few heartbeats.

'Count! You need to get under shelter!' Kay yelled at him.

'No, Captain, I am doing more for our men now,' Sendric replied calmly.

He stayed out in the open, darting from side to side, trying to distract the defenders as the men sought the dubious safety of the base of the wall. But here they were still a target. Sendric looked around for something else that would occupy the defenders — and his gaze fell on the Magicians' Guild.

'Come on! Help cause a diversion!' Sendric waved at the assorted mages.

'Doesn't he know we don't have any magic?' Fernal muttered. 'We should stay here, in safety.'

'We cannot. Now is the time for courage,' Tiera declared. 'Follow me!'

The wizards still held back. Without magic, they felt naked. But when she rushed forwards, they followed.

Sendric saw the wizards racing forwards in a tight group and swore. It was too tempting — they should have split up. Sure enough, the defenders switched their attention to this new target, although that at least gave the soldiers at the base of the wall some respite.

'Get back!' He waved at them, but it was too late. Spears landed among the mages and he saw their leader fall.

'Gello! I'm coming for you!' he shouted up into the night angrily.

'What is going on?' Brother Horna shouted, stalking through the corridors.

'That is the alarm, High One.' An officer bowed hastily. 'The barbarians and demons from Aroaril are inside the city!'

Horna hesitated. Fear had ruled this city for centuries but, without an army or magic power from Zorva, he had nothing to back that up.

'Take every guard, every trainee and acolyte we have to the gate below — leave me just four to bring the girl to the altar instead.'

'At once, High One!'

Horna watched him go, before summoning the rest of the Council. Normally only one or two would be required for this ceremony, as well as a dozen guards to secure the sacrifices. But these were not ordinary times. He wanted all of the Council, bar Onzalez and the Norstaline oaf, to be there when he put the child to the knife. If Zorva did not give them answers, and power, after such an important life, then he did not know what would.

Gello was woken by the horns, a moment before Prent shook him awake.

'They've got men inside, and they're attacking the gate!' he gibbered.

'Get a grip, man!' Gello cuffed him over the head, hard, and walked over to the battlement. It took him but a moment to assess the situation. The band inside the city was a concern but the Tenochs were driving them back and finishing them off. Only a couple were still in sight and surely they could not last long. Meanwhile there were hundreds of men streaming forwards to attack the walls. He needed to show his worth to the various Fearpriests watching and the best way to do that was to throw this frontal attack back in disarray. But he had too few defenders on the wall — and many of them were cowering from the arrows. He needed more men.

'They are attacking the gate! Everyone to the walls!' he bellowed.

The rush of men that answered his call made him smile. Now to kill some of Merren's men. He gazed down and recognised Sendric running around outside the gate. A good place to begin.

'Kill that man!' Gello cried, pointing at Sendric.

The Tenochs tried to obey him but many died as arrows clattered onto the stone battlement.

Gello ignored the screams of his casualties. He wanted to see Sendric die.

Kettering's ragged band seemed to be ignored with all the noise and death going on outside, and atop, the wall. None had a chance to put on trousers or boots, so they ran barefoot across the cobbles, legs stained with water and worse. The few Tenochs in their way were cut down, then they made it to the gate mechanism. Hawke, Leigh and several others strained at the huge winches, hauling open the gate as the others formed a protective circle around them.

'Sire! Below!' Prent almost screamed.

Gello turned back from the wall, where he had been supervising the efforts to kill Sendric and

cursing the incompetents who were failing him —
to see the gates being opened by a pack of muddy,
filthy Norstalines.

'What? I gave orders to finish them off!' he gasped.
Prent just stared at him, so he drew his sword. His
mother had always said, if you wanted something
done properly, you needed to do it yourself. And
Mother was always right. 'To the gates!' he yelled.
He had held back his best men, the Norstalines
and Berellians, from the battlements for just such a
moment. Now they charged down with him.

Leigh left Hawke to get the gate open and braced
the men for Gello's charge. If Gello could get to the
gate winches and shut the gates before Kay's men
were inside, all the sacrifices made until now would
be for nothing.

But as Gello raced over, a lone man ran through
the opening gates.

'Gelloooo!' Sendric howled as he hurled himself at
the man. He aimed a massive blow at Gello's head.

Gello was forced to duck and block, turn aside
from the gate winches. He saw it was Sendric and
the two of them exchanged several blows, Gello's
men forming a half-circle around the duelling pair,
losing all their momentum — until Gello hacked
out, his blade shearing into the old noble's chest.

Sendric collapsed and Gello grinned wolfishly —
then looked up.

The gates were now open, and a horde of
Norstalines was racing through the gap.

Gello turned and ran, Prent half a pace behind
him.

The Berellians and renegade Norstalines who
had followed him hesitated before Kay and his men
hit them from one side, Hawke and Leigh from the

other. For a moment all was chaos as men hacked and slashed at each other but there were more Norstalines in blue pouring through the gates every moment. Not one of Gello's Norstalines or Berellians survived. Of the other gate defenders, some tried to run, and many of these were cut down, while most just threw down their weapons and then themselves, begging for mercy.

'The gates are ours!' Kay shouted, and the Norstalines cheered themselves.

'Where is Kettering?' Kay looked around.

'He sacrificed himself to let us get to the gates,' Leigh said sadly. Even as he spoke, Kettering was being carried over, the spears still sticking out of him. Kay was astonished to see many of the hardened criminals were in tears.

'Look after him, and the Count,' Kay said shakily. 'Hold the gates for us.' Then he led a mixed force of bowmen and infantry off into the dark.

'Leigh!' Kettering coughed.

'Don't talk, man. Just hold on. The magic will be back soon, and they'll heal you,' Hawke said urgently.

Kettering shook his head. 'I think it is too late for me.'

'Rubbish, man! You need to think about what you'll do when you get back to Norstalos! Use your anger to keep yourself alive!'

Kettering smiled. 'You make a better criminal than liar. Anyway, my anger is gone. That's a blessing in itself.' He coughed up blood then, which Leigh wiped away carefully. 'If I did make it back, I'd look up Mabel, the woman I let through the lines,' he said softly.

'That's the spirit. You hold onto that thought,' Hawke told him.

Leigh and Hawke looked at the barely alive Kettering and Sendric, as well as the other wounded.

'Hey, isn't that Barrett's woman?' Leigh asked, pointing at one.

'Aye,' Hawke said grimly. 'And she looks even worse than Kettering.'

The hope that the magic would return flashed between them. For all of them.

Gello and Prent's first thought was to get away from the gates. There was no second thought. Finally they stopped, when the noise of the remaining defenders dying could not be heard.

'What now?' Prent panted.

Gello sheathed his sword on the second attempt, his heart still pounding. He had seen how the Fearpriests rewarded failure. But what was the alternative? Throw himself on his cousin's mercy? Besides, if they had no magic, what could the Fearpriests do to him? He straightened. The Temple was the only safe place in the city tonight.

'Follow me,' he ordered.

Sacrax and his warriors all instinctively froze when the horns sounded.

'They'll know we're coming!' Merren cried. 'Move!'

With just a nod, Martil, Kesbury and a group of Derthals raced towards the front of the Temple and its blood-stained stone steps that led to the top.

Sacrax threw back his head and howled.

His Derthals echoed the call, the strange sound bouncing off the stone walls around the square, then they were loping across the cobbles. They were deceptively fast, for Merren, Milly and Barrett could not keep up with them and dropped behind.

The Temple guards hurriedly shut the gates and began hurling spears. But the wall around the courtyard at the back of the Temple had been constructed to keep curious and fearful eyes out, not as a defensive measure. Barely ten feet high, it was not a serious barrier.

Without pausing, Sacrax and his Derthals raced up. Working in pairs, one warrior bent down before the wall, the second used his back as a springboard to leap up and catch the top of the wall and pull himself up, where they could attack the defenders. These Tenochs were city guards, whose most ferocious opponents until then had been straw targets. Against the Derthals they stood little chance. Sacrax was thinking they would have the Temple at their mercy in a few moments when more Tenochs poured out of the Temple itself, a mixture of guards and red-robed Fearpriests, wielding obsidian knives and axe-clubs.

A handful of Derthals, who had jumped down from the wall to pursue the Tenochs, were caught and killed by this counter-attack.

'Hold here! Help coming!' Sacrax yelled in Derthal. Half his warriors were still on the other side of the wall. They needed time to get up and, besides, his human allies were on the way. Or so he hoped. He led a rush of his warriors to the stairs, where a mass of Tenochs were trying to force their way up and retake the wall.

Karia had almost fallen asleep when the sound of the locking bar being drawn back and the tramp of booted feet made her sit up, heart pounding. Instinctively she knew what was happening.

When the door opened she attacked, biting, kicking, punching and scratching. But without her magic, she was no match for four Temple guards, who carried her, thrashing and fighting, out of her cell and up wide stone stairs towards the altar.

'The Council has decreed you are to go to meet the Great God. Rejoice, for you shall serve Him throughout eternity,' one of them panted as they dragged her up another flight of stairs.

Martil could smell the blood thick on the stones as he climbed upwards. The front of the Temple had not been designed for climbing, for there were no steps, just huge chunks of stone. How much effort had gone into this he neither knew nor cared. He just knew these crudely dressed blocks were precisely the wrong size — requiring he, Kesbury and the Derthals to jump and clamber up them, helping each other as they went. Not only were they about half the height of a man but they were also slick and stained with blood. The horns had stopped blowing by now, and he could hear the sounds of fighting, shouts and screams as the Derthals tried to force their way into the back of the Temple. But he had to concentrate on what he was doing. The square seemed far below him, yet the top seemed no closer.

'This is going to take a turn of the hourglass,' Kesbury grunted.

Martil ignored him, saving his breath for the climb.

Merren had watched Sacrax and his Derthals get over the wall. At first they seemed to be winning easily but the sounds of fighting had only grown heavier and, while almost all the Derthals were now up on the wall, the gate was still shut.

'We're too exposed out here,' Barrett warned, as a spear flew over the wall to land with a scrape on the cobbles near them. 'Perhaps we should wait for Nerrin and the Rallorans, and Kettering and the Norstalines to get here.'

Merren hesitated. She wanted to get inside the Temple, see what was happening and find Karia. But they were horribly exposed here, without even one Derthal to guard them. If a patrol of Tenochs came across them, it would be dangerous in the extreme ... another spear landed near them and she nodded.

'Quick now. We'll wait over there.' She pointed to the closest alleyway.

Gello and Prent slowed down, now the Temple was close. They could hear the sound of fighting, as well as the strange Derthal scream that indicated one had killed an enemy.

'How do we get in?' Prent moaned.

Gello ignored him, as he sneaked down an alleyway. If all else failed, he thought he could climb up the front of the Temple to reach the top. Then he stopped in shock, Prent almost bumping into the back of him. Heading right towards him was his bitch of a cousin, as well as that interfering wizard of hers and some idiot woman in the robes of an Archbishop! He nudged Prent, and gestured. Prent's eyes widened, then he nodded, grinning.

Gello drew his sword, Prent his long sacrificial knife, then they raced down the alleyway.

It was all a blur to Karia. The four men carrying her up the stairs blocked her view of the surroundings but she had seen what went on at the top of the Temple and had no intention of going up there. Martil had told her to do something unexpected if you wanted to gain surprise. So, instead of fighting, she went limp.

The guards, who had been trying desperately to control her struggles, relaxed as she did. Then she arched her back and kicked out, wrenching her right leg free, before slamming her heel into the groin of the one holding her left leg. As he screamed and collapsed, she ripped her arms free and rolled herself into a ball, bouncing down a few stairs before coming up to her feet and running down as fast as she could.

Barrett saw them first.

'Merren! It is Gello!' he yelled. 'Get behind me!'

He wished with all his heart he had the magic to destroy the pair of them as they raced towards him. He had a moment to reflect that this was an embodiment of his favourite daydream — Merren in danger and he was the only one who could save her. Then he hefted his staff and blocked Gello's path, aiming a powerful swing at the former Duke.

Gello ignored Barrett. He wanted to kill Merren, pure and simple. She was the cause of all his problems. She had stolen his throne, she had made him a laughing stock, she had defeated him time and again, turned him into an exile and even made him kill his mother! It was time for revenge.

Gello used his sword to block Barrett's staff, then elbowed the mage in the head, sending Barrett crashing into a wall. He ignored the fallen wizard as he bore down on Merren. He almost laughed as he raised his sword high. She was not even running! This would be so easy — and so satisfying!

Behind him, Prent had knocked the woman Archbishop to the ground and was trying to rip her robes apart with his knife.

Gello could not care about that. He was anticipating the moment when he would strike down his hated cousin. She did not even look afraid! Was she too stupid to understand he was going to kill her? He held back his stroke for a moment, wanting to see the terror bloom on her face before he cut her down.

Karia had barely got down one flight when a Tenoch guard grabbed her.

Shouting and screaming, she fought to get free — but to no avail. Sweating and swearing, the guards hoisted into the air up and began carrying her back up the stairs.

'Hurry!' one grunted. 'The entire Council is waiting for us!'

'Let me go! My dad's coming to kill you!' Karia screamed.

'And that's supposed to make us afraid?' their leader sneered.

Merren stared at Gello, unafraid. She had known Barrett could not hold her cousin back — without his magic, the mage was no match for Gello, who was twice his size. But she was not about to cower and run. Besides, she knew what he was going to do. He would never expect her to fight back, he would want to draw the moment out, try and gloat even then.

She had a dagger at her waist and, as he loomed over her, sword held high, she drew it and took a pace forwards, stabbing upwards.

Gello, his sword still poised for the death blow that would never come, simply ran onto the blade and the pace of his advance helped ram her dagger deep into his throat.

Merren gazed into his astonished eyes as his sword fell to the cobbles, then a gout of hot blood sprayed over her hand, arm and face as he choked on her dagger, an almost comical expression of surprise on his face.

Without a word, she held his gaze, letting him see her absolute contempt for him, before she ripped her blade from his throat.

Blood fountained across the cobbles and he stood for a moment, obviously unable to believe what had happened. Silently he mouthed a word: *Mother*.

Then Gello collapsed to the ground in a pool of crimson.

'You never thought a woman could beat you,' she told the dying man. 'I always told you that would be a fatal mistake.'

Then a horrifying scream made her look up, to where Prent and Milly struggled on the cobbles a few yards away.

Milly could feel Prent's foul breath on her face, as his hands tore at her robes. This was what Tiera and the other girls had been put through. Terror pulsed through her.

'I am going to teach you how Zorva is stronger than Aroaril,' Prent sneered. His size and weight was pinning her down and he was trying to force his knee between her legs. Terrified and furious, she jabbed her thumb into his eye. As he reared back, she grabbed his knife hand, which was trying to lift up her robes, and rammed it upwards.

His agonising scream almost deafened her. Desperately she arched her back, flipping him off her. But all the fight had gone out of him.

She squirmed backwards, kicking him with her feet to get away — then saw what she had done.

Prent was still screaming, his hands locked around his groin, where the hilt of his long dagger protruded obscenely from the front of his robe. Blood was pulsing out over his hands and onto the cobbles with every heartbeat, while he showed no signs of stopping his curdling wails of agony.

Barrett, blood streaming down from a cut on his cheek, forced himself to his feet. He stared at Merren, who stood over Gello, and then at Milly, who was sitting and staring at the howling Prent.

Barrett staggered forwards, reaching out for Gello's fallen sword, to put Prent out of his misery.

'No.' Milly laid her hand on his arm, using it to pull herself to his feet.

'But he'll bleed to death and it could take a turn of the hourglass like that!' Barrett gasped.

'Good,' Milly said bleakly.

Barrett looked at Merren, who nodded her agreement with Milly.

'Come on, we need to see what is going on at the Temple,' Merren ordered.

Leaning on his staff, Barrett followed the two women as they strode back across the square.

Karia had always believed Martil was going to come and save her. He had said so and he had never let her down. Even now, as they dragged her onto the top of the Temple, into the cold night air, she still believed it.

'Dad! Dad! Help!' she screamed into the night.

But no reply came.

The altar was at the very centre of the Temple, surprisingly small, just a stone pillar where the sacrifices could be bent across. Fearpriests, each of them holding a torch, formed an open square around the altar. A brazier smoked beside it and the air was thick with the smell of blood, the stones stained a deep rust brown from years of soaking. Tall stone pillars etched with grotesque carvings leered down at her as she was held across the altar.

It was then that she realised Martil was not going to come for her.

The tears came then, the sobs shaking her small body.

'Don't! Please don't do this!' she begged, but they ignored her, as they had ignored all the pleas of their victims over the centuries.

'Oh Great God! Hear our prayers and receive this offering!' the lead Fearpriest cried into the night. 'We give you this Radiant Child and we hope you will return to us the powers that are rightfully ours!'

The four guards expertly stretched Karia across the altar, one holding each limb, the slightly curved stone digging into the small of her back, pushing her ribcage upwards, to allow the stroke that would open her diaphragm and allow Brother Horna to reach into her chest cavity and rip out her heart.

Around her the Fearpriests were all chanting something in a strange language, its tone sinister. But she could not hear it, could only cry as the knife sliced down.

Nerrin raced into the square, towards the giant pyramid that loomed over the city. He could see lights at the top, hear something going on up there, but he only had eyes for the fight going on at the back, where Derthals and Tenochs fought over the wall.

He could see Queen Merren, Barrett and Archbishop Sadlier, all covered in blood but standing upright and walking towards him, pointing at the battle raging just outside the Temple.

'Sacrax! Get the gate open!' he bellowed.

Sacrax could not get down into the courtyard past the Tenoch spears. Equally the Tenochs could not get him off the wall but he was not here to hold a wall but to break into the Temple.

He heard the shout from the square and glanced over his shoulder to see Rallorans just paces away, with the Norstalines just running into the square now.

Without thinking, he jumped off the wall, landing on a group of Tenochs by the gate, his weight driving them to the stones. Seeing their High Chief in the midst of the enemy, a score of Derthals followed him, landing on the Tenochs as they tried to spear the prone Sacrax.

Winded, the Derthal High Chief staggered to the gate as his warriors fought to give him time and space. With a shout, he threw back the locking bar and hauled it open.

Instantly a thick shield wall of Rallorans drove into the courtyard, slicing into the Tenochs before they could get to Sacrax. The Tenochs fought to stop them, then fought to escape — and died both ways as the Derthals joined the attack.

'Into the Temple! We are running out of time!' Merren shouted from the shadow of the gate, peering into a courtyard filled with dead and screaming wounded.

Nerrin waved to his leading men and, with Sacrax at his shoulder, drove into the Temple door, the shields carving a path the Tenochs could not stop.

Horna's knife ripped open Karia's dress, exposing her skin, pale in the torchlight. The Fearpriest ripped the cloth further, until he could see where he must strike, then raised the knife high.

Around him, the Fearpriest chant had almost reached its conclusion and he prepared to make the final dedication himself.

Then a wordless howl of anger stopped them all.

Horna opened his eyes and watched, with the other Fearpriests, as a monster from their nightmares appeared over the front of the pyramid, covered with the blood of a thousand sacrificed souls.

It had two glittering swords in its hands and it raced at the Fearpriests, roaring its challenge.

'Kill it!' Horna shouted, backing away from the girl, the knife in his hand almost forgotten.

The Fearpriests all had daggers, and they drew them now and converged on the figure.

Martil had told Merren he was in control. But when he heard Karia's desperate cry for help, looked up the face of the pyramid and saw how far he was from the top, he went mad. Nothing mattered but getting to her and nothing could stop him.

From somewhere he found the ability to drive himself up each course of the pyramid, leaping ever upwards, heedless of the slippery stones, the cries of Kesbury and the Derthals asking him to wait for them, the fall that waited for a careless step and his own harsh breathing. As he sprang onto the top of the Temple he saw Karia stretched across the altar, the knife above her, and the Fearpriests clustered around.

His swords leaped into his hands and he raced at the Fearpriests. They tried to stop him but he was among them in a moment, both swords a blur. They were not men, not human to him, they were objects. The Dragon Sword sliced apart all who came near, his fear and anger and hatred driving the deadly blade.

The elderly Fearpriests, clutching only daggers, stood no chance. They got in each others' way and all the time the Sword was killing, killing, killing.

One last head went flying and the remaining Fearpriests, including the one who had stood over Karia, were running for the stairs.

He ignored them, instead focused on the small girl, still being held by the stunned guards, who had watched this warrior slaughter half their Ruling Council.

'You are dead men,' he told them, chest heaving.

The four guards exchanged looks, then let Karia go and rushed at him.

The first had his head split open by the Dragon Sword, the second took a sword through the throat, then the Dragon Sword ripped open the chest of the third.

Screaming in terror, the last — their leader — ran, leaping off the edge of the Temple and falling into the night, his limbs windmilling.

For a long moment, Martil and Karia stared at each other.

Then the spell was broken and they fell into each other's arms, crying with joy and relief.

Kesbury and the Derthals found them like that when they scrambled over the top a short time later.

'Captain!' Kesbury puffed, surveying the man and child locked together in a hug, surrounded by fallen torches and fallen bodies.

Martil ignored them. He only cared about having Karia back. For her part, she just clung to him.

'You came!' she kept saying, over and over again.

'I swore I would. And I won't ever leave you again,' he promised.

'Captain! The Egg! It's still below!' Kesbury insisted.

Behind him, the Derthals were prodding doubtfully at the dead Fearpriests, as well as exclaiming at the amount of dried blood that covered the top of the Temple.

But Martil still ignored them.

'Dad, we have to finish this,' Karia said, wiping tears and blood from his face.

Only then did he nod, and stand, Karia in one arm, the Dragon Sword in the other.

'I can walk!' she said. 'My legs are fine!'

'I don't want to let you go again,' he told her.

She liked the sound of that and snuggled into his shoulder.

'Follow me,' Kesbury said grimly, and led the way back inside the Temple.

'What do we do?' a Fearpriest gibbered, as they paused in their flight on a landing, far below.

Horna took a moment to gather his breath. He had done little exercise in the last few years and the terrified flight from the monster that had attacked them by the altar had left him — had left them all — wheezing and gasping.

'We need guards. Many of them,' he decided.

They began down the stairs again, slower this time — only to meet a handful of blood-spattered guards running up the stairs.

'What is it?' Horna demanded.

'High One! The barbarians are inside! They were led by demons from Aroaril — there was nothing we could do!' the guard babbled. 'There's thousands of them!'

The Fearpriests looked down the stairs, to where faint cries, and the odd scream, could be heard.

Horna glanced back up the stairs, then dismissed that option. The demon warrior was up there.

'We must escape somehow,' he declared.

'But how? There are only two ways out of here!' another Fearpriest cried.

'The prisoners!' Horna exclaimed. 'We must shed our robes and hide among the prisoners. The weak-minded Aroaril-lovers will think prisoners are harmless, and release them!'

'But we have no other clothes!' someone objected.

'Then we find eight prisoners and exchange clothes with them, send them down the stairs in the hope our enemies kill them!' Horna said.

'Which prisoners, High One?'

'It doesn't matter! Just do it quickly, fool!' Horna snarled, and the guards scampered off.

Merren strode across the bloody courtyard and into the Temple, Milly at her side. Barrett had raced back to the main gate, heedless of her orders, of being needed here, after hearing from Kay about the wounded, that Tiera had been hit. She would be angry about that later — there were too many other problems now.

'Bring all the wounded here. As soon as we can restore the magic, we can heal them,' she instructed Kay, before ordering Nerrin to take her inside the Temple.

'Careful, your majesty. We are clearing it out but you never know where they might be hiding — it is a rat's nest in there,' Nerrin warned.

Squads of Rallorans, Norstalines and Derthals were hunting through the lower levels, killing any guards or Fearpriests in red they found, dragging out terrified servants and placing them under guard in the courtyard.

'Have we found their dungeons yet?' Merren demanded.

'Your majesty! Come look at this!' Captain Kay called.

Merren followed him into a huge stone room, almost filled with gold. Bars were stacked along the walls, while jewellery filled seemingly endless wooden chests and spilled across the floor.

'The spoils of a lifetime of evil,' Merren said in wonder, the torchlight reflecting off the glittering piles. 'This is twice, maybe thrice the treasury of Norstalos, before Gello stole it. With this, we can return Norstalos to glory and there will still be more than enough for the poor people of this continent to live on. Kay, I want this guarded. This is our future in here. No child need go hungry again.'

She left the treasure room and followed the advance up through the Temple, uncovering squalid rooms of terrified servants, large barracks with only a handful of guards left and luxurious apartments empty of Fearpriests.

'Where are the dungeons? And where is the Egg?' Merren demanded, but none knew.

The guards returned with eight tunics, all stained foully.

The Fearpriests dressed reluctantly, with Horna urging them on.

'The Aroaril-lovers could be here at any time!' he warned, then handed the eight robes to the frightened guards. 'Now, dress the prisoners and send them down the stairs. As for yourselves, I would advise surrender. The Aroaril-lovers are merciful fools, and we must take advantage of that.'

'Yes, High One.' The guards bowed.

In no time, eight men in red robes were marched over to the stairs and Horna watched in satisfaction as they began running down to where the Aroaril-lovers lurked.

'We shall escape this yet, my brothers,' he announced as the guards locked them into cells.

* * *

'Your majesty!' This time it was Nerrin calling, and the urgency in his tone made her run out of a storeroom.

'Look there!'

Stumbling down the stairs were eight figures in red robes, hands in the air.

Nerrin formed his men into three ranks, spears at the ready. 'Show them no mercy, lads, for they would show us none,' Nerrin told his line.

'Don't kill us! We're not Fearpriests!' one shouted, running slightly ahead of the others.

'It's a trick! Don't listen to them!' Nerrin said immediately.

'We're prisoners!' The speaker pulled back his cowl, revealing himself to be a young man with a horribly scarred face. He turned to his companions and waved at them. They all pulled down their hoods, revealing dirty, scared faces. Like the first, they were all young.

'What is this?' Merren wondered.

'The Fearpriests exchanged robes with us. They are pretending to be prisoners, thinking all prisoners will be released!' the speaker yelled. 'They told us we were free, told us to run down here.'

'Bastards!' Nerrin muttered.

'If it is true,' Merren pointed out. 'Come forward, one by one!'

Led by the speaker, the eight walked down carefully, happy to pull off their robes to reveal they were all dirty, and dressed only in loincloths.

'Well, they all look like prisoners — they're all bruised and beaten, as well,' Nerrin grunted.

'Put them with the servants. Once we have the use of magic again, we shall make sure there are no wolves in sheep's clothing in there,' Merren ordered. 'Nerrin, I want a company up those stairs — if the

Fearpriests are all in the dungeons, then we are safe — but Karia may not be.'

She followed the Rallorans as they raced up the stairs, while Norstalines and Derthals spread out into the different floors they passed.

'How big is this thing?' Merren complained, as her legs began to burn.

'I can smell the dungeons,' Nerrin shouted, as they pounded up one last flight.

'We give up! We are unarmed!' someone shouted.

Out of the gloom a handful of guards appeared. None held a weapon and all lay on the floor, hands over their heads.

'Are there more of you?' Nerrin asked harshly.

'We are the last!' one promised.

'Take them away!' Merren ordered, and they were hustled downstairs.

'What if there are Fearpriests in these cells?' Milly asked. 'How do we tell them apart?'

'Get them out one by one. Compare them. The ones who are clean and well-fed shall be the Fearpriests,' Merren predicted.

But perhaps the Fearpriests had used their short time in the cells wisely. Every man brought out was stinking and dirty, and cowered away from the soldiers.

But there was also one familiar face.

'Ambassador Ezok!' Merren greeted him.

'Your majesty! Thank you for saving me! I have been a prisoner of these foul priests — they were going to sacrifice me. I can help you, I can tell you the hidden Fearpriests in here — just don't kill me! I helped the little girl stay alive, she can —'

'Karia?' Merren demanded. 'Have you seen her?'

Ezok smiled. 'Will you let me live?'

'I shall, if you point out the Fearpriests — and tell me where the girl is.'

'They took her up to be sacrificed.' Ezok pointed upstairs. 'Do I still get to live?'

But Merren was already running up the stairs.

'Don't look at me!' Nerrin stared at his men. 'Two squads after her!' He turned to Ezok, dragging the Berellian to his feet. 'Right, now show me these Fearpriests.'

Merren could hear the Rallorans chasing after her but, with the Fearpriests under guard, she did not fear an ambush. She feared finding a dead Karia and what such a sight would do to Martil.

She had not gone more than a couple of flights up the stairs before she saw a small party coming down towards her, led by a pair of familiar shapes.

'Mummy!'

She nearly stopped in her tracks as Karia shouted and waved at her, then the three of the them were running towards each other, nearly knocking each other over when they met.

'You're safe!' Merren hugged Karia close and it was a long time before they broke apart even a little. The Derthals and Rallorans eased away, giving them room.

'We should never leave each other again,' Karia said gravely. 'We should be a family.'

Merren caught sight of the worried expression on Martil's face, but she just smiled.

'We shall be,' she promised.

'Do you mean that?' Martil and Karia asked at the same time.

'I do.' She laughed.

'But what about the country, what about Count Sendric?' Karia asked.

Merren sighed. 'Sendric might be dead already. But even if he is not, I shall not marry him. I know what I want now — and it is you two.'

She could not finish, because Martil leaned in and kissed her.

Karia squealed with excitement and clapped her hands. She watched them kiss for a while, then patted them both on the head.

'That is enough for now,' she told them.

Martil grinned sheepishly. 'It sounds like this might even be a happy ending from a saga,' he said, to cover himself.

'Not quite,' Merren corrected. 'We still have to find the Egg.'

'Oh that! That's easy!' Karia scoffed.

She led them down one more flight of steps, then into the Council's chamber, where the Egg stood silent. But as soon as Martil entered the room, it began to flash colours, while the Dragon Sword hummed in response.

Carefully Martil drew the Sword.

'Time to end this,' he said, walking forwards.

He stood by the Egg, watching the colours play across its surface. He glanced at the Dragon Sword. The dragon on the hilt had come alive, and its eyes were flashing brightly.

With one smooth move, Martil reversed his grip, so he held it like a dagger, then thrust the Dragon Sword into the top of the Dragon Egg. The blade slid all the way down, until the hilt of the Sword rested on the surface of the Egg. Colours still danced across its surface, but nothing else happened.

'Is that it?' Karia asked.

'Berellian, you might have the promise of the Queen, but I will be happy to kill you, should you try to play us false,' Nerrin told the struggling Ezok. 'Show us the Fearpriests.'

'I can do more than that! I can tell you a great secret!' Ezok gasped.

'Don't play games with me,' Nerrin growled.

'There's a real Fearpriest hidden among the false Fearpriests who came down the stairs!'

'What?' Nerrin and Horna exclaimed at the same time, one much quieter than the other.

'His name is Brother Onzalez, and those guards selected him to play a Fearpriest!' Ezok gabbled.

Nerrin shrugged. 'We have them all under guard. You can show me which one later. Now point out the Fearpriests here.'

Ezok stepped away and hurried down the line of prisoners, until he stood in front of Horna and the others.

'Here they are!' he pointed. 'Now will you let me live?'

'No!' Horna snarled, leaping forwards and wrapping his hands around Ezok's neck.

The Berellian choked as Nerrin and Rallorans charged in. But the other Fearpriests tried to make a run for it at that moment and Nerrin and his men were forced to beat them down. By the time they reached Horna, and had clubbed him into unconsciousness, Ezok was dead, his neck broken.

'Chain these Fearpriests,' Nerrin ordered, breathing harshly. 'And send a message to the guards below. There's a Fearpriest among the prisoners. Not one is to leave the courtyard until Archbishop Sadlier or Bishop Kesbury get their powers back, and can identify him.'

'This is the time when you need a dragon or an Elfaran to tell you what is supposed to happen,' Merren observed, as they stood looking at the Egg.

'I still can't feel any magic,' Kesbury admitted.

'Maybe it doesn't like being in this place of evil,' Karia suggested. 'Why don't we take it up into the air?'

Without any better idea, the Derthals hoisted up the Egg in its cradle, with the Sword still deep inside it, and began to carry it out.

'We should hurry. Dawn cannot be far away,' Merren warned. 'Kesbury, go and get Barrett, drag him here if you have to. Get Archbishop Sadlier, as well as the Magicians' Guild. We must know what is going on.'

Carrying such a weight up stairs would have exhausted men but the Derthals pressed on swiftly, while Martil, Merren and Karia hurried, hand in hand, after them.

They laid the Egg down atop the Temple, a decent distance away from the bloodstained altar and the bodies of the Fearpriests and guards. The sky was lightening now, and dawn was close. But still nothing happened.

'I did what the dragons asked me to!' Martil protested. 'Why isn't it working?'

Nobody could give an answer.

Below, the noise of the battle seemed to have woken the city from its slumber, and the lack of soldiers on the streets seemed to have removed some of their fear. As the sky lightened further with every moment, they could see the square below, see that the Tenochs had left their homes and were creeping out into the square, trying to see what had happened after their night of horns, screams and battles.

But the Egg and the Sword sat, only the occasional swirl of colour any indication something was happening.

A grim-faced Barrett arrived, his eyes red.

'I cannot tell what is going on,' he told Merren shortly. 'Now I am going back to her. And you'll have to kill me to stop me.'

Merren sighed. 'I grieve for your loss Barrett, as I do for everyone who has lost their life. But without the magic returning, there is no future for anyone —'

'I don't care about anyone else,' Barrett said bitterly, glancing across the roof to where Martil sat, oblivious of the Mage's presence and even of his grief, before turning abruptly and hurrying away.

At any other time Merren would have gone after him but not now. She walked back to Martil. Martil knew nothing of Tiera and she saw no need to tell him, for fear he might offer sympathy to Barrett.

'If it is not done before sunrise, all magic shall leave this world, and all life with it,' she said softly.

'I can't believe it could end like this!' Martil groaned. 'Was it something I did, or didn't do? I know I was not the ideal Sword wielder —'

Merren stopped his words with a kiss.

'If it ends like this, then it is how I would want to die. With the two people I most love in the world around me,' she said.

Martil picked up Karia and they embraced Merren, the three of them holding each other close.

'Here it comes,' Martil said softly, as he saw the sun peep above the horizon in the east.

He did not want to close his eyes, did not want to miss a moment of seeing Merren and Karia. Out of the corner of his eye, he saw the first ray of light burst across the sky and brush the Egg with its golden light.

Instantly the dragon on the hilt of the Sword came to life, threw back its head and roared, a challenge that echoed across the city.

'Look!' Karia cried.

The Egg was a riot of colour, blazing brightly. The dragon on the hilt was no longer gold, but a bright silver. It spread its wings and took off, flying high into the sky. Next moment there was a green dragon there, then it spread its wings and flew away. Then gold, then silver again, then red, blue, white — almost too fast for the eye to see, they were created and took off, circling high in the sky above the Temple, others swooping across the square, soaring through the city streets.

At first Tenochs screamed and ducked for cover as dozens of dragons flew over and among them, but the people quickly saw there was no danger.

Children tried to catch them, people waved and pointed as each new one raced through the sky.

'They're so beautiful!' Karia sighed.

Now the Egg was pulsating, beating almost like a human heart. With each beat it grew smaller, while the dragons soaring across the city grew larger, doubling in size each time it pulsed. The tiny dragons, which had flown out just the size of a human hand, were now almost as big as Argurium, and every person in Tenoch could not fail to see them, or be moved by the sight of so many dragons at play. They chased each other, they turned somersaults and loops through the air, their obvious joy could only be reflected in those watching them.

Martil, Merren and Karia were spellbound.

Then the Sword and the Egg, shrunk now to only the height of the Sword itself, simply vanished, exploding into a spray of golden sparks, much as Argurium had done when she had disappeared. But this time the sparks went in all directions, bathing all in their light.

The dragons chased them down, swallowing

them, the sparks dancing inside them as they soared through the air.

'The magic is back!' Karia laughed.

'We must hurry — we may be able to save Sendric and the other wounded,' Milly cried, then she and Kesbury raced down the stairs.

A dragon, gold in colour and with what was unmistakeably a smile on its face swooped low above the Temple, landing lightly on the edge.

'From the dragons, from all life on this planet, we thank you,' it said gravely, its voice high and musical. 'As Wielder, you may ask anything of us and we shall grant it.'

Merren nudged Martil. 'Go on,' she urged.

But Martil shook his head. He put his arms around Merren and Karia. 'I have everything I need,' he said simply.

The dragon bowed its head. 'A good answer. But what about a gift for others?'

'My wounded men', Martil said immediately. 'Save them.'

'None of your men shall die, all shall be healed. And your trip home across the sea shall be both fast and safe,' the dragon promised

'Thank you,' Martil said hoarsely.

'Farewell, Wielder. This Dragon Sword is no more, for it has fulfilled its purpose. But we shall meet again.'

With that it flew away, soaring high into the sky, the other dragons close behind.

The Tenochs almost cried in disappointment to see them go.

'Well,' Karia said into the silence. 'The dragons did say it was an easy task to complete.'

They laughed as they watched the dragons disappear into the distance.

'They've gone but can we? What do we do about them?' Martil pointed to the crowd below, which filled the square.

'Leave them to me,' Merren said confidently. 'Karia, if you can help out my voice? Nerrin, bring the Fearpriests up here.'

While Martil and Karia ate, and tried to clean themselves up, the Tenochs listened as Merren told them they were free, that the Fearpriests would rule them no more. Those who had been brought here against their will could go home, carrying the treasures that had been stolen from them.

'There will be no more sacrifices! No longer will you worship Zorva, no longer will you live in fear! I have freed you but I must return to my own land, so you can decide how you want to be ruled! Is Garas here?'

There was a pause before the Ayan that Milly had healed pushed himself forwards.

'Do you have your people with you?' she called down.

In answer, he waved behind him, and hundreds of Ayans, all dressed in green, fell to their knees.

'You shall have food and gold to take back to your city. As shall all of you. You are free!'

For a moment there was silence, then the Ayans began cheering, followed by the rest of the crowd.

She let them continue, then waved for Nerrin and a squad of Rallorans to bring up the Fearpriests, with ropes magically sealed by Milly and Kesbury, so they could not break them.

'And your first decision is what to do with those who ruled you by fear for so many years!' She waved and Rallorans dragged the Fearpriests to the edge of the Temple roof, where all could see them.

Silence reigned over the square, as the city watched the hated Fearpriests, the men who had terrorised and ruled their lives since they had first drawn breath.

'Kill them!' Garas screamed.

Next moment they were all howling it.

Merren let them chant for the Fearpriests' deaths for a moment longer, then signalled to Nerrin.

One push in the back and the Fearpriests fell from the top of the Temple.

Tenochs screamed with delight, horror and relief as the eight bodies bounced down the Temple before landing with sickening thuds on the square below.

As the echo of the last one falling died away, it was drowned out by cheering. The crowd was crying and laughing at the same time, embracing each other and waving delightedly up at Merren.

'I think that takes care of them for now,' she said decisively.

She signalled to Romon, who moved forwards and cleared his throat. The Tenochs were about to get a full performance from Norstalos' finest bard, and discover a little bit more about the world around them. Whether it would do any good, she did not know. But surely it could not hurt.

Onzalez slipped through the crowd, forcing himself to grin like a madman and embrace total strangers. He had felt his powers return when the dragons had begun to fly and, when the guards were distracted by the amazing sights before them, had taken the opportunity to get over the wall and hide himself in the crowd. First he had to get away, then he could think of what to do next. How he could even begin to regain his power after what had happened here, he had no idea. But he still had followers in Berellia, as well as in other cities on this continent. And, as his father had liked to say, where there was life there was hope.

Martil spent time with his men, the ones he had saved and the ones who had saved him. They deserved much more than his thanks but it was all he could give them for now. Nerrin, Dunner, Ryder, Kay, Kettering — but he did not go near Sendric, or the weeping Barrett.

Barrett cradled Tiera, the tears streaming down his face. Now what would he do? She had been able to bring out the best in him. Without her, the bitterness and anger was swamping him. He could not bear to see that accursed Ralloran again. It was all his fault. The wounded men had been healed but not her. All because Martil had asked for men to be healed and the dragons had taken him literally. That bastard. Martil did not care because he had his happy ending, they all had a happy ending. All except him.

'I'll need to spend the rest of the day trying to finish up here. I'll talk to the leaders of the various cities who want to go home, as well as those Tenochs who are happy to see the Fearpriests gone. Hopefully they can finish what we have begun, breaking the power of the Fearpriests. It feels like we are leaving the job half-done but there is too much waiting for us back home to stay here. At least we'll have time together as we travel back to Norstalos for the grand wedding,' Merren said, as they walked down the stairs back through the Temple.

'Then I shall get a pony, and you'll read to me every night, and we can play catch and dolls and ...' Karia added then drew a breath to continue.

'But,' Merren said firmly.

'But what?' Martil and Karia asked cautiously, looking at each other.

'There are many problems waiting for us back at Norstalos. The country is still in a mess. Even with all the gold we shall bring back, it will be years before life gets back to normal. The people have only just accepted the Rallorans, let alone the Derthals. Aroaril knows we shall have many difficulties bringing them all together. We shall leave Tenoch in a mess, with Fearpriests no doubt still in many other cities. Yes, we have destroyed their Ruling Council and their army; their power is broken but who knows what could happen? And we have not even begun to talk about Berellia. On our southern border will be a country in chaos, one that also has Fearpriests running around. The Rallorans and Avish will probably want to exact revenge from that carcass — who knows what will become of Berellia. Then there is Sendric. He will live but we both know he does not want to see a base-born Ralloran on the throne. After his heroics, he will have won plenty of support from the men, as well. Finally there will be a prince arriving within a year, and how will our little Princess deal with that?'

Martil glanced over at Karia, whose brow was furrowed.

'Are you talking about me?' she asked suspiciously.

Merren smiled ruefully and went on. 'There are years of problems right there — and we have not even got to the biggest problem of all — the Dragon Sword!'

'Aroaril! The Dragon Sword!' Martil stopped.

'Exactly! It's gone! The symbol not just of Kingship but of the country itself is destroyed — how is that going to go down in the backstreets of Wells and Worick, the farms of the north and south?'

'But it has fulfilled its purpose, saved all their lives …' Martil argued.

'And they'll accept its loss that easily, will they?' Merren asked sceptically.

Martil hugged Karia.

'So what are you saying, that I shouldn't go back? I mean, given all that, I can understand why you can't marry me —'

Merren grabbed him by the tunic and pulled him close to kiss him.

'For a clever man, you can be remarkably stupid sometimes. I'm just warning you, this is not going to be a traditional saga ending, where we can say we shall all live happily ever after, with not a care in the world.'

'Well, this isn't a saga. Real life does not end so perfectly,' he pointed out.

'Exactly.' She nodded. 'So, are you prepared to be happy for now and see where we go from there?'

'Well, that's an ending I can live with.' Martil grinned.

They looked at Karia, who had her head on the side, thinking about it.

'Me too!' She smiled and they embraced her.

And, for the first time, a child's laughter echoed through the Temple.